OPERATION BIRDIE

Operation Birdie

WILLIAM ROCKE

MOYTURA PRESS

DUBLIN

This book was typeset by
Gilbert Gough Typesetting for
Moytura Press, 4 Arran Quay, Dublin 7.

A catalogue record for this book
is available from the British Library.

ISBN 1-871305-17-9

The lyrics to "Nobody Does It Like Me"
are reproduced by permission of
Warner Chappell Music Ltd/International
Music Publications Ltd.

Printed in Ireland by
Colour Books Ltd, Dublin.

OPERATION BIRDIE is dedicated to my wife Phyllis.
And to the men and women everywhere who are
addicted to the game of golf.

William Rocke

1

The winding road along the Ayrshire coast had views of mountain and woodland on the right, where clusters of sheep and cattle nibbled short grass. As he negotiated yet another bend, Colm Donohue caught his first sight of Ailsa Craig, rising majestically, dark and menacing, out of the sun-splashed waters of the Firth of Clyde.

He looked at his watch and noted it was past midday. Behind him in the back seat of the car he could hear Joan reciting a nursery rhyme to keep the boys amused. Rory, aged two, strapped securely in his kiddy chair, let out a howl that Joan recognised as the early warning signs of hunger pangs.

'We'll have to stop for something to eat soon,' she said. 'These boys are getting restless.'

'Right-o. How about a hotel in Girvan? We'll be there shortly.' In the rear mirror he caught a glimpse of his wife bouncing four-year-old Michael on her knee. She looked like she could do with a rest from the children. When he had met them earlier that morning coming off the Larne ferry, the sight of Joan, her dark slacks and white blouse accentuating her slim figure, had aroused him. It had reminded him forcibly that it was almost a month since they had slept together.

Now he noticed her hair was mussed and she

1

looked hot and sticky. Being the wife of a touring professional golfer—especially one whose game had yet to reach the potential promised in his earlier days—was certainly no bed of roses. And now there were two extra mouths to feed. Colm reckoned he should have heeded the advice of his former manager and waited before starting a family.

Still, the cheque for £18,000 in his wallet which he had collected for a fifth place in the Scottish Open—it had finished in Gleneagles on Saturday— would please his bank manager, and Joan. He could look forward with some confidence to the start of the British Open just a few days away. That was the big one. This time maybe, his game would come good over the four days of the tournament. Turnberry was one of his favourite courses.

Joan must have been reading his thoughts. 'Are you going to win the Open for us, Colm?'

'Of course. Why not?' he laughed. 'I've only got to beat all the top players in the world. I can do it.'

'Johnny says you're going to make the break-through and win a tournament soon. You might as well start with the Open!'

Colm smiled. Naturally Johnny Davis would say that. Johnny was his biggest fan. It was he who, fourteen years before when Colm was a strapping twelve-year-old with a hurling stick permanently in his hand, had brought Colm along to the local golf course where Johnny was the club professional and had given the young lad his first lessons in the game.

Joan's voice cut across his thoughts. 'Johnny and I had a talk last night after you phoned.'

'Yes. He mentioned it when we met this morning.

He was very pleased with my high finish in the Scottish Open.'

'He wasn't too happy when he read in the papers coming over on the ferry this morning that you could have won outright had your short game been a bit sharper.'

'I expect he'll have something to say to me about that when we meet up later.' Johnny would act as his caddie during the Open at Turnberry. Colm always liked to have the older man along for the major tournaments, even though it was an extra expense that he could ill afford. Bringing Johnny over from the homely Atlantic View Golf Club on the wind-swept west coast of Ireland would eat into his tour budget. But Colm reckoned he owed it to the man who had started him on his golf career. Besides, Johnny Davis was more than a good caddie on the course: he was a father figure whom Colm knew he could rely on in a crisis. Shrewd and knowledgeable, he would be a good man to have around Turnberry.

The British Open! The thought of it made his pulses race. A win there would make him a million-aire overnight. Sure, the winner's cheque this year was only £130,000, but agents would crawl out of the woodwork to sign up the winner and get his signa-ture on lucrative sponsorship and endorsement deals. That's where the really big money was in golf.

As British Open champion, he would not have to travel third class to tournaments. He and Joan could move around the world with a nurse to look after the children. He wished he could have afforded to book the family into the imposing Turnberry Hotel, where many of the big-name professionals would stay during the Open; instead they would stay—Johnny Davis included—in a small guesthouse several miles from the course. At least there would be no hassle there. Joan would like that.

In the back seat of the car the two boys were not resting. Joan leaned forward and whispered: 'I feel like I've been travelling for days.'

'I know, love.' He had phoned her from his Glasgow hotel on Saturday night, advising her to drive with Johnny and the children to Belfast and stay there overnight on Sunday to break the journey. It was a tiring journey, but it was cheaper than flying. In his five years as a pro golfer, Colm was nowhere near the millionaire class of many of the golfers against whom he would be competing at Turnberry.

'What would you say to a holiday in the Highlands after the Open?' Colm called over his shoulder.

'Oh Colm, that would be marvellous.' Joan could hardly believe what she was hearing. They had not had a family holiday in recent years. 'But can we afford it?'

'I have over £18,000 in my wallet that says we can,' Colm grinned. 'We could start off first thing on Monday morning next—sooner if I don't qualify for the final two rounds at Turnberry. Okay, love?'

'The boys will love it. You haven't been with them for ages.' That was one thing she did not like about being a pro golfer's wife, especially one who was barely making a living on the tour. It meant she had to stay at home while Colm travelled. With two young children to look after, she rarely got to see her husband when he was competing. The lifestyle did not exactly make for a healthy marriage. She knew of

4

several couples who had split due to the long separations and the pressures the pro tour imposed. And Joan had often heard whispers of what went on when some golfers looked for relaxation and their wives were not around.

'Hey look. There's a better view of old Ailsa Craig.' Colm pulled the car into a convenient lay-by. 'You know the championship course at Turnberry is called after that lump of rock.'

'Let me have a look.' She was leaning over his seat to get a good view. He caught a whiff of her perfume, saw the outline of her breast through the thin blouse as she strained forward.

'Joan—' She turned to him. He put his hand on her soft hair and pulled her to him, their lips meeting. Surprised at first, she then relaxed. She put her arm around his shoulder and when he turned sideways in the seat she pressed her lips to his. He found them soft, moist, inviting. She broke away.

'No, Colm. Wait—'

'God, Joan, I've missed you.' His voice was thick with passion.

'I've missed you too, Colm—'

Colm tried to face her in the seat, bumped his knee off the gear lever and swore. He pulled her to him and found her lips again. She responded and he cupped his hand around her breast, felt the softness, moved his hand and began undoing the top button of her blouse. 'Come into the front seat, Joan—'

She seemed about to obey his command, but Rory let out a howl and she hesitated. Joan looked at the two boys. 'We can't, Colm. Not here. Not just now. Besides, Johnny will be waiting for us—'

'Forget Johnny, for Christ's sake!' He was working on the second button when Rory let out another howl from the back seat. Joan turned and saw that he had dropped his plastic toy. 'The children—'

'Give him back his toy and come in here—' There was exasperation in his voice.

'But Colm, we can't do it here.' She smiled at him. 'It's a tourist spot. Suppose someone drives in—'

'For God's sake we're married, aren't we?' He jerked his head. 'And we've got those two in the back to prove it.'

'It wouldn't look right.' Joan began to button her blouse. She saw the hunger in her husband's eyes and fondled his cheek. 'Be patient. Wait until we get to the guesthouse.' Colm slid reluctantly back behind the wheel. 'Maybe we could skip lunch and drive straight to where we're staying.' He knew a lot of golfers who stayed off sex during the week of a tournament, but reckoned this was one time he could break that rule—even if it was the British Open that was at stake!

Joan laughed. 'I don't think these two boys will wait that long for something to eat.' She settled into the back seat again. It pleased her that her husband could not wait to get her into bed. It was nice to feel wanted. All those nights sitting at home with only the kids for company, looking at Eurosport on television when they were screening a tournament, to see if she would catch a glimpse of Colm. She envied the wives who could afford to travel with their husbands on tour.

Colm turned the key in the ignition and eased the car out of the lay-by. All those golf studs on tour who boasted of their conquests off the course. He had been tempted a few times, but he had always stood by Joan and the kids. Besides, he reckoned a lot of it was just macho locker-room talk. If even half of it were true, those guys would not have the energy to swing a club, much less compete for four tough days each week on the tour.

BBC commentator Malcolm Jacob stood on the steps outside the Turnberry Hotel, breathed deeply of the breeze whipping in from the Firth, and reckoned it was good to be alive. From his elevated position he saw the Ailsa course spread out below, the clubhouse painted a sparkling white and the flags of many nations flying in the wind, lending a dash of colour and pageantry. Jacob could make out the workmen putting the finishing touches to one of the temporary stands being erected around the eighteenth green. Away in the distance he could see other wood and steel structures being built around the course.

Shading his eyes against the glare, he was able to pick out the television towers, one strategically placed between the first and eighteenth fairways, another at the far end of the links. Soon he and his team would be perched up on one of those, capturing the drama of the Open for millions of armchair viewers around the world. It was a job at which Malcolm Jacob, with his experience of the game allied with his urbane wit, was an acknowledged expert.

He breathed in deeply once more, a well-preserved figure in cashmere sweater and pale blue slacks. It was hard to beat the atmosphere of the

Open—even the Yanks had to admit it was something special. And this time around he had Sally to enjoy it with—what more could a man ask for? Two minutes later he had rejoined her in the breakfast room, admiring her as she deftly spread marmalade on a thin slice of toast.

'Enjoying your breakfast, my dear?'

'We could have had it in bed.' Her grey green eyes teased him over her coffee cup.

'You naughty little devil,' he grinned. 'Didn't you get enough last night?'

'To use a golf term, Malcolm darling, you didn't play a full round. I think you'd had too much to drink.'

'Sshhh! Not so loud.' Jacob glanced around the large room. At the tables he recognised some well-known golfers, agents and media people. The Turnberry Hotel had been booked solid almost a year in advance of the Open tee-off. It was not a place for intimate conversations to be overheard.

'I was tired,' he admitted. 'Driving all the way up from London, then playing eighteen holes at Prestwick yesterday. It was too much. But I'll make it up to you tonight. Promise.'

'Now I know how bored those poor golf wives become while their husbands chase a little white ball into the hole.'

'Careful, my girl. Don't denigrate the great game —one that brought us together.'

Golf had thrown them together at a time when they were both going through a bad patch. Was it really less than a year since they first met—at the Walker Cup clash between the amateur golfers of

Great Britain and Ireland and the Americans at Sunningdale. Malcolm, a former Walker Cup player himself, was as usual among the BBC team covering the event; Sally Penrith had been sent along as production assistant—her first ever golf assignment.

There had been a sexual attraction between them almost from the start. Touching fifty, Malcolm was almost twice her age. But while the flush of athletic prowess had passed and his liking for good food and vintage wine was beginning to show, he could still fill his well-cut sports jackets and matching slacks with distinction.

The fact that he was married did not worry Sally at all. In fact it was a plus in his favour. After a couple of minor affairs with men of her own age she reckoned it was time to go for wealth and experience. Jacob had both in abundance, and his reputation as a womaniser within the BBC made him singularly attractive in her book. He had wit, charm and a job in the City which allowed him unlimited time off for his television work.

Sally knew he also had a wife in Surrey who was teetering on the brink of alcoholism and to whom he was tied in conscience if not exactly in love. She could not make up her mind whether Malcolm was too much of a gentleman to ditch his wife completely or whether he simply liked playing around. Either way she was not particularly worried.

'Don't look now,' Malcolm's voice interrupted her train of thought. 'I see our friend Ricky approaching.'

Ricky Edwards, thirtyish and dressed in trendy Levi jeans and jacket beloved of television directors, wended his way through the tables towards them. 'Morning, Malcolm. Morning, Sally. Didn't quite expect to see you two lovebirds down so early.' The smile playing around the corners of his mouth lent itself to the innuendo.

'I didn't sleep too well last night,' Malcolm responded. 'Tiredness, I suppose.'

'Oh yes. I'm not surprised.' Edwards's laugh was a solo. 'Anyway, it means we can get down to business nice and early.'

'What have you lined up this morning?' Sally asked.

'I'd like Malcolm and his team to come along to cast an eye over our camera angles. We have them set up in the usual spots but we'd like you lot to see if they're okay. Afterwards we'll have you all around a table for a conference to see that we've got everything covered.'

'Splendid, Ricky. I'll alert the rest of the team,' Malcolm replied.

'What interviews have you lined up for today, Sally?' Edwards asked. 'Do you know what time the big boys are arriving?'

Sally had done her homework. 'Most of the home-based pros will drive across today from Glasgow. Lou Menzies'—she mentioned the dour, globe-trotting Australian veteran and holder of the Open title—' flew in last night. He's practising all day and says "no interviews".'

'And the Yanks? What about Escudio, McEvoy, Carlson and the rest?'

'They were playing in the Westchester Classic near New York which finished yesterday and they're expected this evening at Prestwick. Dick Elliott, of course, is already here.' Ricky knew that. The newspapers had carried stories of how America's No. 1 golfer had spent the last week in Ireland with his wife, Susan, playing over a links course which had similar terrain to Turnberry. 'They arrived here a couple of days ago—but of course you know that already, I'm sure,' Sally smiled.

'That chap is certainly giving it a go again this year, despite his past failures,' Ricky said. 'I take it they're staying here?'

'No way. They've rented one of those big houses adjacent to the course. He's had a few practice rounds over the Ailsa already.'

The news did not surprise Malcolm. Now into his thirties, and after more than a decade as a pro golfer, Dick Elliott had won over a dozen major tournaments in his native America and around the world. These included three big ones—the US Open, the Masters, and the American Professional Golfers' Association title. Alas, the last link in the Grand Slam—the British Open—had eluded him over the years. In a decade of trying he had finished second on three occasions and had never been out of the top ten finishers. But he had never held aloft that famous silver trophy.

Two years ago the talented American with the film star good looks seemed to have the title within his grasp when he led by three shots with only four holes to play. That had been at Muirfield, another tough Scottish track. But he had finished ingloriously with two bogeys, triple-putting the last green, and the fast-finishing Englishman, Paul Pender, had pipped him by a stroke. Afterwards the whispering had started: 'Elliott blew it again. The fellow will never win the British Open. The psychological factor, you know.' Dick Elliott knew what was being said about him and it made him even more determined to prove them all wrong.

'Okay, so we know where the big shots are staying. Well done, Sally. Now Malcolm, I'll expect some short interviews for our Open preview. And don't forget the home boys—' Ricky consulted his clipboard. 'Jesus! I almost forgot. What about this fellow Maurelli. That Yank is supposed to be something special, isn't he?'

'He certainly is,' Malcolm agreed. 'And that wife of his, Lisa, is a bit of a cracker too.' Tony Maurelli was the most colourful golfer on the US circuit, a young guy who had come to the top quickly and who grabbed the headlines by treating the media to a champagne party whenever he won a tournament. It was a gimmick that had earned him the title Champagne Tony—and now the flamboyant character was coming over, boasting that he would take the Open at his first attempt.

'Do we know what time Maurelli and his party are arriving?'

Sally nodded and gave Ricky one of her dazzling smiles. 'We certainly do. As you probably are aware, Champagne Tony won the Westchester Classic yesterday. He and his wife were to fly into Prestwick in their private jet today but that arrangement was cancelled.'

She could see the horror spreading across Ricky's face. 'You mean he's not coming?'

'He's coming all right, but they won't be flying in

until tomorrow. I phoned Westchester last night and got in touch with Maurelli's agent. After Tony's win yesterday, his agent had no trouble fixing up an exhibition game in New York today for a $50,000 fee. Marvin Maxwell—that's Tony's agent—reckoned the money was too good to pass up.'

'With him getting ten per cent off the top he would, wouldn't he?' Edwards made a note on his clipboard. 'All right, my loves. That's all for the present. We'll get together later.'

Malcolm watched the director weave his way through the tables, avoiding the white-coated waiters bustling in and out with trays of food. 'My word. What a busy little man.'

He leaned his elbows on the table, moved closer to Sally so that those at the next table would not hear. 'Now, my love. What about you and me?'

'What have you in mind?'

'How about a little holiday when we get through here next Sunday?'

'Sounds interesting. I'd love to see more of Scotland—'

'That's not quite what I had in mind.'

She pretended not to be interested. 'Don't you ever think of anything else?'

'When I'm with you, Sally dear—never! What do you say to a Highland fling?'

'What about Felicity? Won't she be expecting you home after the Open?'

Mention of his wife wiped the smile off Malcolm's face. He thought for a moment, then said: 'I'll phone her, tell her I'm going on a golf trip with some of the chaps.'

Sally looked doubtful. 'Do you think she'll fall for that? I mean with your reputation—'

He waved his hand. 'Don't worry. Felicity is used to my not coming home by now.' Still, it was a bit of a worry. He had not told his wife about Sally, although she must suspect by now that he had a mistress. Maybe that was why she had been hitting the bottle harder than usual lately. He knew it must be lonely for her in the house on her own, with only the cleaning lady coming in and the boys away at school, but dammit he had his own life to live.

Malcolm remembered back to those early years at their local golf club where both their families had been cornerstones. It was almost taken for granted that he and Felicity would marry, which they had obligingly done in due course. They were a feared husband and wife team in open foursomes. He was the better player of the two, representing his county, winning two British Amateur titles, playing for England and once being on the Walker Cup team. Golf aside, their lives had been one long social whirl. Then, like his game itself, things had palled, gone off slightly. He had to have excitement in his life, and with Felicity it just wasn't there any more.

'Telephone call for Mr Jacob.' The voice coming across the p.a. system brought him back to the present with a jolt.

'Wonder who that could be?' Sally asked.

'Maybe something's come up at the office.' But he knew this was unlikely. His partner in the City rarely phoned him when he was on a golf assignment. He excused himself and crossed the room towards reception. He had a sense of foreboding that his well-planned week at the Open at Turnberry was about to be thrown into disarray.

Joan Donohue sat in the back seat of the car, gazing with unseeing eyes out over the Firth of Clyde as they made their way towards Girvan. Five years married to a golf professional, touring with Colm full-time before the babies came, had given her a pretty good insight into the life and times of the men who tramped the world's fairways in search of fame and fortune. It had also introduced her to the women— wives, mistresses and groupies—who tagged along for a slice of the action.

Married at eighteen, just after Colm had turned professional following a meteoric amateur career that had looked to be a stepping-stone to a lucrative lifestyle, she had left her hometown in the west of Ireland and was plunged into a new world. It was a lifestyle for which she soon realised she was ill- prepared.

It awed her at first to be in the weekly company of handsome bronzed men, many of them from different continents whose names she had known once only from the newspapers. She marvelled at the women partners who moved so effortlessly from hotel to hotel, enjoying the pre-tournament parties but staying discreetly in the background when the real action started on the fairways.

'Son,' Johnny Davis had counselled Colm when he was turning pro, 'you have a great talent and soon the opportunities to make big money will come your way. But it won't be easy, neither for you nor for Joan.'

Johnny was right. She had encountered problems from the beginning, the first when she was taken aside by smooth-talking Ron Grantham, whose English management agency had won the race to sign up Colm. He had tried to give her some advice about the tour. It was during the press reception that he had given to hype up Colm's signing the contract. While the members of the media helped themselves to the free bar, Grantham had taken her upstairs to his suite in the Dublin hotel.

'To be frank, Joan, we're not keen on young wives accompanying their husbands on tour. It creates problems, you see.'

'I'm afraid I don't understand, Mr Grantham.'

He studied her face before replying. 'No. Of course you don't.' Ron Grantham had a beautifully cultivated English accent, although he was actually a bookmaker's son from Liverpool. His management stable included first-rank snooker, soccer and golf personalities, plus two of Europe's Formula One racing drivers. He was accustomed to dealing with temperamental, overpaid stars and prided himself on never losing his cool. 'Wives, you see—and young wives in particular—tend to distract their husbands from the business in hand.'

'How so?'

He waited a moment, wondering if she was naive or perhaps having him on. He decided on a head-on approach. 'What if you have a baby? I expect you will take precautions for the first couple of years until your husband makes a breakthrough—'

Joan shrugged. 'Colm and I don't believe in those things. If it happens, it happens.'

'But don't you see that if you do have a baby it will probably mean your having to stay home while Colm plays the circuit. Golfers, like all sportsmen striving for the top, need a good night's rest. They can't be expected to perform at their best on the course if they've been up half the night listening to a baby crying.'

But Joan had stuck to her beliefs and had refused to listen to his advice. And she had enjoyed the tour that summer; it was like a permanent honeymoon, travelling throughout Britain and into Europe and North Africa, managing to live on Colm's winnings, even though they rarely went over the four figure mark each week.

It was strange and exciting. She had even been approached once at the Barcelona Open when she was not wearing her wedding ring. She was sitting at a table in the marquee reserved for players and the sponsors' representatives when a young, handsome Australian, who introduced himself as Jack Hastings, had sat down uninvited and began chatting her up. Joan recognised him as one of the touring professionals who always seemed to have a girl in attendance. She had told him she was waiting for Colm and had sent him on his way with a few well- chosen words!

When she had mentioned the incident to her husband later, he had laughed. 'They say that guy Hastings has had as many birds as he's had birdies. That's why he's never won a tournament—his attitude is all wrong. It happens all the time on tour.'

Two months later Joan discovered she was pregnant. After Michael was born, she continued on the circuit with Colm for a season but it was very difficult and she felt that having the baby and herself along was affecting his game. His winnings dropped during his second year on tour and not long afterwards she found she was pregnant yet again. When the tour started the following year, she decided she would stay at home to look after Michael and Rory and let her husband go it alone.

The new arrangement did not make much difference to Colm's level of winnings. Each week was a struggle to make enough to meet travelling expenses. New talent, some of it from America, was joining the tour and the competition was red hot. At the end of that year his winnings had dropped so low that Ron Grantham informed him that his agency was not interested in handling his affairs any longer. Since then it had been a struggle, although this year looked like it was going to be his best ever. At least he had qualified for the Open having finished in the top five at the Scottish Open at Gleneagles last week—and if his game came together during these four days at Turnberry, anything could happen.

'Here we are, love. This is Girvan.' Colm's voice jerked her out of her reverie. 'Wake up the boys and we'll have something to eat.'

Michael Jacob lifted the telephone indicated by the receptionist and said: 'Hello. Malcolm Jacob here.'

'Malcolm! Oh, thank heavens.'

'Felicity!' Christ! He groaned inwardly. Then panic gripped him. 'Anything wrong?'

'Of course. Why the hell do you think I'm phoning

you—' He sensed she had been drinking. Probably had a gin and tonic in her hand right now.

'What is it, Felicity? Has anything happened to the boys?'

'No. It's me, Malcolm. *Me*, damn you.'

He felt an enormous sense of relief. He was about to say 'Is that all?', but checked himself. My God, she was already on the sauce. He was trying to contain his anger when she spoke again.

'Malcolm?'

'Felicity, have you been drinking? You can hardly be out of bed—'

'Actually, darling, I'm still in bed!' Her laugh was dangerously high and tense.

'Felicity, darling. What is it you want? I am rather busy right now—' Maybe if he showed sympathy instead of anger, he could get her off his back. It had worked before.

'I want someone to talk to, my darling. That's all.'

'Of course, darling. You're lonely. Isn't Mrs Houston there? You two usually have a good old chinwag—'

'She's ill. She phoned earlier. Food poisoning or something dreadful. She won't be in for the rest of the week.'

'Oh.' Malcolm pondered. Trust their stupid cleaning woman to eat something peculiar the week of the Open championship. 'Look, darling. I'm sorry, but I can't come back home just now—'

'That's all right, Malcolm. I understand. I'll come up!'

He felt as if someone had punched him in the solar plexus. 'No, no, darling. You can't. Not this week—'

19

'Why not, Malcolm?' Her tone had changed.

'Because—' his mind raced—'because the weather here is dreadful. We're expecting storms all week—'

There was a pause at the other end of the line and he thought he could hear something being poured into a glass. 'Darling, if you put me off, you'll run into something worse than a storm. I promise.' Another pause. 'Well?'

'It's just not practical, Felicity. Besides, the hotel here is completely booked out. Not a bed available. I'm squeezed into a single room myself. Every hotel and guesthouse for miles around is booked solid. Taken over by golf fans—'

'Rubbish. I don't believe you.'

'Honest, darling.'

'Malcolm, dear. You sound like you're hiding something—or somebody—from me.'

He was waiting for that old chestnut. 'Tell you what, Felicity, as soon as the Open is over on Sunday, I'll fly back home. What would you say to the two of us flitting off to Paris for a few days. We're due a break—' Damn, he would have to postpone his holiday with Sally. He hoped she would understand.

'Malcolm, I'm setting off today. I'll pop a suitcase into the car, stay overnight along the way, and be in Turnberry sometime tomorrow. How's that?'

'No, darling. You can't. I forbid you to drive. Catch a plane to Prestwick and I'll meet you at the airport tomorrow. Phone me back when you've booked the ticket.' He could hardly believe what he was suggesting. But she was determined to come up and he did not want her weaving her way along the motorway, stopping off now and then for a couple of drinks.

'Perfect. Thank you, Malcolm. Oh, and darling—'

'Yes?' Jeez, what now?

'I promise not to be any trouble.'

'Trouble?'

'You know, especially at that stuffy old Golf Writers' Association dinner you arrange every year on the eve of the Open—'

Oh God, he had almost forgotten that! Several years ago he had come up with the idea of the top golf writers from the world press who were covering the Open having a formal dinner the night before the event began. He had succeeded in getting one of the major oil companies to sponsor the dinner and it had proved a spectacular success. This year he had decided to change the format and allow the writers to bring along their partners. The dinner would also be open to the committee members of the Royal and Ancient Golf Society, the ruling body of world golf. Some of the biggest names from among the 150 golfers competing were also invited and a private room had been reserved for the function in the Turnberry Hotel for Wednesday night.

Sally had been looking forward to the big night and she had even brought along a new dress for the occasion. Now he would have to inform her that she would not be going. Worse, with Felicity coming, Sally would now have to move out of his room. Almost in a daze he said goodbye to his wife. Malcolm put down the phone and mopped his brow. He was not looking forward to going back into the breakfast room and telling Sally the bad news.

'You feeling all right, Mr Jacob? Not bad news, I hope,' the receptionist asked anxiously.

'Oh, er, yes. Got a bit of a jolt but I'm okay now.' He forced a smile and, despite the fact that it was still mid-morning, walked into the bar off the foyer and ordered himself a double Scotch. Malcolm Jacob felt he needed it.

Dominick Earley entered the hotel which was in one of Belfast's better class suburbs. The young man behind the desk looked up, recognised the visitor, nodded a greeting, and watched as he entered the lounge bar.

Earley paused in the archway of the lounge, surveying the other occupants. It was a quiet time of the afternoon; the lunchtime rush was over and it was still too early for the regulars who dropped in for a quick one on the way home. Two well-dressed ladies in their fifties sipped sherries and chatted. Almost directly opposite them in another corner of the lounge two men, similarly well-dressed, were enjoying their second whiskies. The only other occupant was the barman, keeping himself busy shining already spotless glasses. He broke off his work to pull the new arrival a half-pint of lager which Earley took to a table at the end of the lounge, facing the entrance.

Dominick Earley, commandant of the breakaway IRA faction operating out of West Belfast, undid the button of his Donegal tweed jacket and sat down.

The lounge was pleasantly warm and he would have liked to loosen his tie but decided against it. With him a neat appearance counted for a lot; it showed discipline and orderliness. It was the lack of discipline, so vital when one was engaged in a guerilla war against the forces of the British Crown and all it stood for, that had made him decide to quit the Provisional IRA. Too many thoughtless and unnecessary killings were taking place; it was time for him to form his own breakaway group. That had been just under a year ago and it was now operating successfully.

There had been no recrimination from the regular Provo unit operating in West Belfast. After all, the ultimate aim of both factions was the same—to rid this part of Ireland of the British Army and bring down Unionism. But while he abhorred the killings and bombings of the rival IRA unit, Earley enjoyed grabbing the headlines. As he sipped his lager, he reckoned the plan he was about to put into operation on the Ayrshire coast of Scotland would do just that. It showed flair and daring; it was a pity he would not be taking an active part in it himself.

His watch showed three minutes past four. Martin Dignam was late. He would have to speak to him about that. If Dignam did not arrive soon, the girl would show up first and that would be awkward. Blast him! The fellow was committed, no doubt about that. But when a member of the unit was ordered to come along to a preliminary briefing session, Earley expected him to arrive on time.

Another full minute passed before he saw the figure of the man he was awaiting framed in the archway. Dignam peered around the discreetly lit lounge, saw Earley, came over and slid onto the cushioned banquette seat beside him.

'You're late, Martin. Four minutes.'

Dignam glanced at his watch, but let the accusation hang in the air for a few seconds. 'So I am. So what's the hurry? You said it was only a preliminary briefing. We're not doing the job today, are we?' He grinned, strong white teeth showing through a thick black beard.

'When I set a time, I mean it. Understand?'

'Yes, Commandant Earley.' The sarcasm in the tone was not lost on Earley, but he let it pass. He decided—not for the first time—that he did not like Martin Dignam. They were both in their mid-thirties, had grown up together and had both joined the IRA in their late teens. In fact he had been on several assignments with Dignam over the years and knew him to be a fearless, albeit sometimes reckless, companion, particularly when it came to a shoot-out with the Brits or with any of the Protestant para-military organisations.

He also knew that Dignam was a bit of a show-off, a fellow who craved action and who was not averse to boasting about his exploits in the pubs and clubs frequented by the unit's members. Dark-haired, athletically built and the owner of a back lane garage in Belfast, he had that moodiness about him that women seemed to find attractive.

'Nice place this.' Dignam surveyed the hotel lounge. 'Makes a change from the smokey backrooms where we used to meet when we were with the other lads.'

'If the Brits or the Prods want to sort you out, they know where to find you in the clubs,' Earley responded. 'I doubt that they'd think of looking for us in a place like this.'

They were silent for a few moments. 'Get yourself a drink, Martin. We're waiting for somebody.'

Dignam went over to the counter, exchanged a few words with the barman and returned carrying a pint of Guinness. He took a long pull, wiped the froth from his beard with the back of his hand and asked: 'So, what's the job?'

'Know anything about golf, Martin?' There was a hint of a smile about Earley's lips.

'Golf? Will you be serious, man? What the hell would I know about golf?'

'I am serious. You're going to the British Open in Scotland. It starts on Thursday. I've got two tickets.' He was enjoying the mystified look on Dignam's face.

'Two? Who else is coming?'

'You'll be accompanied on the mission by Marie Kirk.'

Dignam's eyes narrowed. 'Marie—you mean Patrick's young sister?'

'That's right.'

The look on Dignam's face turned to annoyance. 'Fucking hell. I thought she was in England, studying or something. Last time I saw her she was over for Patrick's funeral.'

'She's back home again. Permanently. She's with us now.'

'But she's only a kid—'

'She's nineteen, Martin. About the same age as you when you got involved.'

Dignam brooded. He took another long pull at his drink before speaking again. 'But for God's sake why pick her for an assignment with me? I mean after the way Patrick died—'

'Forget that. It was unfortunate that he died in that shoot-out at the bank. You didn't. You got away—'

'I was lucky, that's all.' Dignam was angry. 'It could easily have been me instead of Patrick.'

'Nobody blamed you, Martin,' Earley said soothingly. 'You were exonerated after you gave evidence at the investigation. What are you getting worked up about?'

Dignam did not reply. Christ! Was this some kind of joke, or was there a deeper reason for his being teamed up with Patrick's sister? And he did not like the way Earley had smiled when he had said that nobody was blaming him for what had happened. He looked very superior, sitting there in his jacket and tie, like a tailor's dummy. The man had not seen action for a long time; not since he had assumed command. Too busy giving orders for others to take risks. There were several other men in the unit, himself included, who would make a far better leader than big-shot Dominick Earley.

Dignam had known the Kirk family for years. That was what had made Patrick's death all the more tragic. Their house in Dindale Street was a hotbed of Republicanism—had not Patrick's father himself been interned as a youngster during the last war for his attacks on British barracks in the North? Only natural then, that when the troubles broke out again, the son would get involved. Not long after the IRA split in West Belfast, he and Patrick Kirk had been sent on the bank raid. The new unit needed funds to operate and they had been selected for the job, but it had all gone terribly wrong. Martin Dignam did not like to think about it.

'Something troubling you, Martin?'

'I told you. Marie Kirk. Couldn't you pick someone else for the job?'

'It's too late. Everything has been arranged. I'll fill you and Marie in on the final details tomorrow.'

'But—'

Earley's voice was sharp, commanding. 'I said it's too late to change plans now. You're under orders. Understand?'

Their eyes met across the table, each one challenging the other. Finally Dignam said: 'If you say so, Commandant.'

'Good.' Earley's eyes shifted to the archway. 'Here's Marie now.'

Dignam looked over his shoulder. She stood in the archway, a girl of medium height, wearing a skirt that finished just above her knees and a blouse that accentuated her small, well-shaped bust. A bag with a cardigan looped over it hung from her shoulder. Her dark hair was cut short and it made her look older than she was. He watched her as she walked slowly towards them, her high heels sinking into the lounge carpet. The men in the lounge followed her progress with interest. The trip to Scotland might have its compensations after all, Dignam thought.

She said hello, smiling, and eased herself into the seat. 'Hello, Marie,' Earley said. 'You know Martin, of course.'

She looked directly at him across the table. 'Of course. You and Patrick got on well together.'

'Yes.' Dignam felt uncomfortable, not quite

knowing what to say. Instead, he swallowed some Guinness.

Earley rose and went to the bar for a glass of white wine for Marie. Dignam took an unusual interest in the two ladies who were gathering up their parcels, ready to leave. When he looked at the girl again, he found her eyes on him.

'How long were you in England?' he asked.

'Two years. In London mostly.'

'When did you join the organisation?'

'In our house you didn't join the IRA. You were in it from the moment you were born.'

After another pause he asked: 'How's your Dad?'

'Not great. Patrick's death was a big blow. I don't think he'll ever get over it.'

He was relieved to see Earley returning with her drink. 'Here's to Scotland.' Earley raised his glass and they all drank. 'That's where you're going on your first assignment, Marie. With Martin.'

'What's in Scotland?'

'The British Open golf championship, an event shown on television around the world. We aim to use it to get publicity for our struggle.'

Marie looked interested. 'What do you hope to do—dig up the greens? They did that in Portmarnock at the Irish Open a few years ago and it was reported in all the newspapers.'

'Don't tell me you're sending us over there just to dig up a few sods of turf?' Dignam asked, sarcasm in his tone. Marie could feel the tension between the two men. She looked at Dominick Earley, saw his jaw muscles tighten.

'My plan is more daring than that. And it's guaranteed to get a lot more media attention.'

'What the hell is it then?' Dignam pressed. 'A kidnap. A bomb, maybe?' His voice, tinged with excitement, was nevertheless pitched low.

'That's right, Martin. A bomb,' Earley said quietly.

Dignam heard Marie catch her breath. Jeez, she was scared already. He hoped Earley knew what he was doing on this one.

She spoke up. 'The bomb . . . where will it be planted? I mean, will anyone be killed?'

Marie was relieved when Earley shook his head. 'That's not the objective. Look, I can't give you all the details just now. There are a couple of things I want to check out first. We'll meet here tomorrow at the same time for a final briefing. Okay?'

'Can you at least tell us when we leave for Scotland?' Dignam asked. He wished Earley would stop the fencing around. He was milking the situation, showing off in front of the girl.

'You and Marie will catch the Wednesday morning sailing from Larne. You'll be going by car.'

'Want me to nick one tonight?' At last there was a hint of excitement in Martin Dignam's voice.

'No. It's too big a job to risk being picked up for driving a stolen car. I'll hire one'—he laughed nervously—'more respectable. Oh, there's just one more important item. . . .' He looked from one to the other. 'You will be travelling as a married couple. Your husband is a golf fanatic, Marie, who wants to see the Open championship. It will mean sharing a room. Any objections?'

'None from me,' Dignam replied, smiling.

29

Marie felt their eyes on her. She shook her head and Earley saw that she was blushing slightly.

'Okay then, see you both tomorrow.'

Susan Elliott looked at herself in the full-length bedroom mirror and liked what she saw. Although it was eight years since she had walked the ramp as one of America's top fashion models, she reckoned there was still a good living in the business if she ever tired of following her husband on the world golf circuit.

At twenty-seven years of age the threat of wrinkles were still a long way off. Years of careful dieting, no children, lots of exercise—she got plenty of that tramping the fairways with her famous husband—had paid off handsomely. The no children edict nowadays hinged mainly on Richard's obsession to become one of golf's immortals by winning the Open. There were occasions when Susan missed not having babies, but there was still plenty of time. And besides, her husband's sizeable winnings, plus his lucrative contracts, meant that she travelled everywhere in style. Golf could be boring to watch, but it did have its compensations.

She crossed the room to the wide bay window. Richard's agency had hired the house especially for them. Although it was within a couple of long iron shots of the Turnberry clubhouse, it isolated him from the media, the crowds and his fellow competitors. She let her eyes wander over the undulating Ailsa course. He was down there with his caddie somewhere, practising, measuring distances, trying out shots, noting bunker positions. After that he would probably spend an hour on the putting green.

Susan looked at her watch. Almost four o'clock. She could do with another martini sour. Okay, it was the fourth since Richard had left in mid-morning. So what.

Downstairs, she was pouring when Mrs Craigie came out of the kitchen. 'Will you be going out, Ma'am?'

'Yes. I'll stroll down shortly and meet Richard at the clubhouse.' Mrs Craigie came with the house; she was employed by the real owners and was part of the rental deal arranged by the agency.

'Will you both be back for dinner?'

'Yes, Mrs Craigie. Make it eight o'clock. That okay with you?' Richard rarely went out at night during a major championship, and especially not when he was playing in the British Open.

'Och, don't worry about me. I'm here to do your bidding.' Mrs Craigie noted the martini in the glass. Poor thing, alone in a big house like this. You could sense her boredom. To be sure, young golfers nowadays could earn big money—aye, too much for their own good, Mrs Craigie thought. But it was sometimes a lonely life for their young wives.

Susan sat on the seat beneath the window. This was the time that all golf wives hated and she was no different from the rest of them. It was frustrating waiting around for the big event to start, knowing that the best way to help your husband was to keep a low profile. It was not too bad when the darned championship began; at least you could be there with him to share the ups and downs each day. There was no fun standing around on the practice ground looking at your man hit golf ball after golf ball into the distance.

She thought about the first time, nine years ago now, that she and Richard had met. It was at the Parkridge Country Club in Virginia where she, along with a few other girls from the model agency, had been brought along to decorate the occasion. The club's star golfer, Richard Elliott, had won the US Amateur title two days previously in California and the proud members of Parkridge were giving him a welcome home party.

He was twenty-two, tall, rather on the thin side, and not the handsomest among the dinner-jacketed gathering. Someone told her that he was from a well-to-do family and that he was number one in the golf squad at Parkridge College. The word was that his father planned to bring him into the family law firm next year when he graduated.

'But hell, I don't want to become a lawyer. I'm interested in becoming a pro golfer, playing for pay.' He looked at her with his intense eyes. 'Know anything about golf?'

'Nothing at all.'

'I could teach you. It's not difficult. Honest. You're tall, and I bet you could develop a good swing; probably hit the ball a mile. Like to try?'

He had cornered her as soon as he had extricated himself from the crowd of well-wishers seeking to shake the hand of the new US Amateur champion. His mother and father had drifted over and had been introduced: Clark Elliott, in white dinner jacket, tanned, distinguished, and his wife, Magda, elegant in a designer dress. They had chatted desultorily for a while, then drifted off, leaving the young couple alone.

'You're a model, I've seen your photograph around.' She thought him a bit brash, but likeable. He caught her by surprise with his next question. 'How much money do you make a year?'

'Enough.'

'Come on. Tell me. It's no big deal.'

'I make at least two thousand dollars a day when I work.' The surprised look on his face had given her a lot of satisfaction.

'Wow! But you're only a kid.'

She was just eighteen years old then. The next day he gave her a golf lesson and after that they dated a lot. Richard had wanted to turn pro immediately, but his father, bitterly disappointed at his son's decision, had insisted that Richard graduate from college first.

At the end of that year, he had battled his way through the qualifying tournaments at the rookie school to earn his pro card and join the big names when the tour started off in January. He showed such good form that some of the golf writers were comparing him to the young Jack Nicklaus. Richard was snapped up by a top management agency and justified its faith in him by winning the Memphis Open within three months of joining the tour.

By the end of that first year, he had won another tour event and made the halfway cut in all but one of the remaining events. *Golf Digest* voted him Rookie of the Year by an overwhelming margin and at the end of the year he had won over $300,000. He was on his way.

Susan's modelling career was also on the up and

up, which meant that, with the travelling both careers called for, they did not get to see much of each other. It was frustrating, because by then they were sleeping together and had discovered that they were very much in love.

'Tell you what,' Richard said. 'We'll make a deal.'

'What sort of deal?'

It was morning and they were having breakfast in bed in Susan's apartment. By now she had moved her base to New York and was picking up lots of work. Richard had decided to take a week off from the tour, probably, Susan reckoned, to get things sorted out between them.

'Look, we both want to be with each other, right?' She noticed when he had something urgent to discuss with her he always ended his sentences abruptly. 'So—' he turned on the pillow and faced her—'here's the deal. Whichever one of us makes a million dollars first in one year, the other will give up their career so that we can be together. How's that?'

It struck her as being a bit bizarre. When she had recovered from the initial shock, she said: 'But Richard, I couldn't ask you to give up golf. It's your whole life.'

He laughed as though she had said something funny. 'Who the hell says I'll have to give up golf? I aim to beat you to that million, Susan.' She knew his chances were slim.

Susan was now at the stage of her career where her agency was commanding breathtaking fees for her services—and getting them. She also had a couple of tentative film offers to consider.

'You'd never make a million dollars on the tour in

one year, Richard. You'd have to win five, maybe six tournaments.'

'Not really. All I've got to do is win one of the majors—the Masters, the British or the US Open or the PGA. And I can do it. I know I can. The endorsements would be huge.' He stroked her hair, kissed her lightly. 'Is it a deal?'

Once again Susan had the impression that she was being rushed into making a hasty decision. She gambled and lost. The following April he won the Masters at Augusta in Georgia. Susan watched the final round on TV in New York—she was shooting a commercial at the time—and cheered louder than anyone when he sank the final putt. She watched him being presented with the famous green jacket in the clubhouse and reckoned her career was grinding to a halt. No way would she welch on their deal.

A month later they were married in a church ceremony in Oakmont, Virginia. They had to postpone the honeymoon; Richard was hot property since his Masters' win, and his contractual arrangements ordained that he rejoin the tour immediately. Their trip to England in July for the British Open would be their honeymoon. It was held that year in Hoylake, near Liverpool and the weather was dreadful. Richard was one of the favourites to take the coveted title, but he was never in the hunt. He had kissed away her disappointment with a 'Don't worry, honey. We'll be back next year' promise.

In fact they were back for seven years in a row, but the British Open still eluded him. Susan accompanied him to the great courses . . . Muirfield, Turnberry, St. Andrews, Birkdale . . . but it was always

Open failure. Susan had travelled the world with Richard, seeing him win tournaments in Australia, Japan and the Far East, offering solace when his game was off. She had long given up her apartment in New York; now they had homes in Fort Lauderdale, Florida, and one back in Richmond, Virginia.

'When are we going to have a baby?' she had often asked.

'We can't have a baby just yet, honey. You *know* that. Wait until I win the Open and do the Grand Slam. Then I'll cut down on my tournament schedule. I promise. Plenty of time yet.'

'Is there, Richard?'

'Sure, honey.' She hoped that time would arrive this week in Turnberry.

Susan drained the last of her martini. Maybe she would feel better tomorrow when some of the other American golfers and their wives flew in from the States, although she had nothing in common with Tony Maurelli and that sexy wife of his, Lisa, who liked to set tongues wagging with her behaviour.

Then there was Rafael Escudio, the Mexican who was now a naturalised American. He was a mean, swarthy type, a fellow who, it was whispered, had shot to stardom too quickly for his own good. He had a liking for fast women and fast greens. Often she had seen him eyeing her at some function or other on the tour, although he had never made any approaches. She wondered what her reaction would be if he did make a pass.

Susan rose and crossed to the door. On the way she called out, 'I'm strolling down to meet Richard, Mrs Craigie. See you later.'

'For God's sake, Malcolm, you can't ask me to move out of your room. Where do you expect me to go? Every hotel and guesthouse within miles is full.'

Sally glared at Malcolm Jacob. He looked harassed and not at all like the suave, imperturbable golf commentator whose voice was known to millions. 'Sshhh, darling. Not so loud. I did try to put Felicity off. But she wouldn't listen to me—'

They were in the bar of the Turnberry Hotel. It was late afternoon and the place was getting more crowded by the minute. They had just spent several hours working with the television crew and Malcolm had taped a couple of interviews for tomorrow's transmission. This was the first time since breakfast that they had been alone together.

'OK, Malcolm dear, you tell me where the hell I sleep after tonight. You're the one who got me into this mess.'

'Frankly, I don't know. I've tried everything. I've even asked the manager if one of the staff rooms will be vacant.'

'Thanks very much!'

'There is a storeroom in the attic—'

'What!' Sally put her drink down so hard on the counter that some of it spilled. 'I'm not sleeping in any attic. You sleep up there if you wish and let me share with Felicity. We could exchange some interesting stories at bedtime.'

Dammit, why are women always so unreasonable, Malcolm wondered? He was seeing a side of Sally he had not experienced before. He decided to offer one more suggestion.

'What about one of your friends? Perhaps some

of our own girls would let you share with them?'

She levelled her gaze at him. 'I suppose I'll have to do my own begging. I hope your wife enjoys herself in my bed. Frankly, I rather doubt that she will!' Sally finished her drink, uncoiled herself from the bar stool and said: 'Goodbye, Malcolm darling. See you when you sort yourself out.'

With that she turned on her heel and swept out of the bar. Several pairs of male eyes followed her progress, then turned in his direction. Malcolm ignored the curious stares, leaned his elbows on the bar, and made a point of studying the rows of bottles on the shelves.

It was mid-afternoon by the time Colm Donohue and his family arrived at the guesthouse ten miles up the coast from Turnberry. Johnny Davis was already there, sitting outside in the sun, working on Colm's clubs. He waved a greeting as the car slid into the parking area beside the large three-storeyed house.

They were welcomed by Janet and Donald Carlyle, the middle-aged couple who owned 'Seaview', built on an elevation which afforded an expansive view of the firth. 'Bring the wee children in right away,' Mrs Carlyle said. 'You must be all hot and sticky after that drive. The children can play in the back garden; they'll be safe there. I'll give them both a glass of lemonade.'

They registered and Colm carried the suitcases upstairs. The rooms were small but comfortable and his eyes roamed to the bed in the corner. Joan must have read what was in his mind for she said: 'Why don't you go down and chat to Johnny while I unpack. You haven't seen each other for some time.'

Johnny was still lolling in the sun. They sat in silence for a while, enjoying the view across the expanse of water. Finally the older man said: 'You had a good tournament last week in Glasgow, lad. You might have won it if you had been a bit sharper around the greens. I saw the last round on television and spotted a couple of flaws in your game. We'll work on your putting over the next few days.'

Colm said: 'When we stopped off in Girvan, I met Bill White in the hotel. He reckons my game is coming good and thinks I have a useful chance in the Open.' Bill White, a columnist with an upmarket Sunday newspaper, was regarded as one of the more knowledgeable writers on the circuit.

'I'll go along with that, Colm lad. First time I saw you whack a golf ball as a youngster, I knew you had what it takes to become a champion. Remember when you won the Irish Boys' title—you were only fourteen years old at the time. You did everything I told you to perfection that day.'

Colm remembered; pity it was not the same nowadays. If only he could earn enough money on the tour to employ Johnny Davis as his full-time caddie, it would make that vital difference to his game. He was sure of that. The problem was that only those golfers who made a good living on the tour could afford to bring their own caddie along with them. Those who did not earn big cheques each week engaged local caddies at the tournaments. It was not the same as having a regular companion at one's side. The circuit could be a lonely place and a pro golfer needed a buddy, someone at his shoulder, with a word of advice or encouragement at a vital moment during a round. Johnny Davis was such a man.

'I see I'm a fifty to one shot in the betting to take the Open title.'

'That right? I'll have a couple of quid on you at that price. Someone has to win it—and it might as well be you, Colm lad.'

Johnny squinted into the distance, his face, burnt brown after a lifetime spent in the open air, thoughtful. At fifty-five, his firm body was now inclined to fat, but his shoulders beneath the thin silk short-sleeved shirt were powerful and his forearms were still muscular.

'It takes a great golfer to win the Open championship, lad. You've got to have it up there—' he tapped his head—'and down here—' Johnny's finger jabbed his stomach. 'I've heard of golfers who had a chance to win the title getting sick in the locker-room on the last day.' He grinned suddenly. 'But we'll meet that problem when we come to it, son. Now what have you planned for this evening?'

Colm considered for a few moments. 'It's still only four-thirty. How about you and I going into Turnberry and getting onto the course? I could get in a practice round before it gets dark. Might as well start my preparation for the Open today, Johnny.'

He was surprised when he saw the older man shake his head. 'I don't think that would be wise, son. Why don't you go up to Joan? It must be a long time since you were really together. Know what I mean?'

He knew what Johnny meant. It was a great idea! Joan was upstairs right now, unpacking, in the bedroom. The children were safe in the garden. 'But shouldn't I be at least hitting some golf balls?'

'Listen, lad. There are young golfers like yourself on the course right now practising for all they're worth, burning themselves out before the Open even starts! I don't want that to happen to you. Upstairs now and do what you really want to do—'

'Is that an order?'

'Yes!'

Colm jumped to his feet. 'Okay, Johnny, you're the boss—'

'You leave everything to me. I'll drive back to Turnberry, walk around the course, take a few measurements. And I'll book a practice time for us tomorrow.' Johnny rose and made his way to his car. 'See you later, son,' he called over his shoulder.

Colm paused in the doorway of the guesthouse and shouted across the car park: 'When I become Open champion next Sunday, Johnny, I'm going to appoint you my permanent caddie. Okay?'

Johnny Davis waved his acknowledgement. Colm was bounding up the stairs before the car turned onto the main road.

2

The media had descended on Prestwick Airport en masse to record the arrival of Tony Maurelli, the flash, brash American, coming over for his first tilt at the British Open championship. Maurelli's delayed arrival had heightened the journalists' expectation. He had played in Britain only once before but then had been relatively unknown. Now in his fifth year as a pro, he was topping the American money list and his victory in the Westchester Classic was his third in the US this year. Maurelli's game was obviously red hot.

'Let's hope he's brought the bubbly with him.' Whoever it was among the waiting journalists who made the remark was echoing the sentiments of his colleagues. Tony dispensing the champagne after a victory always made good copy and they loved him for it. The post-tournament press conference was never dull whenever Maurelli won.

'Is it true he pilots his own jet?' an eager young photographer asked. 'Think he'll come off the plane with a glass in his hand?'

'Don't worry, even if he doesn't, you'll still get a good picture,' one of his colleagues replied. 'Watch out for that pretty young wife of his. When Tony came over two years ago to play in a tournament at Sunningdale, she got nearly as much publicity as he did. She's a stunner.'

Murmurs of approval greeted this statement. It was true: Lisa Maurelli was certainly a looker. With her dark Italian features and luscious figure, she was every photographer's dream. And she knew how to dress, too. Tony, with his huge physique, almost dwarfed his petite wife, but her figure-hugging outfits, which she wore on the course when she followed her husband during tournaments, meant she was never overlooked. Her behaviour often set tongues wagging and at times outraged the wives of some of the other golfers. Not that the gossip worried Lisa.

Fifteen minutes later the jet, with its blue and white body flashings, had landed and was taxiing along the tarmac towards the arrival building. A room had been set aside for the arrival of Maurelli and his entourage and it had been arranged that he would give a press conference there. The golf writers gazed from the window as their photographic colleagues scampered outside to get pictures of Tony and Lisa as soon as they stepped out onto the flight steps now being put into place.

A few minutes later the door of the jet opened and Tony Maurelli stepped into view. He was dressed casually in a dark, expensively cut leather jacket and light coloured slacks, a sports shirt opened at the neck to reveal a golf pendant glinting among the dark mass of chest hair. In one hand he held aloft a glass of champagne, while he had the other around his wife's waist. She laughed as the wind blew strands of her long, dark hair across her face.

'Jeez, is this guy a golfer or a rock star?' one incredulous photographer asked.

His question was lost amid the cheer that went up from a group of golf fans who had come to the airport to see the arrival of the American superstar.

And Tony Maurelli certainly was not going to disappoint the spectators—nor the television cameras whirring in the background. Amid shouts from the photographers to 'Hold it right there, Tony' and 'Look this way, Tony', the cameras clicked away merrily.

Lisa also wanted to get into the act. She too was holding a glass of champagne which she raised to her scarlet lips at the behest of the eager photographers. She struck a provocative pose that showed off her bosom to perfection, conscious that the wind seeping across the tarmac was lifting her skirt, slit in front, enough to show an expanse of thigh. The photographers were shooting so fast their shutters were in danger of overheating.

'Excuse me, Mrs Maurelli. Would you please turn in this direction? I feel I'm being ignored—'

The speaker was David Megson, a freelance photographer who ran his own agency, specialising in golf. He had a studio in London and travelled extensively on the golf circuit. He was known but was not particularly well liked by all the photographers on the tarmac, many of whom admired his work but considered him cold and conceited. Handsome, thirtyish, a stylish dresser, he rarely mixed with the other working photographers.

Now he stood, camera poised, looking up at Lisa Maurelli with a confident grin on his face. She turned to see who had spoken and those perceptive enough might have seen her smile disappear and a rather panicky look flit across her face. But she recovered her poise almost immediately and said: 'Sorry. I—I didn't notice you at that side.'

'I rather thought you didn't.' His grin was a half leer.

She tore her eyes away from his and tilted her chin, the sunshine catching her hair with dramatic effect. 'This okay for you?'

David Megson lowered his camera slightly. 'If you don't mind, Mrs Maurelli, I'd like you to smile a bit more. You look like you've just seen a ghost.' He was enjoying her confusion.

'Aw, come on, honey. Give the guy what he wants.'

Lisa shot her husband a quick glance. Christ, did the big lug realise what he was saying? No, of course not. Tony was not that smart. It had to be an off-the-cuff remark. Besides, she and this photographer had been pretty careful when they had last met. Still, it was a bit of a shock to see him here today. The nerve of the guy, showing up and talking to her like that in front of all these people.

Lisa put on one of her special smiles—the one that showed off her dazzling white teeth. She turned to just the right angle and let the breeze and the sun do the rest. 'How's that?'

'Perfect.' Out of the corner of her eye she saw him click away busily. Hell, she would show him she had spunk too. 'Had enough—or would you like more?'

Megson lowered his camera and by the smile playing about his lips she knew the innuendo had not been lost on him. 'Thank you. That'll do for now. No doubt you'll give me another opportunity to see you at your best—' his eyes shifted to Tony—'if that's okay with your husband, of course.'

She did not dare reply. Instead she watched David Megson walk back towards the terminal building. He even had the audacity to turn and give her a final wave.

'Hey you guys, I've got a surprise for you. Look who hitched a ride over with us—' Tony's voice brought Lisa back to the business at hand. He had moved further down the steps and now several other figures were emerging from the doorway of the jet into the bright sunshine. The photographers did not recognise, and consequently dismissed as a person of no importance, the portly little man dressed in a sober suit and tie. He was Marvin Maxwell, Tony's manager and the man whose marketing genius had hoisted his young client into the millionaire bracket.

But they immediately recognised the swarthy, stocky figure who came into view next. Dressed smartly in casual jacket and slacks, tinted glasses shielding his eyes from the sun, Rafael Escudio came out unsmiling onto the steps. At twenty-six, he was already very wealthy and a British Open winner two years' ago. A volatile character whose Mexican temperament had often got him into trouble on the golf course and whose relationship with the media verged on the acrimonious.

If as a golfer he had few weaknesses, Escudio certainly had one away from the fairways: he liked women. Not for their brains but for their bodies. Indeed it was known by tournament organisers in Europe that one sure way of getting Rafael to cross the Atlantic was to guarantee him a good time at night rather than offer him appearance money.

That said, Escudio was not too happy about being in Scotland right now. He knew it rained a lot here and bad weather was something he did not like. The Open? Rafael really did not need it and it carried none of the guarantees he liked.

Escudio gave a desultory wave to the waiting cameramen. Bastards. He blamed them for a lot of his problems.

Marvin Maxwell called a halt to the proceedings on the tarmac. 'Okay, fellows, let's wrap it up. Join us in the lounge for a glass of champagne. Tony has a few bottles left over from yesterday.' He led the way towards the terminal building.

A few minutes later the American entourage was ready to hold court. Marvin made sure before the questions started that everyone had a full glass. Lisa was relieved to see that David Megson had made himself scarce.

'You reckon you can win the Open at your first attempt, Tony?' It was the obvious question with which to open the proceedings.

'Sure. Why not? Remember another Tony—Tony Lema? He came over and won it at his first attempt.'

'He cracked a few bottles of champagne in his time. It's said you've been set up as another Champagne Tony for publicity purposes. That right?'

'Hell, no. I'm my own man. I'm gonna be even greater than that guy Lema, you'll see.' Good on you, kid, Marvin Maxwell thought. You're following the script to perfection.

'Lema was obviously a hero of yours. Did he inspire you, Tony?'

'Oh sure. When I was at school, a lot of my buddies wanted to be great football or baseball players. Me—I was a standout. I was an Italian kid in the Bronx who wanted to make it at golf. I always wanted to follow in the footsteps of my hero.'

Like hell you did, Marvin Maxwell thought to himself. Why you big wop, you had never even heard of Tony Lema until I came along and sold you on the idea. But I got to admit you're not without talent; the way you're handling these British newspaper guys makes me wonder if I haven't got you in the wrong job—maybe you should have been an actor!

As the questions continued, Marvin sipped his champagne and reckoned that the only cloud on his boy's horizon just now was not how to adapt his game to a seaside course like Turnberry, but the broad—his wife—who was sitting beside him. She too had missed her calling, Marvin mused. The way she carries on when there are men around, he reckoned she would have made a great hooker. Lucky Tony hadn't seen the way she was playing up to that guy Escudio in the plane on the way over. With his fiery temper, Tony would probably have ditched him in the Atlantic!

Seeing that Tony was in control of the situation, Marvin sank deeper into the comfortable seat and recalled the first time he had become involved with him. Unlike most of the young American golfers who made it to the professional circuit through university, Tony Maurelli had come up the hard way. As a kid he had earned a few dollars a week caddying at a public golf course bordering New York's Italian sector. While other teenagers were going to college,

Tony was working in the pro shop and taking money off any well-heeled adult foolish enough to try to match their golf skills with his.

Five years ago, aged nineteen, he had surprised even himself by winning his ticket to play on the American pro circuit. 'What do I have to lose?' he confided to Marvin, who, as a golf equipment salesman earning a moderate living, harboured plans to become a manager. He reckoned this young kid may provide him with a meal ticket. 'Italian kids from the slums either become waiters, boxers or gangsters.'

Tony had expounded on his philosophy: 'Waiters don't earn big money. I'm too good-looking to be a boxer, and I haven't the brains to become a crook. The only thing I'm good at is playing golf. If you think you can make us both rich, Mr Maxwell, you go right ahead.'

Marvin knew a good opportunity when he saw one. 'Okay, kid. So now you're a professional golfer. So now all you got to do is to go out there and win a tournament. I'll turn you into another Tony Lema.'

'Tony who?'

'Forget it. Just win a tournament for me. Okay?'

That first year had been really tough. 'Rolling those fat cats in New York for ten dollars a time was easy compared to this, Mr Maxwell. Am I going to make it?'

'Keep on asking stupid questions like that, kid, and you're a goner. Of course you're going to make it. Golf is all about confidence. Think winning.'

The tour for Tony and Marvin had meant cheap hotel rooms, cut-price air tickets and sometimes long road journeys in Marvin's second-hand Chevrolet.

How they envied the big boys with their superstar lifestyles and the special invites to tournaments in Europe and the Far East which carried with them a fat appearance cheque.

By the end of Tony's first year he had earned a measly $28,000 on tour, not enough to break even after expenses. Only Marvin's salary and commission from his golf equipment sales kept them afloat. The first two months of the second year opened promisingly enough, with Tony having a top ten finish in the Phoenix Open in January and picking up good cheques in the Hawaiian Open and the Desert Classic in Las Vegas.

Then it happened, just as Marvin had always dreamed it would. Three sub-par rounds, one of them a new course record, and he saw his protégé walking up the eighteenth fairway in the Doral Open in Miami three shots in the lead. The kid was going to do it!

Marvin waited just long enough to see Tony hit a six-iron second shot onto the green for a safe par before scampering into the clubhouse bar and instructing the staff to get a case of champagne over to the press tent immediately. Fifteen minutes later, after the prize-giving ceremony and with the $140,000 cheque safely in his pocket, Marvin and the media were helping Tony celebrate his first tour victory in a shower of champagne.

The press boys loved it. Starved of real personalities on the circuit, they could not wait to get to their fax machines to tell the golf world about this new sensation with the Italian connection. By then, of course, Maurelli was word perfect on the exploits of the late Tony Lema, another Italian who had started off the champagne craze, had won the British Open at his first attempt at St Andrews in '64, then unfortunately had been killed piloting his own plane a couple of years later.

'The kid's another Lema,' screamed the golf writers. Even Maurelli had believed the hype—he obligingly won another tournament later that year and was beaten only in a play-off in the US Open at Pinehurst. Tony's confidence grew as endorsements flowed in, thanks to Marvin's marketing skills; he even got the jet at a bargain price on the strength of a publicity deal. Suddenly the days of travelling to tournaments in a beat-up Chevy were over!

Tony was now in his fifth year as a pro and his win on Sunday in the Westchester was a good springboard for his first attempt to win the British Open. As he helped himself to another glass of champagne, Marvin reckoned he had been wise to keep his boy away from the most coveted golf tournmament in the world until now. The kid was ready for it. Marvin was already figuring out the lucrative sponsorship deals he would set up as soon as Tony sank that final putt at Turnberry.

The only fly in the ointment was Lisa. Just Tony's luck that he should have made his school sweetheart pregnant and be forced by the two Italian families to marry.

The bitch always seemed to be in heat. A few times on the tour Marvin had had suspicions that she was playing around, but he had never been able to catch her out. And even if he had, he would not have told Tony. No way was he going to kill off that flow of golden dollars!

He watched Lisa now, pouring champagne into glasses and taking every opportunity to bend forward, giving the press boys a chance to look down her cleavage. That photographer guy had said something to her on the tarmac. He would have to monitor that situation, so nothing happened to upset Tony.

Marvin let the proceedings run another fifteen minutes, then called a halt. 'Tony and Rafael are scheduled to play a few practice holes together later today. Afterwards you guys can ask them questions about what they think of the course.'

A few minutes later he lead Maurelli, Lisa and Escudio down to the arrivals' lounge where they met up with their long-time tour caddies who had jetted across the Atlantic with them. The caddies had checked the golf bags and other equipment through to the helicopter that would land on the helipad on the front lawn of the Turnberry Hotel. As they whirred their way down the Scottish coast Marvin Maxwell thought back to those long journeys in the beat-up Chevvy. He smiled and closed his eyes.

About the same time that Tony Maurelli was landing his jet at Prestwick, Leonard Morgan was attending to the overheated engine of his second-hand BMW in a lay-by north of Ayr. Damned car! He'd have to leave it in a convenient garage and pick it up later that evening after his practice round at Turnberry. He wiped his hands on a cloth, lowered the bonnet, and joined Liz in the Dormobile. She was lying on one of the bunks reading a magazine. She glanced up as he entered.

'Well, what's it this time?'

'Same old problem. I'm no expert on cars, but I think we need a new carburettor.'

'I think we need a new car. Can we afford one?'

'Sure. When I win the Open Championship.'

She did not appreciate the joke and went back to reading her magazine. After a few moments, she asked: 'How much will it cost to get us moving again?'

'Couple of hundred. Lucky I won that few grand at the Irish Open a few weeks back. How much have we got in the kitty?'

'Not a lot. It cost a bit to ferry the Dormobile and the car across the Irish Sea and back. And last week at the Scottish Open was a disaster. Not exactly a luxurious lifestyle, Leonard darling.'

She was right, of course. It was no fun being the girlfriend of a struggling pro golfer. Fine when you are at the top, but tough when you are at the other end of the scale. Thank heaven he had been one of the lucky ones to scrape through to qualify for the Open. The season so far had been tough going. Sure, there was twelve million pounds in prize money on offer this year, but very little of that had come Leonard Morgan's way. He and Liz had long since given up staying in hotels on their way to tournaments.

Two years ago he had bought a caravan, or a Dormobile as the salesman called it. Now he and Liz drove to golf events, even on the Continent. They cooked, ate, argued and made love in the Dormo. It was tough for a professional golfer, but at least he had the excitement of competition each week to sustain him, plus his dream of breaking into the big time.

What of Liz? How long could he expect her to stay around? They had been together now for five years— she had even caddied for him to save expenses. But he knew it would not last unless he made a break-through soon. A girl with Liz's looks and personality had a right to expect more from life that she was getting just now; like marriage, a nice house and kids, for example.

She had gone outside to stretch her legs. He found her sitting on the stone wall of the lay-by admiring the sea view. 'Don't worry. I'll make some money at the Open, believe me.'

Liz glanced out to where the sun was shimmering off the sea. 'If we ever get there. What do we do in the meantime, sit here and look at the scenery?' At least the weather was good. She would enjoy their stay in this part of Scotland, although she would have en-joyed it a lot more from the terrace of the Turnberry Hotel. Would it ever be any other way of life on the tour for them?

'We'll stay here for an hour or so to let the engine cool down', Leonard said. 'I'll drive slowly into Ayr and leave it in a garage for someone to have a look at it.'

'How do you plan on us getting to Turnberry? This is Tuesday, Leonard. You need a practice round.'

'I know. We'll take a taxi to the course. After I've practised, we'll get another one back to Ayr. I realise it'll hit our budget, but it can't be helped. With luck the car will be fixed by then and we can look for a place to park the Dormo.' He took her hand in his. 'I'm sorry, Liz, but that's the best I can do.'

She did not answer. Instead, she gazed out to sea to where seagulls circled and screeched, wheeling suddenly and settling back into the crevices of the cliff face. The sun was warm, inviting, and Liz would have liked to stretch out and top up her tan. But the car was a worry. The silence was shattered now and then by the roar of airplanes landing and taking off from nearby Prestwick. Tourists flying in to see the British Open and take in a Scottish holiday at the same time, she supposed. God, how she envied them.

She envied also the wives and girlfriends of top golfers against whom Leonard competed week after week, with their nice sports outfits, always with the well-known brand names which were part of their husband's endorsement package. Not for them the indignity of dining in a Dormo; they wore designer dresses to pre-tournament evening functions, travelled first-class, and had their hotel bills picked up by the tournament sponsor.

Liz recalled the only time this year they had enjoyed real money—that was as far back as January when Leonard had taken off for a month to the Far East to play some tournaments there, thanks to an overdraft from his friendly bank manager. She had stayed behind with her parents in Newcastle while Leonard, of whom her parents did not approve, joined the small band of British golfers who were going to Japan and Hong Kong to sharpen their game for the year ahead. Leonard had not won a tournament, but curiously he had come home with a lot of money. When she had asked him about it, he had gone all vague and muttered something about 'getting lucky'. For the first few months of the

European tour, they had lived in comparative splendour, enjoying the luxury of hotel life. But when Leonard's game did not show improvement and the money ran out, it was back to life on the road.

The whirring sound of a helicopter passing overhead interrupted Liz's musings. Bringing some of the American superstars from Prestwick to Turnberry, she supposed. Would Leonard ever rate such treatment on the circuit? Maybe he would have a good Open championship.

Malcolm Jacob entered the arrivals' lounge in Prestwick just in time to hear the announcement that the 2.00 pm flight from London had landed. He hoped even at this stage that Felicity would not be on it. Maybe she had changed her mind and decided not to travel. If so, he would talk Sally into moving back to his room in the hotel and all would be well between them again. Just thinking of getting Sally between the sheets gave him a fleeting moment of pleasure.

'Malcolm!' The voice rising above the hubbub in the arrivals area jarred him back to reality.

'Felicity darling! Lovely to see you.' He swept her up in an embrace. Christ, he thought, now I'm in trouble.

'I was waving furiously but you seemed to be in another world—'

'Sorry, dear. Got lots of things on my mind just now.' If she only knew the half of them—

'Nothing you can't handle, I'm sure.'

Malcolm decided to change the subject. He held her at arm's length, looked her up and down, and said: 'Felicity, you're looking super. Never saw you looking as good.' He wasn't exaggerating. She was dressed in a sleeveless cotton print dress, with a wide white band around her waist. Her legs were bare and tanned and she looked as if she had had her hair done in London before leaving. Looking at her, he found it hard to believe this was the same woman who yesterday was threatening suicide over the telephone, but then Felicity had been prone to swings of temperament this last year or so. It was one of the problems Malcolm found difficulty in coming to grips with.

'Thank you for the compliment, Malcolm.' She gave him a peck on the cheek and held his hand. 'You have a car?'

'I borrowed one from the fleet we've hired. Where's your luggage?'

'There.' She indicated two very large suitcases.

'Heavens, Felicity, you're not coming for a month!'

She laughed. 'You do want me to sparkle, don't you, Malcolm? I am the wife of the BBC's top golf commentator, remember.'

'Of course, darling.'

'It's my duty to look well. You may be stuck away in your little commentary box all day, but I'm floating around on the course, in the press tent and the clubhouse—'

And in the bars, too, no doubt, Malcolm thought. He wondered when he'd have time to see Sally with Felicity around. Things weren't looking too good there. 'Put the luggage in the car and we'll have a little drink,' he heard his wife say.

He made a point of glancing at his watch. 'Really, Felicity, I don't think we have time right now. A lot of the big names are out practising in the afternoon and I've got to be around to do some on-the-spot interviews. . . .' One drink never satisfied Felicity nowadays.

'Oh, come on. The way you're carrying on one would think the British Open couldn't run without you.' She stood in the middle of the concourse, waiting, smiling at him. Once again it struck him how splendid she looked.

'All right then. Just one.'

'Good. See you in the bar upstairs.'

He would have to try to meet Sally when he got back to Turnberry. Throughout yesterday he had done everything possible to get her fixed up with accommodation, all to no avail. Then late last evening she had announced witheringly to him that she was moving in with two girls who were also part of the BBC broadcasting team. 'For your information, Malcolm dear,' she had informed him, her tone icy, 'I'm sleeping on a camp bed supplied by the hotel management.'

Dutifully he had offered to move her things to the other room, all his efforts to make conversation meeting with a stony silence. The next few days were going to be pretty difficult.

Felicity sat at a table in the bar which overlooked the concourse. Prestwick was always busy at this time of year and it was even more so now with the world's top golf tournament being held just down the coast. A lot of people were moving about below but she had no difficulty picking out the tall figure of her husband as he hurried back to join her. Malcolm was hiding something from her, she was convinced of that. More than likely it had to do with another woman. She had sensed it for some time now and after their brief encounter a few minutes ago she was surer than ever.

Felicity wondered if this would be a good time to break the news to him that she was expecting a baby. Her other problem would be to convince him that it was his.

Marie Kirk arrived in the hotel lounge just a few minutes after Dominick Earley. He was seated in the same secluded corner he had occupied yesterday. He nodded a greeting and went to the bar to get her a glass of white wine. She studied him as he chatted to the barman.

Marie judged him to be in his mid-thirties. She knew he was married and that he lived in a house in West Belfast with his wife and two young children. An intellectual type, he had studied law at Queen's University and now ran a small but lucrative solicitor's practice. Marie also knew that he had served at least one term in Long Kesh. From conversations between her father and her late brother, Patrick, she had learned that Dominick Earley had on many occasions at IRA council meetings spoken out against what he termed the needless killings perpetrated by the hard men within the organisation. It did not endear him to the more rabid element, who poured scorn on what they saw as an intellectual trying to muscle in and change the direction of their struggle against the British forces in Northern Ireland.

It did not surprise anyone when Earley, frustrated by the IRA hierarchy blocking his policies, and disillusioned at the continued stalemate among the politicians on both sides, had broken away and formed a splinter group. What had surprised Marie was that her father, whose family had supported the IRA from way back, should have opted to follow him. The shift in allegiance had lead to the death of her brother, and she often wondered if her father had blamed himself for it.

Her two years away in London had been a blessing. She realised that now. No sooner had she returned than her father had insisted that she take her dead brother's place within the organisation. She had the feeling her father was living out his fantasies through her now that Patrick was gone.

What had Earley planned for her and Martin Dignam? Was she really capable of planting a bomb, of killing innocent people? Marie doubted that very much. She had lain awake all night thinking about it, terrified that he might be planning another terrible disaster like that in Enniskillen. It could not be anything like that; Dominick Earley was against senseless killing. She would have to wait and see.

He set the glass of wine down before her, glancing at his watch. 'Dignam's late again.' She sensed there was a game going on between the two men. Marie knew that if she remained silent he might construe it as a touch of nerves. 'Is everything finalised?'

'Yes. You and Martin leave by ferry tomorrow morning.' He took a drink from his glass of lager and she was conscious of him studying her. 'Nervous?'

'No. Not really. Should I be?'

'This is your first assignment. And they say one's first bomb job is always the most difficult.'

'If you didn't think I could do the job, you wouldn't have picked me.'

'True.' There was a silence and she wished Dignam would show up to divert attention from her. 'That boyfriend of yours in London. Was it serious?'

The question caught her by surprise, which was what he had wanted. How did he know about Stephen? Her father, of course. He would see it as his duty to tell everything about her. She saw no point in trying to hide anything. 'If you mean was I in love with Stephen, the answer is yes. He wanted to get married.'

'I'm told his father is a big noise in the Conservative Party. How did you meet him? Did you tell him you were from Belfast, that your family had an IRA background?'

He's checking everything, she thought. 'We met on one of those walking holidays in Wales. Things developed from there between us. Stephen's parents are both doctors, very upper crust. When he introduced me and they started asking questions about my background, I knew it was time to get out.' She was toying with her glass of wine, her eyes lowered.

'They knew about your family background?'

'I told them everything. They made it clear that they didn't want the relationship to develop so. . . .' Marie let her voice drift away.

'Are you sorry you came back?'

'No!' Her answer came quickly. Maybe too quickly, Earley reckoned. She recovered herself. 'Look, as far as I'm concerned, it's finished between Stephen and myself. I told him that before I left. You have nothing to worry about on that score.'

'I'm not worried. Any daughter of Pat Kirk can be trusted.'

'Thank you.' She finished off her wine. 'And don't worry about Stephen, either. I haven't heard from him since. I expect he's taken up with some other girl by now—and she probably votes Conservative.'

After a short pause Earley said: 'I think you are going to be very useful to us, Marie. Girls with your looks can sometimes achieve things that men with beards can't.'

She smiled, although there was a sadness in her eyes. Again Earley was conscious of how attractive she looked. He remembered her as a schoolgirl with her hair tied back; tall, gangly. It seemed such a short time ago now. The two years in London had been the making of her. Now she was a young woman, able to make decisions, ready to step into action. Yes, he had a feeling that Pat Kirk's daughter was going to prove quite an acquisition to the organisation.

Dignam walked in. This time he apologised for being late. 'I got stuck in traffic. The Brits had one of their stupid roadblocks on the Falls Road.'

'That's all right, Martin. Get yourself a drink and sit down.' While Dignam was at the counter ordering a pint of Guinness, Earley turned to Marie and said: 'Oh, by the way, Martin was a bit put out yesterday when he heard you were the one going with him to Scotland.'

'Really?' There was a hint of amusement in her voice. Her eyes flitted to Dignam at the bar. 'I rather thought he liked women.'

'He does. It's just that he didn't like the idea of

62

working with a sister of his best pal who was shot dead.' Earley studied her face to gauge her reaction. 'Understandable, I suppose.'

She shrugged. 'He has nothing to worry about. It wasn't his fault. Your investigation proved that.' When Earley didn't reply, she asked: 'Well, didn't it?'

A pause. 'Yes.'

She noticed his slight hesitation. 'Was there any doubt? You don't seem too sure.'

'Well, there was just the two of them on that bank job. We only had Martin's evidence to go on.'

'But they were unlucky that a British Army patrol showed up when it did. A shoot-out was inevitable.'

'Yes, you're right, Marie. The incident is closed.' He seemed relieved when Dignam came back.

'What's the read for Scotland, then?' Dignam set his drink down carefully on the table. There was no mistaking the tinge of excitement in his voice. He always felt like this when a new assignment was being planned. Martin Dignam liked action—the riskier the better.

'You and Marie take off on Operation Birdie tomorrow morning,' Earley said, enjoying Dignam's puzzled look. 'Know what a birdie is, Martin?'

'Haven't a clue. Something you look at in a camera when you're having your photo taken?'

'It's a golf term. A birdie is when a golfer completes a hole in one under par.'

Dignam looked unimpressed. 'Big deal.'

'You and Marie will be mixing with crowds at the Open championship, so I suggest that you both wise up on golf terms. You're supposed to be a golf fanatic, Martin.'

Marie spoke up. 'I'm fine. Stephen was a member of a club near London. I used to go along and act as caddie for him sometimes.' She smiled at Dignam. 'I'll fill you in on a few things about the game later.'

'Thanks,' Dignam replied, without enthusiasm. Trust Earley to put him in a position where he would be getting advice from a beginner—and a girl at that.

Earley reached into his pocket and took out some keys which he passed across the table to Dignam. 'Here are the keys of a hired Ford Sierra which is parked across the road from this hotel. You drive to Glasgow first and meet up with one of our men there.' Earley leaned forward, his voice falling to a whisper. 'His name is Flavin and he's an expert in bomb-making. He'll provide you, Martin, with a uniform similar to the one worn by the security men patrolling the golf course at night. He'll also give you the device—all you will have to do is set the clock.'

'Where do we plant the bomb?' Marie could hardly believe she was asking the question. My God, was she really part of all this? Maybe she should back out now; tell them she wasn't up to it but that she would keep her mouth closed. But she knew it was already too late; her father would disown her and, besides, the IRA dealt severely with any member who did not carry out instructions to the full. Being a woman would not save her either. 'You said that no one would get killed.'

'Does that worry you—whether someone is killed or not?' Dignam was grinning at her, wiping froth from his beard. 'Bomb deaths make big headlines.'

Before she could answer, Earley cut it. 'There's been too much of that sort of thing lately. What happened in Enniskillen didn't do our cause any good. I've made it clear that we in this unit are not into killing innocent people. Not while I'm OC.'

'So what do we do with the bomb then?' Dignam asked sarcastically. 'Bring it back here?'

Earley chose to ignore the sarcasm. 'The bomb will be used to blow up a monument.'

There was a few moments' silence. Marie felt relieved. At least she would not have anyone's death on her conscience. She saw that Dignam was unhappy.

'A monument! Is that all?'

'Yes, Martin.'

'You mean to say we're going to Scotland, risking our necks, just to blow up a fucking monument? Come on, Dominick.'

Earley did not allow himself to get ruffled. Still speaking in lowered tones, he said: 'This is no ordinary monument. It's a British war memorial erected on a hillock right in the middle of the Turnberry golf course where the Open is being held. My plan is to blow it up early on Sunday morning, just hours before the final round of the British Open starts.' He paused to let his words sink in. 'Think of the headlines that will make around the world, Martin.'

Dignam was not impressed—and the look on his face clearly showed it. Fuelled by the sense of relief that nobody would get killed in the exercise, Marie found herself blurting out: 'I think it's a great idea. The publicity will be enormous.'

'Martin?'

Dignam took a long pull at his Guinness before deigning to reply. 'Personally I think it's a waste of good explosives.'

There was a silence. Marie again could feel the tension between the two men. Earley was staring straight at Dignam. Finally he spoke. 'You can think whatever you like. They're your orders—and I expect you to carry them out. Understand?'

Dignam hesitated before replying. 'You say you want it planted at night. What about security? Are there guards on the course?'

'Yes. Plenty. Golf courses at all major tournaments are patrolled every night. You can bet your life security will be even tighter than usual at the Open.'

'So what do I do—just stroll up with a bomb in my hand, dig a little hole and plant it like it was a bunch of geraniums?'

Earley waited until the other's mirth had subsided. 'You're no beginner, Martin. Don't start acting like one now. You'll go to Flavin's place in Glasgow, collect the bomb and the security uniform; we sent your measurements over to him a few weeks ago.' He leaned back in his seat, glancing around to make sure their end of the lounge was still deserted. This was what Dominick Earley enjoyed, planning an operation down to the last detail—and springing surprises on someone like Martin Dignam.

Dignam was staring into his now almost empty glass, swilling the last of the beer around. Earley wished the fellow would come up with another question. He would enjoy closing the trap again. It was the girl, however, who broke the silence.

'How did you get hold of the security uniform?'

'Yeah.' Dignam looked up from his drink.

'We didn't steal it, if that's what you mean. That

would have aroused suspicion and questions would have been asked. We had some photographs taken and worked it out from there.'

'You seem to have thought of everything,' Marie said. She could not conceal the admiration in her voice.

'I have to. That's my job. But things can go wrong sometimes, and when they do someone can get killed. That right, Martin?' The latter did not reply. Earley continued: 'I was sorry about Patrick. He was a good man. Your father took his death well.'

'Yes.' Her father never spoke about Patrick now. He would see his son's death as another heroic deed in the war to free Northern Ireland. A terrible waste of life. 'I never thought about Patrick getting killed. He seemed so—so indestructible.'

'Nobody is indestructible in war,' Earley replied.

'For God's sake will you both shut up!' Dignam's angry voice carried beyond the confines of the booth in which they were seated.

'Lower your voice,' Earley commanded.

'Patrick's dead. Buried. Let's leave it at that,' Dignam hissed.

'I'm sorry—' Marie said. She was a bit frightened.

'Forget it. It wasn't you who resurrected Patrick,' Dignam replied pointedly. He glared at Earley across the smooth tabletop and there was naked antagonism between himself and his OC. 'Patrick got a good funeral. He's a hero now. Let's not forget the war is still on and that Marie and I have a job to do.'

'Right, Martin. Tomorrow evening at five o'clock you both will be in The Wild Grouse pub in Fortnum Street in Glasgow. Sit there until a man approaches you and asks: "Are you going birdie hunting tomorrow?" One of you will reply: "Sorry, we don't know what you mean." Got that?'

They nodded and Earley went on: 'He'll say: "What I mean is are you going to Turnberry for the Open?" One of you will reply: "No, it's not on our schedule." Mr Flavin will sit down and join you for a drink. You'll then go to his house to collect the items already mentioned and go over final details.' Earley glanced from one to the other. 'Any questions?'

'What day do you want us to arrive at Turnberry?' Marie asked.

'I think Thursday would be soon enough. That's the first day of the championship. You'll be two of the thousands of spectators tramping over the course, so it'll give you a good chance to look around.'

Dignam spoke up again: 'If this golf thing is as big as you say it is, Turnberry will probably be overrun with visitors. Where do you expect us to stay?'

'I've thought of that, too, Martin. Some months ago I wrote to the Scottish Tourist Board and got them to send me a list of accommodation still available in the area. You and Marie are booked into a guesthouse about ten miles from Turnberry itself.' He reached into the inside pocket of his jacket, took out his wallet and extricated a card which he passed to Dignam.

'Here's the address. "Seaview", run by a husband and wife couple named Donald and Janet Carlyle.' Earley grinned. 'A nice family establishment, apparently. Should suit you, Martin.'

'What do we do for money?'

'Oh yes.' Earley reached down for a slim briefcase which he had placed under the table. He flipped it open, took out two brown envelopes and passed one each to the couple. 'These contain two hundred and fifty pounds each. That should be enough to cover the operation. Your ferry tickets are in there also.'

Marie put the envelope into her handbag, Dignam slipped his into an inside pocket. 'Do we have to fix up with Flavin in Glasgow?' he asked.

Earley shook his head. 'That's all been taken care of. I mentioned yesterday that you would be travelling as husband and wife. You're booked into the guesthouse as Tom and Norah Young from Belfast. It'll mean you're sharing a room. I'll leave the exact arrangements up to yourselves.'

'Suits me fine.' Dignam glanced at Marie, but she stayed silent. He reckoned it would be no hardship sharing a room with her for a few nights. But he was under no illusions ... she probably had him sleeping on the couch as of now. Not that it mattered; when he was on a mission, he allowed nothing to get in his way. This one was not exactly his cup of tea, but if Earley wanted to waste his talent blowing up a stupid monument, that was his problem.

'It would be a good idea for you to wear a wedding ring, Marie,' he heard Earley say. 'Can you get one before tomorrow?'

'My father kept my mother's. It's in the house somewhere.'

'And Martin, you'll have to sacrifice your beard for Operation Birdie. Beards and terrorists are synonymous. Policemen at ports tend to look more closely at men with them.'

Dignam nodded. Earley kept them for another hour, going over every detail of the plan again and again until Marie got bored. Finally, he said: 'Okay, that's it. You'll report back to me by telephone only in an emergency, Martin. Good luck to you both.' He did not shake their hands, simply sat there and waited for them to leave.

Outside the hotel a light drizzle had started and the late evening sun was hidden behind angry clouds. It looked as if there might be a thunderstorm. Across the street a group of girls in summer dresses were laughing among themselves, waiting on a bus that would take them into town.

Marie stood on the hotel steps, listening to their giggles and excited chatter. She could be one of them, set for the night out. Instead, she was a member of an illegal organisation ready to set out on a bombing mission to Scotland. She wondered what Stephen would say if he knew. His parents would more than likely tell their son that it was what they had suspected all along.

No doubt Stephen would try to understand. He always had. His philosophy was that she had been born into the IRA and that she was never really part of it of her own accord. She was well and truly part of the organisation now. After Turnberry there would be no way out. She had loved Stephen and would have been happy to spend the rest of her life with him, but that was all in the past now.

Martin Dignam walked up behind her. 'Come on. I'll give you a lift home.'

'It's all right, thanks—'

'It's raining. You'll get wet.'

'I can catch a bus.'

'Why do that when you can travel in style, courtesy of the organisation.' He nodded towards the car at the kerb.

Marie relented. They drove through the damp streets, not talking very much. Fifteen minutes later he pulled up outside the terraced house to which he had been a frequent visitor in the past before Patrick was killed. He refused her invitation to go in and chat to her father.

Colm Donohue stood on the twelfth fairway of the Turnberry course and thought about his second shot to the green. He had driven the ball 270 yards off the tee and was now left with what he reckoned was a wedge shot to the flag.

'What do you think, Johnny? Will a wedge get me here?' A few yards away Johnny Davis rested the heavy golf bag on the turf and shook his head.

'Let me see you hit a nine iron. It's a bit longer than it looks.' After their talk outside the guesthouse yesterday, Johnny had motored back to Turnberry and had walked the Ailsa course in the evening, pacing out the fairways and taking notes of the terrain for his young protégé. Today he was putting those notes to good use in this, Colm's first practice round.

'Right-o. A nine iron it is.' Colm took the club from the bag, squinted the 130 yards to the flag, set himself up carefully for the shot and swung smoothly. A divot of turf flew, the small white orb took off into the evening air, arched, hit pin height. It didn't bite, but ran on towards the back of the green.

Johnny grinned ruefully at his former pupil. 'Sorry, lad. You were right—it was only a wedge. You're striking the ball beautifully.' He made a note in his little book. That error of distance must not be repeated when the championship began.

Colm strode up the fairway, thinking deeply. Yes, Johnny was right. He was hitting the ball really well. He would have another practice round tomorrow— and if he could hit the ball as well during the actual tournament, who knows what might happen.

What a marvellous course this Turnberry was! He had played it several times in his amateur days and had never failed to be impressed by the famous Ailsa links. He knew that during the last war the course had been turned into an aerodrome for use by the British and American forces. He could see away to his left the narrow expanse of asphalt that once had been a runway, and on his right as he strode down the twelfth fairway, on a hillock and outlined against the evening sky, he could see the slim, stone monument which commemorated the dead of two world wars. Unusual to have a war memorial on a golf course, but then Turnberry was something special.

'Hey, what's going on over there?'

Johnny's voice cut across his train of thought. Colm looked across to the other side of the fairway where his partner in the practice round, Belgian golfer Willi Ducret and his caddie seemed to be having an argument. Willi's angry voice, in excited French, carried across the expanse of green and several spectators were looking on in amused silence.

'Are the two lover boys having a falling out?'

'Looks like it,' Colm replied. He was not surprised. He had sensed tension between Willi and his caddie as soon as they had stepped onto the first tee earlier that afternoon. While Willi had been pleasant enough to Colm during the round, chatting in stilted English, discussing particular shots and club selection as golfers do during a practice round, there had been a few sharp words exchanged between the two Belgians in their own language.

Some on the circuit said that Willi Ducret was the tour's first homosexual golfer. Certainly the whispers had started not long after he had arrived on the scene with his caddie, Ben. The two of them were lookalikes: both were in their mid-twenties, slim, blonde and good-looking. Too good-looking, if some of the macho men on the tour were to be believed.

What set tongues wagging was the conduct of the two off the course. At tournaments throughout the European tour they travelled together, ate together, and roomed together. No pro on the tour had that kind of close relationship with the person who carried his clubs. More than once there had been murmurings in the locker room about the carry-on of the two Belgian boys. If Willi Ducret heard the whispers that Ben serviced more than his golf clubs after tournaments, it did not show in his game. A consistent winner since he had turned pro, Ducret was currently in the top twenty money winners on the European tour, and some shrewd observers fancied him to become Open champion at Turnberry. But arguments like the one he was now having would not help his cause.

On the other side of the fairway the excited voices had died down. If the two Belgians had sorted out their differences, it did not show on Willi Ducret's face; he was scowling as he prepared to hit his second shot to the twelfth green. Willi hit the shot too heavily and it came up short, plunging into the bunker on the right of the green.

Willi glowered, flung his club on the turf for Ben to pick up, then marched up towards the green. The drama over, the tiny knot of spectators began to drift away. The young Irishman and the Belgian were not exactly crowd-pullers; up ahead the American duo of Escudio and Maurelli had a big gallery as they neared the end of their round.

'Everything okay?' Colm enquired pleasantly as he and Willi approached the green.

'I am sorry for what happened back there—'

'Don't apologise. Caddies can be a problem sometimes.'

It was true. In a high pressure game like golf, it was vitally important to have the right person with you on and off the course. If the partnership was not working, then the only solution was to split. Over the years there had been some acrimonious partings between caddie and pro on the tour.

Ben was close enough to have overheard the end of the conversation with the Irishman, and he did not like it. After four years of following Willi Ducret around the world, pandering to his every whim as caddie, companion and lover, he was not going to be thrown over now for someone else.

It had all started yesterday, not long after they had arrived at Turnberry from Glasgow, where Willi had picked up a five-figure cheque at the Scottish Open. Willi's manager had booked several rooms at the

Turnberry Hotel well in advance for the select group of top golfers whom he managed, including one to be shared by the two Belgians. One of the advantages of being a soulmate to a successful pro golfer, Ben knew, was that one got to indulge oneself in the best hotels.

The relationship had really begun to blossom when they were aged sixteen and had quit school together in Liège. Not only did they look like brothers, but academically they were on the same level.

Not long afterwards they both got jobs in the bar at the Royal Liège Golf Club. The game was only becoming popular in Belgium then; it was played mainly by the rich and there were few golf courses to which those from the lower class, like Willi and Ben, had access. As employees of the club, where they also caddied for members and helped keep the course in good shape, they were allowed to play the occasional round of golf. Within two years they were so good at the game they were shooting better scores than many of the monied members for whom they caddied.

Whether it was their arrogance on the fairways that eventually caught up with them—they had taken to openly criticising the poor play of the members when caddying—or whether it was the malicious whispers about their relationship while sharing a flat on the club premises that finally got them kicked out, Willi and Ben never knew. One day a letter was handed to each of them. Inside was a single sheet of notepaper bearing the insignia of the club. The manager's message was to the point:

At a meeting of the executive committee last night it was decided that your services with the Royal Liège Golf Club are no longer required. You are required to vacate the club flat immediately.

Willi and Ben had asked for an explanation but to no avail. They had been dismissed and there was no way back. They moved their belongings into a flat in town and contemplated their future together. It was Willi who said 'Why don't we go to England and try to earn our living playing professional golf?'

They bought a second-hand car and caravan and headed for England. It had been decided that Willi, always the better player of the two, would be the golfer and Ben the caddie. Ben would do the bulk of the driving between tournaments and also the cooking.

Willi won his European Tour Player's card in Spain at the qualifying tournaments at his first attempt. But on the tour proper he struggled, a novice up against experienced competitors week after week. Both he and Ben watched the good players during tournaments, studied their techniques and spent hours on the practice ground applying them to Willi's game.

The relationship between the two men raised eyebrows, of course. But they both turned a deaf ear whenever remarks were made in their hearing. Willi and Ben were loners, kept very much to themselves and gave nobody—least of all the tour officials—any cause to complain.

The breakthrough they worked so hard for came

during their third year on the tour when Willi won the Spanish Open in Madrid. With that win came a surge of confidence. The partnership won the Dutch Open later the same year and they signed a contract with one of the tour's leading agents. It was the end of caravanning around Europe for Willi and Ben. After that it was smiles all the way, until yesterday, when Ben had discovered that Willi had taken a fancy to a young waiter in the Turnberry Hotel.

He had dropped his partner off at the hotel and had driven on down to the clubhouse to check out Willi's practice time the following day. He had also dropped into the bar there and had a couple of drinks with one of the other tour caddies with whom he had struck up a friendship. Thus it was some time before he entered the bustling Turnberry Hotel. Willi was not in their room when he went up. Probably having a drink at the bar before dinner, Ben reckoned.

He was right. He could not see Willi at first when he entered the lounge bar. The place was crowded with people, many of whom he recognised—golf officials, pressmen, several well-known golfers and their wives. At the bar he could see the BBC's much-respected commentator, Malcolm Jacob, deep in conversation with a good-looking girl half his age. He noticed the girl was looking angry. Ben smiled to himself. Women—thank heavens they were not a threat. He was so lucky.

He saw Willi waving to him from a table in an alcove. Ben was easing his way through the standing couples when he saw the young fellow seated at the table of his friend. Ben had never set eyes on him before.

'You were a long time,' Willi said, smiling. He saw Ben eyeing his young companion. 'Sit down. I want you to meet Alec.'

The young fellow extended his hand. 'Hello. Nice to meet you, Ben.' He had the bluest eyes Ben had ever seen. He also had a heavy Scottish accent and a limp handshake. Warning bells began to ring in Ben's head. He managed a hello.

'Alec will get you a drink from the bar. Here is some money.' Willi passed several coins to the young man. 'Same again for us and a gin and tonic for Ben.' They watched him wind his way towards the bar.

'Who is he?'

'I told you. His name is Alec. He's a waiter, here in the hotel. He'll be serving us dinner later.'

'Very convenient. Why are you buying him a drink?'

'I happen to like him. So will you, Ben.'

'I doubt it. I don't fancy him as well as you obviously do.'

Willi stopped smiling. 'What's that supposed to mean?'

'Don't play innocent. You know what I mean. You really like him, don't you? I can see the way you look at him.'

'Don't be silly, Ben.' Willi toyed with his glass. 'You see things that are not there. We have been together a long time—'

'Maybe that's the problem.'

'Will you stop worrying. Be pleasant to Alec. He's a very nice boy. You'll see—'

'I'm telling you I don't like it. I want you to get rid of him.'

'Sorry. I don't take orders like that from you.'

Ben had become even more sullen during dinner. Alec had arranged for them to sit at a table in his area of the spacious dining room and had danced attendance on them throughout the meal. The waiter's uniform accentuated his slim figure and Willi's eyes followed him as he passed in and out of the kitchen. Ben could see that his partner was enjoying it all. For the first time in their relationship, he felt threatened.

After the meal Willi insisted on sitting in the lounge, waiting for Alec to join them when he had finished his duties. Usually before a tournament, and especially one as important as the British Open, Willi and Ben would go to their room, watch television or read, then retire early. This evening that schedule had been cast aside. When Alec did join them, Ben stayed outside of the conversation, and made a point of looking at his watch frequently. When Willi tried to get him to talk, Ben pointedly lost himself in a magazine.

Exasperated, Willi finally said: 'Ben, you go to bed. I'll follow you later.'

'It's all right. I'll wait.' Ben was determined to make things awkward. In a few days they would leave Turnberry and head back to Belgium for a short holiday. He would see to it that Willi would forget this little Scot. Tomorrow in the practice round he would put Willi in his place. . . .

Colm untied his golf shoes in the locker room and grinned at Johnny. 'My God! I'm glad those eighteen holes are over. I've never seen a golfer and his caddie act up like that.'

'What on earth was going on?' Johnny glanced around to make sure he was not being overheard. Willi Ducret was at the far end of the room, alone. 'I thought those two fellows were going to start throwing clubs at each other!'

'They must have had a lovers' tiff. Willi seemed very annoyed. I thought he was going to go for that photographer who was taking snaps. They'll have to be very careful how they behave.'

'Do you think they'll get into trouble with the Royal and Ancient officials?' Johnny asked.

'It could well happen. The R & A won't stand for their championship being brought into disrepute.'

As Colm headed for the showers, Johnny shouldered the heavy golf bag. Outside, he stood for a few minutes and watched the last foursome of the day finish their practice round on the eighteenth green. Among the quartet was Richard Elliott, whose personal battle to win a British Open was going to be one of the talking points of this year's championship. The big crowd which had followed the four men watched with reverential silence as the last putt dropped.

As the golfers walked off the green to generous applause, Johnny saw a tall, loose-limbed young woman move across to greet Elliott. Must be his wife, Johnny reckoned. But before she had reached him, a member of a television crew grabbed him by the arm and guided the American towards an interview area. Johnny saw Dick Elliott smile resignedly at the lady before he was led away.

Working for Colm was not likely to expose either of them to many television interviews, Johnny reckoned. That was the way he wanted it. There were a couple of aspects of the young fellow's game that needed work and Johnny did not want any undue interruptions. But right now there was a bag of golf clubs to be cleaned and made ready for the morrow. After that, he would join Colm and his wife for a quiet dinner.

Inside the clubhouse bar Rafael Escudio was sipping a glass of Budweiser. He was alone, but not by choice. He would much rather have been in the company of any one of the pretty girls who were seated at various tables, a couple of whom were making it very clear by their glances that they were open to offers.

A few moments later he was joined at the bar by his caddie, Donny Alvarez, a happening that did not exactly make Rafael's day. He knew Donny was in Turnberry to act as his minder—sent over by his manager, Kirk Kalder, who, as boss of Mega World Promotions, wanted to make sure the hottest golf property on his books was kept away from girls and concentrated instead on winning the Open championship. Indeed, Donny was allowed into the members' bar only because he was caddie for one of the biggest names in the business. Were it not for that he would be banished, like many of his lesser-known colleagues, to one of the local hostelries.

Because of his other business commitments, Kirk Kalder would not be able to make it to Turnberry until later in the week, but he had given specific instructions to Donny before he had left with Rafael.

'Stick like glue to that horny compatriot of yours. I don't want him with any girls.'

'Yes boss. I make sure. I stay close to him. Don't worry.'

'He'll offer you money. Lots of money.'

'I don't take the bribe, Mr Kalder. Honest.'

Like hell you don't, Kalder thought, but what could he do? He would have to trust Donny to do the job.

'If Rafael comes back to the States with a dose of the clap, you're fired. Savvy?'

'Don't worry, boss. Yo comprendo.'

'You'd better. And stop telling me not to worry. The guy just can't get enough of it. He's overpaid, oversexed, and if he keeps on the way he's going, he'll soon be over the hill.'

Donny grinned. 'He find it hard to get a chica into bed with me around.'

'Don't kid yourself. Rafael has given the slip to smarter guys than you. I want him checked out every night.'

Donny took the insult with a smile. After all, he was on a percentage of Escudio's winnings and made good money. Besides, he knew what it was like to be born poor. He never wanted to go back across the Mexican border to that kind of life.

A big problem for Donny was that Rafael, in accordance with his superstar image, was booked into the Turnberry Hotel while Donny was sharing rooms with Tony Maurelli's caddie in a house near-by. It would mean his having to keep a close watch every night.

Maybe Rafael was suffering from jet lag and would retire early tonight? He certainly had not hit the ball well today during his practice round. But

Donny noticed the way the younger man's eye roamed the bar area. Far from being jet-lagged, Rafael Escudio was looking for action. It could be a long night. Donny sighed—at his age he could do without long nights!

Escudio was thinking about that cute little chica, the driver of the courtesy car he and Tony had taken from the hotel down to the course that afternoon. While Tony, his manager and Lisa had squeezed into the back seat, he had sat beside the driver, an ideal place from which to admire the girl's handling of the car—and the shapely knees that showed beneath her smart uniformed skirt. When he had asked her name —she had a tag with 'Elaine' on her uniform—and enquired when she was off duty, she had just smiled sweetly and replied that she was employed to chauffeur the clients and was not allowed to answer personal questions.

Escudio aimed to see more of her later in the week. He would find out who was in charge of the courtesy car service and let the guy know there was money in it for him if he could arrange something with Elaine. What with the AIDS scare, a guy had to be careful whom he picked up these days; but not even that was going to come between him and the beautiful girls who were always available at the tournaments.

'You tired, boss?' Donny asked hopefully.

'No, Donny. Coming to the Open gets me all fired up.'

Donny groaned inwardly. 'Why don't you go to bed soon, boss? We have another busy day practising tomorrow—'

'You want me to go to bed so that you can phone

Mr Kalder and tell him that I'm being a good boy tonight, eh? That what you have to do?'

'I'm here to look after you, boss. I want you to win the Open again.'

'Then let's have another couple of drinks.' Rafael would make sure his minder earned his money on this trip. Over Donny's shoulder he saw the tall figure of Tony Maurelli approach. Tony had entered the bar a few minutes ago and had joined Lisa and Marvin Maxwell at a table. He put a friendly hand on Rafael's shoulder.

'Hey, how about joining us for dinner at the hotel? I reckon on having an early night.'

Rafael could sense Donny waiting for his reply. 'Thanks Tony, but I guess not. I got other plans.'

Tony glanced around the room, his eyes flitting over to where a trio of girls sat sipping their drinks. 'Yeah, I know what you have in mind. I'll level with you, man. This wasn't my idea. Lisa thought you looked a bit lonely, in need of perking up. Come on—I'll even pick up the tab!'

So Lisa wanted him along for the night. He might have guessed. She was a hot little thing and liked men, and the way she looked at him sometimes gave him ideas. But she was Tony's wife and that would be big trouble. As for tonight . . . what the hell, he would give the little flirt the benefit of his company for a few hours. Anyway, Donny was determined to do his duty tonight, so what had he got to lose.

Rafael held up his hands resignedly. 'Okay. I accept. Who am I to refuse a lovely lady.' He turned and nodded to Lisa. She looked pleased. 'Let's go.'

Donny watched them leave the clubhouse,

accompanied by Maxwell. He had reckoned on an early night, but now he would have to hang around until Rafael had finished dinner and make sure he was safely back in his room. You simply could not trust that sex-mad sonofabitch. He would telephone Señor Kalder in a couple of hours, tell him not to worry, that everything was okay. Then he would go to bed.

As they piled into the courtesy car for the short drive up the winding road to the hotel, Lisa allowed herself to be squeezed into the back seat, between her husband and Escudio. She experienced tiny sensations of delight every time the car swung around a bend and her body came into contact with his. She would love to know what he was thinking behind those dark, brooding eyes.

Rafael Escudio was commiserating with himself for their not having the services of Elaine with the shapely legs. His number had not come up this time, but then there would be other opportunities over the next few days.

He applied the same rules to getting a woman into bed as he did to winning at golf—be patient and sooner or later the birdies would come.

3

WEDNESDAY, 15 JULY

Marie Kirk gazed idly out of the car window as they wound their way along the Ayrshire coastline. From the passenger seat she had a bird's eye view of the firth below. The wind from the half-open window flung wisps of dark hair across her face and now and then she closed her eyes to ease the glare of the sun bouncing off the water.

Beside her, Martin Dignam handled the hired car expertly. He turned his head and said: 'Enjoying yourself?'

'It's beautiful. I never thought Scotland could look so good.'

'Everywhere looks good when the sun is shining —even Belfast. I hope the weather holds.' He had the car radio tuned into one of the pop stations— it had been like that since they had left Stranraer—and now and then he hummed along to the beat of the music. With his dark beard shaved off, he looked younger, less like a terrorist, Marie thought. He drummed his fingers on the steering wheel to the rhythm of a George Michael number and she had to admit that they would pass for what they were supposed to be . . . a young couple on a driving holiday, instead of an IRA twosome out to disrupt the British Open. The traffic was getting noticeably thicker as they approached Turnberry.

'Will we pass through the town itself?' Marie asked.

'Yes. We'll go through there on our way to Ayr before we cut inland for Glasgow. It'll give us an opportunity to see what the hell this golf thing is all about.' Dignam was still disgruntled about being sent over to Scotland merely to blow up a monument. Those were his orders and he would carry them out, but he wished they did not have to hang around until Sunday to do the job. It seemed a stupid move on Earley's part.

'Tell you what—' he swung the car into a convenient lay-by, 'why don't we change plans slightly?'

'What do you mean?' He had turned off the radio and was looking directly at her, excitement gleaming in his eyes. She felt a little frightened.

'Instead of driving to Glasgow to meet Flavin tonight, why don't we take a leisurely drive up the coast instead, see some more of Scotland. What do you say?'

'But we can't. We have our orders. Dominick Earley said—'

A look of annoyance crossed his face. 'Oh, forget Earley for the minute. Look, our orders are to complete the mission on Sunday, right?' When she nodded, he went on: 'We'll do that. My point is we don't have to meet this fellow Flavin tonight on the dot, do we? I don't remember Earley naming an exact night, do you?'

'He did—'

Again that impatient wave. 'So I'm changing the orders slightly. Now listen, Marie. We have nearly five hundred quid between us. The fact that we're on a job doesn't mean that we can't enjoy ourselves. This is only Wednesday, we don't have to hang around all that time in Turnberry—'

'But we'll need time to have a good look over the area. Dominick said to make sure—'

The mere mention of his OC seemed to bring out the dark side of Dignam. His face clouded and he said harshly: 'I told you to forget Earley. I'm in charge now.' His anger vanished as quickly as it had risen and he grinned. 'Come on, Marie, what d'you say?'

She knew she should not give in too easily, but she had a feeling he would do what he wanted anyway. 'Where will we stay tonight?'

He threw back his head and laughed. 'Who cares? It's the summer—holiday time. Look around—' He turned in his seat and waved his arm. 'There are dozens of hotels and guesthouses. We'll drive until we find a place. And to set your mind at rest, we'll stop by that guesthouse we're booked into and tell them to expect us tomorrow night instead. I'll even pay them, so that they won't be at a loss. How's that?'

'All right. You're in charge. One thing, though. What sleeping arrangements do you have in mind for tonight?' The question had to be asked sooner or later—and this seemed a good time to settle the matter.

A smile played around the corners of Dignam's mouth. 'I wondered when you'd come to that.' He shrugged. 'I'm easy. We travel as a couple, book one room and I'll sleep on the couch if that's what you want. Okay?'

She nodded in agreement. It was not as if she was a virgin, an innocent abroad. She had slept with

Stephen, after all, but only when she had convinced herself that they would stay together and eventually marry. She had loved Stephen. Now her life had taken a different direction and she must forget about him. She was now a member of an international terrorist organisation and on a mission with a man whose swings of mood she found difficult to gauge. At the moment the sun was shining, Scotland looked splendid, and she did not want to spoil it by thinking too far ahead. Tonight would take care of itself.

'One thing that worries me—'

'What is it now, Marie?'

'Mr Flavin. Won't he get worried if we don't show up in the pub tonight? He might telephone Dominick—'

'Good thinking.' Dignam pondered this, then said: 'I'll make a call to The Wild Grouse this evening, ask for Flavin and tell him not to expect us until the same time tomorrow. Happy with that?'

She nodded, and he turned the key in the ignition. He eased the car out onto the road again and began to whistle along with the tune on the radio.

The telephone rang in room 307. Lisa, still in her dressing-gown, answered it.

'Good morning. Remember me?'

She caught her breath. 'David! My God—' She looked quickly over her shoulder to make sure the bathroom door was closed so that Tony would not hear. She had recognised the English voice immediately.

'Right first time, my darling. Are you alone? Can you talk?'

Her heart pounding, she dropped her voice to a whisper. 'No. Tony's in the other room.'

He sniggered. 'Silly bugger. Why isn't he in bed with you!'

'Because he's standing on his head just now practising his yoga, that's why. His manager came up with the idea. He says it does wonders for Tony's concentration.'

'Bully for him. What does it do for his sex life?'

She let that pass. 'I haven't time to talk. What do you want, David?' As if she did not know.

'When can we get together again?'

'What makes you think I want to?'

'Come off it, Lisa. It's about time we had an encore. Were you surprised to see me at the airport?'

She glanced over her shoulder again. 'I told you. I can't talk right now—'

'Who wants to talk, for Christ's sake!'

He was not going to leave her alone, and maybe she did not want him to. She remembered how easy it had been the last time—and so enjoyable. David Megson had a cruel streak in him, but he was a good lover. Why could it not be the same again?

'Tony is practising today—' My God, what was she saying!

'What time?'

'I heard him tell his caddie to pick him up here at the hotel at two o'clock. He'll play eighteen holes, then go to the practice ground—'

'That should give us at least three hours. Probably more.'

Three hours! That would make up for Tony being out of action at present. He laid off sex whenever he was playing in a big tournament. And when one as important as the British Open came around, it was like living with a monk. 'I'll tell Tony I want to rest this afternoon. He'll believe me—we're going to this big dress-up dinner in the hotel tonight—'

'That's my girl. I'll phone you from the foyer about two-fifteen. If anyone else answers, I'll say it's room service, a wrong number.' He laughed again. 'Same routine as last time, right?'

'Where are you staying?'

'I'm in a hotel a few miles from here. We'll go there.'

'Okay. See you.'

'See you.'

Lisa replaced the receiver, crossed to the window and sat down. They had a suite of rooms at the front of the hotel overlooking the links. In the perfect setting of a warm July day, less than twenty-four hours before the Open would begin, Turnberry was buzzing. By now the 150 golfers who had qualified to compete in the Open had arrived with their retinues of wives, girlfriends, managers, caddies, agents, business associates and fans. Television crews from Britain, America, Australia, Japan and several European countries were covering the event. A second press tent was being erected to cater for the media people, some of whom were seeking last-minute accreditation.

Last night someone had told Lisa that over the next four days almost 100,000 golf fans were expected to follow the action on the Ailsa course. Christ! some people were easily pleased. Lisa preferred a more strenuous form of action! Frankly, golf bored her stiff.

She could not for the life of her see how people could become excited looking at grown men hitting a little white ball into a hole in the ground. It was crazy— and slow. Of course, she never said that to Tony. After all, his being able to do just that better than most of the other guys had helped to get her out of that overcrowded apartment in the Bronx which she had shared with her father, her overly religious Italian mother and her six brothers and sisters. And it did pay for the hefty clothes bills she ran up whenever Marvin Maxwell's back was turned.

Of course there were other compensations; like mixing with the tanned, athletic young men who travelled the circuit. Sure, most of them were a dead loss with their golf-is-my-whole-life attitude. But there was the occasional guy who wanted to stop now and then to smell the roses along the way—like Rafael Escudio, for instance. She often fantasised what it would be like in bed with that Mexican stud.

Lisa fantasised, too, about how different life would have been for someone like her if Tony had been discovered by a Hollywood talent scout instead of that balding little Marvin Maxwell schmuck. He kept a close eye on her activities; she must be careful of him today.

Down below on the putting green in front of the hotel she saw a group of photographers busily snapping away at a couple of big-name golfers practicing. David Megson was among them. She remembered last year when Tony had been invited over to that big tournament at Sunningdale. Excited at first, by the third day of the tournament she was feeeling bored. It was then that she had allowed herself to be picked up by David Megson. While Tony was struggling to put up a good score to justify his £25,000 appearance cheque, she was sipping Margaritas in the clubhouse bar with this casually dressed English freelance photographer with the smooth line in chat and the rather mean eyes. When he suggested they might drive somewhere so that he could take a couple of really good pictures of her, she knew he had other things in mind.

Tony had started his round that day and was not due in for about three hours. Besides, it was starting to rain and tramping a wet golf course was not her idea of fun.

They were in bed within half-an-hour, in the small hotel where he was staying. She was back in Sunningdale in time to wave to Tony as he strode up the eighteenth fairway. The following day, immediately after the close of the tournament, they flew back to New York. David Megson was by then just a fond memory.

Lisa rose and went into the bathroom. She stared at her husband for a few moments. Tony was still in the corner, feet up against the wall, relaxing in his favourite yoga position.

'You nearly all through there, honey?'

He opened his eyes. 'What time is it?'

'Almost ten.' She always felt ridiculous holding a conversation with Tony when his face was where his feet should be.

'Guess we should go down and have some breakfast. I want to hit a few balls before lunch.' He bent his knees, his feet touched the floor and he stood upright, towering over her. 'What are your plans today, Lisa?' he asked as he stepped into the shower.

'After lunch I'll come back up here and rest, if that's okay with you. I feel tired, and we have that dinner tonight, don't forget. I'll join you in the clubhouse later when I get my hair done.' He did not reply and she could hear the water running. This was going to be easier than she thought.

'Say, honey—'

'Yes?' she paused, apprehensive.

'Did I hear the phone ring?'

'Oh yes. It was room service. They had a wrong number.'

Felicity Jacob always knew instinctively when Malcolm was cheating and having an affair. The signs were easy to detect; he either became over-attentive to the point where she wanted to scream 'Stop it, Malcolm, the game is up!', or else he became shifty and nervous, jumping to answer the telephone whenever it rang, unable to sit down and watch television or read a book.

Right now he was having a bad attack of the jitters. She had been convinced of this the day before when, over a drink at the airport, he had told her how delighted he was that she had come up to Turnberry. She did not believe him for a moment. When she tried to make small talk and asked him how work was progressing for the Open, he had answered in a bemused and offhand manner, as though his mind was on other matters.

Last night when she followed him down to dinner, she had caught him in earnest conversation with a girl, a tawny-haired beauty whose casual dress did not hide her obvious attractions. The girl had 'danger' written all over her. Felicity had observed them for a time from the entrance to the cocktail lounge. The lounge was pleasantly crowded with groups of people waiting to go into dinner and so they did not notice her. Malcolm was doing most of the talking, but his companion did not seem at all impressed with whatever he was saying.

Felicity saw the girl turn to go at one point, but he grabbed her arm, restraining her. The conversation lasted less than a minute after that. The girl smiled sweetly—it was her goodbye—and made her way out of the lounge through the crowd. She passed within a few paces of Felicity, who waited a few moments longer before joining her husband at the bar.

'Hi.'

'Oh, hello darling.' He signalled a waiter and ordered her a drink. 'How are things with you? Everything okay?'

For a wild moment she thought he was enquiring about the baby. But how could he—she had not told him about that yet. Felicity recovered quickly and said: 'I'm fine.'

'Good. By the way, we're having dinner tonight with Dick Elliott and his wife.' He looked pleased with himself and she surmised that this was something of a coup.

'Any special reason?' Of course there was. Malcolm did not do things without a reason, not even for the world's number one golfer. Had they been dining alone, it would have been a good time to tell him he was about to become a father again. Now it would have to wait.

'I want to get him along to my dinner tomorrow night. I've got all the top names tied in, including several committee members of the R & A. It'll be a splendid night and if I get Dick Elliott along, he'll be the icing on the cake—he's never accepted an invite to my eve-of-Open dinner yet.'

'I presume you have something in mind for me?'

'It would help if you chatted up Susan, his wife. She used to be a top model, you know. Invite her along on that shopping trip to Edinburgh you're planning for the wives.'

'I thought chatting up pretty girls was your line of business, Malcolm darling.'

Although Felicity was smiling, he felt the barb. 'I don't know what you mean, darling.'

'Who was that I saw you talking to a few minutes ago?'

He paused with his Scotch halfway to his lips, looking suitably puzzled. 'Was I chatting someone up?'

'A girl, tawny hair. Beautiful. One of those bright young things one reads about in *Cosmopolitan*—'

'Ah, you must mean Sally—'

'You actually remember her name. How nice.'

'She's one of our team—a production assistant.'

'Thank heavens. I thought she might be one of those golf groupies one hears about.'

'Sally—a golf groupie? That's a joke.'

'I don't suppose she's married?'

'I don't know. Frankly, I've never asked.'

'Sleeping with anyone?' Felicity was enjoying herself.

'Felicity, please!' Malcolm glanced over his

shoulder. The noise in the lounge was so loud, it seemed everyone was talking at once.

'Is she staying in the hotel?'

'Er, yes, I believe so. All the BBC team is here— boys and girls.'

'How convenient.'

'Felicity darling, you have something on your mind. Why are you asking all these questions?'

'Just curious. Mind if I ask one more?'

'Fire ahead.'

'Tell me, darling, what is her favourite perfume?'

'Perfume? Is this some sort of joke? How the hell would I know what perfume she uses.'

She laughed in a way that worried him. 'Just testing, that's all. Now order me another dry martini, there's a good boy.'

The dinner date with Richard Elliott and his beautiful young wife had gone off well last night. On the surface they looked the ideal couple: he tall, handsome and tanned, Susan elegant in a sheath dress slit to mid-thigh which accentuated her slim figure.

During dinner, in the privacy of the ladies' powder room, Felicity asked Susan about her modelling career and if she had ever thought about taking it up again.

'I think about it all the time,' Susan confided. 'But Richard would not approve right now. He has other things on his mind, like completing the Grand Slam. Why do you ask?'

'I'm organising a shopping trip into Edinburgh for some of the golfers' wives, with possibly a fashion show included. Would you be interested?'

Susan's eyes had lit up. 'That would be just great.

I'll sound out some of the other girls if that's okay with you, Felicity.'

'Do that. 'You sure Richard won't mind your going missing for an afternoon?'

Susan looked straight at Felicity. 'When Richard is on a golf course, nothing else matters to him but winning', she said, a hint of sadness in her voice. 'I've come to accept that as part of life.'

Now it was the following morning, Felicity rose from the dressing-table and considered what to wear. Something chic and sporty she decided. They were fortunate in having a room at the front of the hotel; outside she could see the sunshine bathing the links and crowds of spectators moving around. Her eyes fell on the tiny bottle of perfume on the table. Soon she would be returning it to the person she presumed was its rightful owner. She wanted to look her best for that confrontation.

Felicity let the dressing-gown slide to the floor and studied her naked body in the mirror. At thirty-nine she still had a figure that men admired. Her stomach was trim and her buttocks were under control; those occasional weekends spent at the health farm had paid off. She turned from side to side, taking pleasure in what she saw. Her breasts were full and firm. She placed her hands over them, massaging the nipples gently.

Jon had massaged her breasts like that the night he had followed her home from the golf club. Kissing them, teasing . . . making her cry out in pleasure. He had sensed her loneliness and she had succumbed. . . .

From the range of outfits she had brought, she

selected a smart flower appliquéd cotton top and a pair of white poly-cotton Bermudas. The weather was perfect and she had noticed that a lot of women out on the course were wearing shorts. A light, loose-fitting jacket with large pockets completed her outfit.

Forty minutes later, after a light breakfast, she was mingling with the spectators on the fairways. The tented village was alive with colour and there was a carnival atmosphere about. Felicity strolled past the huge stand flanking the eighteenth green to the area where the television pylons towered above the spectators. Her husband might be in that commentary box right now, making sure everything was just right for the start of play tomorrow.

Then she saw the girl she was looking for. She had a clipboard in her hand and was jotting down notes given her by a man with earphones. Even with the pair of dark shades shielding the girl's eyes, Felicity recognised her. She stayed a short distance off, waiting for the man to leave. When the girl—Malcolm had called her Sally—was alone, Felicity moved towards her.

'Excuse me—'

The girl turned around, surprised. 'Yes?'

'May I speak to you for a few moments?'

The girl looked slightly annoyed, but nevertheless managed a smile. 'I'm sorry. I am rather busy right now—'

Felicity was not going to be put off. 'It will only take a few minutes. I have something that I think belongs to you.'

That got the girl's attention. 'Oh.' A pause. 'Do I know you?'

'I doubt it. But you probably know of me.' Felicity put her hand into the pocket of her jacket and took out the small bottle of perfume. 'Is this yours?'

The girl pushed the shades back into her hair. She stared at the tiny, heart-shaped bottle for a few moments. 'It's certainly the perfume I use.'

Felicity's eyes met hers. 'I found it on the floor at the side of the dressing-table in my husband's room in the hotel.' She nodded to where the Turnberry Hotel towered, white and majestic, in the distance.

'I see.' The girl lowered her eyes. When she spoke, the words were barely audible. 'You must be—'

'Felicity Jacob. Malcolm's wife.'

A silence. Around them the chatter of the crowds went unnoticed. After what seemed a very long time, the girl said: 'How do you do? I'm Sally Penrith.'

'I know. I saw you talking to my husband in the bar last night. I think we should have a chat, don't you?'

'Yes, if you wish.' Sally slipped the perfume bottle into her pocket. 'There's a snack bar over there that serves coffee.'

Out on the course, Leonard Morgan, in a threesome that included Ngaio Ontabe, a Japanese who was a consistent money winner on the Far East and American golf circuits, and Lou Menzies, the veteran Australian and current holder of the British Open title, were teeing off at the final hole of their practice round. They had attracted several hundred spectators. Menzies, the dour forty-year-old who, after two decades of globe-trotting golf, culminating in his Open win last year, was the main attraction.

The fact that his historic win had made the Australian into a celebrity overnight had not changed him. Indeed, his uncompromising attitude and lack of charisma had cost him a fortune. Potential sponsors had backed off, scared of his inability to handle the media. They would be happy to see the last of him as Open champion. Lou Menzies was angry that he was rated only a thirty-three to one shot to retain his title and was determined to prove them all wrong this week at Turnberry.

Leonard Morgan had not enjoyed the practice round. Menzies had been uncommunicative, while Ontabe's knowledge of English was minimal; he smiled a lot but spoke little.

Morgan had just birdied the par five seventeenth hole and he was first up on the eighteenth tee. He had planned to hire a local caddie for the Open, but the garage bill for the car repair had been expensive and, to cut down expenses, Liz was carrying his golf bag. It was a tough chore for a young woman, but she had done it before when money was tight. Now, more than ever, it was essential that he qualify for the final two rounds of the Open and earn a sizeable cheque.

There was a fair smattering of spectators lining the eighteenth tee. In the distance Morgan could see the big stand at the back of the green. It was a straightforward 377-yard hole, no more than a good drive and a short iron—provided one kept the drive straight and missed the yellow gorse running to the right of the fairway. Leonard crossed to the side of the tee where Liz was standing with his golf bag. He was reaching for his driver when he glanced up and saw Stan Tynan. He was alone, standing on a hillock so that he was shoulder high over the forest of heads.

Their eyes locked and Morgan felt his heart jump. Tynan gave him a smile and an almost imperceptible nod of the head. Morgan looked away quickly.

Liz said something that he did not quite catch. Instead, he took the proferred club and, his mind in a whirl, pushed a tee into the turf. When he straightened up, he glanced quickly over the heads of the crowd behind Liz. Tynan was nowhere to be seen. Morgan took up his stance, trying desperately to concentrate on the shot. He swung the club, but knew instinctively he had hit a bad drive. The spectators gasped as the ball took off on a mighty arc to the right and vanished into the yellow gorse in the distance.

'You'll have to do better than that tomorrow, mate.' It was Menzies's first attempt at levity during the round and Morgan was in no mood to appreciate his remark. After the other two had driven off, he followed them down the fairway, his mind racing.

The last time he had seen Stan Tynan was early in the year outside a small hotel just off the motorway from Heathrow airport. Morgan had flown in earlier that day with several other golfers from a month-long tour of the Far East circuit. Tynan had picked him up at the airport, driven to the hotel, and in the car park Morgan had handed over the dozen small plastic-wrapped packets of cocaine which he had squeezed tightly into the false bottom of his golf bag. Tynan had had it specially made after Morgan had agreed to bring back the drug consignment from his trip abroad.

The £10,000 payment had helped himself and Liz live in luxury for a few months on the European tour.

Besides, when he and Tynan had shaken hands in the car park, Morgan had emphasised that it was a once only operation. He was determined to stick to that.

'Are you all right, Leonard?' Liz's voice cut across his thoughts.

'Sure.'

'What on earth happened to you back there on the tee?'

'I lost concentration.'

'You look awful; as though you've seen a ghost.'

He forced a smile. 'I'm okay.' Liz did not know how close she was to the truth. Tynan had come back to haunt him. Morgan glanced into the lines of spectators once or twice as he walked down the fairway, but could see no sign of the fellow. Luckily, a spectator had found his ball in the gorse and he concentrated on making amends for his wayward tee shot. He had to hack the ball out of deep rough and could only make it back onto the fairway about eighty yards short of the green. His wedge shot was not one of his best—it had no backspin and finished about twenty feet past the flag. Still unsettled, he three-putted from there and finished up with a two over par six. He cursed under his breath.

Morgan was making his way through the spectators towards where Liz was waiting when he felt a touch on his arm. 'Hello, Lenny boy.'

Stan Tynan was smiling. Christ! This was all he needed. Leonard decided to play it cool. 'Hello, Stan.'

'Long time no see. How are you, mate?'

'Fine—'

'You haven't made the big time yet, I see. Still struggling, you and your pretty girlfriend.'

Morgan turned to go. 'Sorry, Stan. But I've got to get in some putting practice—'

'Course you have, Lenny boy. But what's the hurry? Let's have a little drink first.'

Morgan glanced around anxiously. There were several uniformed policemen about and he did not want to be seen talking to someone like Stan Tynan. The man was a drug pusher and was probably known to the authorities. In his sporty outfit, complete with sun visor, he looked like any one of the thousands of golf fans walking the course, but the man was a crook. Why the hell could Tynan not leave him alone?

'I haven't time for a drink.' He tried to brush past, but Tynan grabbed his arm.

'I said I want to talk, Lenny boy.' The smile was still frozen in place but the eyes were hard. 'Where can we meet? That Dormobile of yours might be a bit cramped—'

So Tynan knew he and Liz had their trailer near-by. Trust the bastard to have checked up. He must get rid of the man somehow; there were too many people around. If he told Tynan now that he was not interested in another drugs operation, the fellow may get nasty. Better play him along for the present.

'Okay. I'll see you tonight.'

'That's my boy. Where?'

'The Royal Hotel in Girvan. Eight o'clock.'

Tynan relaxed his grip on Morgan's arm. 'You won't regret it, Lenny. I'm setting up something for next year. Big money—it'll take the pressure off; help you shoot better scores.' He winked. 'See you to-night.'

Like hell you will, Morgan thought as he watched Tynan move off, the thin fabric of the man's sports shirt emphasising the corpulent belly that bulged over his belted trousers. A young, athletic-looking minder moved to Tynan's side as they vanished into the crowd. Leonard watched them go before moving across to join Liz.

'Who on earth was that?'

'Oh, somebody I met earlier this year.' He knew that would not satisfy her curiosity and he was right.

'He looks a bit of a rough diamond. What did he want?' Her eyes searched his face. 'Leonard, are you in some sort of trouble?'

He paused before replying. He had never told Liz about Tynan, but now that he had surfaced in Turnberry and wanted to implicate him again, it was only right that she should know. Leonard hoped she would understand. A burst of applause rippled across from the eighteenth green as another three-some completed their practice round. When it had died down, he said: 'Liz, let's go and sit down some-where.'

'It's unbelievable. I never thought there would be so many people here to see a little ball get knocked about!'

Martin Dignam surveyed the panoramic view below through binoculars from the forecourt of the Turnberry Hotel. It was mid-afternoon and thou-sands of fans were out on the course watching the final day's practice round. The size of the crowd had surprised Dignam; if it was like this now, imagine the multitudes when the bloody thing really got under way. What an audience. He hoped they would admire his handiwork!

'Hey! I can see it!' Dignam's tone was excited.

'What?' Marie asked.

He moved closer to her, saying quietly: 'The war memorial. Here, have a look. Over there.'

He passed the binoculars and she followed his pointing finger. She picked it out—a slim column on a grassy knoll away towards the far end of the course. The hillock on which it was situated gave an elevated view of several fairways and greens and she could make out quite a number of spectators watching the action from there.

She lowered the binoculars. 'It's very impressive.'

He shrugged. 'Who cares? A monument is a monument. Not my type of target.'

Earlier, the traffic approaching Turnberry had slowed them down and when they had reached the course itself, they had decided to stop for an hour or so to look around. She could see that Dignam was impressed with the crowds. He had never seen so many people spread over a confined area before and it excited him. What had also excited him, after they had parked their car and gained entry to the course, were the huge temporary stands which had been erected at judicious vantage-points for the spectators.

They had stopped near the eighteenth green to admire the five steel and wood structures, one of them larger than the others, that surrounded it. Workmen were putting the finishing touches to the larger stand. 'How many of these are around the course?' Dignam had asked one of the men.

'About a dozen, I expect.'

'This one here—would that be the biggest?'

'Yes, mate. This is where it all finishes on Sunday evening.'

Marie was glad she knew a bit about golf. Last year she had gone with Stephen to the Open championship at Wentworth, just outside London, for a few days. Dignam had never been on a golf course in his life until today—and it showed.

They had moved away but Marie noticed Dignam looking back at the temporary stand. 'It will be packed on Sunday, I suppose.'

'The tickets for the next four days are probably sold out already,' Marie replied.

He smiled and said 'Interesting.'

'Seaview', when they reached it, basked placidly in the afternoon sun, a haven of peace compared to the hustle and bustle of Turnberry, ten miles down the road. They parked the car outside on the roadway and entered the long front garden with neatly trimmed grass, the rose bushes adding splashes of red and yellow to the scene. A young woman sat at a table under a large blue and white sun umbrella, sipping an orange drink and watching two young children gambolling on the grass.

While Dignam went to speak to the proprietor, Marie looked at the two little boys. One of them kicked a ball in her direction and he clapped excitedly when Marie joined in the fun. She kicked the ball towards the far end of the garden and the two boys ran after it. She watched, then turned to the young woman who was obviously their mother. 'They're lovely children. What are their names?'

'The big one is Michael—he's four, and the

smaller one is Rory. He's aged two.'

Marie studied the girl. She was not much older than herself and already she was a wife and mother. Subconsciously she found herself envying her. 'Are you on holiday? You sound Irish. By the way my name is—' Marie was about to give her real name, but caught herself in time. Jesus, she might have blown the whole operation there and then. She would have to be more careful. The girl was looking at her curiously, waiting for her to finish. 'Er, Young. Norah Young.'

'Hullo. I'm Joan Donohue. We're from Sligo. And no, we're not exactly on vacation—.' She laughed. 'My husband is a professional golfer. He's here to play in the Open.'

'Oh, how exciting.' Marie had recovered from her confusion. She had never heard of a golfer called Donohue, but then she was familiar only with the big names who played the game. 'Is he going to win?' she asked, laughing.

The girl smiled. 'If Colm wins enough money for us to have a good holiday next week, I'll be very happy. He's not one of the fancied superstars.'

Before the conversation could progress, two men came out of the house. The younger man, dressed neatly in slacks and pullover, carried a leather hold-all. He was wearing a sports shirt and Marie noticed that his arms were bronzed and muscular. With him was an older man, a weighty golf bag on his shoulder.

'Come on, children. Here's Daddy,' Joan Donohue called out. The boys came running up from the end of the garden. 'I'm bringing them to the beach while Colm practices,' she said to Marie. 'It can get so boring watching them hit golf balls—'

'Of course.' Marie sensed that she was expected to agree. There was a quick exchange of introductions and she learned that the older man was Johnny Davis, Colm's caddie. He was now loading the golf bag and a picnic basket into the boot of the car. What a beautiful, happy family group, she thought to herself, making a mental note to read the newspapers to see how the sports writers rated Colm Donohue's chances in the Open. He looked very boyish to be competing against the world's top golfers.

'We'll be back here tomorrow night,' Marie said as Joan prepared to join the others. 'I might see you then.'

'That would be nice. The guesthouse is full and they are all golf fans. There isn't anyone else of our age staying, so it'll be nice to have someone to talk to. If Colm plays well during the first two days, we'll be here until Sunday evening at least.'

The children waved goodbye through the back window and Marie responded.

Fate had played a fickle card by having Dignam and herself stay in the same guesthouse as one of the participants at Turnberry. She knew that in all professional golf tournaments, just over half the competitors survived to contest the final two days. Marie hoped the Donohues and their children would not be around on Sunday when the war memorial was blown up. Right now, Marie was not proud of what she was doing.

'Come on. Let's get out of here.' She had not noticed Dignam come out of the guesthouse. 'Who was that I saw you talking to just now?' he asked as they were getting into the car.

'Oh, just a woman and her husband. They're Irish also.'

Dignam's eyes narrowed with suspicion. She was surprised at the harshness in his voice. 'I don't want you holding casual conversations with anyone while we're on this job. Understand? We're on a mission and from now on we keep pretty much to ourselves. That way we don't have to answer any questions and nobody gets any information—'

'I didn't give away any information,' Marie said stiffly. 'We only exchanged a few pleasantries—'

'I don't give a fuck what you call them. Cut them out.'

'Oh, all right, Martin—'

'And another thing—from now on we call each other Tom and Norah. I want us to get used to using those names.'

Marie nodded but did not answer. She was once again seeing the harsh, dedicated side of Dignam: a man programmed to do a job and determined to let nothing stand in his way. He knew she was inexperienced and needed keeping an eye on, but she resented being treated like a schoolgirl.

Dignam started the car and drove towards Ayr and the coast beyond. He told her he had paid for their room even though they would not be spending the night at 'Seaview'. The car radio was on and he sang snatches of the pop songs that blared out. Funny the way Dignam's mood could change so swiftly. Now he was relaxed again, striving to make conversation. Marie found this irritating and made no attempt to reciprocate.

'What's wrong? You're very silent.'

'I'm enjoying the scenery.'

'Worried about tonight?'

'Should I be?'

'Well, I mean we are travelling as husband and wife . . . sharing the same room—'

'Forget it! Don't get any ideas on that score.' Her tone was sharp, icy.

'I see. Patrick's little sister acting the virgin. Come on, I bet you didn't act like that with your old boyfriend—'

'How do you know about Stephen?'

'I checked it out with Earley. When I'm sent on a job with someone, I like to know everything about them. You're not the girl you appear to be, Mrs Norah Young.' He laughed.

She was sorry now she had allowed him to talk her into driving up the coast like this. She should have insisted this morning that they go to Glasgow to meet Flavin and then drive back to 'Seaview' tonight. It still would not have resolved their sleeping arrangements, but at least she would have had company other than his for the evening. The Donohues and their children, for instance. Still, better make the best of the situation now. After all, she was stuck with Dignam for the next four days. She would try to be pleasant.

'Did you know that Colm Donohue is a golfer?'

He grunted. 'I didn't waste my time back there. I checked out everyone who's staying in the place.'

'He's competing in the Open.'

'No kidding.' This time he gave a short bitter laugh. 'I just hope he's not expecting to win the bleeding thing. He might be in for a bit of a shock.'

The bedside phone rang at 2.20 p.m. Lisa Maurelli levered herself onto one elbow and lifted the receiver. 'Hello?'

'Lisa—' His voice was a whisper.

'Hi.'

'Are you alone?'

She sighed. 'What do you think?'

He laughed. 'Let's go, then. I'm down here in the lobby—'

Lisa decided to play David Megson along, make him work for it. 'My, my. You are in a hurry.'

'Come on,' he said impatiently. 'We haven't much time—'

'Three hours at least. Probably more.'

'What makes you so sure?'

'Simple. Tony teed off with his partners roughly twenty minutes ago. They'll be trying out shots and pacing out the course, so they won't play too fast, at least fifteen minutes a hole. Seventeen holes still to play—figure it out for yourself, honey.'

'You've got it all worked out, haven't you?'

'Naturally. But I must be back for Tony to see me on the eighteenth tee. Okay?'

'Right. Now come on down.'

She paused. The guy was so anxious for it, he was not thinking straight. Maybe he did not care if she was caught. 'Use your head. We can't be seen walking out through the foyer together. Too dangerous. Marvin Maxwell might be snooping around. Where have you got your car?'

'In the official car park—the press section.'

'I'll see you there in five minutes.'

'Make it sooner. I'm in danger of coming—' He heard her laugh before the phone went dead.

Lisa swung herself off the bed, glanced in the mirror. She was dressed simply in a halter top and slacks and reckoned it was ideal. As usual at a time like this, she felt a surge of excitement: a mixture of sexual anticipation coupled with the danger of possibly being caught out. Hell, she thought, Tony probably got the same feeling every time he hit a goddam golf ball.

Megson hooted the horn as she walked into the car park and she slid into the seat beside him. He did not say anything, just let his eyes tour slowly over her body.

'Like what you see?'

'Perfect.'

'That's what I like about you English, you're so gallant.' The engine fired into life. 'Where are you taking me?' She giggled at her choice of words.

He matched her mood. 'Here if you like. But I think it might be more discreet at my hotel.'

The official at the gate waved them out and soon they were heading north up the coast road. Lisa found herself admiring the view across the firth, contrasting with the rugged furze-covered hillsides where sheep and cows grazed in the afternoon sun. She was finding her first trip to Scotland a pleasurable experience.

He took his eyes off the road momentarily to glance at her, smiling. His hand left the wheel and fell on her thigh. Megson waited for a reprimand; when it did not materialise, he moved his hand up and down slowly, caressing the shapely thigh that stretched the expensive slacks to their limit. She closed her eyes, gave a low laugh, and slid down further in the car seat so that his hand was at the top of her leg.

His hand was at the zip of her pants, trying to work it down. Lisa stopped him. 'Wait, honey. Be patient,' she said huskily. The car swerved and she opened her eyes in terror, the wail of an angry motorist fading in the distance. 'My God, what you trying to do—kill us?'

'Sorry.' He put his hand back on the wheel.

She was relieved when a few minutes later they pulled into the car park of a hotel. There were not too many other cars around and she assumed most people would be in Turnberry watching the final practice.

'How do I get to your room without arousing suspicion?' she asked as they strolled towards the entrance.

'Easy. I'm in Room 19 on the first floor—turn left at the top of the stairs. We'll go into the bar first and have a drink. Then I'll leave and you follow me up.'

They toyed with their drinks in the almost empty bar, whispering, subjecting themselves to sexual torture. David downed his drink in a couple of gulps and left. She waited until the lone barman had his back turned, measuring a whisky, then slid off the stool and strolled into the foyer. The girl behind the reception desk was chatting to a male member of the staff and did not give Lisa a second glance as she walked towards the carpeted stairway. It was rather gloomy as she went up, but there was a light on the first-floor landing. She had no trouble finding Room 19, which opened at her touch.

David Megson came out of the bathroom as she entered. He had taken off his jacket and was in a short-sleeved sports shirt and slacks. He was thinner than she remembered, but she liked hungry-looking men with slim bellies and equally slim buttocks. Through the thin material of the hip-hugging slacks, she could see he was already aroused.

He did not say anything at first, just crossed the room and locked the door. As he did so, he turned. She strolled over and put her hand on his crotch, squeezing gently. She could feel the hardness.

'My turn,' she said wickedly, looking up into his eyes.

'You little devil—'

He grabbed her roughly, pressing her close to his body with one arm while, with the other, he reached for her hair, pulling her head back so hard, she cried out in pain, her mouth open. He brought his mouth down, hard, his lips finding hers, his tongue forcing itself inside, twisting, probing, seeking a response which was almost immediate. Her arms encircled his neck and her body curved into his.

They finally broke apart, breathless, staring at each other for a few moments like two boxers. Bosom heaving, she stepped out of her shoes, still with her eyes on his. She saw him follow suit; then, as though on a preordained signal, they moved in on each other, peeling off clothes with a speed that excited and left then both panting for breath. When they were both naked, he swept her up in his arms and moved to the only bed in the single room. It was on the small side, but it suited their purpose.

But David Megson did not try to take her sexually all in one go. He surprised her and added pleasure to the encounter by holding off, teasing her, exploring her body with his hands, with his tongue. Lisa writhed and moaned with delight, and when he did finally enter her, she screamed with the intensity of passion, her nails digging deeply into the flesh of his back.

Then it was her turn. She became the aggressor, kneading him, holding him until she again brought forth signs of arousal, then straddling him and working to his rhythmic movements until he came again. Afterwards they lay side by side, exhausted, exhilarated. She asked him the time and when he told her she calculated that Tony would be playing the twelfth hole. She hoped he was having a good day.

David Megson did not talk much, which disappointed her. She liked when someone she was with complimented her. Lisa turned sideways onto him, watching him blow perfect smoke rings towards the ceiling. When he did turn to her, she noticed again that he had rather cruel eyes. 'When can we have an encore?' he said.

She was non-committal. 'I don't know. I'll see how I'm fixed over the next few days.' That would keep him on tenterhooks. Besides, she did not like to make it twice with anybody during a tournament as a general rule. Marvin Maxwell was always snooping around.

'Was it better than last year?' He was leaning over her, stroking her nipple.

Now was that not just like a man—putting the

onus onto somebody else? 'You tell me.'

He laughed. 'Okay, so it was.'

She moved his hand away from her body. 'I must have a shower before I go.' Lisa slid off the bed and padded across the room. At the entrance to the bathroom, she paused and looked over her shoulder. 'Coming?'

'Why not? It's a good way to save time.'

But of course it did not. They took off again under the stinging hot water, soaping each other down, slipping and laughing at each outrageous antic. Finally she broke away, dripping water onto the floor. They dried each other down and got back into their clothes. One last passionate kiss, then she went downstairs alone and out into the car park. He followed a few minutes later and within a quarter of an hour they were back in Turnberry.

Despite her being anxious to make an appearance on the course—she reckoned that Tony, not to mention Marvin Maxwell, would be scanning the crowds for her just now—Lisa consented when David Megson asked if she would pose for a few photographs in front of the clubhouse. As it turned out, it was a blessing in disguise; while he was taking shots of her posing under a sun umbrella, she saw the bulky figure of Tony's manager coming through the crowd. He was perspiring as usual and looked flustered.

'Lisa—'

'Hi, Mr Maxwell.'

'Where the hell have you been?' he hissed, conscious that there were people within earshot. 'Tony's been asking for you.'

She feigned surprise. 'Why? Is something wrong?'

That angered him. 'Nothing's wrong. He just likes to see you around now and then, that's all. Where were you?'

'In my room. Resting.'

'You weren't. I checked.'

'Oh.' She gave him her wide-eyed look. 'Then I must have been out. Getting some fresh air.'

Marvin breathed heavily. It was obvious he did not believe her, but he could not make an issue of it. Not right now. Not with these people around. Instead, he nodded towards David. 'Who's this?'

'A photographer. The man from the airport, remember? We met a few minutes ago and he asked me to pose for some photographs.' She smiled across at David. 'What did you say your name was again?'

'Megson. David Megson.' He played it along beautifully.

'Oh yes. This is Marvin Maxwell, Tony's manager—'

Marvin waved his hand impatiently. 'Come on, Lisa. Let's go. Tony is walking down the seventeenth fairway right now—' He turned to Megson. 'You're all through here, buddy. And remember, next time you want to take pictures of the lady, you contact me first. Got it?'

Megson glared. 'Get stuffed, mate.'

As he was turning on his heel, Lisa called out: 'So long, Mr Megson—'

'Bye, Mrs Maurelli. Thanks for everything.'

She met his gaze. 'My pleasure. Hope you got

everything you wanted—' His laugh followed her into the crowd.

The committee of the Royal and Ancient had ordained that practice rounds on the Ailsa course finish at 6.00 p.m. After that time, a small army of staff, under head greenkeeper Fred Cartwright, would swarm over the course, replacing divots, raking bunkers, and giving the famed Turnberry greens, with their subtle undulations, a final shave before the first threesome of the 150 competitors teed off at 7.30 the following morning.

There had been a minor controversy during the day when two American golfers, Jim Dyer and Cal Olton, had had their only practice round curtailed by R & A officials on the fourteenth hole. They had flown in from the US a few hours before and had made a dash for the first tee, anxious to get their first look at Turnberry. But at six o'clock precisely, they were ordered off the links by two officials. Pleading first, then threatening to quit the Open altogether, the Americans finally had to relent, leaving it to their respective caddies to walk the last four fairways of the course, making detailed notes of yardage, bunkers and pin placements on the greens. Newspaper and television reporters, eager for a good story, had buttonholed Dyer and Olton and had given the duo's acerbic comments about officialdom the full treatment.

When asked to comment on the controversy, Major Patrick Dougherty, the Royal and Ancient Tournament Director, had refused to comment.

Another problem, and a much more serious one

as far as the Open contestants were concerned, was the rough at Turnberry. The pros reckoned that the R & A had allowed it to grow to tigerish proportions and had complained bitterly about it. Their mutterings fell on deaf ears. Pint-sized Taiwan golfer Tai Kai-Chen was quoted as saying, tongue in cheek, that he would not venture into the rough after his ball for fear of getting lost!

As the evening sun set over the deserted Ailsa course, awaiting the assaults of the world's best golfers, American Richard Elliott was installed as firm favourite to win the title at his eighth attempt.

'He has prepared well, is striking the ball beautifully in practice, and seems to have the measure of Turnberry's tricky greens,' Malcolm Jacob told his early evening television audience in a half-hour Open Championship Special. He rattled off a list of names whom he considered could be there or thereabouts at the finish. These included several home-based players, notably England's Sam Joyce and the genial Scot, Sandy McIntyre.

'Rafael Escudio comes into the reckoning also, and Tony Maurelli could equal the late Tony Lema's Open record and win it at his first attempt. Personally, I like the look of Spanish youngster José Chiquero and the equally youthful Australian, Ken Stimpson. But picking a winner of the British Open is akin to predicting which horse is going to win the Grand National,' Malcolm Jacob went on in the breezy style of delivery for which he was renowned. 'Whereas in the National a rank outsider can come good on the day and win, in the Open championship a golfer must keep his game together for all four days—and that's where class tells. Dick Elliott has that class in abundance. In a conversation with him today he struck me as a man without a worry in the world; a man dedicated to achieving his goal—to be crowned British Open champion on Sunday.'

In his room in the Turnberry Hotel, Malcolm scowled at the television set. Unlike Dick Elliott, he had worries galore. The interview had been recorded two hours earlier, not long after Sally had told him about the confrontation in the coffee tent between herself and Felicity.

'The game is up,' Sally had said. 'Your wife knows about us.'

'My God, how? You didn't tell her surely—'

'I didn't have to. She found a bottle of my perfume in your room. Besides, she's a woman. She suspected something.'

Malcolm pondered a moment. 'What'll we do now?'

Sally had laughed. 'I really don't know. I'm sure you'll think of something, Malcolm.'

So far Sally's confidence in him had been misplaced. Which was maybe as well, because he did not want to say anything just at the moment to disturb his wife. Felicity was in the bathroom now, soaking in a tub, sobering up in time for the eve-of-the- Open dinner in the hotel later tonight. Earlier, he had rescued her from the bar where she had spent most of the afternoon.

'Well, Malcolm. So you're playing around again . . . .' He had managed to get her up to their room before she started on him. 'You're old enough to be her father. You do realise that, don't you, darling?'

'We didn't get around to discussing our age difference—'

Malcolm sat down on the bed, thinking. He was not looking forward to the gala dinner tonight. Not with Felicity in this mood. Heaven only knows what antics she would get up to. In half an hour or so she would come out of the bathroom, smiling and chatting as she got herself ready, pretending nothing had happened between them. But he knew Felicity. It would not surprise him if she did something to embarrass him, something irrational to punish him in front of all his friends—including the committee members of the R & A. He would have to watch her carefully tonight.

Good God! What if she was drowning herself in the bathroom right now. Just like her to do something silly like that out of spite. He jumped up, dashed across the room and thumped on the bathroom door. 'Felicity! Felicity! Are you all right in there?'

There were a few moments' silence, then he heard a weary: 'Go away.'

Thank heavens! He came away and sat down again, relieved. At least she had not done anything stupid. He would like to shoulder Dick Elliott's burden right now—all that guy had to worry about was winning the British Open.

4

THURSDAY, 16 JULY

'On the first tee—Leonard Morgan, Willie Lammie and Mr Jim Greene from the Lakes Golf Club in Cumbria.'

The voice of the official starter rang out in the early morning Turnberry air. It was 7.28 a.m., just two minutes before the first ball of the British Open Championship was due to be struck. Throughout the day, at eight-minute intervals, the 150 world class golfers would tee off in groups of three, with the final threesome of the first round not due to finish until late evening.

Over 30,000 spectators, a record for a first day at the Open, were expected. Giant scoreboards, similar to the one near the clubhouse, had been erected at strategic points out on the course to keep everyone, including the golfers, alerted to the hole-by-hole progress of the championship. An early morning haze, giving promise of a warm, sunny day, hung over the Ailsa course. Out in the firth, the huge bulk of Ailsa Craig had yet to emerge from the mist. Already knots of spectators were making their way onto the course, most of them heading for the first tee to see the opening shot being struck.

Morgan, Lammie and the British amateur champion, Greene, were ready to go, with Morgan having the honour of hitting the first ball. 'Even if I don't make the cut, at least I'll get my name mentioned in all the newspapers,' he thought as he fastened the snugly fitting glove on his left hand. He took another look down the first fairway, a fairly straightforward 361-yard hole that dog-legged slightly right. All the holes in Turnberry were named and this one was called, appropriately, Ailsa Craig.

'Good luck, love,' Liz whispered as he selected the club from the bag which she would carry all day. Morgan smiled and gave her a quick peck on the lips. A photographer's shutter clicked. Morgan looked hard at him and a steward moved the offender to a safe distance.

He had decided to hit a three wood off the tee and play for position. He took his stance, willing himself to swing smoothly. He shut out everything from his mind: Liz, their tight financial position, the unexpected appearance yesterday of Stan Tynan . . . everything. Even after he had hit through the ball, he kept his head down until he heard the smattering of applause from the spectators.

They liked it! And why not—he looked up to see his ball finishing between the fairway bunkers, nestling just short of the light rough on the left, roughly 250 yards distant. The ideal position for his second shot to the green. The knot in Leonard's stomach eased. Thank God that first drive was safely away. Maybe it was going to be his day.

That feeling was reinforced ten minutes later when, after hitting his second shot to ten feet from the pin, he sank the putt for a birdie three. What a way to start his Open campaign! As he walked to the second tee he felt a surge of confidence. That was dangerous, he told himself. He must keep his emotions under control.

He got safe pars at the next two holes. Then things happened at holes four and five that would get Leonard Morgan's name mentioned in the early sports bulletins and send spectators scampering across the Turnberry turf to swell the crowd following the opening trio from a small group to hundreds. Morgan birdied both the holes to go three under par after five and provided the Open with one of its most sensational starts ever.

Leonard was in trouble at the 245-yard par three sixth hole. He did not strike the ball well with his three wood and it caught the slope in front of the green, rolling back down a good thirty yards from the flagstick. But the groans of the spectators turned into cheers a few minutes later when he left a wedge shot four feet from the hole and a mighty roar erupted when he sank the putt for a safe par. Meanwhile, his partners were not matching his brilliance; Willie Lammie was already two over par as they walked off the sixth green, while the amateur Greene seemed overwhelmed by the occasion and was four over regulation figures.

As he stepped onto the seventh tee, already ringed with eager fans, Leonard Morgan had to steel himself not to scan the faces to see if Tynan was among them. Christ, he must put all thoughts of Tynan out of his head. So what if he was in big trouble for not keeping that appointment in Girvan last night with Tynan. That threat had to wait.

In the dining room of the Turnberry Hotel, Malcolm

and Felicity Jacob were finishing their breakfast in sullen silence. She could sense his annoyance, and all because she had really enjoyed herself last night at his stuffy old dinner.

She glanced around the large room. Outside, the first trio had teed off an hour ago and Malcolm had been bleeped a few times and given some of the early scores. Felicity hoped that that would take his mind off last night. But when he still did not try to make conversation, she decided to meet him head on.

'Sulking, Malcolm darling?'

He set down his cup carefully before replying. 'Sulking, no. Embarrassed is a better word.'

'Embarrassed? But why? I thought it went awfully well last night. Everyone seemed to enjoy themselves tremendously.'

'You certainly did. You had too much to drink.'

'I did not!'

'You knocked back far too many, Felicity.'

'Rubbish. Some of your journalist friends and their so-called ladies had far more than me.'

He did not outwardly show his anger, but his tone said it all. 'The difference is they know how to behave. You didn't see any of them getting up to sing!'

'I thought I did very well.'

'Did you now?' He leaned forward and, even though his voice was lowered, the words came across the table like machine gun bullets. 'You were not meant to sing. It was not that sort of evening.'

'Really? Then why the hell did you have a piano player tinkling away in the corner?'

'I engaged him to lend a sense of occasion to the

evening—not to accompany boozy ladies doing their favourite party pieces.'

Felicity took the insult in her stride. 'For God's sake, Malcolm, your little soiree was far too formal. All those stuffy Royal and Ancient types; it needed a bit of livening up.'

If looks could kill, Felicity reckoned she was sipping her last cup of coffee. 'If I'd needed a cabaret singer, I'd have engaged one who could sing. And that song. Oh God. . . .' His voice trailed away in painful memory.

It was all coming back now. She had sung her favourite old bluesy number—'Nobody Does It Like Me'. The same song she had sung at the local golf club party a few months ago, that night when Malcolm was away on one of his BBC golf assignments and she had been feeling especially lonely.

> If there's a right way to do it,
> A wrong way to do it—
> Nobody does it like me. . . .

She had taken a couple of drinks too many that night, too. The club lounge had been well patronised for the weekend dance and for most of the evening she had sat at a table with other women members and their husbands, sticking out like a sore thumb. When the dancing was over, someone had commandeered the piano and a sing-song had started. By the time her name was called, Felicity was nicely tipsy, just enough not to care a damn. She had sauntered to the piano and someone had put her sitting on it. She had crossed her legs—that brought a few wolf whistles—

and, with smoke drifting skywards from her cigarette, had launched into her favourite number:

> If there's a wrong way to play it cool,
> A right way to be a fool—
> Nobody does it like me. . . .

Felicity had noticed Jon Selsway looking at her several times during the evening. Whenever she had glanced over to the bar, he seemed to be looking her way, glass in hand, eyeing her over the shoulder of one of his companions. The son of a member, he had never really registered with her before, because she was definitely not into chasing toy boys. Now there he was, smiling as she sang and openly ogling her as she did her Shirley Bassey party piece on the piano.

> When I try to be a lady,
> I'm no lady I'm a fraud—
> And when I talk like I'm a lady,
> What I sound like is a broad—

She had a good voice and could carry a song. But Felicity sensed that, like the rest of the men present, Jon Selsway was enjoying the expanse of thigh she was showing as much as her song. All the same, it was great being an object of admiration again—she had not experienced that sensation for some time now.

> Nobody does it like me—yeah!
> Nobody does it like me!

As she belted out the last few bars she threw her head back and flung her arms wide. Eyes closed momentarily, she could hear the cheers ringing out from the males in the audience. When Felicity opened her eyes again, he was standing before her.

'May I?'

'Pardon?'

He smiled. 'Assist you down.'

'Of course.' She stubbed out her cigarette in the pianist's ashtray. 'Please do.'

He put his hand on her hips and she could feel the strength in his arms as he swung her onto the floor. She had placed her hands on his shoulders, but now withdrew them quickly when she saw that some of the members were looking on with interest. 'Thank you.'

'My pleasure.' He took his hands from her body. 'I enjoyed your number.'

He did not go away, just stood there looking at her, smiling. 'May I buy you a drink?'

She would loved to have accepted his offer, but there were too many eyes watching. Besides, she had already had quite a few and she was worried about driving home. 'Maybe some other time. Thanks just the same.'

She walked back as straight as she could to the table. When she sat down the atmosphere was not exactly cordial. One husband bravely said: 'Good show, Felicity', but a glare from his wife froze him into silence. More than ever she felt out of it at the table.

Felicity sipped her drink slowly, glancing over to where Jon Selsway had been with his mates. She could not see him now and probably he had left. What the hell was she playing at; she was nearly twice his age. In fact she recalled one time when as a schoolboy he had caddied for her!

Since her stint on the piano, conversation at the table had cooled and one couple had pointedly left. Felicity finished her drink, said goodnight and departed. Nobody pleaded with her to stay.

He was waiting for her in the car park, materialising out of the gloom as she approached her car. 'Hello.'

She pretended to be startled. 'Who—Jon! What are you doing out here?'

'Waiting to drive you home, of course. Got the keys?'

'I beg your pardon—' Felicity hoped she sounded suitably shocked.

He had a disconcerting habit of just standing and staring. 'I said I'm here to drive you home, Mrs Jacob. Isn't that what you want?'

He had a nerve, thinking he could pick her up like that. She stared at him in the gloom. He returned her gaze coolly, smiling confidently. My God he had grown up a lot since he had caddied for her. Now he was a handsome young man—and available. He obviously knew that Malcolm was away and reckoned she was lonely—and looking for something.

'What makes you think I want you to drive me home?'

He did not answer. Instead, he held out his hand for the car keys. She hesitated. It was just like a scene out of that film, what was it?—'The Graduate'. Mrs Robinson had certainly enjoyed her joust with the eager young fellow in that movie. Felicity opened her handbag, took out her keys and handed them over.

Suddenly he grabbed her around the waist and pulled her to him. His kiss was gentle, lingering. She responded, arching her body into his. Her coat slipped from her shoulders and fell to the ground. They swayed, locked together, his hand moving down her back to her buttocks, pressing her body to his. Felicity fought for control. She broke off, stepped back, looked at him, saw the smile playing around the corners of his mouth.

'Your place or mine?' he whispered. She was sure that line was from a movie, too.

'Mine.' He came at her again, slowly, his weight pushing her back against the body of the car. She had resigned herself to being taken there and then in the car park when in the distance the door of the clubhouse opened and a shaft of light pierced the gloom. They broke apart, guiltily. Oh no, Felicity thought, that's all I need—to be caught snogging redhanded with a member half my age in the car park. She would never live that down!

Jon fumbled with the keys. 'Quick, into the car.'

She bent down, retrieving her coat. 'For God's sake, hurry!' Voices and laughter drifted across the tarmac. Felicity glanced over her shoulder and saw figures of men and women outlined in the lighted doorway. Jon was already in the driver's seat. She pulled her car door open and flung herself inside, thankful that the exit was at the furthest end, away from the clubhouse and the approaching couples. The car slid into the night.

She had only been back to the golf club once since

then—with Malcolm. Nobody had ever mentioned anything to her and there had been no malicious gossip among the members, according to one of her friends. As for Jon Selsway, he had been there the night she had returned with her husband. He had never tried to get in touch with her since and, whenever their eyes met across the lounge, he merely smiled and looked away.

It was the way Felicity wanted it. She had enjoyed their all-action, all-night encounter in her house but an affair was not her style. Malcolm provided her with creature comforts and she was not really interested in penurious toy boys.

The only problem was that she was now expecting a baby—and she was not sure whose it was. Fortunately, whatever about Malcolm's lack of emotion these past few years, he had always seen fit to perform his duty regularly as a husband, no doubt out of a sense of guilt rather than genuine passion. When she saw fit to break the news to him, she would be grateful for those less than stimulating encounters.

'Morning, Malcolm. Morning, Felicity. And how are we on this beautiful day?' The crisp, businesslike tones of Ricky Edwards brought Felicity back to the present. He had his clipboard in his hand and his identity disc was in place on his Levi jacket. A bleeper dangled from his belt.

'Guess who's burning it up out there'—Edwards nodded his head towards the course—'Leonard Morgan. Three under par after nine holes.' He sat down, helping himself to a slice of toast.

'Good for him,' Malcolm replied.

'He'll blow up, of course,' Edwards said matter of

factly. 'If not later today, then probably tomorrow.'

'Anyone else showing?' Malcolm asked.

'Not as yet. But then all the big names are teeing off later.' Edwards filled him in on the broadcast schedule for the day; a morning, afternoon and late evening session to show the last golfers coming in. The crowds were now pouring in, anticipating low scores from the golf greats as the day wore on.

'I'm told I missed a good party last night.' Ricky chewed on his toast, smiled disarmingly at Felicity. 'I believe you were in particularly fine fettle, my dear.'

'Yes, I enjoyed myself. Everybody did, I think.' She saw Malcolm scowl.

'I hear you did your party piece.'

'I sang a song, yes. A bluesy number.'

Ricky pretended surprise, although he had been told all. 'In that august company—' his eyes flickered to Malcolm, 'that must have been something. I'm sorry I missed it.' Serve that asshole Jacob right for not inviting him.

'Mind if we get back to today's business, Ricky.' The bloody ponce would sit gossiping all morning if he wasn't shifted, Malcolm thought.

'Of course.' Edwards consulted his clipboard. 'I've assigned you Sally again today, Malcolm. That okay? You both work so well together, it would be a shame to part you now.' He jumped to his feet, a smile on his lips. 'Cheerio, must dash. 'Bye, Felicity darling—'

From a hotel room in Luss, a picturesque town on the shores of Loch Lomond, Martin Dignam's phone call to Dominick Earley at the headquarters of the IRA unit in West Belfast had just been put through.

'Hello . . . that you, Dominick?'

'Yes.'

'Dignam here.'

'Oh, hello Martin.' The tone was friendly. 'Everything all right?'

'Everything's fine.'

'Can you talk?'

'Sure. Don't see why not. We're in a hotel.'

'A hotel?' There was a pause. The friendly tone vanished. 'Where?'

'A place called Luss. A lovely spot. Overlooking Loch Lomond.' Dignam waited for the reaction. Another pause, this time a longer one. He would have given anything to have been able to see Earley's face.

'Fuck Loch Lomond. You're supposed to be in Turnberry. At the Open, remember?'

'Yes, I know, Dominick—'

'So why the hell aren't you?'

Dignam grinned to himself. Fuck you too Earley, he thought. I just love giving you a hard time. Aloud he said: 'The weather here is lovely, Dominick. I decided that Marie and I might do a spot of sight-seeing.'

'Have you gone off your bloody head, man!' The voice exploded from the earpiece. 'I didn't send you to Scotland to go sightseeing!'

'Relax, Dominick. That job you want done will be looked after. I can't say much more right now.'

The voice now had a cutting edge. 'Whose idea was it to change plans?'

'I thought it best not to hang around Turnberry too long.' It was a lie, but it sounded good.

'You realise what you've done, Dignam. You've disobeyed orders—'

'Careful what you say, Dominick. You could be overheard.' That's put the bighead in his place!

His warning had a sobering effect on Earley. When the voice from Belfast spoke again, the words were chosen carefully, the tone measured. 'Have you been in touch with Glasgow yet?'

'Everything there is under control,' Dignam replied.

'I want you and Marie in that guesthouse in Turnberry tonight. Is that understood?'

'Yes.'

'I'll phone sometime tonight. If you haven't checked in, I'll send two men over on the ferry tomorrow. Is that also understood?'

'No need for that, Dominick.'

'See that there isn't.' A pause. 'How's Marie?'

'Fine. She's having breakfast right now. I'm looking after her—'

The phone went dead. Dignam replaced the receiver on the cradle and gave it a two-fingered salute. He had angered Mr O.C. Earley but was not going to lose any sleep over that. If the stupid bastard knew what he really had planned for next Sunday, Dignam thought as he went downstairs, Earley would really have something to get miffed about.

He found Marie waiting for him in the foyer. She looked stunning in a pair of red toreador pants and a black top, tied in front and showing a bit of bare midriff. She had some figure—and to think he had spent last night sleeping on the couch!

'You spoke to Dominick?' She asked in a low voice. He nodded. 'What did he say? Was he annoyed?'

'Naw. He agreed it might be a good idea not to show up too soon at Turnberry.'

She looked surprised. 'What else did he say?'

They went outside into the sunshine. It was a beautiful day and couples were sitting or strolling around on the lawn. Dignam lead her away from the entrance to a low, flat wall that led to the car park. They both sat down.

'Well?' Her eyes were on his face.

'About blowing up the memorial on the course? I asked his permission for changing the plan slightly.'

'What do you mean, changing the plan?' There was alarm in her voice. He would have to play her along gently.

'We could leave the monument alone. Plant the bomb somewhere else on the course—'

'No!' She turned on him, eyes blazing. 'You mean kill people? That wasn't the plan—and I don't want any part of it. I'm going to phone Dominick.'

'Wait, Marie. Wait.' He grabbed her arm. 'Who said anything about killing people? The plan would be to blow up the stand at night, just like we aimed to do with the monument.'

'I still don't like it. What did he say when you put it to him?'

'He said he would leave the choice up to me. He's happy as long as we create some disturbance and get the attention of the media.'

She shook her head. 'As far as I'm concerned, it's

the monument or else—'

'Or else what, Marie?' He spoke the words softly, but there was no mistaking the hidden menace.

'I get on the phone immediately to Belfast and tell them that I don't want any further part in this operation.' She pulled her arm away. 'Make up your mind, Martin.'

They faced each other and he could see the determination in her eyes. He smiled. 'Okay, Marie. You win. We'll do the monument.' The stupid little bitch, he thought. Why the hell had he been lumbered with her? When it came to the crunch, the chance to see some real action, she was scared shitless, just like Patrick had been the day he got his. Well, he did not need her co-operation. And that went for Earley also. He would carry his plan through without help from anybody and show the boys back in Belfast what a real leader is made of.

'So there's no change of plan? And nobody's to get killed?' She wanted to push him on this.

'That's right. Scout's honour.'

Was he telling her the truth, she wondered? Probably not. There was something about Martin Dignam that frightened her. He had always been a committed IRA member; she knew that from the early days when he had come to the house to see Patrick. Now there was a ruthlessness about him that she had not noticed before. He did not seem to see anything wrong in killing people, taking innocent lives. She had put that to him last night in the room when they were talking, expecting him to tell her to mind her own business. Instead he had laughed and said: 'We're at war in Northern Ireland—and we

137

must do everything in our power to win.'

'Did Dominick say anything about me?' she asked.

'Yes. He said I was to make sure you had a good day at Loch Lomond. So come on, girl. You know how dedicated I am to carrying out the OC's orders.'

At about the same time that Martin Dignam and Marie Kirk were driving to Scotland's famous scenic spot, Leonard Morgan was surveying a crucial putt on Turnberry's eighteenth green. Down on his haunches, the visor shielding the sun from his eyes, he studied the texture of the green and decided the putt had a slight left to right borrow. He needed this for a six under par round of 66. With the breeze freshening by the hour, Morgan reckoned that such a score would probably leave him the first round leader.

The two thousand spectators in the main stand behind the green watched the drama below. The four smaller stands were also full. Morgan stalked the putt in deathly silence. He knew the nearest challengers to him at this moment were the Japanese Ontabe and a little-known Canadian called Myers, both at two under after nine and twelve holes respectively. He was not worried about them, nor about the big names who had still to start their round.

The clicking sound his putter made when it stroked the ball was clearly audible in the silence. Leonard kept his head down and raised it only when he heard the roar welling up. He looked up just in time to see the ball disappear into the cup. When it dropped, he raised his putter high in the air. On the fringe of the green, standing beside his heavy bag, his girlfriend was jumping about like an excited school-girl.

Morgan exchanged handshakes with his two partners, neither of whom had distinguished himself, and walked off the green to thunderous applause. Television cameras whirred as he hugged Liz. On the way through the crowd to sign his card in the tour-nament director's caravan, he whispered to her: 'Join me in the press tent later, but don't give any inter-views or pose for photographs. We're news right now; I aim to make some money out of it.'

Ten minutes later, seated at a table behind which microphones were being hastily assembled, he was facing a barrage of questions.

'Have you ever lead the Open before, Leonard?'

'Have you ever lead any tournament before?'

'Is it true you made less than £30,000 from tour-naments last year?'

'What's it like travelling to tournaments in a caravan with your girlfriend?'

'Do you envy the big guys being paid all that appearance money at tournaments?'

'That putter of yours was red hot out there, Leonard. Where did you get it?'

'What about the pressure? Think you can shoot another 66 tomorrow?'

The interview over, the reporters dashed off to commandeer a telephone or a fax machine. But still Morgan was not able to relax; some photographers wanted shots of him and Liz outside, holding the magic putter. He vetoed suggestions for pictures of himself and Liz posing outside their caravan, parked on a site five miles away. Anyone wanting those pictures was going to have to pay for them.

The offer he was waiting for did not take long to materialise. He and Liz were still the centre of attention when he felt a tap on his arm. He recognised the fellow trying to get his attention as Terry Shortt, a golf reporter for one of the tabloids. 'I'd like to have a few words with you, Leonard.'

'Sure.' They moved away until they were out of earshot of the other reporters.

'I want an exclusive. You and Liz at your caravan. Mike here', he nodded to where a cameraman stood in the background, 'will take the pictures.'

'Okay. How much?'

'Five hundred.'

Morgan shook his head. 'Not enough. Double it and you're on.'

Shortt hesitated. 'I don't think my editor would go for four figures. Let's face it, it's just after midday. All the big boys still have to go out. You may not even be the leader by tonight, Leonard.'

'I will.'

'What makes you so sure?'

Morgan looked up to where the flags were fluttering on their poles. 'See how strong the breeze is? And it's getting stronger out there. I had the easy part of the day. Nobody's going to beat 66 today.'

He was probably right, Shortt reckoned. Okay, so Leonard Morgan is more than likely a one-day wonder; tomorrow he will blow it, shoot 77 and maybe not qualify for the last two rounds. But right now he was a hero, a golfer with an interesting life-style. Readers were interested in one-day wonders.

As though reading the reporter's mind, Morgan said: 'We'll make good copy, Terry, Liz and me. See this putter. Did you know it was a birthday gift from Liz last year?'

'No kidding.' Terry Shortt exchanged a quick glance with his photographer.

Of course I'm kidding, you asshole, Morgan thought to himself. But isn't that what your readers want to be told over their cornflakes tomorrow morning?

'Okay,' Shortt said. 'A thousand it is.'

'Great. When do I get the money?'

'I'll send off a fax to London now. I'll have a cheque for you immediately we come back from taking the photographs.'

The couple watched Shortt and the photographer depart. 'I don't believe it,' Liz said. 'A thousand pounds for a chat and a few photographs.'

Leonard grinned. 'Forget all that tinned crap we have back in the caravan. Tonight we dine in style up there—' He nodded at the Turnberry Hotel, towering majestically above them. 'Let's relax with a drink while we're waiting for Shortt.'

They were making their way towards the club-house when Stan Tynan stepped out of the crowd. Morgan tried to brush past him, but the big man stood in their way.

'Congratulations, Lenny boy. Great round—'

'What do you want?' Liz was surprised at Leonard's curt tone.

'You know what I want. You didn't show up for our little chat last night, Lenny. I don't like that.'

'I told you yesterday. We have nothing to talk

about. I'm not interested.'

Tynan did not move aside. Instead he smiled at Liz, showing a flash of gold tooth. 'Such bad manners your boyfriend has. I stop by to congratulate him and put some money his way and he tries to brush me aside.'

Morgan remained silent. Tynan took off his sun visor and mopped a ring of perspiration which had formed across his forehead. Liz noticed that his steel grey hair was beginning to thin. When he spoke again, his voice was low and menacing. 'I'm warning you, Lenny. Don't try to push me aside. You'd better go along with what I have planned or else—'

Liz glanced around. Was this really happening— here in broad daylight at the British Open, with hundreds of people within earshot and policemen and security guards in view? Why didn't Tynan leave them alone, get someone else to do his dirty work? Liz decided it was time she stepped in.

'Mr Tynan, Leonard is exhausted right now. He doesn't want to talk to you. He's finished with you, don't you understand? Now will you leave us alone or shall I call those policemen over?'

Stan Tynan glanced over his shoulder to where two policemen were chatting. He turned to face them again. 'Your girlfriend is right, Lenny. You're tired right now, not thinking straight. This is not the time to discuss our deal. But don't worry, you'll be hearing from me again, I promise.'

Tynan replaced his sun visor and moved off into the crowd. Morgan passed a hand across tired eyes. 'I wish to hell I'd never got mixed up with that gangster,' he said bitterly.

'Do you think he means what he says, that he'll be back again?' Liz asked.

'I've no doubt he will. But let's not worry about it right now.'

The official starter's voice rang out: 'On the first tee—British Open Champion Lou Menzies of Australia, Mañuel Luca from Spain and Richard Elliott from the United States!'

The buzz of excitement surged through the huge crowd now ringing the first tee as the three golfers stepped onto the tightly trimmed green sward. A ripple of applause soon died to silence. Both sides of the fairway, all the way down to the green, were lined with spectators, heads turned towards the tee, waiting for the drama to begin.

Dick Elliott studied Menzies as the Australian prepared to tee off. The man looked imperturbable, the essence of composure. Unsmiling, almost grim, the eyes in the bronzed, weather-beaten face narrowed against the afternoon sun. When Elliott had wished Menzies 'good luck' a few moments ago, he had barely acknowledged the greeting. It was as though he was saving every ounce of concentration for the forthcoming battle.

The 66 posted by Leonard Morgan was still the leading score, Elliott noted. The way the breeze was blowing now it was likely to remain so. Dick Elliott had not heard of Leonard Morgan before today and was not worried about his great round; unknowns tended to have their early hour of glory in the Open. When the real pressure came on, they usually cracked.

He had not slept well last night. Usually he had

no trouble sleeping the night before a big event like the Open. He hoped it was not a bad omen.

The Australian and the Spaniard had both hit drives down the middle of the first fairway and now it was his turn. Dick Elliott pushed all thoughts to the back of his mind and concentrated instead on the area to the left of the fairway where he wanted his ball to land. He swung his two iron smoothly, but came across the line and his ball took off too far right. It bounced on the fairway a couple of times and finished in a bunker about 200 yards away.

The spectators groaned and Elliott looked grim. He had begun his four-day Open battle inauspiciously.

On the practice ground bordering the seventeenth fairway, Colm Donohue was hitting the last of the hundred golf balls which he had brought out to loosen up. A couple of hundred yards in the distance Johnny Davis and other caddies were moving about, retrieving the golf balls being rifled towards them by the line of pros. Colm hit the last ball and saw it take off directly on the intended path. He was swinging beautifully, and if that wind kept up, he was confident he could return a good score. Like most Irish golfers, he was accustomed to playing in breezy conditions.

His partners in the threesome for the first two days would be Rafael Escudio and Willi Ducret. Colm was under no illusions—he would be the minor attraction in that company. He had never played with Escudio before and was looking forward to it. The Mexican-American was a colourful character, although right now he was not looking too happy with himself. Colm noticed that Ben was still carrying Willi Ducret's golf bag; he sincerely hoped that the bickering was over between those two.

Rafael Escudio reckoned he had a right to feel irritable. Donny, his caddie, was following instructions from management and was watching him at night like a hawk. And when he had managed to corner Elaine, the courtesy car girl, and asked her to have a drink with him, she had turned him down flat. He was not used to being rebuffed by women to whom he took a fancy at tournaments. Sponsors always made sure he got what he wanted—and that included his pick of girls.

While he waited for Johnny Davis to gather up the remaining golf balls, Colm Donohue thought about Joan and the kids. They were enjoying their trip to Scotland so far. This morning he had driven them to the course and they had all enjoyed a snack lunch in the clubhouse. Afterwards, when he and Johnny had gone out to the practice ground, Joan had taken the boys onto the nearby Turnberry sands. They were down there now, building castles, enjoying the picnic which Mrs Carlyle at the guesthouse had prepared for them.

'Ready, lad? Let's go out there and enjoy ourselves.' Johnny led the way through the spectators, towards the first tee. Colm felt a knot of tension in his stomach and hoped that his game would hold up.

The wind whipping in from the firth had the white horses forming long before the waves crashed on the

Turnberry sands. Occasionally, above the sound of the waves rolling in on the shore, or when the wind shifted slightly, Joan could hear a distant roar from the Ailsa course.

They had been on the beach for over an hour now, the two boys happy to dig away in the sand while she sat on a rug, reading a book, hearing their shrill cries of excitement. Tired of burrowing in the sand, they had rambled off and had disappeared around a promontory of rock. Joan put down her book, rose to her feet and decided it was time to see what Michael and Rory were up to.

She jumped a rivulet and then skirted the rock formation. As she did so, she caught sight of her two offspring; they were gazing up at a young woman who, like herself, had found a hitherto deserted stretch of beach on which to relax. The newcomer had a cardigan thrown casually around her shoulders and was chatting to four-year-old Michael while little Rory looked on bemused.

She glanced up and smiled as Joan approached. 'Hello, are these yours?' The tone was friendly, American.

'Yes. I hope they haven't disturbed you.'

'Not at all. We were just getting acquainted. Michael, isn't it? And what's your brother's name?'

'Ror-ree.'

The girl looked askance at Joan, who volunteered 'Rory.'

'Oh. That's Irish isn't it?' When Joan nodded, she said, 'Congratulations. They're two lovely boys.'

'Thank you.'

'Are you all here on holiday?'

'No,' Joan replied. 'My husband's a golfer—he's playing in the Open.'

'Really? So's mine. I'm Susan Elliott. My husband is Richard Elliott.'

'Oh, of course.' Joan was sufficiently into the international golf scene to have heard of the American superstar. 'How do you do? My name is Joan Donohue. My husband's name is Colm.'

'Colm Donohue?' It was obvious the name meant nothing to her.

'He hasn't won a tournament yet,' Joan added helpfully, 'so he's not well known.' She did not want to embarrass the American woman.

Susan Elliott shrugged. 'Don't worry. I'm sure he will—and when he does—' there was no joy in her laugh—'that's when your problems really begin.' She twirled, pumping Rory up and down in her arms, laughing when he yelled his delight at being on a human merry-go-round. Still laughing, Susan returned the youngster to earth. Her eyes followed him as he toddled off along the sand to join his brother.

'I'd love a couple of kids like yours to keep me busy,' Susan said.

'Why don't you have some?'

'Because Richard and I have a deal.' She dug her hands deep into the pockets of her skirt. '*He* made it, naturally. No children until he completes the Grand Slam. Richard needs to win just one more of the majors—the British Open. That's why we're over here. This is his eighth try.' A roar from the course made them both turn their heads. 'Sounds like someone's just made a birdie,' Susan said.

An awkward silence fell between them. Joan felt

uncomfortable. She was never good at making small talk with strangers.

Susan broke the silence: 'What do you say to a stroll along the beach? We seem to have it to ourselves today.'

'Good idea.' Joan called out to the boys to follow. 'It'll keep them happy.' They walked for a while in silence. They both shared a feeling of helplessness, of being cut off from the drama that was taking place in front of huge crowds just a short distance away.

'It's funny,' Susan mused. 'When we were married first, I used to follow Richard around the course during every round. Now'—she shrugged—'he's so dedicated to winning, I bet he doesn't notice whether I'm around or not most of the time.'

'I'm sure you're not alone. I think a lot of wives who are married to professional golfers get the same feeling.'

'Do you travel with your husband on tour, Joan?'

'I did for a while. Then our first baby arrived soon after we were married. Now it's too expensive. But if Colm ever became famous, I'd make sure the family came first. He always promised it would.'

'Do you think you could hold on to him, if, say, he won the Open this week?'

The question surprised Joan. 'Of course. I don't think winning the Open would make any real difference to us.'

Susan's laugh was bitter. 'Don't you believe it. He'd become a celebrity overnight, get hassled by agents, sponsors, con men, not to mention the media. Suddenly you're on a non-stop merry-go-round. You can't get off, even if you want to.'

148

'I think I could handle it.'

'Good for you. I thought that too when Richard won his first major title. Now. . . .'

Joan decided to change the subject. 'I read in a golf magazine once that you were a top model before you married.' They had left the golf course behind and were approaching part of the beach where caravans were parked on the high ground away from the shoreline. Above the waves, seagulls floated in the strong wind.

'Hey, that reminds me,' Susan said. 'Are you going on that shopping trip to Edinburgh tomorrow —the one organised for the wives? It should be fun.'

Joan shook her head. 'I haven't heard anything about it.' That was the worst part of staying in a guesthouse. The trip was probably the talk of the Turnberry Hotel and the wives who were staying there.

'You must come. It's being set up by Felicity Jacob, the wife of the BBC man. There is a special coach laid on, so there should be lots of room. How about it, Joan?'

'I'd love to go.' She found herself warming to Susan Elliott's friendly manner. 'I'm just not sure about the children—'

'Doesn't your hotel have a baby-sitting service? They all do nowadays.'

'We're not staying in a hotel—'

'Oh.' Susan kicked herself mentally. She would have to remember that not everyone on the tour enjoyed the same lifestyle as herself. 'Isn't there somebody—the lady who owns the place, perhaps?'

'Yes, Mrs Carlyle would no doubt look after the

boys for the day.' She had already offered to do so whenever Joan wanted to see Colm play. It seemed too good an opportunity to miss. 'Yes, put my name down on the list.'

'Great. I'll give you the phone number of the house which we've rented. Call me tonight for the details.'

They turned into the wind to begin the walk back. As they did so, they heard a roar from the course. In the distance, in the late afternoon sunshine, they could make out the red and white of Turnberry's famous lighthouse. The first day of the British Open was now moving to a close, with the hopes of some of the contestants already beyond redemption.

'Time for us to find out how those husbands of ours are getting on,' Susan said.

At 7.30 p.m. precisely Malcolm Jacob faced the BBC cameras to give a summing-up of the first day's play. As he stood in front of the giant scoreboard at the back of the eighteenth green, viewers could see the wind gusting strongly, lifting wisps of his carefully groomed hair.

'There's no doubt that the stiff breeze that has been blowing here at Turnberry for most of this first day of the Open has posed problems for several of the big names. The wind which began to whip up around mid-morning got stronger in the afternoon' —Malcolm saw on the monitor that the camera had switched to show a view of the sea.

As the camera switched back to him, Malcolm went on: 'The last threesome of the day has just finished. That trio included Tony Maurelli, the man hoping to win at his first attempt. He shot a level par 72 to keep himself in touch with today's surprise leader, Leonard Morgan. Morgan was in the first threesome that went out this morning, enjoyed the best of the conditions, and shot a magnificent 66, six under par. Now let's look at the top scores after today's first round—'

Names and scores flashed onto the television monitor. 'There's Morgan, the man who has yet to win a tournament, on top with a 66. Nearest to him, three shots back, are Kiyoshi Minoki of Japan and Mañuel Luca of Spain, both on 69. In third place on 70 comes a four-man group that includes defending champion Lou Menzies of Australia and the young Irishman Colm Donohue, who shot sixteen pars and two birdies.'

The cameras came back on Malcolm Jacob again. 'And what about Dick Elliott, the man who has yet to come through that mental barrier to win his first Open title? He's tucked in there nicely with fellow American Maurelli on 72. Elliott didn't attempt anything spectacular today in the wind; one got the impression that he was playing well within himself and we might see some fireworks from him tomorrow.

'But not all the big names scored well today. Rafael Escudio never looked happy with the conditions, showed a few flashes of temper, and shot a four over par 76. He'll have to improve a lot on that tomorrow if he's to survive the cut.

'Another fancied player to struggle was the Belgian Willi Ducret. He shot a disappointing 77 and will also do well to survive the cut tomorrow.'

Jacob paused, moved a few paces to his left, then continued: 'But enough about the foreign players. Let's salute the real hero of today, our own Leonard Morgan' the camera took the leader of the Open into the shot—'Congratulations, Leonard.'

'Thank you.'

'I think it's only fair to say that you played during the part of the day when there was little or no wind. Were you lucky?'

Morgan shrugged. He was not going to be denied his moment of glory. 'Maybe. But I played well. A couple of putts stayed on the lip. I could have shot a 64.'

'You haven't done so well on the tour this year. How much have you won so far?'

'About £28,000. It's been a bit of a struggle.'

'But this lovely young lady has stuck with you all the way. Come in here, Liz—' She moved into the shot, smiling shyly. It was her first time ever on television and she was nervous. Malcolm looked into the camera and explained to the viewers: 'Liz is not only Leonard's biggest fan; she's also his caddie.'

'Don't you envy those golfers and their wives who travel the world first-class?' Jacob asked Liz.

Of course we do, you silly berk, Liz thought. What a stupid question. Aloud she said: 'Not really. The way Leonard and I live is much more cosy.' They all laughed.

'Now Leonard, a 66 today, but what about tomorrow? Is that putter of yours going to work wonders again?'

'We'll see. I know a lot of people expect me to slip

152

up tomorrow, but I'm not going to. I'm going to surprise them all—yourself included, Malcolm.'

'Good luck to you both, anyway.' The camera zoomed in to a solo shot of Jacob. 'That just about wraps up our coverage of the first day's play here at Turnberry. We'll be back for an early morning report tomorrow at nine a.m. See you then.'

Martin Dignam turned the car into Fortnum Street in Glasgow, spotted an empty parking space, and nipped in. Traffic was heavy at this time of the evening and he and Marie Kirk would walk to The Wild Grouse pub.

The area reminded him of the streets off the Falls Road in Belfast; small, two-up, two-down houses, their neatness spoiled by an occasional splash of graffiti. The local authority had long ago moved most of the inhabitants to more spacious housing estates in the suburbs; Fortnum Street was now inhabited mainly by elderly couples who would see out the rest of their lives in gentile poverty. In the long term, the street was due to be demolished to make way for a new motorway.

They were surprised to find The Wild Grouse pleasantly packed when they entered. Dignam brought over a couple of drinks to the marble-topped table. The clientele was working class and nobody gave them a second glance as they sat in silence. Finally, Marie said: 'I wonder if he is already here.' Her eyes scanned the men lined up at the bar. 'What if he doesn't arrive?'

'Getting nervous?'

'Yes, a little.' She did not mind admitting it. 'I'd

like something to happen.' Marie felt conspicuous in what was obviously a mainly male pub. She was glad that earlier she had taken the precaution of changing out of her toreador pants and bolero top.

'Maybe you should ask the barman about Mr Flavin.'

He gave her an angry look. 'I'm sitting here and you'll do the same unless I tell you different. Understand?'

They fell silent again. There had not been much conversation between them since the incident in the late afternoon on the hill overlooking Loch Lomond. After the phone call to Belfast, they had left the hotel and headed for the scenic drive around the loch. They enjoyed an early lunch in a local restaurant, left the car and had taken a tourist trail into the surrounding hills. Later they had abandoned the trail and found their own secluded spot where she had sat down on the grass. The sun was hot, its rays shimmering on the waters of the loch below.

'It's lovely up here,' she said.

'Aye.'

'So peaceful. It would be nice to stay for a few days.' Marie knew it was wishful thinking.

Dignam was not sitting on the grass like her, relaxing. He was standing by a tree a few feet away, pulling at the leaves, staring at the tiny figures moving below by the water's edge. He seemed on edge, as though something was bothering him. Once or twice she caught him looking at her and she felt uneasy.

'Why don't you sit down, Martin.'

'I don't feel like relaxing.'

154

'Suit yourself. You've been uneasy since you spoke to Dominick this morning. Is everything all right?'

'Everything's just fine. Earley doesn't worry me.' He pulled at a low-lying branch, snapping it in anger. 'And I'm not worried about this stupid job he has sent us on, if that's what you're thinking. Christ, you must think you're with an amateur, a raw recruit. You know how many Brits I've killed so far?' She shook her head. 'Guess. Go on.' His eyes were blazing now.

'I haven't an idea. And I'd prefer not to know.'

'Seven. That's how many. Soldiers, that is. Young kids brought over to do their tour of duty in Northern Ireland, not having a clue what it was all about. Patrick was with me on a few of those jobs, you know that?' His laugh sounded more like a sneer.

'Don't you feel any regrets?'

'Not a one. The only regret I have is that I didn't get more of them.' He bent down again with his back to her, and reached inside his leather jacket which was on the ground. When he turned, she saw he had a small, snub-nosed automatic in his hand.

Startled, she said: 'Martin, put that away. Someone will see you.'

He ignored her request. He pointed the gun at an imaginary target. 'This is what counts in Northern Ireland today. With one of these beauties in my hand, I'm somebody, ready to do his bit for his country.'

He was like a small boy, trying to impress her. 'All right,' Marie said. 'So you've proved your point. Now put the gun away. Please.'

He bent down, slid the gun inside his jacket, turned and gave her a searching look. Marie could feel his eyes burning into her and she felt uncomfortable. She was conscious of how isolated they were up here.

She was relieved when he sat down away from her. Dignam pulled up a handful of grass and picked at it. 'If the Brits weren't there we wouldn't have any excitement, would we? Nothing to bring us onto the streets, plant a bomb now and then. Not to mention the odd bank raid to keep the funds flowing. Me?—I'd be just another motor mechanic poking around under car bonnets all day. Instead, I have variety in my work, waiting for the call to action.' He guffawed.

'But where is it all going to end, Martin?'

He flung the grass away. 'Who the hell cares? Put it this way—who wants the bloody thing to end!'

Marie lay back on the grass. It was difficult to argue with him, and after all she was part of it now. He had known violence all his adult life and now he did not want to, or would not know how to, live without it. He had openly admitted to killing seven soldiers without remorse. How many more people would he kill before it was all over? He did not seem to care; killing and maiming people gave him and his friends some sort of pleasure.

The sun was warming her now and she was regretting that she had chosen to wear the tight toreador pants. Marie was imagining herself splashing in the cool waters of the loch below when a shadow blocked out the sun. She opened her eyes to see Dignam standing over her, staring.

'Jesus, Marie, you look lovely.' His words were barely audible.

'Thank you.' Alarm bells were ringing in her head.

'Patrick's little sister has grown up a lot. You know that?'

She sat up quickly, brushing the grass from her clothes. She was about to get to her feet, when he put a hand on her shoulder, restraining her. She said: 'I think we should go—'

'What's the hurry? We have plenty of time.' He sat down close to her, touched her hair, said brazenly: 'I want you, Marie.'

Her laugh was nervous, forced. 'Patrick would be surprised to hear you talk like that.' A stupid remark, but maybe it would bring him to his senses.

Dignam snarled: 'I told you before. Forget Patrick. He's dead.' It was the catalyst that pushed him towards his objective. He reached out, pulled her to him and kissed her violently. Still with his lips on hers, he forced her back on the grass, his weight pinioning one of her arms. Breathing heavily, he fumbled at her black top, trying to undo it.

My God, he was going to rape her! Marie struggled frantically, twisting her head and tearing her lips away from his. She was surprised at her strength.

'Martin, don't be a fool—'

'Hold still and enjoy it, for Christ's sake—'

He had forced his leg in between hers, and was trying to get his body on top of her. Marie felt a wave of panic sweep over her and prayed she would not pass out. If he was going to take her, it would have to be by force. He had most of her top undone and she could feel his hand pushing its way up under her bra, seeking her breast. She put her hand into his

157

luxuriant dark hair and pulled his face away from hers.

'You bitch—' he snarled. She pulled his head sideways, feeling the weight of his body on hers easing. With a superhuman effort she arched her own body and pushed him sideways off her. Marie scrambled to her feet, her hair wild. She pulled her black top back into place.

Dignam was crouched on the grass, watching her, grinning. 'So Patrick's little sister wants to play—'

'Don't come near me again, Martin!'

He made a grab at her feet, diving full length on the grass like a goalkeeper. But Marie saw the move coming and skipped sideways. He rolled over on his back and laughed again. The bastard was enjoying himself! They were alone on a Scottish hillside and he was playing with her. He was on his knees now, leering.

'Go on, Marie. Run a bit more. I like having to chase you.'

She ran past him, over to the tree where his jacket was. Frantically she thrust her hand into the inside pocket, feeling the comforting steel of the gun. She flung the jacket aside, whirled around and pointed the gun at him. He had climbed to his feet and was advancing on her. When he saw what she had in her hand, he stopped.

'I warn you, Martin, don't come near me or I'll shoot.'

'I don't believe you.'

'I will. I don't want to kill you, but I will if I have to.'

It looked for a terrible moment that he was going

to call her bluff. In fact, he took a step forward, but stopped again when he saw her finger tighten on the trigger. Dignam did not know for sure if she could handle a gun, but this was no time to find out.

'Okay. Stalemate. So what do we do now, Marie?'

'We walk back down to the car. I'll be right behind you.'

'And the gun?'

'You'll get it back later.'

He stared at her, anger in his eyes. His pride was hurt, but there was nothing he could do about it. Not just now, anyway. It was the first time a girl had ever got the drop on him and he was annoyed with himself for letting it happen. He would get his own back by doing the job his way and keep this bloody little bitch in the dark. That would let her know who was boss.

Dignam shrugged, moved across to his leather jacket and picked it up. She watched his every move, the gun pointing in his direction. 'Put that away. It's dangerous. Someone might see you.'

'You should have thought of that a few minutes ago,' Marie replied. She was amazed at how cool she was. They made their way down the hillside, Dignam walking in front and Marie following, the gun hidden under her cardigan which she carried across her arm. In the car she had sat in the back seat while Dignam had driven in sullen silence to Glasgow. She gave him his gun back when they reached the outskirts of the city.

Now they were in The Wild Grouse and still Flavin had failed to show. Marie glanced at her watch. It showed three minutes to seven o'clock.

Where on earth was he? She did not fancy sitting in the pub much longer with a silent Martin Dignam. Another fifteen minutes passed and then a man left the top end of the bar and approached their table. He was in his sixties, Marie estimated, and was soberly dressed in a neat, grey pinstripe suit.

'Good evening. Mind if I join you?' The voice was cultured, soft.

Marie looked up, smiled and asked him to sit. Dignam kept silent.

'Thank you.' He pulled up a chair and placed his half pint of bitter on the marble table top. There was a pause during which the eyes behind the steel-rimmed spectacles scrutinised them. After a few moments the newcomer said: 'Are you going birdie hunting tomorrow?'

Another silence. Marie waited for Dignam to reply. It seemed an age before he said: 'Sorry, mate. We don't know what you mean.'

The face remained impassive. 'What I mean is are you going to Turnberry for the British Open?'

Marie and Dignam exchanged glances. She said: 'No, it's not on our schedule.' She saw the older man smile.

'You're Flavin,' Dignam said.

'Yes. And you're late,' came the mild reply. 'You were meant to be here yesterday. Five o'clock.'

'So we changed our plans slightly. You got my phone call,' Dignam replied.

'Any problems?'

'None that you can help with.' Dignam's sidelong look at Marie, and the cool atmosphere between them, did not go unnoticed.

'I see. Anyway, now that you've arrived, perhaps you'd care for another drink—'

'No thanks. Let's go to your place and talk.' Dignam was already on his feet.

'As you wish.' Flavin finished off his drink, held the chair for her when she rose, and smiled at her 'thank you'. She had an instant liking for him. There was an old-world charm about him that struck a chord in Marie. It made a change from the company she had been keeping lately.

She sat with him in the back seat of the car. Flavin broke off their conversation now and then to give Dignam instructions. In the twenty minutes it took them to drive to a better area of the city, Marie learned that Flavin was a retired schoolteacher. His wife was dead and he lived alone. Originally from Donegal, he had come to Scotland thirty years ago to work and had settled in Glasgow.

Flavin's house was red-bricked, set well back from the road by a large, well-kept garden. The interior reflected the appearance of its owner; an open-plan lounge with shelves of books fitted into one corner, everything neat and tidy and not a thing out of place. The few pictures on the walls were paintings of scenic parts of Ireland, the mass-produced type on sale to the general public and to be seen in hundreds of Irish homes.

'Make yourselves comfortable. Anyone like a drink?'

'I told you—we don't have much time.' Dignam also declined the invitation to sit down. 'You have a bomb and a security man's outfit for me. Let's have them.'

Flavin did not lose his courteous tone. 'Please come with me to my workshop outside.' Dignam followed the older man out of the room. Marie watched them through the bay window as they walked down a paved pathway to a wooden hut at the end of the garden. Flavin took out a bunch of keys and unlocked the door.

She strolled around the comfortable lounge, with its chintz curtains, paused before a cabinet on which was a framed photo of a middle-aged woman, pleasant, open-faced and smiling. Standing there, surrounded by an aura of middle-class respectability, Marie found it difficult to believe that just a short distance away two men were examining an instrument of destruction.

A few minutes later they re-entered the lounge. Flavin was carrying a small tin box with a lid on it. Marie noticed with amusement the name of a well-known British biscuit firm emblazoned on the side. Dignam had a brown paper parcel fastened with cellophane under his arm. Flavin placed the box on the table in the centre of the room, moved to the windows at both ends of the room and drew the curtains. He switched on the lights.

'There it is,' he said, addressing Dignam. 'Do you want me to show you how it works?'

'No need to. I've handled these little babies before. I just prime the timing device, set the clock and let it tick away. Then—boom!' Dignam clapped his hands together to simulate an explosion. He laughed and said: 'You're sure it's big enough?'

'It'll do the job you want on the monument.'

'I'll take your word for it. You're the expert. Now,

about this security uniform—' Dignam picked up the parcel. 'I want to try it out for size.'

'It should be inch perfect. However, if you feel it necessary'—Flavin opened the door to the hallway, and flicked a light switch. 'The bedroom on the right at the top of the stairs.' He watched Dignam go up and then came back into the lounge. 'Please sit down, my dear. I'll make you some coffee. You look worn out.'

He went into the kitchen off the lounge and she followed him a few moments later. He was spooning coffee into a percolator. 'Why do you do it?' she asked.

'Do what?'

'You know what I'm talking about, Mr Flavin. Supply bombs. Help Dominick Earley?'

He turned, gazed at her with his remarkable blue eyes through his spectacles. 'We're not murderers, you know. Not this breakaway wing. Dominick Earley has said many times that he is not out to kill innocent people, and I believe him. Unlike the other lot, he wants Ireland united by peaceful means and that's my philosophy too. When I heard about what he is trying to do and how he is going about achieving it, I went over to Belfast and talked to him. I was impressed.'

'But I still don't understand why you're involved. You're an educated man, Mr Flavin.'

He smiled. 'I'm also an Irishman. I was in the movement as a young lad in Donegal. I'm still involved, even though I'm over here thirty years or more. Please sit down.'

Marie sat down at the round wooden kitchen

table. He poured two steaming mugs of coffee.

'Where did you learn about explosives?' she asked him.

He stirred his coffee, smiling. 'You ask a lot of questions, young lady. I learned from books, magazines, army manuals. It's not too difficult to pick it up.'

'You've never been caught?'

'I've never even been questioned. I don't look the terrorist type, I suppose. Not like your friend upstairs.' He paused. 'You don't like him, do you? It shows.' Marie shrugged but remained silent.

'I don't like his attitude,' Flavin said matter-of-factly. 'He's dangerous. There's something about him that's not quite right. You watch yourself, young lady.'

Marie smiled, remembering the afternoon episode. 'I can take care of myself.'

Footsteps descending the stairs interrupted further conversation. They went back to the lounge, just as Martin Dignam entered. He was dressed now in serge trousers and a dark sweater, with a flash with the words Olympic Security on both shoulders. A cap, dark blue shirt and matching tie completed the outfit. 'How do I look?'

'Splendid,' Flavin said. 'I told you it would be a perfect fit.'

Dignam studied himself in the mirror over the fireplace. 'I shouldn't have any bother getting onto that golf course at night in this outfit. What do you think, Marie?'

It was the first civil remark he had made to her since Loch Lomond. 'I think Mr Flavin has done a good job,' she said coolly.

Dignam nodded. 'Now it's up to us, isn't it?' His good humour had returned and he seemed to have brushed aside what had happened between them earlier. When he had changed back into his own clothes, they waited, on Flavin's advice, for darkness to fall completely before transferring the tin box and the brown paper parcel to the boot of the car. They buried both underneath the sets of golf clubs which they had brought over as a decoy.

'Goodbye—and good luck.' Flavin stood on the kerb and spoke through the car's open window. He gave them instructions back to the motorway. 'Careful you're not stopped by the police.' He looked at Marie. 'Goodbye, young lady. Remember what I said—and take care of yourself.'

As the car sped off, Marie glanced back through the rear window. Mr Flavin waved after them. He looked like a benevolent grandfather seeing off a favourite daughter. She smiled to herself, visualising the shock on the sedate avenue if ever the retired schoolteacher's extra-curricular activities came to light.

'What are you smiling about?' Dignam asked. He seemed to want to make friends with her again.

'Oh, something that's just occurred to me. You wouldn't appreciate it.'

The rain began to fall heavily before they were halfway to Turnberry and strong gusts of wind got up. Marie reckoned if the weather was like this tomorrow she would view the Open on television from the comfort of the guesthouse lounge.

5

FRIDAY, 17 JULY

The clatter of the wind blowing with almost gale force against the bedroom window woke Colm Donohue from an uneasy sleep. Light was seeping through the closed curtains. He had a sudden stab of panic, as he always did when he had an early tee-off time and there was a fear of being disqualified for arriving late. The alarm clock on the bedside locker showed 6.10 a.m. and he relaxed. In yesterday's first round he had had a comfortable 1.25 p.m. tee-off time; now, as was the custom in the British Open, times were reversed and he was one of today's dawn patrol, due off at 7.50 a.m.

He reached over and switched off the alarm. The movement woke Joan, who opened her eyes and asked: 'What time is it?'

'Six-ten. Time for Johnny and me to get moving.'

'Are the children still asleep?'

'Yes.' There was no sound from the other room as yet. Clad only in his pyjamas, Colm sat on the edge of the bed while he put on his socks. The wind rattled the window again. Amazing the change in the weather from yesterday. But then this was Scotland. 'It's going to be tough out there today,' he whispered as he dressed.

'Nervous?'

'A little.' No point in telling her he had had

trouble sleeping last night. Still, as a youngster in the west of Ireland he had grown up battling against the Atlantic winds on the golf course. If those conditions kept up throughout the day, the big names might struggle and outsiders like himself could have a chance. In this game you looked after yourself and to hell with the other guy's problems.

He showered, shaved, and ten minutes later was ready to go downstairs. Joan was bravely fighting off returning to sleep when he re-entered the bedroom. 'Bye, love.' He bent down and kissed her lightly on the forehead.

'Bye, Colm. And good luck. You know I won't be at the course today.' She had told him about meeting Susan Elliott and the invitation to go shopping to Edinburgh with the other wives. She had yet to get someone to look after the children, but Joan remembered that the young Irish girl whom she had met briefly in the front garden two days ago had taken a liking to Rory and Michael. It was unlikely that the girl— Norah she had said her name was—would go to the course today with the weather as bad as it was. Joan would ask her to keep an eye on the children while she was in Edinburgh.

Johnny Davis was already in the dining room eating breakfast when Colm entered. Outside in the hallway the heavy golf bag, clubs cleaned and primed, was lying in readiness, along with a couple of hold-alls containing towels and changes of clothing for both men. Johnny had seen to everything.

'How are you feeling, son?'

'So-so.'

'Eat a good breakfast. It'll be a long day. You'll

only hit a couple of dozen golf balls on the practice ground this morning. I don't want that wind wrecking your swing before you start.'

Colm nodded in agreement. Anything that Johnny Davis said was okay by him. The old guy had one of the shrewdest golf brains in the business. In addition, Johnny was a steadying influence, always ready to give advice both on and off the course. Colm knew he would be relying on his friend a lot today.

'What do you make of that?' Johnny passed one of the morning tabloids across the table. He pointed to a story on the front page. 'Looks like our partner Willi Ducret is in a spot of trouble.'

Colm glanced at the story. It was in one of the newspapers not renowned for its good taste. In the centre of the page was a photograph of Willi and his caddie, Ben, obviously taken during that practice round a couple of days ago when they were having their row. The story hinted at sensational developments between Ducret and a handsome young waiter in the Turnberry Hotel with whom he had become friendly, and Willi's long-time friend Ben. 'Top Golfer in Love Triangle' the headline screamed. The reporter who had broken the story promised further revelations 'which will rock the world of golf and make the members of the sedate Royal and Ancient sit up and take notice, not to mention the committee of the Professional Golfers' Association.' Willi's manager was denying all allegations and was threatening to sue the newspaper.

'Ducret could be in trouble for bringing the game into disrepute,' Colm said.

'It's not our problem who is gay or who is in

trouble off the course,' Johnny came back. 'Our job is to go out there today and shoot a score that will get us into the final two days of the Open. Keep that in mind.'

Johnny is right, of course, Colm mused later as they drove down the coast towards Turnberry. The whole secret of getting to the top in golf, as in any other sport, was to be ruthlessly single-minded; to think about nobody but yourself.

'Our objective today, son, is to concentrate hard and don't try to do anything spectacular. And don't worry if you find yourself over par—nobody is going to shoot a record score here today. So take it easy.' Johnny glanced sideways at his passenger. The young fellow was not looking good. Must not let him get too uptight.

'Yes, Johnny. I'll remember.' Colm began to feel more relaxed. He was not in this alone. On the rare occasions that Johnny Davis caddied for him at a major tournament like the Open, he noted that the older man always spoke in the plural. It was his way of emphasising that they were a team, that while it was Colm's job to hit the shots, he had someone at his shoulder with whom he could share the pressure. For Colm it was a comfortable feeling.

But partnering someone like Willi Ducret, who right now was the centre of media attention, could only add to today's problems. Although the tee-times had been switched around, the threesome partnerships remained the same today, so that Colm would again be playing with Rafael Escudio and Ducret. They were two of the more fancied contenders in the Open, but he had managed to outshine them yesterday. He was banking on doing it again.

Colm knew that Escudio was also having problems—and not only with his game. During yesterday's round the American had looked angry throughout, exchanging sharp words in Spanish with Donny, his caddie. On several occasions Escudio had glowered into the gallery when he considered that a spectator had moved unnecessarily. The American's behaviour had caused resentment among the fans.

Johnny must have been reading his thoughts. 'If that guy Escudio starts throwing tantrums like he did yesterday, ignore him completely. Got that? The word is he's got women problems.'

Just as they were arriving at the course, wending their way through the cars that were already filling the enclosure, they heard the weatherman on the radio warn that the high south-easterly winds that were lashing most of Scotland were expected to last most of the day, accompanied by heavy squalls of rain. As they made their way from the car park to the locker room, they saw that the winds were already taking their toll on some of the pavilions in the tented village. Two of them had come adrift and workmen were frantically trying to right them again before play began.

Inside the warm locker room Colm was changing when he looked up and saw Rafael Escudio going through the same procedure across the aisle from him. Colm smiled a greeting. It was returned with a barely perceptible nod of the head. Yes, he thought to himself, it is going to be a really tough day!

As he struggled into his lightweight waterproof

golf gear Rafael Escudio was blaming the terrible British weather, and the lack of a woman, as the reasons why he was not feeling so good. He had hoped to win the Open at Turnberry, but his poor round yesterday made that unlikely now. Also the weather had turned against him. He would much prefer to spend the time in bed with a woman than playing golf in a gale.

That courtesy car girl, Elaine, would suit him fine. For two evenings he had kept watch on her movements from the lobby of the Turnberry Hotel. She was always pleasantly efficient, smiling at him, saying 'hello' and 'goodbye.' Last evening she had again smilingly refused to accept his invitation to go for a drink when she had finished work.

'Why you say no? We could have a nice evening together.'

'Thank you, but—'

'No but. Just say yes.'

'I've explained to you—' the smile had disappeared from her eyes—'our services extend only to driving the car. Sorry, Mr Escudio.'

Rafael knew this was not true. Many times in the past he had been able to make it with chicas—and in different countries, too. Of course he could have tried for one of the other courtesy car girls. But he fancied this one, Elaine. The fact that she was playing hard to get only made him more determined. The way she was treating him was irritating Rafael, as was the presence now in Turnberry of his manager, Kirk Kalder, who had flown in from America last night. Now he would have to be extra careful.

Rafael had a plan. He would get talking to Elaine's

boss in the clubhouse bar after today's round, buy the guy a drink, and let him know there was money in it for him. That approach had worked before.

At 7.45 a.m. precisely the threesome of Donohue, Escudio and Ducret were walking down the first fairway after hitting their drives. Gusts of rain, whipped by a 35-mile-an-hour wind, were blowing directly into their faces. Despite the terrible conditions and the early hour, knots of spectators were dotted at intervals along both sides of the fairway. Wrapped in waterproofs and huddled under sturdy golf umbrellas, the hardy fans were determined to enjoy the second day of the Open Championship.

Colm walked to the spot in the light rough on the left of the fairway and surveyed his second shot to the green. Yesterday, from the same side but from thirty yards further on, he had hit a nine-iron shot pin high. Today, into the wind, he reckoned he might need a five iron. He was away first and, after a short consultation with Johnny, hit his five-iron shot on to the green, albeit about fifteen yards to the left of the pin. The secret today would be to swing smoothly; very difficult when one was being buffeted by a strong wind.

Five minutes and two putts later he was walking off the first green with a par four, the only one of the trio to have achieved that. Both Escudio and Ducret had taken bogey fives and the scowls on their faces became even more marked.

'Like I said earlier, we're not going to have a fun day with these two.' Johnny passed the remark to Colm as they made their way towards the second tee. 'But not to worry; we're not out here today to make polite conversation!'

On the second hole, with the wind howling over his shoulder, Colm hit too big a drive and his ball carried all the way to the first bunker on the left side of the fairway. His recovery shot landed in a smaller bunker twenty yards on. From there he made the front of the green and earned a big round of applause from the wind-blown spectators when he slotted in a huge par-saving putt. Ducret and Escudio played the hole in more orthodox fashion, splitting the fairway with their drives, hitting the green with their second shots, and both two-putting.

As they walked to the third tee Colm noticed that there were now almost double the number of spectators following them as when they had started out almost half-an-hour ago. He knew they were not braving the terrible early morning conditions to see him, a long-shot Open contender. Obviously the big attraction was the story of Willi and Ben which had broken in the tabloid that morning. Golf fans enjoyed a bit of scandal on the course.

If they were conscious of the furore they were causing, the Belgians gave no sign. Both were maintaining a stony silence. Indeed Colm had yet to hear Willi pass one remark to his caddie during the round. That all changed, however, after they had parred the 462-yard par four dogleg third—the longest par four hole on the course—and moved on to the next.

At the fourth, a 167-yard par three played to a raised green, all had hit good long irons and, despite the gale, the three balls were nestling on the putting surface. Colm missed what would have been a welcome birdie by a few inches, then tapped in.

Escudio studied his twenty-footer, missed by a fraction on the left, and also tapped in for par.

Ducret's fine four iron into the crosswind had finished only twelve feet from the hole. He was on his haunches studying his birdie putt when Ben moved behind him and muttered something over Willi's shoulder. Spectators ringing the green saw Willi turn around and glare at his caddie. Either Willi did not want his one-time friend's advice or else he considered he was being given the wrong line to the hole. Amid an uneasy silence he putted and missed. After finally holing out, he crossed to where Ben was about to pick up the golf bag and flung his putter to the ground, muttering something to Ben in an angry voice before turning away. Ben glared after the retreating Willi and looked as if he was going to quit there and then. Instead, he picked up the golf bag and followed to the fifth tee.

The golf writers in the crowd spotted the incident. They immediately got out their short wave radios and sent the news back to their colleagues in the press tent. The battle of words between the homosexual pair would make a juicy news item for the early editions—and there was still a long way to go in the round!

'Everything organised with the wives, my dear? The coach will be here about ten-thirty.' Malcolm Jacob gazed out of his bedroom window in the Turnberry Hotel at the near-gale blowing outside. The idea of being stuck up in a commentary box under those conditions did not exactly cheer him up.

'Everything's fine, thank you, dear,' Felicity replied. 'I informed all the girls last night of the arrangements.'

'You will be taking in that Edinburgh Castle tour which I also laid on?' Malcolm enquired hopefully.

'You must be joking, darling. Not in this weather. We'll just take in the shopping.'

'Pity.' He swore under his breath. Damn, that would mean they would be back in Turnberry earlier than expected. Less time for him and Sally. She was still angry with him.

'Malcolm?'

'Yes. What is it, dear?' He was hardly listening now. He had just seen Sally go down the front steps and get into the special BBC minibus on her way to the course. He could grab the seat beside her if he hurried.

'There's something very important I want to talk to you about.'

He turned from the window, looked at his watch. 'Can't it wait? I'm due on the air in fifteen minutes—'

'It really is important. For both of us—'

'Sorry, dear. Must fly.'

'It will only take a few minutes.'

'Tell you what—' he was struggling into his duffle —'I'm due a break at eleven-thirty. Why don't you meet me in the press tent and we'll have a cup of coffee?'

'Haven't you forgotten something? I'll be halfway to Edinburgh by then.'

'Ah, yes. Then I'm afraid, darling, it'll have to wait until this evening. Can't waste any more time now.'

She rose as he moved to the door. 'I'm sure when

you hear what I have to tell you, you won't consider it a waste of time.'

'No. Of course not. I didn't mean it that way, darling. Have a good time in Edinburgh.'

Felicity was left staring at the slammed door.

At the 'Seaview' guesthouse Joan Donohue was waiting for the taxi which would take her to Turnberry. She was looking forward to joining Susan Elliott and the other wives on their trip to Edinburgh, despite the bad weather. She had dressed Michael and Rory in their best and they were now waiting in the lounge of the guesthouse for her new acquaintance, Norah, to show up and take charge.

'You sure you'll be able to manage them, Norah?' Joan asked when the young woman entered the lounge a few minutes later. She hated leaving the children with anybody.

'No problem,' Marie Kirk replied. She had still to get used to being called by her new name. 'We'll have great fun, won't we boys?' She laughed at Michael and Rory, who stared back at her.

'Your husband won't mind your having to take care of two toddlers, will he?' Joan thought he had looked annoyed when she had mentioned it this morning at breakfast. Later she had seen the couple arguing and it had made her feel guilty.

'Don't worry about it. I'm sorry he was so abrupt. My husband is shy. He doesn't like talking to strangers and thinks I should follow his example.'

'Oh.' Joan decided not to pursue the subject. She was glad when the girl asked: 'Any word of how your husband is doing today? It must be very difficult playing golf in this weather.'

Joan looked at her watch. 'He should be halfway through the round. There's no word yet. I suppose I should be out there cheering him on.'

Outside the wind was still howling. Looking out, all they could see was a mass of grey, low-hanging cloud over the sea. A taxi pulled up outside and they all piled in. The taxi would drop Joan off at Turnberry, then bring the boys and their nanny-for-a-day to the Royale Hotel, several miles inland, which boasted a children's complex and an indoor heated swimming pool. There was also a toddlers' corner. The boys would enjoy themselves there.

At Turnberry the cream-and-blue tourer coach was waiting outside the hotel entrance. Inside in the foyer the group of women who were going on the outing to Edinburgh were gathered, chatting excitedly in small groups. Before she went into the hotel, Joan gave the boys one final hug and warned them to be on their best behaviour during the day.

When she had disappeared inside, Marie said to her two charges: 'Well now, we're going to enjoy ourselves too, aren't we?' The taxi turned and headed down the winding road from the hotel. Across the Girvan Road, Marie could see the flagpoles swaying in the wind, giving some indication of the dreadful conditions on the Ailsa course.

'Look there—' the taxi driver pointed—'another one of the hospitality tents has come down. I'd no' like to be a golfer today.'

As the taxi climbed inland away from Turnberry, Marie looked back through the rear window at the scene. Despite the dreadful weather, the crowds were still out in their thousands. Martin Dignam was among them, out there somewhere, watching, making mental notes. They had argued last night when she had informed him that she was taking charge of the two boys today. He had reminded her forcibly that she was on a dangerous mission and that he was in command. Nevertheless she had insisted on having her way, a factor which had increased the enmity between them.

The Royale Hotel was a large, modern edifice on its own grounds just outside the village of Kirkoswald. It was popular not only with golfers because of its proximity to Turnberry, but also with well-to-do families who came north across the Scottish border and availed of it as a base from which to tour the Ayrshire countryside.

Happy that her two charges were safe under the watchful eye of the play area supervisor in the basement, Marie strolled upstairs. Mid-morning tea was still being served and she ordered a pot and some scones. She was helping herself to a second cup when a voice behind startled her.

'Marie!'

She turned, hardly daring to believe that it could be him. 'Stephen!' She put the teapot down with a clatter.

'My God. It's really you. When I noticed you first I wasn't sure—'

They stared at each other for several long seconds. Marie's mind was racing, already seeking answers to the inevitable questions she knew would come. 'Hello, Stephen.'

'What a coincidence. It's lovely seeing you again, Marie.'

'Thank you. I—it's lovely seeing you, too.' They were still staring at each other, each of them lost for words, their minds racing back in time to London, her flat, and the nights they had spent together there. It all seemed so long ago now, Marie thought, yet it was barely six months since she had told him that it was finished between them and that she was returning to Belfast.

'Won't you sit down, have some tea—'

He was seated beside her before she had finished the sentence, his eyes never leaving her face. Her smile hid the panic now rising in her. He would ask questions and she would have to be careful how she answered them.

'What on earth are you doing here, Marie? In Scotland of all places?'

She poured tea for them both. 'That's exactly what I was about to ask you, Stephen.' She was desperately playing for time.

'I'm up here to see the Open. Mum and Dad were coming to Turnberry for a week, so I decided to tag along.'

Of course! They were a golfing family and it was only natural that they should be here. She recalled the occasions when she had accompanied them to golf outings around London, happy to be with Stephen, despite the aloofness of his parents to a girl whom an eminent physician like Dr Wilfrid Trafford did not consider a suitable catch for his son.

'Are your parents staying in this hotel?'

'Yes. I saw them off to Turnberry an hour ago. I

didn't fancy going.' He grinned. 'I suppose you could call me a fair weather golfer.' He broke off, looked directly into her eyes. 'I'm darned glad I stayed, Marie.'

There was no mistaking his meaning. Marie's mind was still spinning. Meeting Stephen again like this, so unexpectedly, was disturbing. What would he say if he knew the real reason why she was in Turnberry? Marie had not given him the answer to that question yet. She had lied when she had told him she did not love him and now she would have to lie to him again. She wanted to reach over and kiss him and tell him everything and ask him for help but she knew that would be dangerous. Marie knew if Martin Dignam even found out that Stephen was in the area, his life could be in danger.

It was not quite as simple as that now. In London, Stephen had been in love with Marie Kirk, a girl from Belfast. She was travelling now as Norah Young, a member of a breakaway IRA unit, a recruit on her first mission. She was in too deeply to back out and start again with Stephen. The organisation had ways of dealing with anyone who had a change of heart.

'Tell me you're glad to see me again, Marie.' He looked very handsome, sitting there dressed in a lightweight navy sweater, his shirt open at the neck. He had broken his nose some years ago playing rugby at college and she had often teased him about it, saying it made him look more like a boxer than an aspiring doctor. They had laughed about it a lot.

'I am glad to see you, Stephen, but—well, something's happened since we last saw each other.'

'What is it? It can't be more important than you

and me getting together again, Marie. I love you, and I know you love me, despite what you said in London. I should have never let you go back to Belfast. We've had arguments, Mum, Dad and I. I was going to follow you over—'

He took her hand and squeezed it. She saw him staring at something. He was looking at the wedding ring on her finger. 'My God!' He looked into her eyes and she saw the pain. 'Is that what you meant when you said something had happened?'

He was giving her an easy way out and she took it. It was one way to stop him getting involved. She would do it for his sake. 'Yes. We're here in Turnberry on our honeymoon.'

It was as though she had slapped him in the face. 'You never mentioned anyone else.'

She shrugged. 'There was someone from a long way back. We were childhood sweethearts—' She saw the mixture of pain and bewilderment in his eyes. 'I'm sorry, Stephen.'

His hand slid from hers. 'I'm sorry too, Marie. I hoped that you and I—that there might still be a chance—'

'I know.'

He forced a smile. 'I suppose I should say congratulations.'

'Thank you.'

'He's a lucky fellow. Do I get to meet him? Are you staying here in the Royale?'

'No.' She shook her head. 'We're on the other side of Turnberry.'

Panic gripped Marie. What if he asked her what she was doing in a strange hotel sipping morning tea without her new husband? She would have said goodbye, got up and left, except she had to collect Michael and Rory from the playroom. Thankfully it was Stephen who came to her rescue.

'Oh well, that's it, then. Isn't it?' He stood up and she also got to her feet. 'Goodbye, Marie.'

'Goodbye, Stephen.' My God, was this how it was finally going to end, in a strange hotel in Scotland surrounded by people sipping mid-morning tea?

He leaned over and she thought he was going to give her a peck on the cheek. Instead, he kissed her full on the mouth. Surprised at first, she could not help herself responding. After a few delicious moments she pulled away. Marie could feel several pairs of eyes looking their way.

'I'm sorry—' He was about to turn away but she stopped him.

'Stephen . . . I'll always love you. You know that.'

He turned and was gone, striding across the lounge towards the elevator. She watched him until the door opened and he disappeared from view. Marie sat on for a few more minutes, oblivious to the other people around her. She had done the right thing, of that she was almost certain. And yet.

She rose and went downstairs to the playroom, her mind still in turmoil.

David Megson reckoned this could turn out to be his lucky day after all. Earlier this morning he had taken one look at the rain-lashed Turnberry course and had come to the conclusion that taking pictures of golfers, indistinguishable in their wet gear, was not for him.

182

He would accompany the wives on their trip to Edinburgh instead and hope that something turned up. A few words with Felicity Jacob in the foyer of the hotel and everything was hastily arranged. She was only too pleased to have a photographer with them to add a bit of excitement. The women, designer outfits peeping from beneath plastic rainwear, would enjoy a photographer along as well.

Lisa Maurelli too was glad to have David Megson on the trip for company. The two of them sat together in the back seat of the coach, listening to the excited chatter emanating from the multi-national group of wives and girlfriends, all eager to see what Edinburgh had to offer. Lisa looked a knockout in a tight-fitting, white, one-piece boiler suit which showed off her tanned skin to perfection. The zip was judiciously undone to display an ample amount of bosom. Glancing down the golden cleavage helped to pass the hour-long journey for David Megson.

Arriving in the Scottish capital they quickly transferred out of the wind and rain into one of the city's most exclusive stores. They were greeted by the manager and a bevy of salesgirls, who conducted them on a tour of the various departments.

'Later, girls,' Felicity Jacob announced before they dispersed, 'the management has laid on a lunch in the rooftop restaurant and this will be followed by a fashion show specially set up for us.'

During the lunch Felicity, fortified by several glasses of champagne, called for silence and announced that she had a surprise for the gathering. 'As you know girls, we have among our group today a lovely lady who, until she gave up her own career a few years ago to accompany her husband around the golf circuit, was herself a famous model.'

Down the table Joan Donohue, who was sitting beside Susan Elliott, heard her friend exclaim: 'Oh my God—'

'What's wrong?' Joan whispered.

'I think my past may be about to catch up with me.'

'—you all know who I'm talking about, of course,' Felicity was saying. 'Susan Elliott!' There was a buzz of talk and then handclaps. 'Will you take a bow, Susan?'

Susan rose to further applause. She smiled, said 'thank you' and sat down again quickly. She was totally unprepared for what Felicity came up with next.

'As a special treat for us today, girls, I'm going to ask Susan to make a comeback to the ramp and join the other models in the fashion show. Now she may need some persuading, so put your hands together and show her how much we'd love to see her back in action again.'

'Oh no, I couldn't—' Susan began. But her voice was lost under an enthusiastic burst of applause from the crowded table. Everyone was looking at her.

'Please, Susan.'

'Come on, honey. Don't be shy.'

'We'd love to see you do it—' The enthusiasm was rising in waves. Susan felt trapped, but strangely elated. She too had had a few glasses of wine. It would be interesting taking on some of those younger models.

'Don't let us down.'

'Come on, it's only a fun thing.'

'All right. I'll do it.' Susan got to her feet to loud cheering. Richard would not be too pleased if he found out what she was about to do, but what the hell. Maybe it was time she began to think of herself as a person in her own right again.

'Splendid, Susan.' Felicity was beaming at her. 'I knew I could count on you.'

'We are honoured that a famous model like yourself is taking part in our show,' the pin-stripe suited manager was smiling at her. At the far end of the restaurant Susan could see the ramp, with the psychedelic lighting flashing on and off, hear the bouncy music. She could feel all the old excitement rising within her.

'I hope I'm doing the right thing,' she whispered to Joan.

'Don't do it if you don't want to,' Joan said. But it was too late. Susan's eyes were alight with the challenge. She really wanted to get up there and be the centre of all eyes again.

At the far end of the table David Megson could hardly believe his luck. Imagine, Susan Elliott, the one-time darling of the ramp, the girl whose face had featured on fashion and photographic magazines the world over, was about to make a comeback—and he was right on the spot. It was better than photographing sodden golfers at Turnberry any day of the week!

A short time later, prancing down the ramp on her first showing, Susan simply dazzled. It was as though she had never been away. Tall and slender, her hair loose and tumbling over her shoulders, she looked stunning. Eyes sparkling with the thrill of it all, she was the big star—and she was enjoying every moment.

She showed off a succession of designer outfits with a combination of seductive and insouciant charm that had her audience applauding wildly—and the other models eyeing her enviously. Susan smouldered in an off-the-shoulder black evening dress; looked chic in a three-quarter length jacket and tartan skirt, and was positively a knock-out in a shimmering cocktail dress with a deep cleavage down the back. The manager had insisted that she be given pride of place in the line-up and when she jived down the ramp for the finale in a beach skirt slit to the thigh and a skimpy top to match, the female audience jumped to its feet as one and applauded wildly.

The department store manager, his eyes still on the ramp, leaned over and said to Felicity Jacob: 'Marvellous. Absolutely brilliant. She could go back to modelling tomorrow and name her own price for a day's work.'

Out front, David Megson was clicking away furiously. He knew he was sitting on a good story. Picture editors would pay handsomely for what he had in his camera.

A short while later Susan, her eyes sparkling with excitement and champagne, rejoined Joan's table. 'How did you enjoy the show?' she asked as she helped herself to another glass.

'It was tremendous. You looked terrific, Susan.' Joan sipped her orange juice. She was feeling a bit overwhelmed by it all and kept thinking of Colm. He would have completed his round by now. She wondered how he had coped. She should have been there. . . .

'I must say I enjoyed it. Didn't think I would but I did.' Susan was on a high, enjoying the con- gratulations that were coming her way.

Felicity came up with the pin-striped store manager in tow. 'Darling, you were quite superb. Mr Edgar is raving about you.' Mr Edgar, tall, slim and almost completely bald, beamed at her.

'Thank you both. I never realised how much I missed the business until today. I'll have to think seriously about making that comeback.' Joan wondered what Susan's husband would say to that.

'You looked as though you'd never been away from the ramp,' Felicity gushed on. 'I have my eye on that little cocktail number. I just hope it looks as well on me as it did on you.' She turned to Joan. 'What about you, my dear? See anything you fancied?'

'No. Not really.' Joan had been astonished at some of the prices called out during the fashion show. She knew she should not have come on this trip. The wives were buying almost everything in sight, flashing bank cards and cheque books. All she planned to buy were two outfits for Michael and Rory and an off-the-peg dress for herself. She was thankful when the store manager and Felicity moved on, leaving Susan and herself alone. Susan was more herself again. She was glancing anxiously around the room.

'Looking for someone?' Joan asked.

'That photographer who was taking pictures. Do you happen to know who he is?'

'No. Except that he's English. I heard him talking to Lisa Maurelli on the coach.'

187

'Those photographs he took—' Susan had a worried look. 'I want to know what he plans doing with them.' The excitement that had been there earlier had now completely disappeared. Richard wouldn't like what she had just done. She scanned the room; David Megson was talking to Lisa Maurelli at a table. She did not want to make a scene about the photographs. She would tackle him later when they got back to the hotel.

'Easily the best round of the day so far. And when you consider that this young Irishman had to battle not only with the terrible weather but also with the distraction caused by one of his playing partners, you'll appreciate his achievement.'

From his commentary box above the eighteenth green Malcolm Jacob was giving a rundown on the morning's play on the second day of the Open. High in his elevated position he could see the white rollers crashing on the Turnberry sands, whipped up by the near-gale which had sent scores in the second round soaring. So far not one golfer in the world-class field had broken par today—and it was unlikely that anyone would, given the prevailing conditions.

Colm Donohue had walked off the eighteenth green almost an hour ago after completing his round. Hot and sticky under his rain gear, he nevertheless felt pleased with himself. His ability to handle a high wind had paid off with eighteen straight pars for a 72. A lot of the golf writers filing their early copy were describing it as one of the greatest rounds ever at Turnberry.

But great as Colm's round was—and it made him

the early leader in the clubhouse—the news that really grabbed the headlines was the shouting match out on the course earlier between Willi Ducret and his caddie. Veteran golf scribes had never witnessed anything like it.

The trouble between the two fair-haired Belgians had erupted on the final nine holes. The one-time friends were openly at war with each other. It was obvious that Willi blamed Ben for leaking the story that had appeared in one of the morning tabloids. Several times during the round they were heard exchanging angry words and Willi, who had shot a five over par 41 for the first nine holes and had given up hope of qualifying for the final two days, had taken to flinging his clubs to the ground after each shot, instead of handing them back to a glowering Ben.

The championship official accompanying the Donohue/Escudio/Ducret threesome had a quiet word with Willi and his caddie, warning them of their conduct. But to no avail. The battle of words and bad temper continued between the two as the threesome neared the end of the round.

Things came to a head at the sixteenth hole, known in Turnberry as the Wee Burn. It measures 409 yards and has a stream running across the fairway just in front of the green. Always a dangerous hole, it was particularly so today into the teeth of the wind. Most players were laying up short of the burn with their second shots and hoping to get their par with a chip and a putt. That was the sensible approach. Rafael Escudio had done just that with his four iron.

Then it was Colm's turn to hit his second shot. He was also selecting an iron from the bag when Johnny said quietly. 'Go for it, son. Across the burn. You can make it.'

Colm hesitated. It seemed a suicide shot. 'You really think I can do it, Johnny?'

'Definitely. You're pumped up right now. You'll make it with a two wood. It'll show the rest we mean business.'

The young Irishman made his decision—he would risk it, on Johnny's advice. He reached into the bag, took out the wooden club. The crowd roared, knowing he was going for the green.

The buzz of excitement died down as he took a couple of practice swings. As he lined up it seemed the wind increased in volume. Keep the swing smooth, he told himself; don't try to overhit. Colm took one last look up towards the distant flag, settled himself once more, and swung. He kept his head down and went right through the shot. As soon as the ball took off, the applause began and he knew he had hit a good one. He narrowed his eyes against the wind and saw the ball complete its arc and begin to drop.

Christ! It looked to be heading for the burn! But there was a mighty roar from the spectators as it made it over, bounced on the front of the green, and ran several yards past the pin. He had made it!

Then it was Ducret's turn. He and Ben were again arguing. Everyone was looking at them as their voices rose. Willi, it appeared, wanted to try for the green, Ben was advising against. After much gesticulating Ben took an iron club from the bag and handed it to Willi. The latter took the club, flung it to the ground, then reached into the golf bag and took out a wood. Ben scowled, said something in a loud voice to his partner in French, then retired to a safe distance.

Under the circumstances, Willi's attempt to clear the burn was always doomed to failure. He swung, did not make proper contact, and watched his ball take off on a low trajectory. It bounced once on the fairway then disappeared into the distant stream. He looked after it for a few moments then turned and shouted something at Ben. Spectators saw Ben's face contort with rage. Then he flung the heavy golf bag to the turf, turned on his heel, and stormed off.

There were a few moments of stunned silence before the crowd realised what was actually happening. Then they began to talk excitedly among themselves. Ben was quitting!

A stern-faced championship official moved across the fairway to Willi. Briefly he explained that Willi would either have to carry his own bag for the rest of the round or get someone else to do so. And of course the incident would be reported to the championship committee. Fortunately a young fan stepped out of the crowd and offered to carry Willi's golf bag for the few remaining holes during which the Belgian dropped a further three shots to par.

Malcolm Jacob caught up with Sally just as she was entering the refreshment tent reserved specially for the media. He called her name.

She turned, didn't smile. 'Oh, hello.'

'Hey, what's wrong? I've got the impression you've been avoiding me lately.'

191

Sally looked at him coolly. 'Does that surprise you, Malcolm?'

'Well yes. Let's have a cup of tea and a sandwich. We'll talk about it. You grab a table—'

'I don't think I want to talk about us. I don't see the point.'

'Why not, for heaven's sake?'

'Because it's finished between us. Understand?'

She turned to go, but he put his hand on her arm, restraining her. 'Sally, don't be so hasty. What do you mean, finished—I really don't understand.'

'Don't you? Then ask your wife.'

Malcolm tried to brush that aside. 'Look, I know Felicity is on to us, but we shouldn't let that interfere with our relationship. We love each other, for God's sake. Tell you what, she's in Edinburgh today with the wives; won't be back until some time this evening—'

'So? What are you suggesting?' Sally knew what was in his mind. But she wanted to see if he was really callous enough to voice it.

He looked at her, wondering what the hell was going on. Why on earth was she not responding? 'I thought seeing as how you and I have a few hours to spare we might—you know—' Malcolm broke off and grinned.

'You want us to go to your room, jump into bed, and have a quick screw. That it, Malcolm?'

His smile vanished. 'I say, Sally, that's putting it a bit crudely—'

'But that's what you have in mind, isn't it?'

'Well . . . yes.' He was beginning to get annoyed. 'Look here, Sally. What the hell is wrong? Is it something Felicity said?'

She faced him. 'Remember one thing, Malcolm. I am not a whore. I'm a one-man woman. I expect the same loyalty from whoever I'm sleeping with.'

'Of course. It is something Felicity said, isn't it?'

'Yes.'

He breathed deeply. 'Come on. Out with it.'

'You mean she hasn't told you already?'

'Told me what? If you know what it is, you tell me.'

'No. That's your wife's pleasure. She's the one who's expecting the baby.'

Sally turned and walked away. Malcolm did not follow her. He wanted a drink all right—but it had to be something stronger than tea.

It was well into the afternoon when the rain that had been falling all day ceased. But the wind never let up. It blew just as fiercely from the sea as ever, turning the Ailsa course into a bigger monster than usual. By now the last threesome of the day had teed off and the golfers who were still out on the course were able to dispense with their wet gear. It might help some of them to improve on their round by a shot or two; for others the change for the better in the weather had come too late. They would miss the cut, pack their bags, and head down the motorway to the next tournament.

In the clubhouse bar Colm Donohue was enjoying a well-earned drink alone. Earlier he had answered a barrage of questions from the media, all eager for him to give a blow-by-blow account of his great round. It had been quite an experience for him to face the press.

He could not remember when he last had that pleasure. But he had enjoyed it. Unlike Joan, who always felt uncomfortable with strangers, he loved being in the limelight.

When Colm was an amateur, Johnny Davis had told him once: 'You've a good personality, Colm. Charisma is what they call it nowadays. It's a good thing to have if you ever make it to the top as a pro.'

Well, he had not made it to the top yet. But right now he was leading the British Open—and already the agents and managers were beginning to sniff around. That made a welcome change, too. He saw Ron Grantham making his way towards him. His former manager was smoking one of his slender cigars and smiling. Grantham pulled up a chair and sat opposite, signalling to a waiter as he did so.

'Great round today, Colm. Congrats.'

'Thanks, Ron.' The waiter was despatched for a large Scotch and another drink for Colm.

Grantham exhaled some cigar smoke, studied Donohue through the haze. 'Are you going to win the big one?'

'Too early yet to say. There are still two days to go. Too many good golfers around.'

'None of them will beat your score today, though.'

'Let's wait and see.' Donohue remained silent. Grantham had sought him out for a purpose. He was taking his time leading up to it.

It did not surprise him when his former manager said: 'I'd like to take you on again, Colm. I always thought you had the potential. You just made a couple of bad decisions.'

Like getting married too young, and getting

lumbered with a wife and two kids when he should have concentrated on his game. Colm Donohue knew that Ron Grantham would not come out and say that, but it was what he meant. 'What do you say—about my managing your affairs again? If you listened to me, you could really go places on the circuit, earn real money.'

'I'll think about it, Ron. There have been a couple of others putting out feelers. You understand.' The guy had a nerve, coming back after ditching him when it looked like he was not going to make it. He would hold on for a couple more days. If he had a high finish in the Open, his hand would be strengthened when it came to wheeling and dealing.

If Grantham was disappointed that the current leader of the Open was holding off it did not show. 'You think about it, Colm. I'll be around. And good luck tomorrow and Sunday.' He smiled. 'Give my regards to that wife of yours, won't you?'

He watched as Ron Grantham moved across to the crowded bar. Then he turned his attention to the television set showing today's round in progress. Leonard Morgan was on the screen. The first round leader and his two partners were playing the par three eleventh hole, a 177-yarder which was into a cross wind. The caption on the picture informed viewers that Morgan was three over par for today's round so far. The Englishman had not 'blown up' as many had predicted. Conversation in the bar died as those in the room paused to hear how Leonard Morgan was progressing.

'. . . he has just drilled a beautiful four iron into the heart of this green and has left himself with a putt of about six feet for a birdie,' the commentator's voice told viewers. 'This man Morgan is really putting it up to the big guns in the Open championship.'

Two minutes later the viewers in the bar saw Morgan confidently slot in his birdie putt. A cheer went up, but it died down as quickly as the commentary was taken up again.

'It's a day when the golfers out there are just hoping to keep as close to par as possible. And doing that for the first nine holes were the fancied American duo of Tony Maurelli and Dick Elliott, who reached the turn in 38; although I've just been told that Elliott has just bogeyed the fifteenth and sixteenth holes, which is bad news for him. And watch out for current Open champion Lou Menzies—the Aussie needs to par the last two holes for a very good round of 74. That would put him right up there among the leaders with a 144 total.'

Across the other side of the crowded lounge, Rafael Escudio was introducing himself to Eddie McBain, the man in charge of rostering the fleet of courtesy cars operating at the Open. The official championship programme carried a picture and story on Ed McBain, smiling in front of a row of gleaming Ford Granadas. The caption stated that McBain was this week 'at the service of the world's top golfers.' Rafael Escudio was about to put that statement to the test.

'Excuse me.'

Eddie McBain turned aside from the group of associates with whom he was drinking. He immediately recognised the handsome, swarthy young man who was addressing him. Oh no, McBain thought, another complaint.

'Hello. What can I do for you?' He smiled, tried to look pleasant.

'A little favour, maybe. First, I buy you a drink.'

'Oh, very kind of you.' McBain relaxed slightly. So it's not a complaint. People who are going to start bitching don't usually start off by buying you a drink. 'I'll have a large Scotch.'

Escudio caught the eye of a barman and ordered two drinks. The clubhouse bar was very crowded. 'You know me—Rafael Escudio—'

'Of course. Open champion two years ago.'

'That's right.' Escudio grinned, his capped teeth showing white against his dark skin. 'I got lucky.'

'How did you do today?' McBain asked affably, wondering what the hell this was all leading up to.

A shrug. 'Okay. I shoot a 76 that should qualify. That weather'—Escudio waved his hand—' it is terrible.'

'Not like Mexico, eh?' McBain laughed. Rafael tried not to look offended. He did not like being reminded of poverty and sleeping four in a bed. He had left all that behind him when he had run away, sneaked across the border into the US and discovered golf.

The drinks had arrived. He picked his up. 'Salud.' He studied the big Scotsman as McBain knocked back most of his in one gulp. This guy looked easy. Escudio reckoned he could do business.

'Well. . . .' McBain replaced his glass on the counter. 'What can I do for you? Everything okay with our car service, I hope.'

'Sure, sure. Everything fine. The cars are fine, the

197

service is fine. And the girls. . . .' Escudio let his voice trail off.

'They are fine too, I hope.' McBain grinned. He had an idea what was coming.

'They are beautiful, your girls.'

'Glad you like them. I pick them myself.'

'You have good judgement, Mr McBain.'

'Och, thank you. And just call me Ed. Everyone does.'

'Sure.' Rafael paused, sipped his drink. 'This favour, Ed. I like one of your girls.'

'Aye.' Where had he heard that one before?

'I want to . . . how you say, get to know her a little better. You know what I mean?'

Of course I know what you mean, McBain thought to himself. You're another of those randy golfers with an eye for the birdies. He had dealt with them before, the superstars who, apart from their appearance money, demanded other services when they came over for a tournament. It did not apply only to golfers, to be fair. He had run into this sort of deal with businessmen who used the fleet, big spenders who did not believe that the service ended in the hotel car park. It was one of the hazards—or advantages—of using pretty girls as drivers.

Ed McBain knew all the pitfalls. In the past year he had had to fire two of his girls for extending the service to male clients. Not that he had any objection to any of his girls earning some extra money on the side; their crime was that they had tried it on without making sure their boss got a share of the proceeds. Ed reckoned he had to guard against that sort of sharp practice.

He finished off his drink and did not object when his companion repeated the order. 'Which one do you fancy, Rafael?'

'A chica called Elaine.'

'Elaine, eh?' McBain swilled the whisky in his glass. 'Nice lass. Very independent.'

'You can fix?'

'Maybe. I take it you want to have more than a little drink with the lassie?' Escudio nodded. McBain pondered. 'It'll cost money.'

'I pay. Don't worry. How much?'

This was always the tricky bit. How badly did the guy want it— and how much was he prepared to pay? Escudio had won the Open and was one of golf's superstars. No sense in letting the product go too cheaply.

'Five hundred pounds. Cash.' He could see the Mexican converting it into dollars.

'She is very expensive. No?'

McBain shrugged. 'My girls are very high class. They turn down a lot of offers. I'm not even sure Elaine will play ball. She's new in the job.' He thought she would. She had a two year-old son and no husband in sight. She could probably do with some extra money. 'When do you want me to set it up, Rafael?'

'Tonight.'

McBain shook his head. 'Sorry. She's on the late shift. And I have a very tight schedule. I should be able to line her up for you tomorrow night. How's that?'

Rafael Escudio swore under his breath. Just his luck—the weather was bad and now he could not have the girl. 'When is the next time you see her?'

'She'll be back on duty around lunchtime to-morrow.'

'Okay, Ed. I check with you then.'

'Cheers.'

'Salud.'

McBain watched the dark-haired golfer ease his way through the crowd towards the exit. He wondered which was more important to Rafael Escudio right now—winning the Open again or bedding Elaine McVicar. Ed reckoned he knew the answer to that one: some men had a peculiar sense of values. He would put the proposition to the newest recruit of Courtesy Cars tomorrow. As usual he would be diplomatic about it. If she went for it, he would see she was well compensated for her night's work—two hundred and fifty pounds into her hand and the following day off. No one could say that Ed McBain did not look after the welfare of his girls.

It was getting on towards evening when the luxury air-conditioned coach powered up the winding driveway and stopped outside the Turnberry Hotel. A babble of female voices filled the air as the wives of the golfers who had gone on the shopping trip to Edinburgh descended the steps and stood around in small groups, excitedly discussing the day's adventure. Many had gift-wrapped parcels in their arms and entered the hotel quickly out of the stiff breeze which was still blowing. A few of the women were gathered at the back of the coach, waiting to collect extra large purchases which had been stored in the boot.

Susan Elliott said goodbye to Joan Donohue and watched her get into a taxi. She knew Joan was anxious to get back to the guesthouse to see the children. 'You have my phone number. If you and Colm want to drop by for a drink this evening, feel free to do so. The men won't want to stay up late, of course, but we could spend a pleasant few hours chatting.'

'Thanks for the invitation. I'll see what Colm says.' She liked Susan Elliott, even though their two lifestyles were worlds apart. But right now she wanted to get back to see the children and find out what Colm had scored in the second round. She said a silent prayer that he had qualified for the final two days of the championship.

Susan waved goodbye then glanced around. She saw David Megson with Lisa Maurelli at the other side of the car park. He had put his photographic gear into his car and they were deep in conversation. Slowly the day trippers drifted into the hotel until she, Lisa and the photographer were the only ones remaining outside. Susan followed the last of the wives into the foyer, left her parcels at reception, then came out on to the hotel steps again.

Lisa and David Megson had just ended their conversation. By the way he was glaring after Lisa, it did not seem to have been a particularly friendly chat. Susan waited until Lisa had disappeared inside, then skipped down the steps and ran across the tarmacadam space. The photographer was about to slide in behind the wheel.

'Mr Megson!' He turned at the sound of her voice. When he saw who it was, he looked surprised.

'Yes?'

'Mr Megson, I'm Susan Elliott—'

'I know who you are. Something I can do for you?' He leaned on the open door of the car. His voice was not very friendly.

'You took some photographs this afternoon.'

'Lady, I took a lot of photographs this afternoon.'

'You took some of me on the ramp.'

'That's right. You certainly stole the show, Mrs Elliott.' His eyes travelled over her body. The wind had whipped her coat open, and the light dress she was wearing was pressed tight into her figure, outlining the curves of her shapely breasts and thighs. She was beautiful, no doubt about that.

Conscious of his scrutiny, Susan pulled her coat around her. 'Mind telling me what you plan to do with those photographs, Mr Megson?'

He did not reply immediately. 'Dunno. Haven't thought about them yet,' he lied. 'Why?'

'I wouldn't like any of them to appear in the newspapers. Not until the Open is over, anyway.'

'Oh, I thought all models liked to see their photo in the newspapers. You must be different to the rest?' He was being unpleasant, she knew. That tiff with Lisa had left him in a bad mood.

'I know this is an unusual request but—could I buy that film from you? I don't want those photographs used.'

'You're joking.'

'I assure you I'm not, Mr Megson.'

He decided to play her along. 'Okay. How much?' This was turning out better than he had thought.

Her gaze did not waver. 'Name your price.'

Jesus! The bird was serious! She would do almost anything to stop those photographs being published. Why, he wondered? It was not as if she had gone topless, for heaven's sake, like a Page Three girl. He had something she wanted very badly and he would see exactly how far she was prepared to go to get it. He had spent a fruitless day with Lisa Maurelli, arguing and cajoling her, trying to get her to come to his hotel again, but without success. He guessed the little nymph was lining up someone else for a bit of action.

C'est la vie. Time to move on to someone else— and Susan Elliott was class. Funny, a lot of models would go to bed with you to get their photo in the newspaper; now here was one who was perhaps ready to do the trick to keep her photo out. All he had to do was to play his cards properly.

'Supposing I don't have a price, Susan. Know what I mean?'

His using her first name irritated her. She tried not to lose her cool. 'I have a good idea what you have in mind, Mr Megson. Maybe you'd like to spell it out.'

His eyes searched the sky above her head. He had a half grin on his lean face. He closed the car door, leaned back casually against it. 'What if you were to call around to my hotel tomorrow—say when that husband of yours is out on the course. I'd have the negatives printed up by then—'

'And?'

'We could come to some, shall we say, arrangement.' His gaze came down from the sky and he looked directly at her. 'I am not interested in money.'

Susan held his gaze. 'Let me get this straight, Mr

Megson. You want me to go to bed with you. Right?'

'Right.'

Susan's hand came up quickly and scored a perfect hit on Megson's face. The slap sounded like a pistol shot, whipped away on the breeze.

She turned on her heel and strode quickly towards the hotel entrance. Behind her an angry David Megson was feeling a stinging cheek. He watched her as she went up the steps and into the hotel. He would make the bitch pay for that, Megson vowed as he got into his car and drove away.

Malcolm Jacob looked down from his elevated commentary position behind the eighteenth green. He was gazing on the wide expanse of fairway, back over 400 yards to the tee where the threesome had driven off. It was past six o'clock in the evening now and a long day's golf at Turnberry would end within the next hour, with roughly half of the 150 competitors due for the chop at the end. Leonard Morgan would not be one of those; right now it looked like the outsider would be the leader going into tomorrow's third round.

The wind was still howling in from the firth. Best score today was still Colm Donohue's 72, which had shot the young Irishman into contention. In general, scores had soared and it looked likely that the cut-off would be as high as an eight over par 152.

'Malcolm!' His boss's voice broke in on his train of thought. Too late he realised he had missed a cue—again.

'What the hell is wrong with you?' Ricky Edwards hissed.

'Sorry. What was that?' They were looking at him anxiously in the commentary box.

'You were asked would the cut-off be at one fifty-two?' The question came across on his ear piece.

'Oh yes,' Malcolm agreed without even thinking. 'That's what I estimate, too.'

He would have to concentrate. Must not let his mind wander again. But my God—a baby! He glanced at his watch. Felicity would be back by now, probably in their room resting. He would have to watch that she did not drink too much. He had read somewhere that too much alcohol was bad for pregnant women. Forget about that now. Concentrate!

'If one fifty-two is the cut-off point,' he picked up on the commentary, 'then Willi Ducret, whose caddie walked out on him today, will just about scrape in. But will he be allowed to continue? The championship committee is to hold an emergency meeting after today's play—'

No wonder Sally was annoyed with him. Her sympathies would lie with Felicity, who was expecting his baby. But why on earth had his wife not told him? Maybe it wasn't true. He only had Sally's word for it.

A baby! My word, had Felicity not taken precautions when they made love? Obviously not. He would have words with her about that!

'Let's look at the leader board right now—' Jacob paused until the required shot appeared on the monitor. 'There's Leonard Morgan on top, outright leader at three under par. One behind is Irishman Colm Donohue on one forty-two. On level par one fourty-four there's a group of five—Luca of Spain,

205

Minoki of Japan, another Englishman Sam Joyce, the Scot Sandy McIntyre, and Lou Menzies. The Aussie had a seventy-four today, great shooting in the conditions.

'But, my word, what has happened to Dick Elliott —it looks like his Open jinx has struck again. He went to the turn in a respectable thirty-eight shots, but after that came disaster. He took forty shots on the back nine for a seventy-eight and a two round total of one fifty. That will leave him a long way behind the leaders going into tomorrow's third round.'

Malcolm pushed all thoughts of the baby into the back of his mind as a long range camera shot picked up the huge figure of Tony Maurelli striding down the last fairway. 'Tony has hit a massive drive and needs a par for a seventy-six today. That's four over par overall and just seven shots off the pace. Tony is still in contention—'

After the camera showed another member of the threesome, Canadian Ben Dwight, hit his second shot to the green, it focused on the third member of the group who was playing his second shot from very deep rough. 'Now here's a man we certainly won't be seeing tomorrow,' Malcolm informed his audience. 'Australian Jack Hastings, or Handsome Jack as he's known on the circuit. Yesterday Jack shot seventy-nine, and he's heading for an eighty-two today. No way is he going to make the halfway cut—' Viewers saw Hastings barely get his ball out on the fairway with his next shot. 'Never mind,' Malcolm continued his banter, 'Handsome Jack is a fun-loving fellow who enjoys his golf, unlike a lot of his fellow professionals—'

Down below, also taking an interest in Jack Hastings, was Lisa Maurelli. Her husband was about to play a seven iron to the green, but Lisa's sympathies were with Jack. 'That poor Australian,' she pouted to Marvin Maxwell who was at her side. 'All this way to play in the British Open and he doesn't even make the cut. I think we should ask him to have dinner with us tonight.'

Marvin gave her a sidelong glance. 'That guy plays the European circuit and makes a living. He doesn't look too unhappy to me— and I don't think we should invite him to dinner tonight.'

'Why not?' Lisa asked, as Handsome Jack fluffed his chip shot to the green. 'I think he's cute.'

'He's an also-ran.' Marvin retorted. 'The guy hasn't got a golf brain. From what I hear he spends more time in the night clubs than he does on the practice ground.'

Lisa giggled. 'Sounds like he could be fun.'

At 8.00 p.m. Marie Kirk and Martin Dignam sat down to dinner at the 'Seaview' guesthouse. The food was plentiful but not elaborate, cooked by Mrs Carlyle herself and served to the dozen or so paying guests by her husband and a young local girl, brought in when the demand required it. Across the room Marie could see Colm Donohue and the older man who caddied for him finishing their soup. Joan was not at the table with them and Marie reckoned she was upstairs putting the children to bed. A few minutes later Joan entered the dining-room and smiled a greeting.

'How are the children?' Marie asked.

'Fine. They went asleep immediately.'

'I'm not surprised. They used up a lot of energy today,' Marie laughed.

'I hope they weren't too much trouble for you,' Joan said.

'Not at all. I enjoyed myself. We had a great time. They're two lovely children.'

Dignam waited until Joan was seated across the room. 'You two are getting very friendly.' He paused. 'I don't like it. People who get friendly ask questions. Let her look after her own kids in future. Got that?'

She nodded and they ate the rest of the meal in silence. Marie was glad for the respite. It gave her an opportunity to think about the meeting with Stephen. What an amazing coincidence that they should meet up again the way they did. It had brought him back into her life when it appeared to be all over between them. He still loved her and she hated to have had to lie to him about being married. The hurt on his face when he had seen the ring would stay with her forever.

They were sipping coffee when she glanced up and saw him studying her. 'You're very quiet. Anything happen today that I should know about?' Dignam asked. She shook her head, but he still had his suspicions.

While she had been involved with the children Dignam had gone to Turnberry and driven down a side road to the deserted sands. With a near gale blowing, it was the last place anyone would think of coming to today. He had taken the tin box and a short-handled spade out of the boot and walked along the sands, head down against the wind, until he found what he wanted—an overgrown pathway that lead to an area of scrub and gorse. Here he had buried the tin box, noting the area well before moving off. Driving around with a bomb in the boot was too risky; he would collect it tomorrow night when he came to do the job proper.

Afterwards he had retraced his steps to the car and had driven back to Turnberry to the Open, joining the thousands of hardy spectators tramping the course. Dignam was particularly interested in access from the beach and the five stands ringing the eighteenth green. It had been a valuable afternoon of recon- naissance, but there was still some work to do.

'Come on outside. I want to have a few words,' Dignam said to Marie. They left the dining-room and, although they had the garden to themselves, he took no chances. He waited until they were at the furthest point from the house before saying: 'Sometime after midnight tonight I'm going back to Turnberry. I want to get on to the course again, see how they patrol it. It'll be a dry run for the real thing tomorrow night.'

'Want me to come with you?' Marie asked.

He shook his head. 'No. We'll go straight up to our room now. About midnight when the coast is clear I'll slip out the front. What I have to do won't take long. I should be back before it gets light.' Dignam paused, waiting for her to say something. Her silence irritated him.

'Aren't you going to wish me luck? I mean we're in this fucking thing together!'

'Good luck.' Marie turned on her heel and went back into the guesthouse. He stared after her for a few moments, then followed.

It was not a particularly scintillating evening. Marie spent most of it reading a book, lying clothed on the bed. Martin Dignam prowled around the room, restless, occasionally looking at his watch. It seemed an age until he reckoned it was safe to go.

Less than an hour later he was driving down the same rutted track that he had traversed in the afternoon. To his left, away from the sands, he could see the lights of an encampment where holidaymakers were sleeping in their caravans and mobile homes. He took the brown paper parcel out of the car boot and changed quickly into the Olympic security uniform. From the driver's compartment he took out the small, snub-nosed automatic and slipped it inside his belt, pulling the heavy navy sweater over it. It was unlikely he would have to use the gun, but Martin Dignam rarely travelled anywhere without it.

From the car boot he also took a hand lamp. Looking along the beach he could see in the distance the outline of the lighthouse against the darkened sky. The gale had blown itself out and there was almost no wind now. Clouds occasionally drifted across the moon, obscuring the pale light reflecting from the sand and the sea.

He made his way along the sands for several hundred yards. During his reconnaissance today he had noted the location of the Portacabin from which Olympic Security operated. It was situated near the entry to the tented village which ran almost the whole length to the left side of the eighteenth fairway. That was across the far side of the course from the beach. Dignam reckoned a spot near the fourth or the eighth green was the best place to gain entry to the course. Both were quite a distance from the Olympic Portacabin and, being almost inaccessible from the beach, were not likely to be heavily patrolled.

Moving along the beach in the direction of the lighthouse, it took him a while to find the spot he was searching for. He had marked it yesterday while he was walking the course during the Open but it looked different from the beach and in the darkness it was difficult to pinpoint. The terrain was rocky and he had to make his way gingerly through an area of spiky gorse and whin bushes before scrambling up the sandy bank. It was perfect; he was now at the extreme end of the course and the eighth green was less than a hundred yards to his left.

Dignam brushed sand and grass from his trousers and looked around. At various parts of the course he could see single headlights spearing the darkness, moving in various directions. In fact one was coming up the ninth fairway towards him. He switched on his hand lamp and moved forward to the eighth green. The headlight picked him out, came nearer, blinding him.

A voice with a strong Scottish burr floated through the darkness: 'Hullo, there.'

'Hullo.' This was the big test. He moved out of the glare of the beam, saw the bulky figure of a man astride a wide-wheeled scooter studying him.

'Wha are ye doon so far from base? Foot patrols are to stay aroun' the clubhouse area.'

'Aye, that's right. But I got a wee bit bored patrolling the same patch and decided to come for a stroll up here.' Dignam was grateful that his Belfast accent was not too far removed from the native dialect.

'A stroll, and ye with no rain gear, especially after the weather we've just had. Sure ye must be off your head, mon!' Dignam saw that the other had on water-proofs. Christ, he was close to making a hash of it.

'Nae worry. I'm on my way back now—' He began to move away.

'I'd stay in your designated area if I were you. The boss nae likes his men to leave their posts. See anything suspicious?'

'Nae a thing.'

'Good. Away wi' ye now and leave patrolling the coastline to us wheelies.' There was a roar from the engine and he was gone.

Dignam breathed a sigh of relief. He had passed the first test, thanks to Flavin and his duplicate uniform. But he would have to be more careful twenty-four hours from now when he would be carrying a suspicious square tin box. It was time to make his way down the course towards the clubhouse and the eighteenth green.

He strode over the turf towards the cluster of lights in the distance, skirting the valley to the right of the fifteenth fairway. He walked the length of the sixteenth fairway, crossing the bridge at Wilson's Burn, and cut across open country again to where an arc light lit up the entrance to the tented village. Twelve hours ago thousands of golf fans had scrambled over Turnberry's hillocks and spring heather; now the course lay ghostly silent, awaiting another onslaught on the morrow.

As he neared the tented village, Dignam saw security men on foot, several with guard dogs. One or two of them nodded but no words were exchanged. He cut onto the eighteenth fairway, avoiding the tented village and the Olympic Security cabin. No point in taking unnecessary risks. As he approached the eighteenth green, the outline of the giant stands loomed into the night sky. There were five in all, Dignam noted, the two biggest on either side of the manicured grass sward, the three smaller in the middle. He smiled in the darkness; he had a good choice of where he could plant the bomb!

He reckoned the large stand to the right was the most promising. It was on the far side of the fairway from the tented village and was in shadow. He strolled casually around the back, taking note of the darkened area beneath where the steel and wooden structure angled down to meet the turf. He shone the lamp into the area. Ideal! Had he had the biscuit box with him now the job could have been completed.

Dignam looked into the darkness. A headlight bounced about as a scooter came up the first fairway and he could see several shadowy figures moving about not far away. Bringing the bomb along tomorrow night would be very risky; he would have to choose his moment carefully. Next time he would come on to the course from the beach near the fourth tee. From there he would keep to the rough, staying away from the fairways, which seemed too well patrolled. One worry was that the stand under which he wanted to put the bomb was fairly close to the clubhouse. But there was nothing he could do about that.

Twenty minutes later Martin Dignam was back in his car, had changed back into his ordinary clothes and was driving towards the guesthouse. It had been a useful dummy run. He hoped the real one would go off just as smoothly.

6

SATURDAY, 18 JULY

At three minutes to 7.00 a.m. the foyer of the Turn-berry Hotel was pleasantly busy when Lisa Maurelli came out of the lift. She was dressed casually in a Boss track suit and a pair of white moleskin slip-ons. A brightly coloured headband held her dark hair back from her forehead.

She strolled to the reception desk, conscious that several pairs of male eyes were following her progress. 'Good morning.'

The young man behind the desk, looking smart in his red and tartan waistcoat, smiled the way he had been told to do in management school. 'Good morning. Mrs Maurelli, isn't it? May I help you?'

Lisa gave him one of her very special smiles. She liked people to recognise her. This young man would go far. 'I'd like to order a pot of coffee, with milk, no sugar. And some thinly sliced toast. No butter.'

'Certainly. Breakfast is being served now—'

Lisa shook her head. 'I'm having that later with my husband in our room. I'm ordering the coffee and toast for maybe half-an-hour from now.'

The young man's eyes fell on the towel draped over her shoulder. 'You're going to the pool?'

'The sauna, actually.'

He thought it was a very early hour for a young lady to be taking a sauna, but he let it pass. 'If you're looking for a massage, I'm afraid the masseuse won't be on duty until nine o'clock.'

She flashed her warm brown eyes at him, a smile playing provocatively around the corners of her lovely mouth. 'Not to worry. I've already taken care of that.'

His eyes followed her as she sauntered down the far end of the foyer towards the pool and sauna entrance. The young man had already backed Tony Maurelli to win the Open—and he would lay even money that Tony's wife had nothing on under that track suit!

The swimming pool lay shimmering and un-disturbed as Lisa entered the hotel's leisure complex. She thanked her lucky stars that there were no early birds among the guests. At the far end of the pool, up three tiled steps to another level, were the changing rooms and the men's and ladies' saunas. She was climbing the steps to the upper level when Jack Hastings popped his head out of the men's cubicle.

She had not been able to swing it with Tony for Handsome Jack to join them for dinner last night—Marvin Maxwell had seen to that. 'No way, Tony. You're still in with a great chance of winning this goddam Open. You, me and Lisa will have dinner and then it's early to bed. I don't want you chewing the fat half the night with that has-been Hastings.'

'Sorry, honey,' Tony had said apologetically. 'Marvin's the boss.' When was her husband going to tell that fat manipulator to get lost?

But Lisa had still got what she wanted. They were relaxing in the clubhouse lounge, with Marvin hovering like a mother hen, when Jack Hastings came

216

up to them. He extended his hand. 'Best of luck over the final two days, Tony. Sorry I won't be around.'

Tony shook the profferred hand. 'I'm sorry too, Jack. It was a pleasure playing with you. Hope we meet up again somewhere.'

'I hope so too,' Hastings replied, his eyes flitting to Lisa. Tony had introduced them and she thought of how it was with some men that they lose their sexiness up close. Not so with Jack Hastings—he was coming on strong.

'Are you staying around till Sunday to see Tony winning the Open?' she enquired.

'I had planned to push off tomorrow,' Hastings had replied.

'Pity.' Their eyes met over her Bloody Mary.

After a couple more minutes of desultory conversation he left to join some buddies across the room. During the short time it took them to finish their drinks, Lisa glanced over several times and once caught Jack Hastings looking at her. She smiled.

When they left a short while later, her cry of distress halted Marvin and Tony on the steps of the clubhouse. 'Hold on a moment, boys. I left my cigarette lighter at the bar.' She was back through the doors before Marvin could object.

Jack Hastings spotted her as soon as she entered the lounge. He said something to his buddies, rose, and came over. 'Hello again. Forget something?'

'I'm back to look for my cigarette lighter—'

He gave a quick glance at the bar. 'I don't see it around. You sure you left it behind, Lisa?'

She looked into his eyes. 'No, it's in my handbag.' They both laughed. Lisa said: 'I can't stay now.

217

You're not really leaving tomorrow, are you? I mean not first thing?'

'You got something to offer that might interest me more than the Dutch Open? It starts next week in Haarlem—'

'What do you say to an early morning sauna in the Turnberry Hotel?'

'Just the two of us?' He savoured the thought for a moment. Hell, it would hardly matter if he skipped one practice round before he teed up in Haarlem. Come to think of it, that was the story of his life. 'What time?'

'How about seven a.m.? Tony will still be asleep. Get yourself an early morning call wherever you're staying, big boy.'

'Don't worry. I'm an early morning riser.' He had laughed at the innuendo.

His parting shot came to mind now as Lisa reached the top step in the sauna area and he emerged from the men's cubicle. He was naked save for a towel around his waist. She saw tiny rivulets of perspiration running down his body. He had a deep chest, matted with crinkly, blond hair.

She stood on her toes, put both arms around his neck, and kissed him. His arm encircled her waist, pressing her body on his. They stayed like that until she finally broke away, panting.

His voice was a husky whisper: 'Hurry, girl. Get changed.'

'First things first.' He watched as she took a square of white cardboard out from the folds of her towel. She reached into her track suit pocket, took out a tiny box of drawing pins and affixed the square of cardboard to the outside of the sauna door. On it was printed: Out of Order.

'Clever girl,' he grinned, reaching for her again.

She restrained him. 'Wait. I won't be a moment.' She went outside and entered the ladies' changing room, pulled off her track suit. The young man at reception was right—she was wearing nothing underneath. Lisa draped the large white towel around her, tucking it under her armpits. Body tingling, she came out of the dressing-room, crossed to the sauna and slipped inside.

He was waiting for her, sitting on the middle ledge, the towel now lying across his knees. The rivulets of perspiration were running down his long, lean body, towards his navel, then down further, towards the tops of his thighs. She could see the bulge under the towel and it excited her.

He did not say a word, sat there staring as she unhooked the towel from under her armpits and let it fall around her feet. His eyes raked her body and he gave a low whistle.

'Your masseuse has arrived,' Lisa said. She padded slowly across the hot sauna floor, feeling the dry heat already beginning to prickle her skin. Reaching out, she slid the towel slowly from Jack Hasting's knees. He leaned his back against the ledge behind, closed his eyes, and let her go to work.

In the 'Seaview' guesthouse Marie was awakened by the buzz of Martin Dignam's electric shaver from the bathroom. She glanced at her watch. 8.15 a.m. She had heard him come in during the night but had pretended to be asleep. Everything must have gone well; he was humming to himself.

Dignam appeared in the bathroom doorway. 'Morning.' He was in trousers and vest. She noted that the couch on which he had slept last night was already tidied, the blanket neatly folded across one of the ends.

She returned his greeting, watched as he came into the room, pulling on a dark poloneck sweater. He ran his hand over his chin. 'You know I can't get used to shaving again. I can't wait to get back to Belfast to let the beard grow.' He crossed over to the window and gazed out.

Last night after Dignam had left, she had phoned Stephen on impulse. She had blurted out that she had lied to him earlier in the day, that she was not married and was therefore not in Turnberry on her honeymoon.

'What are you doing here then, Marie?' he had asked, puzzled.

'Stephen, I can't tell you that. Not just now.'

'Why not?'

'It's too dangerous. I don't want to get you involved.'

He spoke quickly. 'Marie, are you in trouble? Tell me.' When she did not reply, he went on: 'You are in trouble. I knew I shouldn't have let you go back to Belfast.'

'I don't want you involved—'

'To hell with that. I *am* involved. Where are you staying?'

She hesitated. 'I—I can't tell you that. It's too dangerous.'

He was getting exasperated. 'Marie, I love you, do you realise that?' His words made her heart jump. 'We can work things out together.'

'Oh, Stephen—'

'I want to see you, Marie. Now, tonight.'

'No! Not tonight—tomorrow.' The words were out before she could stop them.

'Where?'

'At your hotel. Three o'clock. If I can't make it, I'll phone. I can't say much now, Stephen.' She was afraid that Dignam might return unexpectedly.

'Marie, take care. Remember I love you.'

'I love you too, Stephen.' Now, in the cold light of morning, she wondered if she had done the right thing. If Martin Dignam found out, there was no telling what action he might take. He would see Stephen as a threat to the whole operation—and Dignam was not a man to let anything or anybody get in his way. He was a trained killer, programmed to do a job. She was under no illusion about his ruthlessness.

'Aren't you going to ask me how I got on last night?' Dignam was standing by the bed, looking down at her. It was almost an action replay of the scene overlooking Loch Lomond.

'How did you make out?' she asked levelly.

'Pretty good. No problems. There would be no difficulty putting our little baby in place when the time comes.'

'When do we leave for Belfast?'

'We check out of here tomorrow morning.' He was at the window again, peering out. 'There's a sailing from Stranraer to Larne at twelve-thirty.' That would get them back to Northern Ireland before the fireworks began in the late afternoon. Of course Marie would be suspicious Sunday morning when she woke up to see the monument still standing. So what—by then it would be too late for her to do anything except ask questions.

The way he was acting disturbed her. That day at Loch Lomond he had hinted of changing the original plan and she had put her foot down. But how could she be sure where he had planted the bomb unless she accompanied him when he did the job—and that was simply not on. Perhaps there was a more subtle way of getting him to reveal his hand. . . .

'That war memorial—won't it be risky planting a bomb there, even at night? I mean it's very exposed—'

He did not take the bait. 'You let me worry about that. Okay?' Dignam took his leather jacket from the back of a chair and put it on. From the inside pocket he took out the automatic pistol, fondling it. 'You're a smart girl, Marie, but you ask too many stupid questions.' He swivelled, pointed the pistol directly at her. 'I'm in charge of this operation. I make the decisions. Your job is to help—not poke your nose in where it is not wanted. Savvy?'

He put the gun away inside his jacket. 'I'm going down to have breakfast. Then I'll phone Earley in Belfast, tell him that everything is going according to plan.' He paused and grinned. 'My plan, that is.'

There is a saying among golf professionals that a tournament really only begins on the third day. That's the day when those in the lead begin to come under pressure; when the tour-hardened superstars knuckle down to the task at hand and make the charge that shoots them up the leaderboard, poised to strike on the final day.

As the thousands of spectators flocked on to the course, now basking in bright sunshine, in contrast to yesterday's wind and rain, the sensational news that greeted them was that Belgian golfer Willi Ducret was out of the Open.

'Disqualified for bringing the game into disrepute' was the official verdict handed down by the Royal and Ancient committee members. They had convened an emergency session late last night, in time for the early editions of the morning tabloids. Ben had gone public on his homosexual relationship with his long-time friend Willi and the story was splashed across the front pages.

'That's the big talking point this morning here in Turnberry, even before a ball had been struck in the third round,' Malcolm Jacob told his morning television audience. He looked directly into the camera and intoned solemnly: 'An hour ago Willi Ducret left Turnberry in a car with his manager. Neither of them would comment on the newspaper allegations.

'Now let me fill you in on another of this morning's sensational happenings—and this concerns Dick Elliott. He teed off just over an hour ago and has birdied three of the first four holes to shoot up the leaderboard and bring himself right back into contention. He's fighting hard to win the title and beat that Open hoodoo. He's moved out of range of our cameras so we can't show you him in action right now—'

223

Viewers saw Malcolm Jacob's expression change. 'Hold it! I'm just getting word from the course that Elliott has in fact just birdied the fifth. What a charge—he's really burning it up out there—'

In the lounge of the 'Seaview' guesthouse Colm Donohue sat listening to Malcolm Jacob retailing the latest news from the course. He and Johnny had finished breakfast an hour ago and he was feeling nice and relaxed before they headed for Turnberry. He was paired with Leonard Morgan today and they would be the last twosome off at 2.25 p.m. It was now only 11.00 a.m. and Johnny had advised that they relax at 'Seaview' rather than go to the course and get caught up with media interviews and well-wishers.

Outside on the lawn he could see Joan and the girl she had become friendly with sitting in the sunshine chatting, while the two little boys chased each other about the garden. He was glad that Joan had met that girl with the Northern Ireland accent; they seemed to get on well together.

'Four under par after five. That's some shooting from Dick Elliott,' Colm said, watching the television screen.

Johnny did not seem impressed. 'Not to worry. He has a lot of shots to make up. There's a jinx on that fellow Elliott. He's never going to win the Open.'

Listening to reports of another record-breaking crowd milling over the Ailsa course today, Colm felt a tightening of his stomach muscles. Nerves! He had never suffered them during a tournament before—but then he had never been one shot off the pace in the British Open before with just two days to go. He must remain calm, not let the pressure get to him.

My God, it would be terrible if he blew up today—in front of all those millions of television viewers around the world. Better not think about that. Be positive. Treat it as just another round of golf, that's what Johnny said. That is the secret.

'How are you feeling, lad?' It was as though Johnny was reading his mind.

'Okay. A little uptight.'

'That's understandable. Just remember you won't be the only one like that. They'll all be feeling nervous. The difference is that some will handle it better than others.' Johnny gestured to the TV set where Dick Elliott was about to drive off from the sixth tee. 'Even he will feel the old nerve ends tingling—see, what did I tell you!' Johnny exulted as the camera followed the American's ball into the right-hand rough.

They fell into silence. Johnny studied his young companion, seeing in his mind's eye a fourteen-year-old star of the local hurling team, a youngster with a good eye who had the makings of a strong, controlled golf swing. He had taken the young fellow under his wing, coached him, taught him all he knew, had seen the young man leave his home fairways for those of the world circuit. Now he was on the threshold of a big breakthrough.

But would the young fellow's nerve hold? If it did, Colm was on his way to superstardom, and Johnny reckoned there would be a place on the bandwagon for him too. He was not too old to harbour hopes of joining up with Colm as his full-time caddie. He had the experience and the knowledge to weld them into a winning combination. And here at Turnberry,

Johnny Davis reckoned on taking the first steps to achieving that goal.

'Tell you what, let's have a glass of something long and cool.' Johnny rose from his chair. 'It will help you to relax. After that we'll head for the course and some practice.'

Susan Elliott was seated at the window of their rented bungalow, her legs curled up beneath her. She stared unseeing at the sun-dappled lawn, with its neatly trimmed grass, the sprays of gladioli peeping up between the rose bushes. Across the road the first fairway of the Arran course, Turnberry's other golf track, had been given over to car parking, such was the crowd pouring in to see the third day of Open action. The sun's glare bounced off the phalanx of car roofs, shimmering in a heat haze that was sending temperatures soaring.

In a corner of the room a television set was turned on and Malcolm Jacob's voice was giving the up-to-date happenings on the Ailsa course. Susan heard Richard's name being mentioned. He was now half-way through his round and appeared to be heading for a very good score. But she found it hard to concentrate.

Instead, Susan's eyes were on the headlines on the front page of the tabloid lying in front of her on the floor. Richard had read the story out to her at breakfast, just before he and his caddie had left for the course. His words were still on her mind:

'That guy Ducret . . . he's finished. He'll never be able to hit a golf ball straight again after headlines like those.'

226

'Surely it is not the end of the world. He's got to learn to live with newspaper headlines and get on with winning tournaments,' Susan had replied.

Richard had looked at her almost in disbelief. 'Honey, you should know better than that. Do you have any idea what it's like out there? A golfer's got to concentrate like hell, blow his mind of everything but finishing ahead of the other guys. You can't do that if you have something like this hanging over you.'

Susan had not the heart to pursue the subject. All she knew is that she would have to see David Megson again, plead with him not to use those photographs. Yesterday she had let rage get the better of her. It was a mistake. She would have to swallow her pride and beg him to let her have the photographs taken of her on the ramp. She would have to offer him so much money that he would not be able to turn her down.

If the photographs appeared in the newspapers, there was no doubt that it would have a devastating effect on Richard, probably kill off his chances of winning the Open. He must not be upset right now at any cost. Before leaving he had vowed he would shoot a 65 or better today. There was such determination in his voice that she knew he would do it.

It was almost three hours since Richard had left in the courtesy car with his caddie. Since then she had been sitting at the window, thinking, her eyes drawn intermittently to the tabloid on the floor and the television screen in the corner. Now her mind was made up.

'Mrs Craigie?'

'Yes?' The housekeeper came in from the kitchen.

'I'm going down to the course. I want to see Richard play the last few holes.'

Mrs Craigie gestured towards the television. 'He really is in form today. It looks like he is going to break the course record.'

They both watched. On screen Richard was studying a putt, his lean face tight with concentration. The commentator said it was the twelfth green and that 'Dick Elliott is going for yet another birdie—his seventh of the day—to go six under par for this round. Remember he dropped a shot at the last hole.' The spectators were six deep around the green. Susan saw her husband strike the putt smoothly and there was an almighty roar when it went in.

A few moments later she left the house and walked in the bright sunshine past the coloured hospitality pavilions towards the entrance proper. Inside, she saw David Megson near the press tent talking to a girl. She waited until the girl had moved away before approaching him. He saw her coming and stared coldly at her.

'I'd like to speak to you for a moment, if I may.'

'Come to apologise, did you?'

'Yes, in a way. I'm sorry.' Susan paused, waiting for him to smile and say forget it. He remained silent, just stared at her. 'About the photographs. I want them back.'

His eyes showed a flicker of interest. 'You know the price. Are you prepared to pay?'

Susan felt her face colouring. 'I'm talking about money, damn you. Name your price.' A couple of spectators had recognised her and they stopped, staring at the two of them. She was relieved when they moved on.

Megson waited until they were out of earshot. 'You must be really crazy about that guy out there—' he nodded in the direction of the course.'

'Well?' He was playing cat and mouse with her.

'You're too late. I've already sold them—to a Sunday tabloid. Tomorrow you'll rate as much space as your husband.' He laughed.

She felt herself go cold. Eyes blazing, she faced him. 'Why did you sell them to a newspaper when you knew I'd have doubled any price you were offered?'

He rubbed his cheek with his hand. 'Let's just say I don't like being slapped around by anybody—especially a woman.' With that he turned and disappeared into the press tent.

Colm Donohue fired the last of the golf balls into the distance on the practice ground and felt reasonably satisfied with the result. He had just spent an hour or so hitting shots with a variety of clubs and felt nicely loose and relaxed. Inside, however, he was nervous, very nervous, and he hoped it did not show. Earlier his performance on the putting green had attracted a good crowd of onlookers, a tribute to his high spot on the leaderboard.

His watch showed 2.15 p.m. He and Leonard Morgan were due on the first tee in ten minutes. Not far away Morgan was being interviewed by an American TV unit. Donohue himself had been interviewed by the same group a short while ago. He always liked giving interviews. It did not happen very often but when it did he was always very confident of his ability to carry it off well.

As he and Morgan walked together towards the first tee, a TV camera focused on the two surprise players of the Open championship. Spectators stopped in their tracks and stared, some wishing the duo good luck as they passed.

'How are you feeling, mate?' Leonard asked in a low voice.

'Bloody nervous. And I don't mind admitting it,' Donohue replied.

'Same here. I didn't sleep too well last night.'

'That makes two of us. Been approached by any agents?'

'Three so far.' Leonard Morgan grinned. 'A couple of days ago nobody wanted to know. Now I'm hot property. Funny old game, isn't it?'

A burst of applause greeted them as they stepped on to the slightly elevated tee. A tournament official approached them. 'Gentlemen, I'm told that Dick Elliott is on the eighteenth green and putting for a birdie that will give him a 63 and a course record. Before you drive off, I think it would be advisable to wait until he has putted out and the crowd has settled.'

Colm Donohue swallowed hard, his mouth dry. A 63! Christ, Elliott was really putting the pressure on. He glanced over his shoulder in the direction of the eighteenth green. Although the huge spectator stands blocked his view, he could visualise the fans leaning forward in their seats, willing Dick Elliott's historic putt in. The silence was uncanny.

Suddenly it was broken by a thunderous roar. He

knew what that meant—the American had sunk the putt. Donohue did not dare look at Leonard Morgan. He must shut everything out of his mind. Johnny must have read his thoughts. 'Forget what's happening elsewhere on the course, son. Let's concentrate on our own game.'

'On the first tee,' the starter's voice rang out, 'current championship leader Leonard Morgan of England and Ireland's Colm Donohue. Quiet, please!'

Again a silence fell. Already the bush telegraph around the course was informing spectators of Dick Elliott's record round. The crowds lining both sides of the first fairway were growing by the minute, anxious to see how the two outsiders would stand up to the pressure.

They did not have long to wait for their answer. Morgan took a two iron for safety off the tee, blocked it out right and saw it land in a bunker. His partner fared little better; Donohue pulled his three-wood drive left and it finished in heavy rough. The crowd groaned when the championship leader splashed weakly out of the bunker, then chipped on badly, leaving himself a twelve yard putt to save par. The Irishman could only hack back on to the fairway from the rough, chip on, and also leave himself with a long putt for a par.

Heads began to wag knowledgeably among the spectators following the twosome. 'The third round always separates the men from the boys,' and 'watch 'em crack now' were two of the remarks overheard in the gallery.

The crowd groaned again when Colm Donohue

missed his putt and had to settle for a bogey five. 'That's an unnerving start for the young Irishman and not what he wanted at this opening hole,' Malcolm Jacob commented from his vantage point high above the green. 'Leonard Morgan also looks likely to drop a shot here.'

The Englishman gave his putt a lot of study. He settled over it, struck it confidently—and a mighty roar went up when it went into the hole. Leonard's smile of relief as he walked off the green said it all.

At the second hole the leading pair again struggled. Morgan drove badly from the tee, did not make the green with his second shot, chipped on and had to sink a tricky eight-foot putt for par. Colm Donohue pulled his second shot left of the green, played a delicate chip shot over a bunker, then brought gasps from the spectators when his three-foot putt ringed the cup before dropping in. Two rather fortunate par fours.

'We're playing like two old ladies,' Leonard Morgan muttered to his partner as they made their way towards the third tee. Colm grimaced and nodded.

'No doubt about it,' Malcolm Jacob mused into his microphone, 'nerves are beginning to show with these two. That marvellous sixty-three of Dick Elliott has a lot to do with it. That makes him two under par overall and the leader in the clubhouse right now.

'And he's not the only one closing the gap on Morgan and Donohue. We've just heard that Tony Maurelli has played the front nine holes in thirty-four shots. That's also two under par, so he's making a move. Defending champion Lou Menzies is playing two holes in front of the leading pair and has just birdied the fourth hole to go one under par for today's round. And what about big Sandy McIntyre—' Jacob's voice lifted with excitement— 'he's giving his big following here at Turnberry something to cheer about—he is two under par after seven holes and moving into contention.

'Other news is that Luca of Spain and Minoki of Japan, who are both playing together and who started out today only three shots off the pace, are both one under par after six holes. So it's getting very tight at the top. The pressure is really on Morgan and Donohue right now. Let's see how they play the third hole—'

Meanwhile, as the drama unfolded out on the course under a hot afternoon sun with the wind beginning to blow, Dick Elliott was facing a battery of photographers and reporters in the press tent after his great round. Showered and changed, with his beautiful wife at his side, he looked very relaxed.

Elliott dealt easily with the usual string of questions from the media. That putt for the record on the eighteenth green came in for a lot of comment. 'It was a beauty,' he conceded. 'I was confident it would go in.'

'Are you going to win the Open at last?' someone asked.

'I reckon this is my year,' the American replied coolly. 'Forget about that jinx. I'm going to win it tomorrow for Susan.' He gave his wife a big smile. 'She's been my greatest supporter over the years.'

'Do you think your husband is going to win tomorrow?' Susan had seen David Megson among the gathering and she knew he had been waiting for the right moment to put his question. When it came, she hardly dared answer.

'Go on, honey,' her husband said. 'You tell 'em.'

'Of course he's going to win,' she blurted out.

'What makes you so sure? Anything could happen yet.' Megson was enjoying himself.

'I don't care what happens. Richard will win because he's the best golfer out there!' Her reply brought a resounding cheer from the assembled pressmen.

When it died down, David Megson said: 'Let's just wait and see.' Susan was glad when the questions started up again.

Marie Kirk paid off the taxi outside the Hotel Royale and walked into the spacious foyer. Stephen came forward to greet her, relief on his face. 'Marie! Thank God—I was afraid you wouldn't come.'

'Sorry I'm late. Turnberry is jammed tight. It was difficult for the taxi to get through.' He lead her into the hotel's coffee dock, guided her to a corner table. When the waitress had taken the order he said: 'What have you gotten yourself into, Marie?' He lowered his voice. 'You said it was something to do with the IRA.'

She nodded, then blurted out: 'I'm here with someone to do a job at the British Open.'

Marie saw the horror on his face. 'A job? You mean a bomb?'

Again she nodded. 'The war memorial on the course—'

'Oh my God!'

234

'It's not as bad as it seems, Stephen. Nobody will get killed. Those are the orders. The memorial will be blown up tonight—'

He was appalled. 'But Marie, we can't let this happen. We must tell the police, have this other person arrested. What's his name?' He presumed it would be a man.

'Dignam. Martin Dignam. He's dangerous. A fanatic.'

There was a pause. 'Where is he now?'

'At the Open. Probably surveying the monument.'

He pondered a moment. 'We must go to the police right away. Turn this fellow Dignam in. The police will exonerate you, Marie. We could go away together, abroad somewhere.' His hand reached out, found hers. She found comfort in his touch. For the first time in almost a week, she felt a surge of happiness, of longing. It was a long time now since she and Stephen had touched, made love, and she realised that she was quivering slightly. She wanted him again, badly. He was strong, protective, and he loved her. If only they could find a way out of this mess together.

'We can't take a chance of going to the police,' Marie whispered. 'I'd probably be arrested, jailed. We wouldn't be together for months, Stephen, maybe years. I couldn't bear that.'

'I couldn't either, Marie.' He kissed her, tenderly at first, then passionately, oblivious of the stares of an elderly couple having a sedate tea opposite. A discreet cough told them that the waitress had arrived with the coffee.

Marie poured, drank hers black. Stephen was looking at her, a hunger in his eyes. He brought his mind back to more urgent matters. 'What should we do about Dignam, Marie?'

'See what you think of this: tomorrow morning, after the memorial is destroyed, Dignam and I drive to Stranraer to catch the Larne ferry. Once there, at the last minute, I'll refuse to get on the boat. If you meet me there later, Stephen, we can go away together. The job would have been completed and probably the IRA would have no further interest in me.'

Marie could see he wasn't too happy with that. 'What if Dignam turns nasty in Stranraer when you tell him you're not going back?'

'Like I said, I'll spring it on him at the last moment. He'll want to get on that boat urgently. He can't risk missing it. Besides, the terminal will be packed with people. He can hardly force me on to the ferry at gunpoint.'

'You said he was a fanatic—'

'Yes, but he's no fool. Martin won't want to draw attention to himself. There will be police around too, remember.'

Stephen pondered for a few moments. Finally he said: 'Okay, Marie. Play Dignam along for now. But for heaven's sake be careful. He's dangerous. Where are you both staying?'

She told him, laughed at the expression on his face when she informed him that she and Dignam were travelling as man and wife. 'Don't worry, he's been sleeping on the couch and he's obsessed with getting the job done.' She did not tell Stephen about the incident with Dignam at Loch Lomond.

They finished their coffees. Stephen was studying her. She was beautiful, her dark hair contrasting with the pallor of her skin, her red lips moist and inviting. She looked so vulnerable, and she was in such danger. 'I love you, Marie.'

'I love you too, Stephen.'

'I hope I'm letting you do the right thing. I don't want anything to happen to you.'

'I'll be careful, I promise.' She looked at him, silent, inviting. He kissed her again and she felt herself responding. She broke away reluctantly, said: I'd better go—'

Stephen sensed her reluctance. 'Must you?' The question hung in the air. Marie was silent, afraid. Seeing Stephen again, knowing he was on her side, changed everything between them. 'The hotel is practically deserted,' he whispered, 'everyone is away in Turnberry. We could go to my room ...'

She hesitated for just another moment, said: 'Oh, Stephen—'

They rose together, walked into the foyer, crossed to the elevator. The elderly man in the coffee dock noticed they were holding hands as the doors closed behind them. He smiled to himself, poured more tea for his wife.

Back at Turnberry, on a sun-splashed course where the wind was beginning to whip up as the afternoon wore on, Leonard Morgan and Colm Donohue were still struggling. Both had played the first nine holes of the third round in 37 shots, one over par, and the pack was closing in.

'The pressure of being at the top of the leader-board in the Open is telling on Morgan and Donohue, as we thought it would,' Malcolm Jacob commented as he took over from a colleague during the afternoon's televised transmission. 'Indeed only some incredible putting from Morgan—he sank no less than five single putts to the ninth—has kept him with a share of the lead.

'Donohue has been very wild off the tee and has had to play some remarkable recovery shots from the rough to hit the greens in regulation. I'm told they have both parred the tenth and eleventh holes and they should be coming into range of our cameras shortly.'

All things considered, Jacob was very pleased with himself. He had just had a very pleasant lunch with Felicity, during which they had discussed the baby again. His wife wanted to have it and he had surprised himself by backing her all the way. Becoming a father again had made him feel good. Last night in bed when he had told Felicity that he knew about the baby, they had had a very calm and civilised talk.

They had kissed, agreed to give their marriage another go for the sake of the baby, and Malcolm had amazed himself by promising to turn over a new leaf. It would not be easy, but he would shoulder his responsibility like a man and give up these sordid affairs. Well, for the present at least, Malcolm reckoned!

A roar from a nearby green brought him back to the present. The scores of the golfers who had completed their third round was coming up on the monitor and he told viewers: 'Look at all those big names grouped together ... Australian Lou Menzies shot a seventy-one today and is just one shot behind the leader in the clubhouse, Dick Elliott. Also on two-fifteen are Japan's Kiyoshi Minoki, Scotland's Sandy McIntyre and American Tony Maurelli, who had a great sixty-five today and is now hotly tipped to win tomorrow. We have Tony with us here, so we can ask him how he rates his chances—'

The camera moved back and the big figure of Maurelli came into the shot. 'Congratulations on today's great round, Tony.'

'Thank you.' Tony gave his easy-going smile into the camera.

'How confident are you of winning the Open at your first attempt?'

'I'm sure going to give it a helluva try tomorrow. I think I can do it.'

'Tell us about some of the highlights of your round today.' Tony dutifully obliged, and when he was finished Malcolm asked: 'Will you be able to handle the pressure tomorrow? It's going to be very tight at the top.'

Maurelli shrugged. 'Thanks to my manager, Marvin Maxwell, I know how to handle pressure. I'm into yoga.'

'That helps you relax?'

'Sure. Marvin has me standing on my head for half-an-hour every morning. At night too. It's very relaxing, gets my mind together.' Tony knew Marvin would be pleased with that.

'And does it work?'

Tony grinned. 'You ask my wife Lisa. She'll tell

you how relaxed I am during a tournament.' Viewers saw Tony put his arm around Lisa's shoulders and hug her as she came into the shot. 'You tell 'em, honey.'

Lisa smiled into the camera. 'Tony is so laid back sometimes it's difficult to tell if he's alive,' Lisa said drily. She snuggled up to him. 'But I know how to look after my big baby, don't I honey?'

'Thank you, Tony Maurelli—and good luck tomorrow.' The camera focused back on Malcolm. 'Now we'll go out on the course to see if we can pick up the final twosome of Leonard Morgan and Colm Donohue. . . .'

The huge gallery following the two outsiders saw them playing some poor shots and some remarkable recovery strokes from the fourteenth hole onwards. At the long par four fourteenth, playing straight into the wind, both Morgan and Donohue were in the rough off their drives. Leonard had a good lie, but his four-iron second bounced up the fairway and into a bunker. Colm did not try to do the impossible with his second shot, but on the advice of Johnny Davis he hacked out on to the fairway and came up 100 yards short of the green. He then hit a superb wedge shot that pitched past the pin, spun back, and finished three feet from the hole.

Leonard Morgan came out of the bunker on to the green about ten yards from the hole. It looked as if he was about to drop another shot, but his putter was red hot and the ball went into the hole for a par. The Irishman sank his tricky three-footer for his par.

They each scrambled a par three at the short fifteenth hole where Donohue overhit a four iron and

240

got a free drop when his ball landed near the temporary stand at the back of the green. Again he played an excellent chip shot which ran down the green to a foot from the hole. Morgan's badly hit five iron off the tee came up on the fringe in front of the green, but his putt, with a big left-to-right swing, was perfectly judged and finished up two feet from the pin.

The sixteenth hole should have been a disaster for both of them. After useful drives the two of them underhit their second shots and were lucky not to finish up in the infamous Wee Burn. There were gasps from the crowd when the Irishman, whose ball had stopped on the downslope, chipped up far too strongly. The ball was heading towards the back of the green when it hit the flagstick and stopped within four feet of the hole.

'Now I know what they mean by the luck of the Irish,' one sports reporter was heard to mutter.

Beside him veteran golf scribe Bill White sucked on his pipe. 'That's the kind of luck you need to win the Open,' he said.

The 500-yard par five hole at Turnberry—the seventeenth—is considered to be the most vulnerable on the course. The pros reckon it is a great birdie opportunity, and all day it had yielded up as many birdies as pars; in fact Dick Elliott had eagled the hole on his way to his record 63. But there was to be no such good fortune for either Morgan or Donohue. After perfect tee shots into the valley fairway, they both missed the green with their second shots. Each chipped and two putted for a disappointing par five.

As they made their way to the eighteenth tee,

Colm turned to Johnny. 'I'll be glad when this round is over,' he said.

'Forget it, lad,' Johnny hissed so that the crowd ringing the tee would not hear. 'Hang in there. We're doing okay.'

Colm glanced at the nearby scoreboard. Johnny was not too far off the mark. Dick Elliott was now co-leader in the clubhouse with the elegant Englishman Sam Joyce who, after a 70 today, was being heavily backed to take the title. The quartet of Maurelli, McIntyre, Minoki and Menzies had now been joined by Canadian Bill Dwight on 215. It was still anybody's tournament, with the winner tomorrow likely to emerge from that lot. And a par for both of them at the last hole would leave Donohue one shot off the lead and put Morgan one stroke ahead going into tomorrow's final round.

A hush descended on the crowd as Leonard Morgan teed off. The tension crept into the shot; he turned his right hand over in the hitting area and there was a groan from the gallery as the ball zoomed into the evening air, went left, and plummeted into the rough. Leonard managed a smile at Liz as he replaced the driver, but she could see the strain on his face.

Then it was the Irishman's turn—and a round of applause rippled out as his drive split the fairway. Colm sighed with relief.

Morgan's ball was almost unplayable in thick, clinging rough and he had to have two hacks at it before he got it back on the fairway. There was another groan of disappointment when his fourth shot made one of the greenside bunkers. The packed stands burst into applause when Donohue's second shot—a seven iron—settled into the heart of the green.

Again a hush descended in the evening air as Morgan settled himself into the bunker. It was a fairly straightforward shot for most pros in ordinary circumstances. But this was the British Open, and it came as no surprise when Leonard took too much sand with the shot, which came up short of the hole, leaving him with a ten foot putt for a two over par six. Once again his putter came to the rescue and the ball went into the hole. The crowd gave him a big hand, but it had been a costly hole for Morgan and it meant he was no longer leading the Open. He consoled himself with the fact that he had shot a 74 when it could so easily have been an 80. One more good round tomorrow and he could still become Open champion.

Colm Donohue did not fancy his twelve-foot birdie putt at all. It was across the slope of the green and there was not much room for error. He had not had a birdie all day. If he made the putt, he would be in a three-way tie for the Open lead!

He got down on his haunches and studied the putt. 'Left lip,' Johnny advised, looking over his protégé's shoulder. Donohue nodded, straightened up, took a few practice swings, then stood over the ball and held his breath. He looked up just in time to see the ball turn slightly over the last six inches and drop into the hole.

He waved his acknowledgement of the crowd's applause.

'Thank heavens that's over,' Donohue said to

Leonard Morgan as they shook hands and walked off the green.

'You can say that again,' was the grim rejoinder. 'We played like two bloody amateurs, but got away with it.'

'Good luck tomorrow, Leonard.'

'Thanks, mate. Same to you.'

After they had been to the Official Marker's tent to check and sign their cards, they were ushered towards the press marquee. On the way several photographers waylaid Leonard and asked him to pose with Liz and the putter that had kept him in the championship race. Leonard duly obliged and was so caught up in the drama that he did not see Stan Tynan observing the scene from a distance.

Tynan was still smarting from the brush-off he had received two days ago. He reckoned it was time that Lenny and his girlfriend were taught a lesson.

Even as Leonard Morgan and Colm Donohue were facing the media in the crowded press marquee, the pairings for the final day of the Open championship had been decided by the championship committee. As he studied the typewritten sheet on the notice board in the caddies' changing-room, Johnny Davis grimaced.

They had paired Colm with Dick Elliott—and even worse, they were the last twosome out on to-morrow's final day. He had hoped they would have paired Elliott with the other co-leader Sam Joyce, leaving Colm to go out with any of the men sharing second place. The pressure would not have been as great playing with one of them.

Partnering a superstar like Dick Elliott on the final day of the British Open would test the mettle of even the most experienced tour pro. Thousands of fans would follow the American tomorrow, willing him to shoot another great score and win. It would be a severe test of nerve for Colm. Still, the young fellow had proved today that he had the 'bottle' to win. That birdie at the eighteenth had impressed the pundits.

Johnny was making his way towards the club-house when he heard his name being called. He turned to find Joan approaching through the crowds that were now streaming from the course. She was dressed simply in a lightly patterned summer outfit that he suspected had not cost a fortune but which accentuated her neat, slim figure.

'Hello, Joan. Where have you been all day?'

'Watching play from the stand behind the eighteenth green—with Susan Elliott.'

She saw Johnny's weather-beaten face break into a grin. 'Looks like you'll both be back there again tomorrow. Colm and Dick Elliott are paired together. They'll be the last two out.'

'Oh. Susan and I are in for an interesting afternoon, then. Where is Colm now?'

'Still with the press boys, I think. After that I believe some agent or other wants to talk to him.'

'Another one?' Joan asked. Colm was certainly in demand these days.

'He's hot stuff just now, your husband. And if he wins the big one tomorrow'—Johnny smacked his hands together in anticipation—'the sky's the limit for you and the kids.'

'And for you also, Johnny. You got him started.

And you've been a great help to him this week. Colm says so himself.'

He looked uncomfortable at the compliment. 'Come on, Let's go and find him.'

Half an hour later they joined Colm in the clubhouse, where he was engrossed in talks at a table with two young smartly dressed men and a very attractive looking girl. When he saw them he waved, but did not join them immediately. Joan noticed that her husband was listening intently to what each of the trio was saying, and that the girl seemed to be doing most of the talking. They had 'management agency mani- pulators' written all over them.

Joan and Johnny found a table and when he fetched two drinks from the bar he noticed her glancing across to where Colm was sitting. 'I wonder who that girl is?' Joan mused. She knew the scene on the circuit, even though she did not travel it often nowadays. Every pretty girl was a danger.

It was another fifteen minutes before the conference at the other table broke up. Joan saw Colm and the two young men stand up and shake hands. The blonde girl did not rise; she sat there, smiling, sipping an exotic looking drink from a long glass. She put it down and let Colm shake her hand, smiling at him and looking cool and confident. He finished his drink, then joined Johnny and Joan.

The two men had a brief discussion about tomorrow's pairings. She let them talk about it for a while before congratulating her husband on his round and then asking him: 'Who were those people you were talking to just now?'

Before replying, Colm glanced over to where the

trio were still talking. 'They're the Varley brothers from London. They've just set up their own management agency, into sports and entertainment in a big way. Mega stuff, if you believe all they say.'

'They look very young to be into that game,' Johnny said suspiciously.

'Just what I was thinking myself, until I got talking to them,' Colm replied. 'Don't let their youthful looks fool you, Johnny. They know what they're talking about. And they have a lot of big names on their list. I was very impressed.'

'Who's the girl?' Joan asked. 'She looks very impressive, too.'

Colm was prepared for that. He had noticed how Joan had kept glancing their way during the discussion. He would have to play it cool, or she might decide to put her foot down, spoil what was looking like a pretty interesting deal. 'That's Samantha Cruise, their top PR girl and management consultant. Very high profile.'

Joan looked over again. 'She's very attractive. Is she married?'

'Dunno. Never bothered to ask. I was too busy listening to what was on offer.'

What he did not tell Joan was that if he signed up with Varley Brothers Management, he would probably be seeing a lot of Samantha Cruise. She looked after the golf end of the business, flying out to locations on the tour during the season to discuss deals and negotiate for the firm's clients. And if he put in a good round tomorrow and won the Open, he would be Samantha's top priority for the year. He had to admit it was an interesting prospect.

Johnny finished his beer. 'Okay, Colm. Let's go. We've got some things to sort out on the practice ground. We've got to get everything right for tomorrow.' He turned, 'Sorry, Joan.'

She smiled. 'I'm used to it by now, Johnny. I'll go back to the guesthouse. I suppose Mrs Carlyle has had enough of Michael and Rory by now.'

On their way out Colm introduced them to Mark and Peter Varley and Samantha Cruise. As she left the lounge Joan made a point of kissing her husband goodbye. She turned and saw that Samantha was looking their way with interest. Although the blonde girl smiled and waved, Joan felt just a bit uneasy.

Rafael Escudio was having dinner with his manager, Kirk Kalder of Mega World Promotions, in the Turnberry Hotel. Despite the sumptuous surroundings—not bad going for the son of a boozy Mexican father—he was not enjoying the meal. He would much rather have had Elaine McVicar sitting across the table from him right now. Instead there was a manager who had flown in this morning and who obviously was not happy with Rafael's performance in the Open so far.

In today's third round he had shot an indifferent 74 for a 226 total—twelve shots behind the leading trio. Rafael knew his chances of winning this year's Open were now gone. Tomorrow's final round was a mere formality. But what the hell, he was not particularly worried. What was important right now was that he get a woman. And not any woman, but that shapely one who drives the courtesy car and who was driving him crazy. He fantasized about getting the girl to his room, watching her strip and making love to her between the sheets.

Ed McBain had called up to his room earlier today to collect his £500. 'I have to tell you, Rafael, it took a lot of persuading to get you fixed up. I had to threaten to fire Elaine before she would agree. Only for she needs this job badly she would have told you to get lost.'

'I no worry,' Rafael had grinned. 'I like them to pretend they no want it. Makes it more interesting—'

Only problem was that Kalder had shown up today. Fuck Kalder. He wanted this girl somehow.

'Remember you're flying out of here with Tony Maurelli first thing on Monday morning. Got that?' Kalder ordered. The Canon Sammy Davis Memorial Open was starting in Hartford, Connecticut on Thursday. He wanted Rafael there on Tuesday for two days' practice. It was time for the number one golfer in his stable to win another ranking tournament. Sponsors were getting edgy.

'Donny tells me you've been behaving yourself here,' Kalder said, tucking into his grilled steak. 'So how come you're shooting in the mid-seventies?'

Escudio gave a Latin shrug of his shoulders. Funny they can never throw the habit, Kalder thought. A Mex is a Mex however much money the bastard earns. 'I no like the rain and the wind—', Rafael began.

'It wasn't raining today and you shot a seventy-four,' the manager growled. 'Your mind must be somewhere else.'

Rafael shrugged again, let that one pass. He knew that Kalder was angry with him. Had he won the

249

Open again, there would have been rich pickings. But he did not owe this guy anything. Sure, Kalder had taken him under his wing when he was a nobody, struggling to make it into golf's big time. On his way to superstardom his manager had taught him how to behave, what fork to use. But Kirk Kalder had made a good living out of him in the eight years they had been together.

'You've got to take care, Rafael. It's getting tougher on the tour now, with all those college kids coming through. There's a lot of competition—and if you don't watch it you'll burn yourself out—' Kalder took a sip of wine—'end up back in that shack in San Fermin.'

Get lost, Kalder. You always bring that up to frighten the shit out of me. That and AIDS. Rafael fought to control the anger building up in him, just as he had had to learn to control his temper on the golf course. His skill on the tour had lifted him from an overcrowded, dirt-floor shack in San Fermin to millionaire class and there was no way he was going back there. And women . . . he'd had his first girl at 12; Trudy the American teenager who had come across to Tijuana for a weekend with her parents, looking for excitement. There had been a lot more women since then—far too many to count. He made big money now and he was going to enjoy it, not like a lot of the robots on the tour. Like his pal Tony who spends more time standing on his head in the bathroom than he does in bed with his sexy wife. Escudio reckoned that was an awful waste of hot talent.

'Don't worry, Kirk. I win again soon. You see.'

'Better make it sooner than later, kid. Your price is going down. I'm being pushed by the sponsors.'

'They think I'm finished, washed up?' Escudio's eyes flashed in anger.

'Hell no, Rafael. You're not thirty years of age yet. You've got another ten years at the top at least—if you look after yourself.'

Rafael grinned. 'That's what I like to hear you say, Kirk. And you tell those asshole sponsors—'

He broke off, staring over his manager's shoulder. The girl had arrived! She was standing in the entrance to the dining-room, looking around for him. Christ! the fool of a Scotsman had sent her in without warning! He saw her say something to a waiter, who then pointed in their direction. She looked over but stayed where she was. Escudio breathed a sigh of relief. Maybe he could get away with it.

Too late! Kirk Kalder had caught him staring and was following his gaze. Jesus Christ, the manager groaned inwardly. Not another one! Does this guy ever get to sleep? Aloud he said: 'Okay, Rafael. Who's your friend?'

'A girl . . .'

'I can see that. Don't try to tell me she's your new caddie.'

'No, no. She drive one of the courtesy cars. She take me on a little drive tonight, show me the sights—'

'Like hell she will.' Kalder threw down his table napkin.' I'm getting rid of her right now!' He half rose.

Escudio grabbed his manager by the forearm. Kalder could feel the strength in the grip. 'No, Kirk.

You don't interfere. Sit down.' They stared into each other's eyes across the table. Kalder sat down slowly.

'That's better.' Escudio smiled, trying to ease the tension between them. He glanced across at the girl. She was still waiting.

'What do you know about her?' the manager asked tersely.

'Her name is Elaine. She is a nice girl—'

'How the hell do you know? You don't care. She could be a whore, give you the clap—' He banged his fist on the table, but not hard enough for the other diners to hear. 'Good God, Rafael. This is Turnberry. You're playing in the fucking British Open!'

'So?'

'Do you know what you're doing? What you're putting at risk?'

'I go for a drink with Elaine.' A flash of the white teeth. 'And tomorrow I shoot a sixty-six. You wait and see, Kirk.' He rose, eyes focused on the girl.

Kirk Kalder watched him wend his way through the tables, saw him take the girl's arm. 'Like hell you will,' he muttered under his breath.

Rafael guided the girl away from the dining-room, towards the foyer. 'I'm so pleased you come—'

'Forget it.' Her voice was cold like her eyes. 'I'm here only because Mr McBain ordered me.'

'You like a drink first?'

She stopped, faced him. 'No. I'm not staying. I have to go—' For the first time Rafael noticed she was wearing a jumper and slacks under her coat, not what he would have thought appropriate for a romantic evening. 'What you mean, you not stay—'

'I can't. I have to drive back to Glasgow tonight.

My mother phoned to say my son, Jamie, is ill. It will have to be tomorrow night.'

She was moving away, but he stopped her, grabbed her arm roughly. 'I don't believe you. You have no son—'

'Let me go!' She tried to pull away but his grip was firm.

'You come with me or else I tell McBain.' The bastard had taken his money and now the chica was running out on him.

'I don't care. I'm telling you the truth. I have to go to see Jamie—' Her eyes were blazing and she again tried to break free.

People were beginning to stare. He could not afford to make a scene. Escudio put his face close to hers. 'You come tomorrow night. Or else I get you fired. Okay?'

'Yes.' He was not sure if she meant it. He released her arm and she ran to the swing doors and out into the dusk. Escudio swore softly to himself. A few minutes ago he had been looking forward to a long night, easing that ache in his groin. Now it was getting worse by the minute. He was going to phone McBain but decided against it. What he needed right now was a woman—even one to talk to. Rafael headed for the bar to see who was available.

Leonard Morgan stared into the half-light seeping through the minuscule windows of the mobile home. Something—or someone—had woken him from an uneasy sleep. A movement outside. . . .

Yes, there it was again. Somebody moving around, whispering. An early morning couple passing on their way through the site, perhaps? Leonard sat up, glanced at his watch: 3.25 a.m. Christ, didn't they have any consideration for someone with a chance of winning the Open? He had only just been able to get to sleep.

Beside him Liz stirred. The bed that converted into a couch during the day barely accommodated two adults and any movement invariably caused wakefulness. 'Something wrong?' Her voice was drowsy with sleep.

'I heard something. Somebody moving about and whispering.' He listened but there was no further sound.

'Try to get some sleep, Leonard.'

What the hell do you think I've been trying to do for the last four hours, Leonard almost blurted out. A loud banging on the door brought him wide awake.

'Morgan ... Leonard Morgan—' more banging on the thin panels. 'Open up. Police!'

Leonard pushed back the sheets and jumped out of bed. It was a warm night and he was only wearing shorts. 'Who is it? What do you want?'

'I told you—Police. Open up. We want to ask you some questions.' The voice was gruff.

'Do you realise what time it is? Can't it wait until morning?'

'No!' The door panel shook again. 'We have a search warrant. Open up or we'll break it down.'

The police! What on earth—Tynan, that was it! Enraged at being turned down, he must have tipped off the police, probably with an anonymous phone call. Now they had come checking.

'For God's sake open up, Leonard, or they'll smash it down.' Liz had flicked on the bedside light and was sitting up, a sheet pulled up to her chin to hide her nakedness.

Leonard turned the key, slid back the bolt. He was thrown backwards as the door was pushed open violently and two men barged their way in, moving swiftly into the interior before he could stop them.

'What the hell—' Leonard recovered his balance, stepped forward. The other two seemed to fill the interior and there was very little room to move. He noticed that neither of the men was wearing a uniform and that one had a very crooked nose. 'What's this all about?'

'Shut up!'

'What have we got here, then?' The one with the crooked nose reached over, gave the sheet a jerk. Liz cried out, trying to cover her exposed breasts with her arms.

'Lovely.' Broken Nose's companion leered.

'You bastard'—Leonard tried to reach forward but was pushed back roughly.

'Careful, mate. It wouldn't do for you to get hurt right now, would it? I mean not with you going to win the Open tomorrow and all that.' He laughed.

'Who the hell are you? You're not police—'

'That's right, Lenny boy. They're not cops.'

The voice was familiar. Leonard spun around. Stan Tynan had just stepped inside. He too was grinning. 'Sorry for the late call.' He closed the door behind him.

There was a silence in the confined space. Tynan's eyes roved over the mobile home, coming to rest on

Liz. She pulled the sheet up around herself. The two heavies seemed to be waiting for instructions.

Leonard tried to keep the fear out of his voice. 'Hello, Stan. What is it you want?'

'Oh, prepared to talk now, are we?' The big man's voice lost its pleasantness and became harsh. 'Pity that wasn't your attitude a few days ago. It might have saved you this.'

'Okay, Stan. I'll play ball. Do whatever it is you want—'

'Leonard, do you realise what you're saying,' Liz burst out. 'You don't want to have anything to do with drugs, with this creep.' She turned, looked up at Tynan. 'Why don't you get out of here? Leave us alone—'

'Quiet, Liz.' Leonard sat down beside her on the bed. These thugs meant business. Better not to antagonise them.

'Don't worry, Miss. We're going. But first the boys are going to teach your Lenny a lesson—'

Tynan's laugh sent a chill down her spine. My God, Liz thought, they're going to do something to Leonard, make sure he would not be able to play tomorrow! She wanted to do something, scream maybe, but she was afraid they would silence her quickly. Instead, she watched Stan Tynan push his way between the two heavies to where Leonard's golf clubs were standing in the far corner.

'See you brought your gear home with you for safe keeping, Lenny. Good thinking. Without your favourite clubs, you'd be struggling again. That right?'

Leonard's jaw tightened. He had an idea what

Tynan had in mind. He watched as the latter straightened up the heavy golf bag, fondling the club heads peeping over the rim.

'Either of you boys ever play golf?' Tynan asked.

The duo shook their heads. 'One of you like to try?' The two exchanged glances, puzzled.

'Here, Benny.' Tynan took out Leonard's putter. 'You look like you could hole a few long putts—just like Lenny done over the past few days.' He passed the club over to Broken Nose. 'But be careful out there . . . it's dark. Don't hit a rock or anything with that valuable club.' He grinned. 'Know what I mean?'

Broken Nose took the putter, laughed. 'Sure thing, boss. I'll be extra careful.'

He went out, closing the door behind him. There was a silence in the mobile home, broken only by the sound of Tynan flicking his lighter into life as he lit a cigarette. Then they heard it—the sound of something striking the stanchion outside. Once, twice, three times. Liz felt Leonard go tense beside her. She put a restraining hand on his arm.

A few seconds later Broken Nose entered. He held up the putter, the head of which was now at right angles to the shaft. He was grinning. 'Sorry, boss. I guess I'd never make a golfer.'

Tynan and the other heavy laughed at the joke. 'Here, let me see what you've done.' He took the club, examined it, laid it gently on the pillow beside Leonard. 'I'll be in touch with you later in the year, Lenny boy.'

He signalled to the two heavies to leave. Turning in the doorway he said: 'Best of luck today.' He closed the door behind him.

They both stared at the door for what seemed an age. Then Liz buried her head in his shoulder, sobbing. He patted her shoulder gently.

'Don't worry, baby,' Leonard said, 'I'll borrow a putter from one of the other pros tomorrow. Maybe even buy a new one.' The visit had taken less than fifteen minutes. In that short space of time Leonard Morgan knew his dream of becoming Open champion had all but disappeared.

At about the same time that Leonard Morgan's unwelcome visitors were departing, Martin Dignam was checking his watch and setting the timer on the bomb.

His watch showed 3.43 a.m. Perfect. By this time tomorrow afternoon he and Marie Kirk would have disembarked from the ferry at Larne on their way back to Belfast. He reckoned on stopping off in Northern Ireland at some hotel where the final stages of the British Open were being shown on television. That would be interesting.

Ever so carefully he inched the hands around the dial until they showed 3.40, glancing around nervously to make sure no security guard was approaching the eighteenth green just now. He was underneath the smallest of the five stands that ringed Turnberry's final green. Twelve hours from now it would be packed with spectators looking at the final stages of the championship. He could do what was necessary now; nobody would spot him unless they probed right underneath the dark recess.

A short while earlier he had driven down the track

towards the beach, just as he had done the previous night, parked the car and walked along the beach. He had a bit of difficulty finding the pathway that lead into the area of scrub and gorse where he had buried the tin box. He panicked a little before he eventually found the spot. With it safely tucked under his arm he had made his way through the mounds of gorse and scrub, avoiding the open beach on his left for fear of being spotted.

He was already attired in the Olympic Security uniform. Dignam reckoned that if he were stopped by anyone, he would bluff his way out by telling them he had found the bomb on the course. He scrambled up a steep bank and a few seconds later was on the golf course proper. Across in the distance he could see the arc lights of the tented village; also in the distance the whiteness of the Turnberry Hotel was visible. He knew he would have to hurry; it would be getting light soon.

He had planned his route beforehand from the map of the course which he had purchased a few days ago. He had surfaced at the fourth tee and now made his way past the third green, keeping the boundary of the course on his right. In the semi-darkness he walked on briskly towards the second tee. When he reached there he veered left, making his way up between the first and second fairways, avoiding the clubhouse area. The ground was rough and he had to go carefully.

He had gone about a hundred yards and was abreast of the three small bunkers on the right of the first fairway when he saw the lights of the patrol buggy coming towards him. Dignam bent quickly and placed the biscuit box in the rough, then stepped out on to the smoother turn of the first fairway. The headlights of the buggy picked him up.

'Hullo there.' The voice had a distinct Scottish burr.

'Hullo.' He could make out only the outline of the driver behind the glare.

'Everything all right down below?'

'Aye. I've just checked along the boundary out as far as the fourth tee. No problems.'

'Good. Let's hope it stays that way. Have ye had a break yet?'

'No.'

'Away with ye then and get something to eat.'

'I'm on my way. See you.'

'See you.' The headlights swung around in an arc and the buggy headed back down the fairway. Dignam waited a few moments, then retraced his steps into the rough grass and retrieved the tin box. He could make out other lights bobbing about on the course, but they were all a distance away and he was not worried.

A short while later he was in the shadow of the largest stand at the eighteenth green. That had been the most dangerous part of the operation so far. He had had to make his way down towards the club-house area to get to the smaller stand. Despite the danger, he grinned to himself—they had given him five choices of where to plant the bomb!

Dignam could hear voices drifting his way from the tented village. It was now or never; the first streaks of dawn were beginning to show. He gave one last look around before moving swiftly beneath the steel and wood structure. Bending low, he made his way under the scaffolding until he was at the point where it met the turf.

Here the earth was soft and clammy. Dignam got down on his knees, placed the box aside and took out a short, squat steel spade, the type used by campers, from inside his tunic. He began to dig. Despite the damp chill of early morning, he could feel beads of perspiration forming on his forehead.

He had the hole he wanted dug within the space of minutes, glancing over his shoulder into the darkness, fearing a shout from someone asking him what the hell he was up to. It did not come. He checked that he had set the timer for 3.40, almost twelve hours away, checked that the device was primed. It was spot on. Placing the lid back on the box, he filled the area around it with earth and dead fern. When he was finished, he reckoned it would be difficult for anyone at first glance to tell that a hole had been dug there.

Stuffing the spade back inside his heavy navy sweater, he brushed the caked mud from this trousers. Upright now, he made his way out from under the stand. Just in time—a couple of security men were making their way across from the tented village. They passed within twenty yards of Dignam and waved to him. He returned their greeting and watched them tramp away towards the far end of the golf course.

Torch in hand, he walked briskly across the damp grass in the direction of the fourth tee. Less than twenty minutes later he was back in his car and had changed his clothes. As he drove back to the guesthouse he could see the red glow in the sky, heralding the dawn.

Dignam allowed himself a smile. It looked as if it was going to be a very good day.

7

SUNDAY, 19 JULY

Marie Kirk came out of the bathroom and began to dress. She was puzzled; while under the hot shower she had listened to the early morning news on the radio, anxious to hear how the media would treat the story of the war memorial being blown up. It would surely get prominence in the newscast. She was very surprised when the news highlights finished and it was not even mentioned.

Of course the events at Turnberry did get prominence, but only the fact that there was a three-way tie for the lead between American Dick Elliott, England hope Sam Joyce and young Irishman Colm Donohue. But there was no mention of a terrorist bomb having gone off on the course during the night.

As she dressed, Marie glanced at Dignam, still asleep on the couch. What had happened? Had something gone wrong? She had been awake when he had left for Turnberry in the early hours to plant the bomb. He obviously had not carried out those instructions. Why had it not gone off? Had Dignam changed the plan after all? She was tempted to shake him awake and find out. It would do no good. He would tell her when it suited him.

Marie went downstairs. In the sunlit dining-room a couple of guests were having breakfast. They looked up, bid her a pleasant 'good morning', then went on with their meal. Marie strolled out into the tiny foyer and touched the bell at reception. She just had to know if anything had happened. Within a few seconds Mrs Carlyle came out of the family's living quarters.

'Good morning, Mrs Carlyle.'

'Morning—and a beautiful one it is too.'

Marie waited, the landlady looking at her expectantly. No mention of a bomb blast up the road in Turnberry. She said: 'We'll be checking out immediately after breakfast, Mrs Carlyle. Perhaps you might have the bill ready.'

'Of course. I hadn't forgotten. You'll be wanting your breakfast soon. Moving on up into the Highlands, your husband said—' When Marie nodded, Mrs Carlyle went on: 'But you'll stay long enough to see the finish of the Open, I'm sure. Wouldn't it be something if I could boast after today that the British Open champion once stayed here.'

Just then Colm Donohue entered the guesthouse. He was dressed in a track suit and looked as if he had been out jogging. He smiled a greeting and went upstairs without speaking. When he was out of sight, Mrs Carlyle said: 'I don't think that young man got much sleep last night. Their room is directly over ours and I heard a lot of movement during the night. And he was up and out at six-thirty this morning for a run. I only hope the lad can eat his breakfast—'

Marie went back upstairs. Dignam was in the bathroom, shaving. She could hear the whirr of his electric razor. She crossed the room and flung open the bathroom door. He was wearing only a pair of briefs.

His eyes shifted from the mirror to her. 'Hey, I didn't hear you knock—'

'The bomb. It didn't go off.' He continued shaving. 'Martin, the monument—it's still there. What happened?'

'Nothing.' He switched the razor off and studied his face carefully in the mirror, ignoring her.

'Martin, we're in this together. I want to know—'

He turned, grinning. 'Like you said, Marie, the bomb didn't go off. Not yet.'

'What are you playing at? You know the orders—the monument was to be blown up during the night—'

'So I've changed things round a bit. From now on we do things my way. Okay?'

My God, what did he mean? She wanted to scream at him, but she knew that would be a crazy thing to do. Instead, she would have to remain calm and let him think she was going along with his plan, whatever it was.

'All right, Martin. We'll do it your way, if that's what you want.' She turned and walked back into the other room, saying casually: 'Where is the bomb, anyway?'

He followed her out, blowing into the razor head to clear it. 'Maybe there is no bomb now. Maybe I've gone soft, lost my nerve—like your brother Patrick did when we were on that bank job together.'

The remark about her dead brother stung Marie but she ignored it. There was more important business to attend to. 'Dominick Earley won't like it if his orders are disobeyed—'

'Fuck Earley.'

'He'll know by now the monument hasn't been blown up. Shouldn't you tell him why—'

He grabbed her roughly by the arm. 'We're telling that bastard Earley nothing. Understand?' She nodded. 'Let him find out for himself.'

He released her and pulled on a T-shirt. 'Now let's get down and have some breakfast. Then we'll pay the bill and get out of here.'

On the way downstairs, she made up her mind to ring Stephen. Why had she not thought of phoning him earlier? He too would now know that the war memorial was still standing and would be wondering what was happening. She prayed he would not phone the guesthouse and ask for her. That would make Dignam suspicious. She would find some excuse to slip away and phone.

Halfway through the breakfast, she rose and said she was going to the toilet. There was a public telephone in the alcove off the foyer, out of sight of the dining-room. Fortunately it was free. She breathed a sigh of relief when she was put through to Stephen without undue delay.

'Stephen, thank God—'

'Marie, what the hell's happened? The monument—'

'I know, I know. Listen carefully, Stephen, I haven't much time.' She glanced round. There was no one within earshot. 'Dignam has changed the plan—'

'What's he up to now?'

'I don't know. Either he's not going through with it, which is unlikely, or else the bomb is timed to go off under the monument during the tournament!'

266

'Jesus! he must be mad! What shall we do?'

'You'll have to phone the police. Make an anonymous phone call. Tell them there's a bomb there—' Marie glanced at her watch. 'It's not yet nine o'clock. Play is not due to begin for another hour. There should be no spectators near the monument for at least the next two hours and by then the police should have found the bomb—'

'Will I say it's the IRA?'

'No! If you do, they'll block the Larne ferry. You don't have a Northern Ireland accent. They'll suspect a crank call, but they'll search anyway.'

'What about you?'

'I'll be all right. Hurry, Stephen!'

She went back into the dining-room. Her heart was pounding but she made an effort to put on an air of calm. They were finishing their breakfast when Mr Carlyle came in and told Dignam there was a phone call for him at reception.

'Did the caller give his name?'

The proprietor shook his head. 'No. Just said it was very urgent.'

Dignam's eyes flickered to Marie. When he spoke, his tone was friendly. 'Will you do us a favour, Mr Carlyle? Tell whoever it is that my wife and I are not here right now—that we checked out a short while ago.'

If Mr Carlyle was surprised at the request, he did not show it. He smiled and said: 'Right-o. If that's what you want.' He had always suspected that there was something not quite genuine about these two, that they were not really man and wife. It was probably the girl's husband on the phone. Still, it was not his business.

Dignam watched him go. 'I bet that was Earley on the phone, wondering what the hell was going on.' He gave a short laugh. 'He'll know soon enough.'

Marie kept silent. Twenty minutes later they paid the bill. In the foyer Marie said goodbye to Joan and the children, who were just going into breakfast.

'Colm is in bed,' she said. 'Sleeping at last. He didn't get much rest last night.'

'Good luck to both of you. I hope he wins. I'll be watching out for you in the stand at the eighteenth.' Joan came to the entrance and waved them goodbye.

The traffic was heavy as they drove towards Turnberry. Even in the car Marie could sense the excitement in the air. It was a beautiful, clear morning and crowds on foot lined both sides of the roadway as they neared the course . At the entrance to the Turnberry Hotel, a couple of policemen were on duty, trying to keep the traffic flowing. The hotel itself looked white and magnificent against the blue skyline.

'Blast!' Dignam exploded as once again the line of traffic came to a halt. He looked at his watch. They were in plenty of time for the 12.30 sailing from Stranraer, he had made sure of that, but the sooner they were out of Turnberry, the better he would like it.

Once past the entrance to the course, the traffic eased. Dignam relaxed noticeably, even began humming to himself as he drove up the slight incline out of the town on the road to Girvan and the ferry port. He drove on for a while, then eased the car on to the grass verge, almost opposite the spot where earlier in the week they had stopped to catch their first real sight of the golf course.

'Why are we stopping here?'

Dignam looked sideways at her and grinned. 'You want to know where I've planted the bomb?' He got out of the car. 'Come on.'

Marie joined him at his side of the vehicle, wondering what she was going to hear next. He took her by the arm, waited for a gap in the traffic which was almost bumper to bumper going the other way, then moved to the other side of the road. From their elevated position they could see part of the eighteenth green of the Ailsa, hidden from view almost completely by the five temporary stands around it. Even at this early hour the stands were beginning to fill up.

'Magnificent, isn't it? Dignam surveyed the scene, hands dug into his leather jacket.

'Yes.'

'It's ten thirty-five now. Just think, in a little over five hours from now—boom!' He clapped his hands together and laughed.

Thank God they could not see the war memorial from here. It would be cordoned off if there was a bomb scare. Dignam might have become suspicious.

'It wasn't such a bad memorial,' Marie said.

'Yeah. But who's interested in blowing up a fucking memorial. Not me, baby.'

The words chilled her heart. Dignam had made it clear all along that he considered the memorial a useless assignment. But what was his alternative? She had to play it cool.

'So where did you plant the bomb?' she asked

casually.

He laughed again. 'Where it will do some real damage. Can't you guess?' Marie followed his gaze. He was looking towards the only part of the course that was in view from where they stood ... the stands around the eighteenth green. Surely not under one of those!

'Which one?' She had to steel herself to ask the question.

'That small one facing directly down the fairway. See—' he pointed.

Oh God, she was sure that was the one in which Joan and the other woman, Susan Elliott, had reserved seats. Soon they would take their places, watching together as their husbands came down the eighteenth fairway in the late afternoon.

She whirled round. 'Martin, you can't do it—'

'Why the hell not? We'll be safely back in Northern Ireland before it happens.'

'It's murder. You're going to kill hundreds of innocent people—'

'So what?' His voice was harsh and his eyes wild. 'People get killed all the time in Northern Ireland and nobody cares.'

'But blowing innocent people to bits won't help—'

'Think of the headlines, the publicity we'll get all around the world.'

Marie knew there was no use arguing. She would have to find another way. Dignam was crazy, a psychopath. He enjoyed killing people. He had even planned to watch the horrible thing on television when they were safely in Northern Ireland after the short ferry crossing. Dignam had to be stopped somehow.

'Martin, you can't—I won't let you—'

He came closer, grabbed her roughly by the arm and pulled her to him. Car drivers on the slow descent to Turnberry looked out in mild surprise at a couple having what looked like a tiff. They kept crawling forward.

'You know your problem, Marie?' he hissed. 'You're scared. Like your brother.' His face came close to hers. 'He didn't want to shoot it out with the RUC during the bank raid. He wanted to run for it. I told him if he did, I'd shoot him myself.'

The coldness of the words shocked her. 'So that's how Patrick got killed—'

'Yeah. And I'd like to think that the bullet that killed him came from a policeman's gun. Know what I mean Marie?' He was forcing her towards the roadway. 'Come on. We're wasting time.'

They crossed the road to the car, Dignam forcing his way between the vehicles, his hand gripping her arm. Marie's mind was in a daze, shocked by what she had learned in the past few minutes. But she knew she would have to remain calm. Dignam must be foiled at any cost.

She would have to get to a telephone and alert Stephen. Again the question was how? It was little more than an hour's drive to Stranraer and the ferry. She would get Dignam to stop for something in Girvan. A drink, maybe. She had to get to a telephone.

Back in Turnberry, Susan Elliott was staring at the

centre-page spread of a Sunday tabloid. It lay on the floor of the living-room where Richard had flung it a few moments ago before storming angrily out of the house. The caption over one of the pictures of her was in bold print: 'The Vamp of the Ramp' . . . a figment of some caption writer's fertile imagination.

The editorial boys had certainly gone to town with David Megson's pictures. Pride of place in the layout was a full-length shot of her modelling a skimpy beach outfit. The slit sarong showed a provocative length of leg and had over it a caption equal to the occasion. She had not realised on the ramp just how low-cut that shimmering cocktail dress had been; Megson had somehow contrived to get an elevated shot that accentuated her svelte figure but that showed an excess of bosom. At one time she would have been thrilled to have been given that kind of space in a newspaper. But not now; not today.

Her eyes raced over the story under the pictures again: 'While husband Dick endeavours to overcome a hoodoo and win the British Open, his wife Susan, bored by being on the sidelines for so long, decided to grab some headlines herself. Once rated the world's top model—she gave it all up to follow her husband around the fairways—Susan made a surprise return to the ramp during the week in Edinburgh at a fashion show staged especially for a group of wives of golfers playing in the Open.

'As David Megson's exclusive pictures show, Susan Elliott could regain that top spot should she ever decide to return permanently to the ramp. Now it's up to husband Dick to deliver the goods at Turnberry today.'

She had shown the tabloid spread to him at breakfast; better that way than to have someone ask him about it when he got to the course.

He had flung aside the paper after he had looked at the pictures. 'You never told me you were doing this.'

'I'm sorry, Richard. It wasn't planned. Felicity Jacob was in charge and asked me—'

'You could have said no, for God's sake.' He was very angry.

'I didn't realise the photographer was taking pictures until it was too late—'

'No, of course not.' He was being sarcastic.

'Don't you believe me?'

'No! What did you have to do to get a spread like that—sleep with the guy!'

She recoiled at the words. She could not believe that this was her husband talking. 'Is that what you really think?'

He faced her, eyes blazing. 'What the hell am I to think, Susan? I've suspected lately that you wanted to get back to work, that you're bored. You saw your opportunity to get publicity with Megson and took it—'

'Richard, that's just not true.' The tension must be getting to him. He had never talked to her like this before.

'No? Try telling that to our friends.' He had brushed past her. 'Oh, forget it, Susan. You've got what you wanted. Thanks for putting me in the right frame of mind for today.'

'Richard, wait—'

He turned at the door. 'I said forget it. Go talk to

your photographer friend.' He stormed out.

Susan went to go after him but changed her mind when she heard the door slam. She reckoned she needed a stiff drink. She knew it was no state of mind in which to send a husband out to win the British Open.

On the course, the first twosome, back markers Rafael Escudio and the Swede Arne Hargasson, had already teed off in their final round and were playing the third hole. Rafael had birdied the first two holes and was feeling pretty good, despite his disappointment with the chica last night. He had got that sorted out first thing this morning. Before going to the practice ground, he had buttonholed Ed McBain. The chief of Courtesy Cars had expressed surprise at the girl's last-minute cancellation of her date with Rafael and promised to put it right.

'Leave it to me. I'll sort her out. Either she does what I tell her or else she's fired.' The possibility of his having to return the £500 was hurting McBain badly.

He was back before it was time for Escudio to tee off, grinning broadly. 'Same time tonight. Same place.'

'No mistake this time, eh?'

'She'll be there. You have my word. She needs her job badly.'

Rafael hit a cracking four-iron second shot right into the heart of the third green. The crowd roared its approval. He waved and smiled. He always played well when he knew there was something to look forward to that night.

Outside the locker room, Colm Donohue was signing autographs before going in to change and head for the practice ground. In the last ten minutes he had given short interviews to British and American television stations and had chatted to a group of members from his own club who had flown in specially from Ireland that morning to give him support.

He had tried to appear calm and confident throughout, but really he felt terrible and wondered if he was going to be physically sick. Now he knew what pressure really was! A short distance away he could see Johnny Davis waiting with his clubs and a bag of balls. Maybe when he hit a few practice shots he would feel better. Donohue was about to enter the locker room when he heard his name being called. He turned to see Samantha Cruise approaching.

'Hello, Colm. Ready for your big day?'

He shrugged casually. 'Ready as I'll ever be.'

She studied his face. 'Are you feeling all right? I hate to say it, but you don't look great.'

'I didn't sleep too well last night. I'll be okay when I get out on the course. Waiting around is the problem. You wanted to see me about something?'

She hesitated. 'It can wait.' No sense in putting more pressure on him.

'Come on, Samantha. Out with it.' He could see his caddie growing impatient.

'All right. I know you haven't signed up with us yet, but Peter and Mark put out some feelers last night on your behalf. They reckon if you become Open champion today they can make you a million-aire. No problem.' He felt his stomach lurch as she

275

continued: 'There's an exhibition game lined up for the Open champion at Wentworth tomorrow at noon. You get paid twenty-five thousand pounds. We've provisionally hired a plane to fly us from Prestwick to London.' She paused. 'Maybe I shouldn't be telling you all this—'

Twenty-five thousand pounds! For just one day! That was half of what he had won all last year on the circuit. 'All I've got to do is go out there and win the Open.'

'You can do it.' Samantha looked around. 'Where's your wife?'

'Taking care of the kids. I've sent the car back to bring her to the course later.' Last night he had been told that he would have the use of a courtesy car. It was a luxury he had never enjoyed before.

She smiled. 'See, you're in the big-time already.' He noticed for the first time that she was in a pair of Bermuda shorts which did wonders for her figure. 'Good luck today. I'll be cheering for you.'

The locker room was almost deserted when he entered, save for a trio of attendants in blue smocks, one of whom carried his hold-all to a designated space. Most of the competitors were either on the course or on the practice ground. From his place in a corner he could hear Sam Joyce joking with one of the attendants. Donohue envied him his easy-going manner.

A couple of minutes later Sam Joyce popped his head around the corner of the line of lockers. 'Best of luck today, Colm.'

'Thanks, Sam.'

'Nervous?'

'A little.' Christ, what a lie. He felt nauseous. The last thing he wanted to do was play golf. His hands were sweating.

'Not to worry, everyone's a bit uptight. I hardly slept a wink last night. Ended up putting on the carpet at five a.m. Honest.'

Colm forced a grin. 'Thanks again, Sam. I appreciate that.' They shook hands and Joyce went outside.

When he had gone, Donohue felt a lot better. Hell, he was letting it all get to him. He would have to relax. If only his stomach would stop heaving. He should really not have had such a big breakfast. Colm knew if he could get sick, he would feel better.

Lou Menzies appeared around the end locker. 'How are you feeling, mate?'

'I'm fine, thanks.'

'You certainly don't look it. Bet you're shaking in your shoes right now, eh?' Menzies leaned casually on the locker and laughed, a hollow sound without mirth.

Colm continued lacing up his golf shoes. This obviously was not a courtesy call. 'I said I'm fine.'

The Australian stepped closer so that his voice would not have to carry. 'It'll get worse, mate. The pressure, I mean. Wait until you see those crowds out there. The cameras will be on you all the time—unless you blow it early, of course—'

'Shut up, Menzies!'

'—and when you have to make a short putt and you just know that you're going to miss. Your hands start shaking—'

'I said shut up!' Colm straightened up and took a step forward, his fists clenched. 'Clear off, you hear?'

The Aussie backed away.

'Sorry. Did I upset you, mate? Didn't mean to—' He paused at the end of the row and hissed: 'You've never been there before, cobber. I have. Remember I'm only one shot behind you. I'll be breathing down your bloody neck all day!'

Then he was gone. Colm felt dizzy. Nausea engulfed him and he knew he was going to be sick. He walked quickly down the locker room to the toilets, brushing past an attendant who said something he did not catch. Inside his spikes echoed on the tiled floor. He found an empty cubicle, and barely had time to lock the door before he threw up.

Five minutes later, feeling a lot better—Menzies unknowingly might have done him a big favour— Colm walked out of the toilet. This time he gave a muttered 'thanks' to the attendants when they wished him good luck.

'That goes for me too.' The tall athletic figure of Dick Elliott emerged from behind a row of lockers, his hand extended. They shook hands and his rival's warm smile made Colm feel even better.

Outside he found Johnny waiting for him. 'Are you all right, lad? You look like you just threw up.'

'I did, but I'm okay now.'

'Did something happen in there?' Johnny asked. They were walking towards the practice ground and people were stopping and staring, pointing him out. 'I saw Lou Menzies come out a few minutes ago', Johnny continued. 'He was looking pleased with himself.'

'He tried to get at me.'

'The bastard! I'll sort him out.'

'No you won't, Johnny. Forget it.'

'But he has no right to—'

'If you start a row now in front of everybody, you'll attract attention, put *more* pressure on me—'

'How do you feel now?' Johnny asked anxiously.

'A lot better now that I've got rid of that big breakfast!' the younger man grinned. 'Now let's get out there and hit some golf balls.'

Marie Kirk sighed with relief when Stephen answered the phone.

'Stephen, it's Marie—'

'Marie!' He sounded relieved. 'I'm glad you rang. There was no bomb under the war memorial. The police searched—'

'I know. Listen carefully. I haven't much time. There *is* a bomb. Dignam put it under one of the small stands at the eighteenth green, the one facing down the fairway—'

'Oh Jesus—' He stopped. 'He's mad, crazy—'

'Stephen,' Marie glanced around the corner of the bar of the hotel lounge in Girvan where she and Martin Dignam had stopped for a drink. Their table was still deserted. Dignam was in the gents' toilet and could come out any minute. He must not catch her on the phone.

'Yes?'

'You've got to get on to the police again. Alert them—'

'I'm sure they won't believe me. They'll think I'm a crank or something—'

'You'll have to convince them. They can't afford

to take a chance.' Marie glanced around nervously again. 'I've got to go, Stephen—'

'Wait! One last thing. What make of car is Dignam driving? And the colour?'

'It's a red Ford Sierra. Registration UCI 487.' She would have to put the phone down. Dignam might come out at any moment.

'Where are you phoning from?'

'Girvan. Goodbye, Stephen. I love you.'

'Marie, be careful. I love you, too—'

She replaced the receiver. As she was walking back to the table, the door of the gents opened and Martin Dignam came out. He looked at her suspiciously. 'Where've you been?'

'Having a look around. Stretching my legs.' That seemed to satisfy him.

'Come on. Let's finish up here. It's nearly eleven-thirty. I don't want to miss that ferry.'

Back at Turnberry, Sergeant Hugh Tomkins popped his head around the door of the Portacabin which the Strathclyde police were using as their headquarters at the Open. He addressed himself to Detective Inspector Alec Torsney, the man who was in overall charge of policing the event.

'That young man is on the telephone again, Inspector. The lad who was on earlier about the bomb—'

Torsney, fiftyish but with the body of a man who kept himself in shape, turned from the small window from which he had been scrutinising the huge crowd milling about outside. 'What does he want now, Sergeant?'

'He says there's another bomb—a real one this time—under the small stand at the eighteenth green.' The Sergeant coughed and cleared his throat. 'He sounded frightened.'

'Really?' Inspector Torsney sighed. 'The eighteenth green?' He turned and looked out of the window again. From where the Portacabin was situated, to the left of the first fairway and backing on to the Girvan road, he could see the back of the small stand. He knew that by now it would already be packed with spectators.

'What do you think, Sergeant? Another hoax?'

'You saw him. He didn't look like a nut case to me. Hoaxers don't volunteer themselves up to the police like he did.'

The Inspector pulled at his ear, a habit he had when he was thinking. What the Sergeant said was true. The young man did not look the type who got pleasure out of phoning in false alarms. He had appeared genuinely surprised when the sniffer dogs had not turned up anything.

And, yet, hardly any major sporting event went by without at least one bomb scare—usually phony. Still, no matter how many phone calls were received, they all had to be investigated. He could not take a chance.

'Where's he phoning from now, Sergeant?'

'His hotel. Says he's just got another phone call from his girlfriend. She and the bomber, Dignam, are supposed to be heading for the Stranraer ferry. This time he gave me the description of the car they're supposed to be driving. A red Ford Sierra. Want me to put out an alert for the car?'

'First tell that young fellow to get himself down here immediately.'

'Right, sir.' Torsney went back to the window. Earlier this morning, after Stephen Trafford had told them about his girlfriend who had turned informer, he had phoned the 'Seaview' guesthouse and had spoken to the proprietor.

Yes, of course Mrs Carlyle had remembered the couple. They had left only an hour ago. No, neither she nor her husband had noticed anything unusual about them. Of course, she had suspected all along that they were not really married, but surely that was not a crime? They had given an address in Northern Ireland, but she got lots of tourists from there.

Torsney looked across to the crowd lining the first fairway. As a golfer himself—a useful eight handicapper and a member at Turnberry—he was proud of the British Open. It was the greatest golf tournament in the world as far as he was concerned. And he was damned if a despicable organisation like the IRA was going to disrupt it.

If he cleared the stands at the eighteenth green, the world would see it on television and the IRA would gain enormous publicity from their stunt. There was no way he was going to let that happen— and he would take full responsibility for the consequences at any inquiry.

Besides, he was not entirely convinced that there was a bomb there.

'Sergeant!' When Tomkins came in from the outer office, Torsney said: 'Contact our men with the sniffer dogs and get them over here. Also the bomb disposal lads. Tell them to keep a low profile. We'll try not to alert the crowd that we're searching for a bomb. I don't want a stampede out of the stands in front of those television cameras. Besides, people could get injured.'

Tomkins hesitated. 'You're not clearing the stands then, sir?'

'No.' The Inspector's voice was firm.

'Right, sir.'

Torsney picked up the phone and dialled. 'I'm getting on to our divisional unit in Stranraer. They have a helicopter there, checking the traffic flow here. This time I'll get them to see if there's a red Ford Sierra, registration UCI 487, heading their way.'

Within seconds Torsney was talking to his colleague, Inspector Dan Renton, in Stranraer. 'Is your 'copter airborne, Dan?'

'Has been for the last couple of hours. There must be a record crowd at Turnberry today.'

'There is. Contact your helicopter and see if they can spot that Ford Sierra. If they do, ring me back immediately.'

'Leave it with me, Alec.'

Outside, in what he reckoned was the area of the fifteenth green, there was a loud roar. That would be the first twosome, Escudio and Hargasson. Despite the urgency of the situation, Torsney could not resist looking at the giant scoreboard near the clubhouse. He saw that Rafael Escudio was having a good day— four under par for his round. On the first tee Mañuel Luca and Bill Dwight were starting their last eighteen holes.

He saw a quartet of policemen in uniform alight from a van with two dogs in tow. He exited and went over to them. The two dogs were moving about restlessly, pink tongues lolling out.

'Men, I want this as low key as possible.' Torsney's Scots brogue was clipped, short. 'Those five stands are packed with spectators. I don't want any panic.'

'Which one is it, Inspector?'

Torsney nodded. 'That small one opposite. It's not like the war memorial where we saw that the ground had not been dug up. The workmen have mucked up everything under there—'

'Leave it to us.'

He watched the men and dogs move away. Several spectators in the immediate vicinity gave curious glances, but kept on moving, drawn by the cheers nearby.

Sergeant Tomkins approached. 'I didn't bring too many of our own men, Inspector. Just enough for a presence.'

'Good. Where are the bomb disposal lads?'

'In the van. I told them to stay out of sight.'

Torsney walked over to where he had a clear view of the eighteenth green. In the bright sunshine, thousands of golf fans were seated on the tiered wooden structures in the stands, awaiting the two-somes who would soon begin to finish their final round on the undulating green sward below. It was a colourful scene, the men in tee shirts, sun hats and visors, shading their eyes; the women in slacks and shorts, some with floppy hats.

Torsney recognised Susan Elliott from her pictures in the morning newspaper. She was seated near the front and was chatting animatedly to a young woman. He bit his lip in anxiety. Christ, if things went wrong, he would be for it. The media would crucify him! He saw Tomkins moving swiftly over, with Stephen Trafford in tow.

Tomkins said: 'They've found it, sir. In a tin box!'

The Inspector's expression did not change. 'Right. Get the dogs back in the van and let the other lads have a look!' As Tomkins hurried off, he turned to Stephen Trafford. 'Come over here, lad. I want a word with you.'

They were moving away when a policeman with a mobile phone approached. 'You're wanted on the phone, sir. Inspector Renton in Stranraer.'

Torsney took the phone piece. 'Hello Dan. Torsney here.'

'Alec,' Renton's voice was controlled, business-like, 'we've spotted your man. He's about fifteen miles from Stranraer. Should be there in about twenty minutes. The girl is in the car with him.'

'And we've located the bomb. Right under the stand.'

He heard Renton swear under his breath. 'Great work, Alec. You've got everything under control, then?'

'Aye.' Torsney hoped he was not being too premature. As he spoke, he could see a couple of men in khaki uniforms disappear under the stand. One of them was carrying a long, slim steel box of a type used by handymen. 'How are you going to handle your end, Dan?'

The other's mirthless laugh came over the phone. 'I've already alerted our anti-terrorist squad here in Stranraer. We'll be ready for them.'

'A shoot-out?'

'I hope that IRA bastard is stupid enough to want one.' The line went dead.

Inspector Torsney handed the instrument back to the constable. He had almost forgotten about Stephen Trafford.

'What was that about a shoot-out?' Stephen asked.

'You heard. That's the way it's shaping up.'

'But Marie is in that car—' Stephen said, aghast.

Torsney sighed. 'Sorry, laddie. It's out of my hands now.'

Stephen faced the older man, his hands clenched, desperation in his voice: 'But they can't shoot Marie. She's not a terrorist—'

Torsney shrugged. 'I'm sure they'll do what they can.' Personally he didn't hold out much hope.

The Inspector was pacing up and down when, five minutes later, one of the soldiers came from under the stand. There was mud on the knee of his khaki outfit.

'Everything under control?' the Inspector asked.

'Aye. Shouldn't take long. Maybe twenty minutes.' He looked around. 'Why aren't those stands cleared? It's regulations.'

'Forget the regulations. There's no way the Open is being halted.' Torsney was taking a chance and he knew it. He would face the music tomorrow when it was all over.

Dignam heard the roar of the helicopter, took his eyes momentarily off the road to see it wheeling away, and said: 'I don't like it.'

'What's wrong?' Marie asked, as casually as she could.

'That bastard buzzing around up there. What the hell is he at?'

'Monitoring the traffic flow, I expect.'

'Like fuck he is! That's the third time he's come down for a look. I don't like it.'

Marie prayed silently that the helicopter would go away. Dignam was edgy. A couple of times she had noticed him patting the bulge under his leather jacket where the gun was, as though reassuring himself that it was still there.

A sign flashed by: Stranraer 15 kms. They would be there soon. She thought of Stephen, wondering if he had been able to convince the police about the bomb. The helicopter hovering overhead surely meant that he had. Her heart was thumping madly. What would happen when they arrived at the ferryport? In the distance across the firth she could see the town with the Larne ferry docked and waiting. Less than ten minutes later they were in the outskirts of the town. The helicopter was no longer with them.

Dignam slowed down, waited for an oncoming vehicle to pass, then made a right turn into the ferryport. He could see rows of container trucks and cars in the distance already lined up, ready to drive on. He was all set to join the queue when a man in a Sealink uniform waved them to a halt.

Dignam rolled down the window, 'Something wrong?'

'A slight delay in loading, sir. We're letting the trucks on first and requesting car drivers like yourself to form a line over on that side of the ferryport.' The

Sealink man pointed.

Dignam looked at the vast empty space into which he was being directed. 'That line of cars over there seems to be moving—'

'Yes, I know, sir. But would you please facilitate our loading procedures. Thank you for your help.'

Dignam slowly wound up the window. There was something wrong. He moved the car slowly forward, its wheels moving noiselessly over the tarmac. In the rear-view mirror he saw the man in the Sealink uniform staring after them.

Marie tensed. Something was going to happen; she could feel it in the air. Her throat felt dry and she wanted to scream to relieve the tension.

Then it began. Suddenly there was a screech of tyres on the tarmac and about thirty yards ahead two sleek, dark-blue cars shot out from behind a row of empty container trucks. The second car jerked to a halt past the first, blocking Dignam's way completely. The doors burst open and men with guns at the ready jumped out into the bright sunlight.

Dignam's trained mind reacted immediately. Before the first of the men was clear of his vehicle, he jammed his foot down on the accelerator and made a screeching U-turn. The car shot back towards the exit. Three of the men who had jumped from the police cars dropped to their knees and let off a volley of shots from their pistols and Uzi machine guns.

Marie heard the shots thudding into the car's metalwork. The back windscreen shattered. She screamed.

'Get your head down!' Dignam shouted. He was crouching down behind the wheel, driving at breakneck speed towards the exit of the ferryport.

Too late! Two Landrovers were moving into place, blocking both the entrance and the exit gates. Dignam swore, clawed at the wheel again and gunned the car to the right towards the lines of parked cars and container trucks which had been waiting to drive on to the ferry. Several people jumped from the path of the speeding car, their frightened faces passing in a blur.

Marie could see the two police cars speeding across the tarmac in pursuit, one heading directly after them, while the other sped towards the top end of the line of cars and trucks. The trio of men who had fired the first shots were now running across the tarmac also, shouting to people to keep out of sight.

Dignam knew they had him cut off. He reached inside his jacket for the revolver. He would show that fucker Earley and the whole world what the IRA was made of!

'Martin, give up. Please. We'll be killed—' Behind her another bullet came through the windscreen, showering them both with glass.

'Shut up, you cowardly bitch! The bastards won't take me alive!'

A group of truckers dived for cover under their vehicles as the Sierra sped down the line, pursued by another car from which a man was leaning, firing shots. Families in motor cars cowered with their children under the seats.

Ahead the police car screeched to a sideways halt. A couple of men jumped out on the far side of the vehicle and began firing shots. The Ford's front windscreen exploded in a shower of fragments and

Marie felt the car swerve crazily. Bent over double in her seat, she wondered if Dignam had been hit. He was crouched over the wheel, steering with one hand, the gun in the other. His eyes were wild, not with fear, but with excitement.

They were almost on top of the stationary police car now and she was bracing herself for the crash. Dignam pulled at the steering wheel and the Ford veered to the right, smashing into the rear of the police car and slewing it around so that the men behind it had to jump for their lives. Marie screamed with pain as she was thrown forward against the front panel.

There was another burst of fire and the Ford skidded crazily. The two back tyres had been hit. Dignam turned the car to the right around the line of trucks, past the gangplank and the gaping hole of the ship's loading bay. But their speed had gone and the second police car was almost on them.

The time had arrived and Dignam knew it. He slammed down his foot on the brake pedal and the car jolted to a halt. 'Okay, you fucking bastards, come and get me,' he screamed. His voice was hoarse and Marie noticed that he had a wound in the neck.

She flung open her door, tumbled out and hit the concrete hard. Behind her she could hear Dignam opening his door and letting off shots. Luckily the Ford had slewed around so that the car was between her and the policemen, who were now pumping bullets towards their target. Marie shut her eyes and rolled her body across the few yards of tarmac until she was under the chassis of a big container truck. She lay there, curled up, whimpering with fright. She opened her eyes only when the firing had stopped.

She could see feet surrounding the Ford, and hear voices barking orders. The container truck was high enough for her to get to her knees and she crawled out on all fours into the sunlight.

'There's the girl!'

Marie put her hands into the air. 'Don't shoot, please,' she screamed hysterically. She was pulled roughly to her feet and told to face the side of the container truck with her hands held high against it. Someone was shouting orders, telling his officers to keep the crowd of onlookers back. She glanced over her shoulder. The Ford's two front doors were open and she could see Martin Dignam slumped sideways in the driver's seat, one leg out on the tarmac. His revolver was on the tarmac also. One side of his face had been blown away and there was blood all over his leather jacket.

Marie quickly turned her head away, nauseated.

At Turnberry the sun beat down relentlessly from a clear blue sky, the low scoring reflecting the ideal conditions. The bush telegraph was buzzing with news of early starters playing extremely well and it sent hordes of spectators scampering across fairways. The stewards were having a hard time trying to control the crowds as excitement mounted.

'On the first tee, co-leaders Colm Donohue from Ireland and Richard Elliott of the United States. This is the final partnership of the day. Quiet, please!' A hush settled after the official starter's command.

Donohue and Elliott shook hands. The latter had won the toss and elected to drive off first. The Irishman looked at his watch: 1.15 p.m. As he studied the American, he could sense the tension of the spectators.

A burst of applause greeted the American's perfect three-wood tee shot to the middle of the fairway. Donohue turned to select a club, also a three wood. 'Good luck, lad. Remember—swing slowly,' Johnny whispered.

Then he was standing over his ball, ready to drive off. He got the proper arc, made good contact, and as his head came around on the follow-through he saw the ball soar into the sky, curve, bounce along the middle of the fairway and come to rest a few yards behind Dick Elliott's. More applause. As he walked down the fairway, lined on both sides with spectators, Colm reckoned that it would take a 68 or better today if he or Elliott were to win the Open. Some good early scores had already been posted, with Rafael Escudio the best of the day so far with a 66.

In the BBC commentary box, from where he had magnificent views of both the first and eighteenth fairways, Malcolm Jacob was welcoming viewers to the final day's play. 'As you've heard on the news, there has been an IRA attempt to disrupt the Open and one terrorist has been killed and another detained in a shoot-out at Stranraer ferryport. Officials here will not comment on the incident, except to say that today's play in the Open is going ahead as planned.'

Jacob paused, 'And what a final day this promises to be. Just look at that leaderboard—' Captions appeared on screen. 'Current leaders right now are Bill Dwight of Canada and Spain's Mañuel Luca.

They've had an incredible four birdies each in the first seven holes that they've played so far and that puts them both on four under par.

'In second place at three under is our own Sam Joyce, and Lou Menzies. The Australian has birdied the first and second holes and looks in form to retain his title. At two under are the overnight leaders Colm Donohue and Dick Elliott, both of whom have just parred the first hole.'

Jacob let this information sink in. When he spoke again, his tone had just the right touch of professional sadness. 'Alas, it looks as if Leonard Morgan's brave bid to win the Open is over. The man who captured world headlines by surprisingly leading the championship for the first two days has three-putted the first four greens and has slipped from one under to three over par. Amazingly, having putted so well during those first three days, he arrived here this morning without that favourite club. When asked what had happened to his old putter, Morgan refused to comment. He had to buy a new putter from the pro shop here—and it's just not doing the business for him!'

Jacob broke off suddenly. 'Before we continue with this commentary, we're going back briefly to the newsroom for an update on that IRA shoot-out at Stranraer.'

Out on the course, Elliott and Donohue were having a head-to-head battle that revived memories of the epic Watson-Nicklaus duel that had taken place at Turnberry on the final day of the 1977 Open. After splendid second shots to the second green, packed tight with spectators, the American superstar had rolled in a magnificent 18-foot birdie putt.

Hardly had the cheering died down when the young Irishman, from almost the same distance, rattled in his putt, also for a birdie. The battle was on in earnest!

'I fancy Elliott. He's so determined.'

'Nae, mon, he has that mental block.'

'Aye. He'll freeze. Wait and see.'

'Lou Menzies has just birdied the sixth.'

'The Canadian is in big trouble at the eighth.'

'Our Sandy is making up ground after a bad start. He's only two behind the leaders now.'

'Look at Tony Maurelli. He's still there with a chance.'

'The young Irishman is looking good.'

'No way. He'll crack when the pressure is really on.'

Throughout the afternoon, cheers and bursts of applause were heard from different parts of the course. The packed stands at the eighteenth green resounded to loud applause when a young Englishman, Tim Stack, holed out there for a 65. It gave him a two under par total of 286 which, to judge by the scoring out on the course, would be nowhere like a winning score.

By the time they had completed the first nine holes, Dick Elliott and Colm Donohue had shared seven birdies. This left the American, who claimed four of those birdies, a clear leader by two shots over the Irishman who had bogeyed the par four eighth hole. Menzies and Joyce were sharing second place now with the Irishman. A shot further back lurked Tony Maurelli, Japan's Kiyoshi Minoki, and the

Spaniard Mañuel Luca. It was still anybody's championship.

The two police cars arrived at the station in Stranraer with sirens screeching and the squad car lights flashing. Already a group of newsmen was at the door. Stephen Trafford could see a couple of television cameramen setting up across the road. There was a yard in the back of the station where other police cars were parked, but Sergeant Tomkins had to slow down because of the crowd blocking the entrance.

'Blast those reporters!' Inspector Torsney showed his annoyance. 'Let us out here, Sergeant.'

They were barely out of the car when the questions began flying.

'Can you confirm it was the IRA?'

'Who's the man who was shot?'

'Who is the girl, Inspector? What's her name?'

'Is this young fellow her boyfriend?'

The Inspector shouldered his way through the crowd, ignoring the questions. Cameras were raised and, as Stephen went up the steps behind Torsney, he covered his face with his hands. The policeman at the door came out and made a passage for them, then stepped back to block the entrance.

Inside they were brought into a room with a bare, wooden table, around which four men in plain clothes were lounging. Marie Kirk was seated at the top of the table, a policewoman standing directly behind her. There was also a uniformed policeman in the room and Stephen noticed that the windows had bars.

'Stephen! Oh, thank heavens—' Marie went to rise, but the policewoman restrained her.

'Marie, thank God you're safe. When I heard about the shoot-out. . . .'

She buried her face in her hands and her shoulders shook. Her sobs were the only sound in the room.

'It's all right, Marie. It's all over.' Stephen moved across the room. Nobody stopped him. He put his arm around her shoulder and she lifted a tear-stained face. Her hair was a mess.

'She has had a rough time,' one of the plainclothes men said. He was older than the others and looked to be in charge. 'I'm Inspector Roddy of the Strath-clyde Division.' He nodded to Inspector Torsney. 'Hello, Alec. Sorry to have dragged you away from Turnberry.'

'Can't be helped, Tom. What happened?'

'After you phoned, we picked up the suspect's car and tracked him and the girl here to Stranraer. We were waiting for them at the ferryport. There was a shoot-out.'

'It was horrible.' Marie cut in. She held Stephen's hand. 'I think he suspected something when he saw the helicopter, but he wasn't going to be taken alive. I pleaded with him but it was no use—'

'Don't say any more just now, Marie,' Stephen counselled. 'I'll get a solicitor and you can make a statement.'

'The young lady has already made a statement, sir,' Roddy said.

Stephen looked at him. 'But you might have waited until she had a solicitor—'

'It was a voluntary statement,' the Inspector explained patiently. 'The young lady wanted to help all she could. She says she has nothing to hide and it's best that she co-operates.'

'It's all right, Stephen. I know what I'm doing.' Marie seemed to have recovered some of her composure.

There was a silence in the room. Then Inspector Torsney said: 'So it was the IRA.'

'Aye,' his colleague nodded. 'Two of them sent over from Belfast. The girl and this fellow, Martin Dignam. We've checked him out with the RUC. He's a well-known terrorist.' Inspector Roddy turned to Marie. 'She's apparently a new recruit.'

'Marie isn't really one of them,' Stephen said, his eyes darting in turn to the two senior policemen. 'She's not a terrorist. If it had not been for her, there would have been a lot of innocent people killed at the Open today.'

'I'm not denying that, lad,' Roddy said.

'She risked her life to tip you off about the bomb,' Stephen persisted. 'She's innocent.'

Inspector Torsney coughed and said 'That's for someone else to decide.' There was no sympathy in his voice.

Again a silence fell. 'What happens now?' Stephen asked. There was no answer. Nobody seemed to be in any hurry to do anything.

Inspector Roddy rose from his chair. 'Do you want to go over to see the body, Alec?'

'Where is it?'

'Still at the ferryport. The forensic boys are over there now. I have to warn you it's not a pretty sight.'

Marie flinched at the words.

'Aye. Why not? The media hounds outside are looking for action.' Inspector Torsney glanced at his watch. 2.40 p.m. If he got a move on and Sergeant Tomkins made good time back to Turnberry, he might still catch the last few holes of the Open. He might even be lucky and get a trip back by helicopter.

'This is a crucial putt for young Donohue. He's two shots off the lead and if he drops another here, it could be curtains, the end of a brave bid to win the Open—'

Malcolm Jacob's voice trailed off and the camera zoomed in on the Irishman as he sat on his haunches surveying the ten-foot putt on the fourteenth green. The thunderclap of cheering from the packed stand that had greeted Dick Elliott's birdie putt a few moments ago had died. Now the outright leader, the American looked at last as if he was on his way to achieving his greatest triumph.

'Don't forget that slight borrow, lad.' Colm heard Johnny's voice over his shoulder. 'Aim two inches to the left of the hole.'

Colm straightened up, took a couple of practice swings, then stood over the putt. Johnny's assessment was correct, but the green was fast and he had to get the pace exactly right. He stroked the putt, keeping his head still. The roar from the crowd welled up, then turned to an enormous groan as the ball horseshoed around the hole and hung on the lip. It stayed there, hanging into the hole, but did not drop.

Colm waited, hoping. The crowd held its breath.

In the strong sunlight, he took off his sun visor, wiped a ridge of perspiration left by the headband. His eyes were transfixed on the ball, willing it to drop into the hole. Thousands of pairs of eyes were on the white orb. Would it drop? Johnny Davis walked across the green and stopped behind the hole so that his shadow fell across the ball. Eight, nine, ten seconds elapsed, then it happened—the ball dropped out of sight! There was a mighty roar of relief from the packed stand.

'That's an old trick,' Johnny grinned as the marshalls guided them through the spectators to the fifteenth tee. 'When sunlight is cut off like that, grass constricts slightly. Not much, but enough to make a difference.'

'You foxy old devil,' Colm retorted as they stepped up to tackle the 209-yard, dangerous par three fifteenth hole.

Malcolm Jacob was telling television viewers that the Open championship was now effectively between Donohue and Elliott. 'The American is having another great round. He is now seven under par overall, five under for today's round. That means he's two shots ahead of his playing partner, Colm Donohue, and four ahead of Tony Maurelli, Sandy McIntyre and Sam Joyce.

'Lou Menzies, who began so promisingly today, has blown it. We've just seen him having a disastrous double-bogey at the fifteenth hole and he is now only one under par. And sadly Leonard Morgan continues to have problems with his putting. He has three-putted six greens so far today and is now out of it. The heat and the pressure are beginning to tell.' The camera picked up Elliott and Donohue on the tee. 'But not on these two, especially Dick Elliott. Those who thought that he might have had other things on his mind have been proved wrong—'

Elliott indeed had managed to shut out the hurt of what Susan had done. Those pictures in the newspaper confirmed what he had suspected for some time—that Susan wanted back in the limelight. Time to face that problem later. As he followed his shot to the green over 200 yards away, he saw his ball bounce just short of the smooth surface, take the roll off the bank and finish up only twelve feet away. He knew he was looking at another birdie opportunity.

By contrast, Donohue did not hit his four iron well. He watched anxiously as his ball headed towards that dreaded drop down the bank on the right. If it went down there, all would be lost. It got a lucky final bounce and stayed on the top of the ridge. He had been fortunate, but as he walked towards the green, he knew he would have a tough time saving his par.

Three minutes later he was waving his club in the air and the spectators were applauding deliriously. He had floated the ball out of the rough with a wedge and it had caught the bottom of the bank and raced across the green to the hole, hitting the flagstick and nestling between it and the rim of the cup. He had managed to get a birdie. Incredible!

The crowd was hushed as the American stood over his birdie putt. If Donohue's near-miraculous shot had shaken Elliott's nerve, he did not show it. His putt rolled across the green carpet and went right into the centre of the hole. Another birdie! He acknowledged the applause with a wave.

As he made his way behind Johnny towards the sixteenth tee, Donohue caught sight of Samantha Cruise. She was walking with the crowd, but her eyes were on him. She smiled, gave him a little wave which he reciprocated. Damn! He should be concentrating.

Both he and Elliott made pars at the sixteenth hole. The flag was placed towards the front of the green and the creek known as the Wee Burn awaited any golfer playing short and trying for a birdie with an uphill putt. The two Open contenders played safely to the back of the green, then two-putted down the slope for their safe pars. The crowd was shouting encouragement to Elliott now, but he barely acknowledged the cheers. His face was a mask of grim determination. Two shots ahead with just two holes to play; he must not let it slip now.

'You have to get a birdie here to have any chance,' Johnny muttered to his young partner as they walked towards the seventeenth tee. Down in the valley where the fairway stretched into the distance, the spectators were three and four deep. Some had climbed up on to the brown hillocks to get a better view.

On the tee, as Colm Donohue took out the driver, Johnny whispered: 'Go for it now, lad. You've got nothing to lose.'

Dick Elliott prepared to drive. The swish of the club and the click as he made contact with the ball were the only sounds that broke the silence. There was wild applause as he hit a beautiful shot right down the valley and into the middle of the fairway.

The American was shutting the door with every shot.

Donohue gritted his teeth. He must not give up. This was golf and anything could happen. His driver made perfect contact with the ball and as his head came around he saw it fly up against the blue sky, then bounce and run along the shallow valley of the fairway. It finished a few yards behind Elliott's ball. They walked after their tee shots, each keeping his distance from the other. The time for pleasantries was over.

Earlier in the week Johnny had paced out the course, noting landmarks on his yardage chart. Now as Donohue stood over his ball, he turned to the older man for advice. 'What do you reckon?'

'I reckon this is where you're going to hit the shot of your life, lad. A three iron—and I want to see it land right in the heart of the green. That will put the pressure on him.'

'Okay.' There was no questioning the choice of club as far as he was concerned. He had every confidence in Johnny's judgement.

It was Donohue's turn to hit first. Across the fairway he could see Elliott looking over. He took a couple of practice swings, studied the flag in the distance. Suddenly the confidence that Johnny had in him surged through his veins. He knew he was going to hit a great shot!

Up in his commentary box Malcolm Jacob was informing viewers: 'We're told that's a three iron Donohue has in his hands. I hope he has enough club. There are the practice swings, now here is the shot—' Jacob's voice went up an octave—' and it looks like a very good one indeed!'

The camera caught the ball in flight. It seemed to hang a long time in the air, then it began its arc. It bounced a couple of times on the fairway and began its run towards the green.

'My word, look at this!' Malcolm Jacob's tone was ecstatic. The crowd in the stand at the green, and those ringing it from elevated hillocks, burst into rapturous applause as the ball ran on to the green, slowed, rolled with the contour, and finished up three feet from the flagstick. Back down the fairway Johnny Davis was grinning from ear to ear.

Across the other side of the green sward, Dick Elliott registered no emotion. From where he stood he could not tell exactly how far his rival's ball was from the hole, but by the way the crowd had applauded he sensed it was darned close. He must not think about that now. What he had to do was hit the green with his next shot, take no more than two putts, and that would leave him in the lead playing the last hole. He selected a four-iron from his bag, took his customary single practice swing, and hit smoothly through the ball.

'Dick Elliott has hit his second shot—and I do believe he's pushed it slightly!' The camera tracked the ball as Malcolm Jacob fell silent. 'Yes, it's heading towards that bunker to the right of the green . . . oohh, it's missed the bunker, but it's in the light rough and I think Elliott will have to chip over the end of that bunker to get anywhere near the flag. A very difficult shot indeed.'

The crowd, hushed now, was nevertheless tingling with excitement as both golfers approached the green. So far during the championship, this par five hole had yielded 29 eagle threes and over 250 birdies. Now it looked as if it was biting back.

Dick Elliott walked up to the green, skirted the bunker, and surveyed his ball in the rough, his face grim. It was not a good lie; it was nestling down in the light grass and he knew that when he chipped it over the edge of the bunker, it would be difficult to get the ball to stop near the flag. Donohue's ball was a lot closer to the hole than he had figured.

He played an excellent wedge shot under the circumstances. It popped up into the air, cleared the corner of the bunker and landed on the green. It ran towards the hole, missed hitting the flagstick by a hairsbreadth, and finished up six feet past the cup. The applause was generous as the American came on to the green. Now he was under pressure to hole the birdie putt. If he did not and the Irishman sank his, he would have lost his two- shot lead and they would be all square playing the final hole.

Elliott was willing himself to sink the putt. The problem was there was a big left-to-right swing on it. Both he and his caddie stalked the putt from all angles before deciding on the line. Two practice swings, then he stood over the ball and nudged it towards the hole. It broke off line just a fraction of an inch too late. The crowd gasped when the ball stayed above ground. Elliott tapped it in for a par. This time the applause was sympathetic.

He watched Colm Donohue duly sink his putt for an eagle three. The crowd went wild and there was a stampede towards the eighteenth tee and for vantage points all along the eighteenth fairway.

As the two golfers stepped on to the final tee a roar

erupted from the distant last green. Instinctively they both glanced at the giant scoreboard near the tee. Already it was being changed to show that Englishman Sam Joyce, who had earlier birdied the seventeenth, had also done the same at the final hole. He had finished with a final total of seven under par, one shot behind the co-leaders. Tony Maurelli and Kiyoshi Minoki were already in the clubhouse with six under, so Maurelli's attempt to win the British Open at his first attempt had failed.

'Realistically, unless both Donohue and Elliott make a mess of this last hole, one of them must become Open champion,' Malcolm Jacob told his television audience. 'Up to a few minutes ago, one would have given odds on Dick Elliott at last achieving his life-long ambition. But now . . . well, maybe the pressure is getting to him.'

In the stand behind the eighteenth green, Susan Elliott focused the binoculars up the sweep of the fairway. 'They're on the tee now,' she said to Joan. 'Like to have a look?'

Joan shook her head. 'No thanks. I'm too nervous.' She was twisting a tiny handkerchief in her fingers.

Susan smiled. 'I know the feeling.' In fact her stomach was churning over. Richard just had to win this time. If he failed, they were facing an uncertain future.

'Donohue is about to drive,' Malcolm Jacob said in that special voice he used for occasions of high tension. 'In ordinary circumstances, this is not a particularly difficult par four, but in the Open champion-

305

ship the players use the eighteenth tee of the adjacent Arran course, so it makes the hole 431 yards long with a sharp dogleg left. There are two bunkers down that side and thick gorse down the right-hand side where Nicklaus's ball was trapped back in the epic Open of 1977.'

A pause, then Jacob's excited voice: 'Donohue has driven—and the crowd seems to like it! And why not—just look at that . . . a magnificent drive right down the middle of the fairway.' Viewers saw the ball bounce and come to rest on a fairway burnt brown by the sun.

The camera zoomed in on Dick Elliott as he prepared to drive. There was a look of grim determination—or was it strain?—on his tanned face. His swing was as smooth as ever. Thousands of heads turned to watch the flight of the ball and applause broke out when it was seen to split the fairway.

'Two excellent tee shots,' the commentator intoned. 'Elliott's ball is about five yards ahead of Donohue's, so it will be the Irishman to play first. I reckon he has a shot of about 160 yards to the green, so he'll be hitting perhaps a seven iron—' Down the fairway Johnny Davis and his young protégé were surveying the shot to the flag. Donohue had placed his drive in the ideal spot on the right of the fairway. It gave him a clear shot into the green, one of three at Turnberry around which there are no bunkers. But there are a lot of awkward little grassy mounds just short of the putting surface. He did not want to land on one of those and get a bad bounce.

'What do you think, Johnny?'

'You're really pumped up now, lad. Give a seven

iron everything you've got.'

Once again Donohue did not question his caddie's judgement. He lifted the club from the bag, took a couple of practice swings, paused, and let his thoughts dwell for a moment on the stand at the back of the green. Joan would be there, he knew, probably praying silently. He addressed the ball, shut everything out of his mind, and swung.

'Oh-oh, he's tweaked it, I'm afraid,' Malcolm Jacob said. The camera followed the ball as it bounced on to the green, short of the flag and to the left. It was not a good shot and did not have any backspin. The crowd groaned as it ran past the flag and finished on the apron of the green.

'The tension you see,' Jacob's tone was sympathetic. 'A simple shot that most amateurs would have landed on the green. But of course when the Open is at stake—'

All eyes were now on the American. The door had been opened to him with that slack shot from his rival and he knew it. Millions of television viewers saw him select an eight iron from his bag. Dick Elliott was ice cool as he surveyed the shot, measuring where he wanted the ball to land.

He swung at the ball smoothly, knew he had made good contact. The ball was still in the air when the crowd's roar grew in volume. Thunderous applause broke out as the ball bit into the green six feet past the flag, took backspin and came back to stop level with the hole about four feet away. Shouts of 'great shot!' rang out and Elliott allowed himself a smile.

The 150-yard walk to the green was accompanied

by tumultuous applause. Both men saluted the vast crowd, taking off their sun visors and waving to right and left. Those close to them could see the strain on both golfers' faces. Dick Elliott had experienced it all before—here at the Open, at Augusta during the Masters, at Muirfield Village last year when he had won the US PGA title. He had welcomed similar applause in Australia and Japan. But this was something special . . . he had the British Open within his grasp.

For Colm Donohue it was a dream come true, unnerving but unforgettable. Had someone told him last Monday when he and Joan had arrived in Turnberry that he would be getting this kind of reception from the crowd on the last day of the Open, he would have said they were crazy. Now people were rising to their feet and applauding him. He looked for Joan in the stand, but could not see her.

The cheering continued as Dick Elliott placed a coin behind his ball, picked it up and gave it to his caddie to clean. There was no doubt where most of the crowd's sympathy lay; they wanted him to win the title that had eluded him for so long. Across the green, Donohue sensed the feeling of spectators but tried to shut it out of his mind. The £60,000 runner-up cheque would be welcome, but he was determined to take the title.

He got down on his haunches and lined up his putt. It was all of twenty-four feet, he reckoned, and the first few feet of that was through the apron of the green where the grass was slightly thicker. He would have to be careful not to three-putt—that would leave him tied with Sam Joyce for second place and cost

Joan wanted to avoid the subject. 'How is Richard?'

'A bit down. He's refusing all requests for interviews.' She managed to smile. 'Can't say I blame him. The questions some of those reporters ask. They deserve to have their noses punched.'

'Don't worry, Susan. I'm sure he'll get over it. They have to, don't they?' Joan could hardly believe that she was giving advice to someone like Susan Elliott.

Susan obviously felt a need to talk to someone. 'I think he blames me for everything. We had a blazing row last night. I think this might be the end of Richard and me. We're slowly drifting apart.'

'Oh no.'

'We've been near to this before. It's just that this time I don't see much hope. He's absolutely determined to try for the British Open again next year. Right now I've had enough of the tour—'

'What will you do, Susan? Go back to modelling?'

'Who knows? Anything to make me feel a full person again. I might try something in the film line.' She broke off. 'I'm sorry. I shouldn't be boring you with my problems. Where's Colm today? I bet he's busy—'

Joan told her and also filled Susan in on her talk with Mark Varley. When she had finished, Susan smiled ruefully. 'Welcome to the club,' she said. 'No, I'm sorry. Forget I said that. At least you and Colm have something going for you—the children.' She looked wistful. 'Maybe that's where Richard and I went wrong—'

They chatted for a few more minutes before Susan

finally rose. 'Time to go, I'm afraid.'

They hugged each other. Joan said: 'We must keep in touch.'

'Of course. I'd love that, Joan. You have my address. Let me know everything that happens. And good luck to you and Colm. You both deserve it.'

Joan watched her ease her way through the tables. At the exit, she turned and waved. Joan felt a slight unease.

On the hotel steps the Tony Maurelli entourage was almost ready to depart. All the baggage had been loaded on to the helicopter waiting on the heli-pad and soon he, Lisa, Marvin Maxwell, Rafael Escudio and their caddies, plus a couple of American golf correspondents to whom they were giving a lift, would head for Prestwick, transfer to Tony's jet, and take off for New York.

'What the hell is keeping Rafael?' Marvin Maxwell asked, glancing at his watch impatiently. 'If we don't get going soon, we'll miss our take-off time in Prestwick.' He paced up and down. 'The guy is probably still in his room giving a quick one to that broad he's been chasing all week.'

Lisa giggled. 'Marvin, darling, all you men think of is sex.'

Marvin scowled. Lucky for you they do; you're only too happy to accommodate them all! Lisa's early morning trip to the sauna a couple of days ago still haunted him. He had hung around in the foyer after she had passed through on the way back to her room. Not long afterwards he had observed that Australian guy Jack Hastings emerge, looking as if he had had a good workout in the sauna.

'I think something's happened to Rafael,' Tony said. 'Did you notice him during lunch? He hardly ate a thing and looked real worried.'

'If the guy doesn't show up soon, we're leaving,' Marvin growled. 'I want you in good shape for the Hartford Open this week.'

'Any plans for playing again in Britain this year, Tony?' one of the golf writers asked.

Maurelli looked at his manager. Marvin shook his head. 'No way,' he answered. 'There are lots of big money tournaments coming up in the States shortly and Tony will be concentrating on them. Come December, we'll head for Japan and the Far East—'

'Including Australia—' Lisa put in.

Marvin looked at her. 'Who said anything about Australia?'

'Tony did.' She snuggled up to her big husband for the benefit of a photographer she saw hovering in the background. 'Didn't you, honey?'

'When?' Marvin asked harshly.

All eyes turned on Tony, who looked uncomfortable. 'I guess I did promise to bring Lisa to Australia. She wants to see them kangaroos and koala bears. She's crazy about them.'

Like hell she is, Maxwell thought to himself. You big asshole, the only thing your wife is crazy for in Australia is that guy Hastings. The broad would not know a kangaroo from a fucking boomerang! Aloud he said: 'Sorry to disappoint you both, but Australia is not on our schedule.'

Lisa shot him a dirty look. 'Oh yes it is!'

'I said it's not—and that's final.'

'Honey,' Lisa pouted. 'You promised. Show this little man who's boss.'

Just then Rafael Escudio came out of the hotel. Everyone was so relieved to see him that the argument was forgotten. Besides, the guy looked so worried that there was obviously something the matter with him.

'Hey man. You okay?' Tony asked. 'You look awful.'

'I feel awful.'

'You looked okay at dinner last night,' Marvin Maxwell said. 'Did something happen to you afterwards?'

'Maybe something you ate,' one of the golf writers said solicitously.

Rafael gave him a baleful look. 'Come on, let's go,' he said impatiently.

'You see a doctor as soon as we get back,' Tony said. 'You sure want to be in shape for the Hartford Open.'

Rafael Escudio was planning on missing the Hartford Open. As soon as he landed in New York, he was catching a plane for San Francisco. There was a doctor in an AIDS clinic there he wanted to see urgently.

Joan spent most of the afternoon playing with the children in the hotel crèche or browsing aimlessly through the shops in the foyer. The pace was winding down now after the activity of the past week. She found it all rather frustrating; her husband had won the greatest golf prize of all, yet here she was confined to the hotel, waiting for a phone call from him to relieve the boredom. Was this the start of being a superstar golfer's widow? Was this what Susan Elliott had hinted at when she said 'welcome to the club'?

It was late evening when the phone rang in her room. She was sitting at the window from which she had a magnificent view of the Firth of Clyde.

She had expected to hear Colm's voice. 'Hello?'

'Joan?' Disappointment. 'This is Mark. Peter and I are down here at the bar. Something has come up.'

'What is it?'

'Would you like to come down and join us for a drink?'

'I can't. I'm with the children.'

She sensed his annoyance. 'Of course'.

'What is it? Have you heard from Colm?'

'Yes. Well, not exactly. Samantha phoned. She says they won't be back tonight. Something has come up.'

'Oh.' Joan felt a stirring of unease. Had she not suspected something like this ever since he had set eyes on the blonde Samantha? 'What's happened?'

'Sam has arranged a meeting first thing tomorrow morning in London with the manufacturers of the clubs Colm uses. It's a big money deal.'

'Can't it wait until later?'

'Better to strike while the iron is hot. I'm sorry, Joan, but business is business.' His voice was brisk, authoritative, and she did not think he sounded very sorry.

'I want to ring Colm, have a chat, tell him the children are asking for him.'

'That's very cosy, but unfortunately I don't have a number where you can contact him right now. They've finished at the golf club and Sam is bringing Colm off to meet some more people. I expect he'll ring you from his hotel later tonight.'

Joan did not like the idea of being cut off from her husband. 'Did Samantha give you the name of the hotel where Colm is staying?'

'Oh yes. The Ormonde in Bayswater. We always put our clients up there when they're in London.' He gave her the telephone number.

'And Samantha? Where does she stay?'

Mark Varley obviously got the drift of her question. 'Oh, no need to worry about Sam. She has her own flat—in Islington. Try ringing the Ormonde later tonight. Colm should be back by then.'

'Thank you.' Joan replaced the receiver.

In the bar Mark rejoined his brother. 'Trouble?' Peter asked.

'She wasn't too happy about him having to stay overnight.'

'I didn't think she would be.' Peter lit one of the slim cigars they both enjoyed. 'What about Sam?' He exhaled a jet of smoke. 'Is she playing up again, do you think?'

Mark swirled the brandy around his glass before replying. 'I hope not. I warned her after that last time. Playing around with the client is definitely not on.'

'Did you remind her of that when she phoned?'

'Naturally. Jeez! We don't want any hanky-panky with the British Open champion. Imagine the head-lines!'

'I just hope Sam got the message.'

At about the same time that British Airways flight JI 469 was taking off from London to Johannesburg, Commandant Dominick Earley was calling to order the meeting of the council members of the breakaway wing of the IRA over which he had command.

The six-member council was meeting in the upstairs room of a hotel in West Belfast, which the unit used as an occasional meeting place. The room was not very large and the oblong mahogany table around which the five men and one woman member sat took up most of the space. The muted hubbub of conversation filtered up from the crowded bar below.

In front of every member was a copy of the morning edition of the Irish News, opened at the obituary page. Prominently displayed was a death notice beginning: 'It is with deep regret and sorrow that the Council of the Ardoyne Brigade of the Irish Republican Army announces the death, while on active duty in Scotland, of Comrade Martin Patrick Dignam.' Above the death notice was a photograph of a bearded, unsmiling Martin Dignam, looking not unlike Che Guevara, black beret at an angle.

'When is the body expected home, Commandant?'

'Don't know. The British will try to hold it as long as possible.'

'What are the burial plans?'

'They will follow the usual procedure. Full military honours. Comrade Dignam's body will be taken to his mother's house. She is his only living relative. As you know, two of his brothers were killed by the British Army while on active duty some years ago. The body will remain overnight in the house and this unit will mount a guard of honour—' Earley paused and looked around the table. 'Any questions?'

'It says in the paper that Mrs Dignam does not want any military display at our comrade's funeral. She wants the body to go straight to the church and requests no military presence there or in the graveyard.'

Earley's stare ordained silence. 'This brigade is in sole charge of Comrade Dignam's funeral.' There was a murmur of approval. 'From the house the body will be escorted to Milltown Cemetery by a guard of honour. At the graveside, after the prayers, a volley of shots will be fired.'

He looked around the table. 'Of course there will be a British Army and also a police presence. We must be prepared for trouble. Right now we can only wait for Comrade Dignam's body to be released.' Earley cleared his throat. He knew what they were waiting for. Better that he start the discussion before one of them began asking questions.

'The next important item on the agenda is what went wrong with "Operation Birdie"?' A silence. The look on their faces said it all. 'I regret to have to inform you that "Operation Birdie" failed because someone informed the British police. . . .'

'We know who it is and the media seem to be in no doubt', one of the members cut in. 'Marie Kirk. Her photograph is all over the newspapers. Where is she now? She must be found—'

Another man thumped the table. 'The traitor is probably on her way into hiding with her English boyfriend. I agree. She must be found—and made to pay for her treachery.'

A chorus of approval. 'She's a disgrace to her dead brother's memory. Wherever she is, she must be found—and punished.'

The woman spoke up. 'It was a mistake to send her on this mission in the first place. Why weren't we told about her former English boyfriend? Was he checked out beforehand?'

'And why did Comrade Dignam disobey orders?'

'The reason was we sent one of our best men to Scotland to blow up a silly monument. That was a mistake—'

'Silence!' Earley's shout of command was honoured. He sensed the danger in the room. His judgement—worse, his leadership—was now in question. He must give answers. More important, he must show strength.

'Questions have been asked about the failure of "Operation Birdie". I'll answer those questions. But first I want to deal with the matter of Marie Kirk.' He had their attention. 'A show of hands from those who deem her guilty of informing—' Five arms shot into the air.

'Unanimous. Next we will find out in what country she and her boyfriend are hiding. It may take time. I have already made contact with our comrades abroad, in Europe, America, Australia and parts of South America and South Africa. Our contacts in the postal service here have been instructed to open all letters to her father and to her other relatives in Belfast. I will arrange to have her father's telephone tapped.' There were murmurs of approval.

'And when we find her . . . ?' The man with the quiet voice left the question unanswered.

'You all know the penalty for traitors.' Dominick Earley took a deep breath. 'Death. I want your vote, comrades.'

He saw the arms shoot upwards. 'Unanimous.'

Christ, he did not want this to happen. Another young life targeted, wiped out. They would find Marie Kirk, just as they had found all the others who had tried to run away. Nobody could hide forever. He had just signed the girl's death warrant. 'Now to the remainder of our business.'

Meanwhile, the hostess on the British Airways flight to Johannesburg had distributed newspapers to the passengers. Most had left them aside and were dozing off to sleep or chatting.

Not so the young couple—honeymooners, the air hostess reckoned—who had asked for a copy of every newspaper she had available. She could not help but notice that they were both engrossed in the same story—the aftermath of the attempt to plant a bomb at the British Open and the subsequent death of the IRA terrorist.

The air hostess liked to study people, guess their backgrounds. It was part of her job and, besides, it helped pass the time on long flights. This couple were definitely honeymooners, off to South Africa to start up a new, exciting life in one of the big cities.

The air hostess sighed. What she wouldn't give to swap places with that girl right now!

It was nearly nine o'clock when Colm at last phoned. Joan heard his voice, was relieved. And yet she could not quash her annoyance. While he was in London being wined and dined, she was up in Turnberry in him about £10,000. Behind him Johnny was also studying the line.

'It's a straight one, lad. Go for it. Don't leave it short. Remember the old saying: never up, never in.'

The crowd was still as Colm took his practice swings. Then he stood over the ball. The last thing he re- membered before stroking the ball was Johnny Davis's words. His heart was pounding, but he took a deep breath and made a smooth stroke.

Oh God, he had hit it too hard! He knew it as soon as the ball took off. It moved through the fringe grass and when it hit the surface of the green, it gained added momentum. It looked to be racing towards the hole and would probably finish about six feet past—

But it was dead on line! When he tilted his head sideways, Donohue saw that he had got the ball going right at the hole. The roar that was welling up from the crown turned into a thunderclap as the ball hit the back of the cup, jumped an inch into the air, then disappeared from view. Unbelievable! He had made a birdie!

The crowd was going wild. He looked up, his mind in a daze. Across the far side of the green, he saw a group of spectators throw their hats into the air. He was conscious of Johnny thumping him on the back and suddenly he felt very tired.

'The tension here is almost unbearable,' Malcolm Jacob made an effort to keep his voice under control. 'A minute ago Dick Elliott looked certain to win the Open. Now he needs this putt of four feet to force a play-off. I watched his face immediately after Donohue's putt dropped in. He showed no emotion at all. But, my word, he must be shattered. What a tough time to have to make a four-foot putt!'

The stewards finally got the crowd under control. Dick Elliott waited until every sound had died away before moving. He studied the line of the putt intently, first from the front, then from the back of the hole. Finally he stood over the ball, moved the putter blade back—

The crowd gasped as the American stepped away from the putt. 'Something, or someone, has disturbed him,' Jacob told his audience sotto voce. 'A slight movement somewhere. . . .'

Dick Elliott went through his putting routine again, methodically, painstakingly, leaving nothing to chance. Silence again as the putter blade moved back, came forward and touched the ball. It rolled slowly, agonisingly towards the hole. The roar of approval in thousands of throats turned to a great moan of anguish as the ball stayed on the right lip of the cup. Dick Elliott stared at it, as though he could not believe what he was seeing. He waited, saw there was no chance of it dropping in, then took a pace forward and tapped it in single-handedly with an air of resignation. He turned and strode across the green, hand outstretched, towards the new Open champion.

'Jeez, Colm, you've done it!' Donohue disentangled himself from Johnny's embrace to shake the American's hand. Stewards, officials and television cameramen were piling onto the green.

'Congratulations. You deserved it.' Elliott's handshake was firm, warm, but his smile was tight.

Colm was still in a daze. 'Thanks. Sorry about how it ended—' He hoped he was saying the right thing.

'Forget it. You've won. That's all that matters. Good luck.' Elliott moved off quickly through the crowd, brushing past a man with a microphone. He would face the ordeal of a press conference later. Right now he wanted to be alone.

Up in the stand, Joan and Susan were on their feet, being jostled by excited spectators. 'Oh, Susan. I—I don't know whether to be happy or to cry,' Joan said. She was near to tears.

Susan smiled bravely. She was feeling shattered, but tried not to show it. 'That's the way it is in this game. Don't worry, Richard and I will survive.' In the circumstances she wondered if she had said the right thing.

Rafael Escudio watched the final minutes of the championship on television, seated at a table inside the members' lounge in the clubhouse. The thickly carpeted lounge, with its oak-panelled walls and historical pictures of past champions crowned at Turnberry, was pleasantly crowded. There were several other golfers, with their wives, in the room, but Rafael was waiting for someone and he had a table to himself.

The Open trophy had been presented to the new champion—a young guy Escudio had never heard of before he came to Turnberry—and now the fellow was being interviewed on television while photographers clambered around, taking pictures of him and his pretty young wife.

Escudio gulped a mouthful of beer and wondered about Dick Elliott. The guy was never going to win the Open. Just did not have the balls for it. But one thing Elliott did have was a very sexy wife. He often speculated about what Susan Elliott would be like in bed. He would give a British Open win to see what was hidden under that cool exterior.

The talk around the clubhouse was that Elliott was furious with his wife for flaunting herself in front of a photographer, and that Susan had threatened to quit travelling with him and wanted to resume her modelling career.

He saw Ed McBain enter the lounge. The boss of Courtesy Cars had a face that was red from the sun and he looked in need of a drink. McBain glanced around the room, spotted Escudio and eased his considerable bulk through the intervening tables.

'Sorry I'm late. Just had to watch the finish on the eighteenth. Christ! Did you see Elliott freeze over that putt—'

Escudio held up his hand. He felt no sympathy for Dick Elliott and anyway he had had enough golf for the week. He was here to talk about something else. 'You like a drink?' Before McBain could reply, he had waved a bow-tied waiter over, ordered a double whisky and another beer for himself. 'Everything okay for tonight? The chica—she is coming?'

'Och aye, of course.'

'No problems?'

'No. Not after I threatened to fire her if she didn't show up tonight. Is nine o'clock all right with you?'

'Fine. We have a few drinks first, maybe in the hotel.' His voice took on a suspicious tone. 'You sure her kid won't get ill again tonight?'

'That was genuine, I assure you,' McBain said. It was a blatant lie. He knew that Elaine could not stand the sight of the Mexican. McBain reckoned he could make some extra money if he played his cards right.

'It will cost you extra, Rafael, I'm afraid.'

'What you mean?'

McBain leaned forward. 'Let's face it, the Open is over. My girls are free to go from seven o'clock tonight. I had to pay Elaine extra to stay around.'

Rafael knew he was being squeezed, but he wanted the girl badly. 'How much?'

'Another hundred pounds will cover everything.'

He was not going to give in to this asshole too easily. 'Is too much.'

Damn, McBain thought. I've blown it. He swallowed a large mouthful of whisky and put down the glass. He'd give it to this Mexican bighead straight. 'Okay, Rafael, I'll tell you exactly what the problem is. Elaine doesn't fancy you one bit. Sure, she's been with laddies before, so she tells me, but she's always fancied them. With you—nothing.'

He heard the Mexican mutter under his breath. 'This chica, I want her. Understand?'

' Then you're willing to pay?'

Escudio nodded. 'You make sure she is in the hotel tonight. I make sure she enjoys it. I do things to her that will make her change her mind about me.'

'Of course.' The fellow was taking the insult to his manhood seriously. There was still one item to be settled. 'When do I see the money?' McBain asked.

'Finish your drink and come with me. We go to one of the banks here. Okay?'

When Dick Elliott's putt on the eighteenth green failed to drop and her husband became British Open champion, Joan Donohue knew that her whole life would change. What she was not prepared for was how quickly it would happen.

She had no problem getting to him in the immediate aftermath of his victory—the media seemed only too anxious for the two of them to be photographed together—she with her arms around him, urged on to kiss him on the cheek. Frankly, she found it all a bit embarrassing.

Joan was grateful when it was over and Colm was ushered away into the tournament director's tent to check and sign his scorecard. Only when he had completed this was he officially declared Open champion and presented with the famous trophy. Then it all started again; hordes of photographers and television cameramen asking them to pose this way and that, with Colm holding the Open trophy aloft.

Then it was into the press tent to answer more questions and pose for more pictures. Joan noticed that the Varley brothers and the blonde Samantha were in close attendance and talked to Colm whenever he had a few minutes free. Occasionally her husband would look over to where she was standing and wave to her to come across, but she knew she would only be in the way if she went over. She felt slightly detached from the proceedings.

The next few hours passed in a haze of activity. Johnny Davis, released at last from the tensions of the past few days, and a celebrity now in his own right, went off with a few of his fellow caddies to knock back some beers in a local pub.

Colm finally tore himself away from his pursuers

and, with the Varleys in close attendance, he and Joan found a table in the corner of the clubhouse lounge. Although over two hours had elapsed since he had sunk that precious putt, his face was still flushed with excitement. He told Joan he would be signing a contract with Varley Brothers Management. She was hurt that he had not consulted her before doing it, but she let it pass.

'Are you sure you're doing the right thing, Colm?'

'Yes. I like the Varleys. They're young, ambitious. And they guarantee they'll make me a million while I'm Open champion. It's too good an opportunity to miss, Joan.'

'It sounds great.'

'I'm flying to London first thing tomorrow morning for an exhibition game sponsored by some industrialists. It's worth twenty-five thousand pounds.'

He stopped when he saw the look on her face. 'What about our holiday?'

He reached over and squeezed her hand. 'That'll have to wait, love. Just think—twenty-five thousand quid. For just one game of golf.'

'What about me and the children?'

'You stay here, love. I'll be back tomorrow night. The Varleys are flying me down by private plane from Prestwick.'

'They're going with you?'

He hesitated. 'No, only Samantha. Mark and Peter are staying in Turnberry tomorrow to fix up some other deals for me.'

'Oh.'

'Don't worry. You and the kids will be well looked after. We're moving out of the guesthouse and staying up there tonight—' he gestured towards the Turnberry Hotel which they could see through the window. 'How's that for style, eh?' He laughed.

'Can we afford it?'

'You must be joking—the Varleys are picking up the bill.'

'The Varleys obviously are trying for an upmarket image.'

'That's right. It's the type of image a British Open champion needs.'

'And Johnny. What about him?'

A pause. 'What about him?'

'Is he included in the package? Does he fit the Varley image?'

She saw he was looking uncomfortable. 'I don't know.' He paused. 'What the hell is wrong, Joan? I've just won the most prestigious of all tournaments in the world. We should be happy. Instead we're arguing.'

'I'm worried about us, Colm. Can we survive all this? Everything is happening so quickly—'

'Oh, for heaven's sake—' This time he did not try to hide his annoyance. 'What is there to survive? I'm not going to change just because I've won the Open, am I?'

But he was changing already. Joan could sense that. The story of the IRA bomb being planted under a stand during the Open was on all the evening newscasts. Everybody in Turnberry was talking about the incident. Colm knew that she and Susan Elliott had been sitting in one of those stands at the eighteenth green, yet he was so caught up with his victory and what lay ahead that he did not seem to realise that she might have been killed.

Joan had been shocked when she had seen a television picture of the girl she had known as Norah, the girl who had played with her children, tied in with the attempted bomb blast story. To think that they had stayed in the same guesthouse as the IRA bombers without suspecting anything.

Colm Donohue had other things on his mind. And they were not all pleasurable. Later this evening he and Joan and the children would move into the Turnberry Hotel and tonight the Varleys were giving a dinner in his honour to which some media people and a couple of prospective sponsors were being invited. It would herald the launch of the newly crowned British Open champion.

Colm had insisted that Johnny Davis be invited to the dinner. It would be one of the last occasions they would share. After tomorrow's exhibition game in London, he would be dispensing with Johnny as his caddie. Varley Brothers Management had said they would take care of all the details. They wanted an upmarket image for their young Open champion and Johnny Davis did not fit into that category.

Epilogue

MONDAY, 20 JULY

Stephen Trafford had spent an almost sleepless night. Through a window in the small, cheerless room at Prestwick Airport where he had been waiting for almost an hour, he could see the first streaks of dawn begin to appear. Earlier a woman in a blue smock had brought in a jug of coffee with cups on a tray and the young police constable had poured. Stephen's lay almost untouched in the cup. Instead, he lit another cigarette, got up and crossed to the window.

The police constable glanced at his watch. 'Shouldn't be too long now,' he said helpfully. 'They'd make good time from Stranraer at this hour of the morning.'

Stephen nodded. He hoped nothing had arisen to complicate matters. But what could happen at this stage? The Home Office had given the order to release Marie. His father had been told she would be taken to Prestwick to meet him. So why the delay? Had there been a last-minute hitch? The first flight to London was not due out for several hours yet, at 6.00 a.m. He would have to wait it out.

Yesterday, after his arrival at the police station in Stranraer, he had been allowed to spend several hours with Marie, talking to her under the watchful eye of the woman police constable. Outside, the army

318

of reporters and cameramen had grown, all anxious to get a glimpse of the girl at the centre of the British Open bomb plot.

'Oh, Stephen, I'm sorry.' She had been allowed to wash and put on some fresh make-up. But her eyes were still red-rimmed and her knee showed out through a rip in her toreador pants.

'Don't apologise, Marie. You did the right thing. If it wasn't for you, there would be hundreds dead in Turnberry right now.'

'What's going to happen to us? I'm sorry I got you into this mess, Stephen.' She could not blame him if he departed right now, before the media really got hold of the story and his name was splashed all over the newspapers. As the son of one of the country's leading physicians—his father was strongly tipped to be in the Queen's next honours list—Stephen was an obvious target for sensational headlines. Besides, he had his own medical career to think about. The last thing he needed was to be connected with someone like her.

Instead, Stephen had outlined a plan for their future together. He would return to Turnberry, make a clean breast of it to his father, and tell his parents he was going to marry Marie whatever happens. He would ask his father to phone some of his influential friends in the Conservative Party; get them working quickly to have Marie released so that they could go away, make a life together. His father knew people at Westminster who could pull strings.

Marie had stared at him when he told her what he intended to do. 'The police would never let me go.'

'Why not?' He leaned forward, lowering his voice

319

to a whisper. The policewoman rose to her feet, eyes and ears alert. 'You're not really an IRA terrorist, Marie. You didn't want to see people killed or maimed. So you informed the police. You deserve to be let go.'

'But why should your father help? He never liked me.'

'Mother will persuade him to try. It's our only chance, Marie.'

He had been hustled out of the police station, his face covered with a blanket, and into a police car beside Inspector Torsney. The car had been driven off at high speed, through a police barrier at the end of the street which had successfully delayed the cars of the pursuing newsmen. Outside the town they had driven to a Territorial Army base and been taken by police helicopter back to Turnberry.

In the helicopter he had again sounded out Inspector Torsney on the chances of Marie being set free. The Inspector had been non- committal. 'An order like that would have to come from the very top. Besides, I think that young lady would be better off in jail.'

'What do you mean?'

Torsney looked at the eager face beside him. He wondered if this young man realised what he was letting himself in for. 'The lassie's an informer. She's a marked woman. The IRA have a way of dealing with informers.'

When Stephen's parents had returned from Turnberry, they found him waiting for them in the hotel. In the quiet of their room, he explained all that had happened during the past few days, starting

with his surprise meeting with Marie in the Royale
Hotel on Friday. Wilfrid Trafford had listened to his
son in stony silence.

'I love Marie and we want to go away together.
I'm pleading with you, Dad, to help. Make a few
phone calls to London, request that she be freed.'

At first Wilfrid Trafford had refused point blank
to help, as Stephen expected. It was his mother who
prevailed upon her husband to do what he could.
Finally his father said: 'I'm doing this not for you or
your girlfriend, Stephen, but for your mother. She
thinks you and this girl will have a happy life
together. Personally, I doubt it. By now the IRA will
know it was she who alerted the police. They are
ruthless. They will hunt both of you down wherever
you go.'

'I'm willing to take that chance.'

His father had looked at him for a long time before
replying. 'I think you are being extremely foolish,
Stephen.'

It was the start of a long night of phone calls
between Turnberry and London. Wilfrid Trafford
had influential friends in the Conservative Party,
including several cabinet ministers, and some friends
in the Home Office. A big problem was that, being
Sunday, it sometimes took several phone calls to
track down the required person.

It was past 2.00 a.m. when his mother summoned
Stephen back to their room. On the table were the
remains of another round of coffee and sandwiches.
His father was looking tired and, when he spoke,
Stephen noted the coldness in his voice.

'It's all arranged. The call has just come through.

The girl is to be released from custody. She has co-operated fully with the police and now she is free to go.'

'Thank you.' Stephen noted that his father still did not call Marie by name. She would be taken to Prestwick and he would join her there. His mother, tearful, had asked him where they would eventually go.

'I don't know yet. Somewhere I can practice. America perhaps—'

'The IRA is very strong in America,' his father had said.

'Somewhere in Africa, then. There are plenty of opportunities there for young doctors.'

'What about money?' his mother asked. 'Have you enough?'

'Yes. We can manage. I'll pick up some cash in London.' He had kissed his mother goodbye and shaken hands with his father. 'Goodbye. I'll get in touch when we've settled somewhere—'

Now he was in a room at Prestwick Airport waiting for Marie. In the stillness of the early morning he heard a car pull up outside. A minute later the door opened suddenly and she was ushered in. She had obviously been allowed access to her belongings because her torn toreador pants had been replaced by a pair of jeans and a matching tunic. The redness had disappeared from her eyes and she was smiling. They embraced and kissed as the young policeman prudently looked out of the window.

A discreet knock on the door signalled that it was time to go. Marie and Stephen followed the two policemen out on to the tarmac and boarded the waiting British Airways plane by a gangway at the rear. All the other passengers were already on board. The flight took off on schedule for London.

The two scaffolders dismantling the temporary stand at the rear of the eighteenth green saw him first; a lone figure approaching in the early morning sunshine down the fairway from the direction of the houses bordering the famous course. It was barely eight o'clock and a blanket of serenity lay over the Turnberry course.

Today the course was not scheduled to open until nine o'clock for members and visitors alike. Off the coast, the early morning mist was beginning to lift and soon the stony bulk of Ailsa Craig would appear. It would be another hot day.

'I've heard of golf nuts, but that laddie takes the biscuit,' the young scaffolder said to his mate. 'If it's practice he wants, he should be at home in bed with the wee woman.' He laughed at his own wit.

His older companion did not join in. Instead, he stared at the lone figure on the eighteenth green. There was something familiar about him. The scaffolder put aside his wrench and shaded his eyes against the early morning glare. Yes, he was not mistaken—he had seen the lone golfer too often on television to be mistaken. It was Dick Elliott.

He watched as the tall, athletic figure spilled out a dozen golf balls on to the green from a small leather hold-all. He prepared to putt. Selecting a ball, Dick Elliott placed it four feet away from the hole, on the exact spot from where he had missed the vital putt yesterday. He paused to survey the line, then stroked the ball towards the hole. It went into the centre of the cup. Selecting another ball, he moved it with the putter head to the exact same spot, stroked it, and watched it also disappear into the hole. He seemed oblivious to the two men up in the stand watching him.

'What's going on?' the younger one asked his mate.

'Shut up, laddie, and watch.' A fourth ball had disappeared into the hole.

'Who is that?'

'Dick Elliott.'

'Who?'

'Forget it. Go back to work!'

The younger man did not obey the order. He too sensed that what was happening out on the eighteenth green was not simply some golf fanatic getting in a bit of early morning practice. He sat down and watched.

Dick Elliott stooped down, removed the four balls from the hole, then lined up the other four in the exact same spot as before. Each one disappeared first time into the hole. When the last one had gone in, he stood there in silence, staring.

Up in the stand the older of the two scaffolders got to his feet and applauded. His mate stared at him, wondering what the hell was going on. The sound of the applause rang out sharply in the morning stillness and jerked Dick Elliott back to the present. For the first time he seemed to realise that he had had an audience. He turned to the man who was applauding and waved in acknowledgement.

The scaffolder waved back. He had just witnessed

the man who was rated the best golfer in the world trying to purge himself of the mental agony of failure. It was something to tell his mates over a drink.

Dick Elliott scooped up the golf balls and replaced them in the expensive leather hold-all. Susan would be awake soon—she was an early riser. His manager had arranged for a mid-afternoon flight from Prestwick for them, but he would try to get out earlier.

Susan, his manager and his wife had dined last night in the house. The splendid meal had been eaten almost in silence, with the telephone off the hook. Afterwards, when the other couple had left, he and Susan had had a blazing row. He had said a lot of hurtful things, accused her of getting back at him for not wanting a family until he had achieved all his ambitions in golf—the Grand Slam, to be able to walk in the footsteps of the greats like Hogan, Nicklaus and Player.

Susan had cried and gone to bed. He had sat on in the lounge alone, steeling himself to switch the television on around midnight to watch highlights of the day's play. In bed, the mental picture of him missing that vital putt had kept him awake for hours.

Dick Elliott walked off the eighteenth green. He did not want to go back to the house just now to face Susan. He decided instead to walk along the deserted beach.

Rafael Escudio came back to consciousness slowly, sated by sleep and the pleasurable aftermath of a night of intermittent sexual activity. The space in the bed beside him was empty, the covers flung back. He sat bolt upright, called out. There was no response.

He glanced at the bedside locker on her side. The ten crisp £20 notes were still tucked under the table lamp where she had left them.

He was not surprised. When he had offered them to her as an added inducement, she had not tried to contain her anger. 'Keep your filthy money,' Elaine had said, eyes blazing. 'I'm not doing this job for payment. I was ordered to do it. Understand?'

Rafael lit a cigarette, inhaled, and flopped back down on the pillow. For someone who had not tried to hide her disgust at what she was doing, she had performed pretty well. Not exactly ten out of ten, but very close to it. He preferred the chicas who had to be ordered to do the job, the ones who had to succumb to pressure from the boss. The challenge then was to see them begin to enjoy it.

Elaine had played it cool all the way through. When they had gone to his room just after midnight, she had looked around briefly and had gone into the bathroom. A few minutes later she had come out, kicked off her shoes, looked at him and said: 'All right, let's get started.' Her hands were already at the buttons of her dress.

He had moved across to her, close, so that she could sense his maleness. He got a whiff of her perfume, like he had that first time in the car. She smelled beautiful. 'What's the hurry. We got all night.'

'I won't be staying all night. I want to get home to see my son.'

'You don't go until I say so. That was the bargain with your boss.'

Her eyes flashed. 'I don't care what Mr McBain says.' She let her voice go flat. 'Come on. I want to start and get it over with.'

'So do I, chica, so do I—' He thrust forward, his hand sliding down the silk of her dress, finding her rounded buttocks, pressing her to him. She could feel his arousal; her eyes told him so.

'Let's go then—'

He bent down, his lips eager for hers. She hesitated at first, then responded. When he tried to force his tongue through her open lips she drew her head back, not willing to give in too easily to him. Yes, he would enjoy fighting this one.

He was out of his clothes first. He enjoyed standing naked in front of a new woman. He had a good body and it gave him pleasure to see them staring at it, unable to conceal their admiration, however much they despised him.

He was moving towards her when she said: 'Aren't you going to wear something? Take precautions—'

'No. I no like that way.'

'Aren't you worried about AIDS?'

'Why you ask?'

She did not reply. Elaine was naked now. She had a beautiful body, long slim legs, shapely buttocks. He noted that her belly was not quite flat, it bulged just a little, the way he liked a woman's stomach to be. He always found that a big come-on. Her breasts were superb, full, pear-shaped, the red nipples standing erect, awaiting his touch.

She put one knee on a chair at the end of the bed, moving it between the two of them. His eyes travelled down her body, stopped at the black patch of pubic hair. 'How do you know I'm clean?'

She was taunting him, reversing the role that he liked to play. He kept his gaze on her body. 'I no care.' He moved a step closer.

'I could be a carrier—'

Rafael sprang at her. But she was too quick. She was off the chair in a flash, using it as a shield between the two of them. His eyes gleamed—this was turning out to be better than he had expected. Except for the talk about AIDS . . . she was trying to frighten him, spoil it for him.

He grabbed the chair, jerked it out of her grasp. Again she stepped backwards.

'Come on, chica. Be nice.'

'No!'

'Why not?'

'I didn't want this. And I don't particularly like you.'

'Why you come then? For the money—'

'You know why I came.'

'I give you more money. Look.' He turned, scooped his pants from the floor, took out a roll of notes and counted out ten. He leaned across the bed, slid them under the lamp standard. 'See?'

'I don't want the money. You won't enjoy what you're getting. Why don't you just let me go?'

Rafael's harsh laugh cut her short. 'I no let you go, chica—' This time she was not quick enough. He grabbed her wrist, pulled her roughly to him. She could feel his hot breath on her face, the hardness of his passion below.

'You like a lot of girls. You want to fight, do it the hard way. Okay, let's have fun.' This time there was no escape. He pressed his weight against her so that they both fell on to the bed. Elaine prayed it would be over quickly.

He lay back on the pillow, watched the cigarette smoke curl up towards the ceiling. She had fought him like a tigress, but he had won. And not only once, but several times during the night. On occasion, her submissiveness to his every demand had helped heighten the level of his passion. Now she was gone out of his life, bearing the bruises of their encounter. Who knows, maybe he would see her at next year's British Open.

Rafael squashed out the cigarette in the ashtray, swung his legs out of the bed and padded into the bathroom. His blood froze when he read the message she had left scrawled in lipstick across the mirror. It read: 'Welcome to the (AIDS) club, chico.'

It was near to midday when Leonard Morgan drove back to the caravan park. He drove around the perimeter road to the area where the Dormobile was parked. Liz was sitting outside in a deckchair, enjoying the sunshine and reading a magazine. She watched him as he parked and got out.

'Well? What happened?'

He did not answer immediately. Instead he went inside, opened the refrigerator and took out a bottle of beer. 'Like a drink?' he asked from the doorway.

She shook her head, waiting for him to report. He sat down on the doorway step and took a swig from the bottle. 'Everything ready to roll?'

'Yes. Everything's packed.' The next tournament was the Dutch Open at Haarlem. Ordinarily that would mean a ferry across the Channel to Holland.

But this time he had a surprise for Liz; with the money he had won yesterday at the Open, he planned to fly across to Holland, doing it in style for a change. They could leave the Dormobile at Liz's parents' in Newcastle. It would do her good to stay in a hotel for a change: after the encounter with Stan Tynan and his thugs, she needed perking up.

The memory of his play at the Open yesterday still haunted Morgan. Without his favourite putter, the final eighteen holes had been a nightmare. Leonard had three-putted seven greens during the round, tumbled down the leaderboard and finished tied for seventeenth place. But that was worth over £8,000, his biggest ever cheque as a pro.

'You went to see Tynan this morning, didn't you, Leonard?'

'Yes. He wanted me to meet him. It would have been dangerous not to go.' There was an angry silence between them.

'I think you should go to the police.'

'And admit to smuggling drugs into the country?' Leonard gave a harsh laugh. 'I'd be put away for five years at least. That would be the end of everything.'

They fell silent. Liz lay back in the chair, her eyes closed. She had been with Leonard now for three years and their relationship seemed to be going no-where. The last time she had been home, her mother had quizzed her about the situation. 'You're twenty-four years old now, Liz. There's still time for you to make something of yourself. Travelling around in a Dormobile with someone who doesn't make enough money to support you properly is no life for a young girl. Finish it now before it's too late.'

She opened her eyes. 'What does Tynan want you to do?'

'A little job—'

'What is it?'

'Same as before—bring in some stuff when I come back from the tour during the winter. He's promised to back me for six weeks out there—all expenses paid.' Leonard broke off, came over beside her, ran his finger up her bare leg.

'Forget it, Leonard. I'm not interested. That's final.' She picked up the magazine and began reading again.

An hour later they were on the road, taking a route that cut inland from the coast. Liz was silent and he knew she was mulling over the latest development. Okay, so maybe he had been a fool to succumb to the temptation to smuggle drugs that first time. He had believed it was a once-off job. Now he was in too deep to get out. Besides, a six-week all-expenses-paid tour of the Far East circuit would help him get his game into shape for the big tournaments in Europe next year, maybe even help him make a breakthrough. In time Liz would probably see it that way too.

She broke the silence at last. 'Leonard.'

'Yes?'

'I'm not going to the Dutch Open with you.'

Even though he had been expecting it, her decision came as a shock.

'I want time to think a few things over between us. I'll stay with Mum and Dad for a few days.'

'Sure, if that's what you want, Liz. I'll come back to Newcastle, pick you up there. Okay?'

She kept looking straight ahead. 'I expect I'll have myself sorted out by then.'

Malcolm Jacob drained the last of his coffee and smiled across the table at Felicity. 'Enjoy your lunch, my dear?'

'Yes, thank you.'

'Everything packed and ready to go?'

'Almost. It won't take long.'

'Don't rush,' he said solicitously. 'I'm looking forward to our holiday in the Highlands. It'll be like a second honeymoon. Just the two of us—'

'Three,' Felicity smiled.

'Yes, of course.'

He still found it difficult to believe that within six months he would become a father again. Indeed, considering the infrequency of the sex act with Felicity, it was a bloody miracle! Amazing, though, how the knowledge of impending fatherhood had brought them closer together these past few days, Malcolm thought. Felicity was changing, too. She had not been drinking as much of late.

And Sally? The fact that she had given him the brush-off after she had learned about the baby had not hurt his vanity. Learning that he was still sleeping with his wife must have hurt her, even though she had not said as much. Besides, women were very protective towards each other. Time to settle down now, take care of Felicity and the baby, stop looking at other women. For the present, anyway.

'When you've finished packing, don't attempt to lift any of those weighty suitcases, dear. I don't want you doing any heavy work in your condition.'

When Felicity had gone upstairs, he strolled out into the foyer. Suitcases were everywhere and guests were busily settling accounts before departure. He saw a few familiar faces, smiled a greeting and stopped to chat to several.

Outside, from the hotel steps, he looked over the famed Ailsa links. The flags had been taken down, most of the hospitality tents had disappeared or were being packed away on trailers, and workmen were dismantling the temporary stands and television masts around the course. Jacob sighed. There was no more desolate sight than a golf course once the stars and the crowds had departed. He had experienced the same feeling of emptiness many times in different parts of the world.

He heard footsteps, turned, and saw Sally approaching. She had an overnight case in her hand and looked smart in a crisp white blouse and tight skirt. But so young! Why had he not noticed that before? She put down her case and looked over the course.

'My first Open championship, and I can't honestly say it's been an exhilarating experience. . . .' She let her voice trail off. 'How is Felicity?'

'Fine. A lot better than when she arrived. She's looking forward to having the baby.' He realised it was not the most discreet remark to make.

'I suppose you are too. Even at your age.'

He winced. Christ, he thought, the way women change. A few days ago the fact that he was approaching the half century didn't worry Sally. Now she was kicking him where it hurt most. 'Going back to London on your own?' he asked.

Before she could reply, a voice called out: 'Sally, my pet. Sorry for keeping you waiting—' Ricky Edwards came out of the hotel, followed by a young attendant, wheeling a trolley on which suitcases were stacked. He came over and kissed Sally on the cheek. 'Ready to go?' He grinned at Malcolm.

She picked up her overnight case. 'Lead the way.' Ricky took her arm and motioned the hotel attendant to follow them. 'See you sometime, Malcolm,' he said over his shoulder.

Jacob watched them walk towards a taxi, trying not to be envious. Why should he be? He had Felicity—and the baby. Time to face up to life. One could not do that with a girl like Sally. Not really, with Sally, one had to be in the fast lane. It was him yesterday, Ricky Edwards today, somebody else tomorrow. Felicity was not like that. She was trusting, faithful to a fault, a wife a man could be proud of. It was about time he began to realise just how fortunate he was.

Upstairs, Felicity was studying herself in the mirror. In a few months from now the baby would begin to show. She hoped when it arrived that it would look like Malcolm; the probability was it would not.

After lunch Mark Varley asked Joan if she would like a drink. 'A brandy, perhaps? To celebrate.'

She shook her head. 'No thanks. I hardly touch the stuff. I'll have another coffee.'

He signalled a waiter and she sensed that he was finding her a bit of a puzzle. Perhaps boring might be a better word. He was sizing her up to see how she would fit in as the wife of the personable new Open champion. But she had never been good at making conversation with people she hardly knew and Joan suspected she was not rating very highly with Mark Varley. She wished Colm was here right now.

'What time did you say that Colm is expected back from London?'

Mark Varley pulled on a slim cigar. 'Hmmm, around nine o'clock, I reckon. That phone call a few minutes ago was from Samantha. She said the exhibition game had gone splendidly, big crowd, everyone wanting to meet Colm. Sam said he handled it very well.' He smiled. 'Of course we knew he would, didn't we?'

'Why will they be back so late if the game is already over?'

If Mark Varley found her questions trite, he was too shrewd to show it. 'Playing eighteen holes is only part of the deal,' he explained. 'There's a golf clinic afterwards, then the dinner for the specially invited guests. Colm is expected to stay for that. After all, we are getting twenty-five thousand for the day.'

The waiter came with her coffee and his brandy. Mark Varley was speaking again. 'I do hope we've seen the last of the police. Do you expect them in again?'

'No. Colm and I told them all we knew last night. They asked us about the girl we now know to be Marie Kirk, and that fellow Dignam. We helped as much as we could.'

'Good.' His tone became more businesslike. 'Now, you and the kids . . . what is your schedule for the week?'

'Colm had planned a short holiday for us—'

He shook his head. 'Sorry, I'm afraid that's out now, Joan. Colm must be in Holland by Wednesday morning for the Dutch Open. I've already negotiated his appearance money for that event. And before that, there are a lot of other engagements to be fitted in.'

'What about us? Me and the children—'

He smiled, showing beautiful white teeth against his tan. 'Don't worry, Joan, you and the kids will have your holiday with Colm. But not just now.' He paused, then went on: 'Look, let's get one thing straight. For the next year or so, you're going to have to get used to sharing Colm with a lot of other people. We're going to market him, package him, sell him to the highest bidder. How does that grab you?'

'Frankly, it doesn't.'

Varley took a deep breath and looked at her quizzically for a few moments. Then he glanced over his shoulder. 'See that fellow with the spectacles and the gaudy sweater over there?' She nodded. 'He's a golf writer. I could go over to him right now and sell him Colm's story for serialisation. You know the sort of stuff—"My climb from rags to riches, how winning the Open has changed my life." Three episodes at not less than ten grand an episode.'

'What's stopping you?'

'It would have to have a sex angle.' He smiled mockingly at her. 'Know what I mean?' When she did not answer he said: 'When do you plan to return to Ireland?'

'I haven't any plans. We could go down to London, meet Colm, travel to Holland with him this week.' She was determined not to be pushed into the background.

'We'd rather you didn't do that, Joan,' Mark Varley replied quickly. 'It will be hectic over in Holland for Colm. It would be best if you and Johnny Davis went back home and allowed us to do some serious business.'

Joan put her coffee cup down with a clatter. 'But Johnny can't go home. He's Colm's caddie—'

She stopped. Mark Varley was shaking his head. '*Was* Colm's caddie, I'm afraid.' He held up his hand when he saw she was about to cut in. 'Let's be honest, Joan. Up to now Colm couldn't afford a regular caddie on tour. He brought Johnny over for the Open only because he was a friend—and experienced. But he's nearly sixty years of age. Too old. We need someone younger to fit in with the blueprint we have for Colm.'

'What you're saying is that Johnny doesn't fit the image.'

'That's just about it.'

'Does Colm know about this?'

'Yes. It was a management decision. Don't take it out on your husband.'

Joan wondered what Johnny Davis thought of it all. This was the ugly face of big-time golf. Aloud she said: 'What plans have Varley Brothers Management for me and the children?'

The remark stung him. 'Oh, come on now. You want the best for your husband, don't you? Like I said, we'd prefer if you and the kids went back home for a couple of weeks while we set Colm up. I have an idea he's going to be big. Very big. He looks good,

337

speaks well, relates to people, and has a pleasant, relaxed manner. All he has to do is produce the goods on tour.'

'What about our holiday?'

'Give Peter and me a month and I'll guarantee you and Colm a holiday in Bermuda, or the Caribbean. Anywhere you wish—all expenses paid. How's that?'

Everything was being decided for them, taken out of her hands. Joan knew she must sound ungrateful, complaining when already the big money was beginning to roll in. But it was demoralising all the same. She looked over Varley's shoulder and saw Susan Elliott standing in the entrance to the dining-room. She waved. Susan saw her and came over.

'Hi.'

'Hello, Susan.'

'I came to say goodbye. Richard and I are leaving soon for the airport.'

'Thanks for dropping by.' Joan broke off and introduced Susan to Mark Varley. He rose, shook her hand and said: 'I'm sorry, but I have to dash off. I've a few urgent phone calls to make. Excuse me.' He nodded and was gone.

Susan's eyes followed him across the room. 'So the big money boys have moved in.' She sat down. 'Be careful how you and Colm handle it, Joan. Don't let them take over. It's great at first: the big money, travelling first class, staying in the best hotels. When your husband is a golf superstar, you think you've got it made—' She gazed out of the window for a moment. 'Just don't let it ruin your lives.'

an almost deserted hotel. But if her greeting was cool, he was excited and did not seem to notice anything amiss.

'It's been a fantastic day, Joan. I'm only sorry you couldn't be here—'

'So am I. But someone has to look after the children.'

'Of course. How are they?'

'Fast asleep. They're tired and excited. They have been asking for you.'

'Look, love, don't worry about today. We're going to have a great year. You and me—the whole family. We're on our way, believe me.'

'Tell me about today.'

'It was unbelievable. They couldn't do enough for me. Everybody wanted to meet me, shake my hands, buy me a drink.' He was talking very fast and Joan reckoned he was still on a high. 'We had a chauffeured limo at our disposal, the top table for dinner—and I earned twenty-five grand into the bargain. How about that?'

'What about Samantha?'

'Samantha? What about her?'

'Where is she now?'

'I don't know. Back in the office, or in her own place, I expect. I'm phoning from my hotel, The Ormonde.' Another pause. 'Joan, is there something bothering you?'

'No. Nothing. What do you plan on doing for the rest of the night?'

'I'm going to watch some television and have an early night. I'm absolutely tired out. First thing to-morrow I'm meeting the directors from the company who make my golf clubs. We're negotiating a new contract—Samantha says she won't settle for less than a quarter of a million pounds. I'm telling you, Joan, the money is just rolling in—'

'You know about Johnny?'

That brought him up short. 'Yes. It was terrible.' The excitement had gone from his voice. He was back down to earth. 'I didn't want it to happen, but it was out of my hands.'

'Couldn't you have stood up to the Varleys? Insisted on retaining Johnny as your caddie for at least a few months? He helped you to win the Open, Colm, for God's sake.'

'I know, I know.'

'If it wasn't for Johnny Davis, you wouldn't even be playing golf—'

'Don't go on about it, Joan. We'll only have an argument. The Varleys know what they're doing. Johnny was well looked after financially, believe me.'

Joan did not answer. Were the Varleys going to run their lives from now on? She and Colm should have had a lot of things to discuss, but it was not turning out that way. Maybe it was because they were at different ends of the country, talking by telephone instead of over dinner. Now that he was Open champion, Joan supposed she would have to get used to chatting to her husband long distance.

Colm was speaking again: 'By the way, Johnny left a few hours ago to fly back to Prestwick. I told him to drop into the hotel to see you.'

'How is he taking it?'

'He's fine. He knows the score. Don't worry. I told the Varleys to write him a cheque for ten thousand pounds. He'll be happy with that.'

Joan thought it sounded like blood money, but she did not say as much. They chatted for a few more minutes, then Colm said: 'I'd better go now, Joan. I've a busy day tomorrow. I'll phone you sometime.'

'When are you going to Holland?'

'Wednesday, I expect. Take care—and remember me to the kids—'

'Oh, one more thing, Colm. Is Samantha going to the Dutch Open with you?'

'Of course. You're not worried, are you?' He laughed.

'Frankly, yes.'

'Oh, for heaven's sake, Joan.' He sounded tired and irritated. 'You have nothing to worry about. You know I never did fancy blondes, anyway.'

Colm replaced the receiver on its cradle and looked across the hotel room to where Samantha Cruise was sitting in an armchair, smiling at him. He wished she had really gone back to her office, instead of coming back with him to his hotel.

'The little wifey asks a lot of questions, doesn't she?'

Colm shrugged. 'She's seen a lot of marriages break up on the tour.'

'That so?' She crossed her slender, sun-tanned legs, showing a provocative length of thigh in the process. She watched him endeavour not to stare. 'You told a little white lie—about my being back at the office. Why?'

'I suppose I didn't want Joan worried.'

'Should she be worried? I mean this is strictly business between us, isn't it?' She was playing a game, smiling at him, looking at him from beneath her long eyelashes.

'Whatever you say, Samantha.' He was trying not to look at her. 'Sorry, but I'm a bit tired, and we do have a big day tomorrow. Do you mind . . . I want to have a bath, get into bed—'

'Mmmmm, sounds lovely. That's exactly what I had in mind myself—' She rose and walked slowly towards him. He watched her. She had a beautiful figure. She had taken off her jacket and her silk blouse had one button extra undone so that the valley of her breasts showed.

She smiled. 'You have a lovely bathroom—it seems such a shame to waste it on just one person.'

Samantha was standing close to him now, smiling up at him. All he had to do was to reach out, undo another button on her silk blouse. . . .

He thought of Joan alone in the hotel in Turnberry. He had never been unfaithful to her. Sure, he had seen other guys cheat on their wives when they were abroad. It was all part of the lifestyle. A golfer was not a machine; he needed some form of relaxation from the frustrations and pressures of the game. Maybe just this once with Samantha; after that it would be strictly Joan and the kids.

Their eyes were still locked. 'Why don't you be my guest—in the bathroom?' Colm heard himself say. He reached out and began to undo the button.

Samantha stepped back quickly, still smiling at him. 'I'll take you up on that, darling—some other time!' She crossed the room and picked up her jacket from the chair. At the door she turned and said: 'Your wife will ring again in an hour, checking on you. By then, Colm, you should be in bed—alone. Bye, see you tomorrow.'

He was left staring at the closed door. Outside, Samantha walked down the carpeted corridor and entered the elevator, conscious of the admiring glances from the two middle-aged men with their wives as she stepped in. She reckoned she was going to enjoy her year looking after the new British Open champion.

Not long afterwards the telephone rang in Joan's room. She grabbed it before it wakened the children, who were asleep in the other room. 'Hello?'

'Mrs Donohue? Reception here. There's a Mr Johnny Davis in the foyer to see you.'

'Thank you. Tell him I'll be right down.' She checked that the children were still asleep, then went downstairs. Johnny rose from a chair to greet her. He was in the outfit he usually wore when he caddied for Colm and she guessed he had just arrived at Prestwick and driven to Turnberry.

'I'm on my way to Stranraer to catch the midnight sailing to Larne, Joan. Just dropping in for a few minutes. Like to have a drink in the bar?'

'Love to, Johnny.'

The bar was practically deserted. At a table Mark and Peter Varley were entertaining a group of soberly suited men. Johnny saw them and paused briefly. For a moment Joan thought he was going over to them. Instead, he lead her to a table well away from the Varley group.

He ordered a double Scotch for himself and a glass of white wine for Joan. When the drinks came, he raised his glass. 'Here's to yourself and Colm.' He downed half the liquid.

Joan sipped her drink. She had always admired Johnny Davis, but never more so than at this moment. For a man who had suffered the disappointment of his life, he was taking it all philosophically. Maybe he was putting on a show for her sake.

'You've heard I won't be working for Colm?'

'Yes. He told me.'

'I got the sack. From those two little jumped-up buggers.' He glanced across to where the Varleys were sitting.

'I'm sorry, Johnny.'

'What the hell. Not to worry.'

'Colm should have stood up for you. I told him so. He owes everything to you.'

He waved her protest aside. 'I don't want you blaming him. It's not Colm's fault. I just didn't fit the image, I guess.'

Joan sighed. 'That makes two of us.'

His shrewd little eyes searched her face. 'What d'you mean?'

'I don't think I fit the Varleys' image either.'

'Aye, but you're Colm's wife. They can't push you aside too easily.' He drank some more whisky. 'The pro game is tough these days. A lot tougher than when I was on the tour. Too much money and not enough fun, that's the problem. And too many management sharks like those Varley boys about. In my day we managed ourselves.'

They sat in silence for a while, then Joan asked: 'What are your plans now, Johnny?'

He rubbed a stubbly chin. 'I'm off back to Atlantic

View. I'm a bit of a celebrity back there now, you know. We get a lot of foreign visitors to the club during the summer—American and British mostly. They'll all want to play a round with the old pro who caddied for the Open champion.' He laughed. 'Don't worry about me, Joan. I'll make a bit of money.'

'I wish you were with Colm, Johnny. He needs you.'

'Tell the truth, Joan, I wish I were with him, too. But—' He shrugged. 'Colm needs you also, Joan. You and the kids. He's going to have a great year. Make sure you're part of it. Be with him as often as possible.'

'I will.' She had the impression he was trying to tell her something. 'How did you get along with Samantha today?'

He shrugged. 'Okay. She's a smart lass. Knows what she wants, and goes after it. I'd keep an eye on her, Joan, if you know what I mean.' Before she could pursue the topic further, he looked at his watch. 'I'd better be pushing on if I'm to make that sailing. But before I go, there's something I want to do—'

As they rose to go, Joan noticed Johnny take a folded slip of paper from his jacket pocket. 'Know what this is?' He held it up. When she shook her head, he said: 'It's the cheque for ten thousand pounds with which the Varley boys paid me off.' His voice took on a hard edge. 'I want to return it to them—'

Joan was aghast. 'Johnny, for God's sake. Don't do anything foolish. You earned that money—'

But it was too late. Johnny Davis was already halfway across to the Varleys' table. She watched in amazement as he said something to the brothers, then tore the cheque several times and showered the table with the pieces. Nobody said anything as he turned on his heel and left.

When she caught up with him in the foyer, he was grinning from ear to ear, not looking like a man who a few moments ago had torn up what for him was a small fortune. 'I enjoyed that,' he said. He and Joan burst out laughing.

Johnny's car was parked at the front of the hotel. It was still dusk and the darkness had not completely closed in yet. The dark hulk of Ailsa Craig was barely visible out in the firth, while below on the links a quartet of enthusiastic golfers was walking off the last green.

Johnny Davis surveyed the scene, his weather-beaten face impassive. Joan guessed he was reliving some of the great moments of the past week out there. No doubt he could even hear the roar of the Turn-berry crowds. They both stood in silence, savouring the moment.

Finally he spoke. 'You know, Joan. It was a hell of a week—and I'm proud to have been part of it.' He turned and kissed her lightly on the cheek. 'Bye, love. Tell Colm I'll be watching out for him in the Dutch Open.'

'God bless you, Johnny,' Joan said softly. She watched him as he skipped down the broad steps of the hotel, his agility belying his years. He opened the car door, turned and waved.

Joan returned the wave and watched until the vehicle had wended its way up along the road that skirted the Ailsa course. She waited on the steps until the car's tail-lights disappeared from view.

Then she turned and re-entered the hotel. She suddenly felt very alone.